It all started
with a #Filthy Tweet

SOCIAL

NEW YORK TIMES BESTSELLING AUTHOR

JA HUSS

By JA Huss
Edited by RJ Locksley
Copyright © 2017 by J. A. Huss
All rights reserved.
ISBN- 978-1-936413-87-4

SOCIAL MEDIA SERIES BOOK ONE

FOLLOW

NEW YORK TIMES BESTSELLING AUTHOR

HUSS

Chapter One - Grace

#HappinessIsADirtyHashtag

SOMETIMES you just need to stop talking, and right now I should totally take that advice because the airport bartender is giving me that look as I chatter away about nothing in particular. Bebe is in the bathroom freshening up before we make the final leg of our journey to spend four days and three nights on Saint Thomas courtesy of KFLK radio in Denver.

My mouth is still going and even though no one is paying any attention to me, I can't stop talking and they all start shooting me looks. I get these looks a lot. I can't stand silence, it drives me crazy. So I'm a talker. I'm a gabber. I'm what they call... *social*. I pin things, I share things, I plus things. I like, I follow, and I comment.

But most of all... I tweet. I'm a tweeter. I live for the Twitter. I chirp good morning like a little blue bird from my bed in the AM and then chirp good evening again every night.

Even before social media took over the world I was this girl. From my very first year I have been one of those butterflies. Yes—I'm putting my hand up to stop the protests—my very first year. Because my first birthday picture was of me whispering a secret into my big brother's ear.

And after social media took over the world I embraced this girl. My bestie, Bebe, and I have this whole social thing down to a science. We are the champions of chatter, the proponents of prattle, the backers of blather. We are the goddesses of gossip and we own this shit. We take bubbly optimism to a whole new virtual level. Our motto is *Happiness is a #Hashtag* and we live life knowing the fairy tale is possible, even if you only get it online.

Who needs reality anyway? Reality is being orphaned at thirteen. Reality is foster homes and loneliness. Reality is a risk ripe for disappointment.

But thank God for Bebe and her family. They welcomed me in with open arms and instead of something tragic, I became the poster child for surviving and came out the other end not only intact, but better than ever.

But back to my mouth—and by extension, my fingertips since they do all my talking on Twitter—it has a mind of its own.

And that mind is very dirty.

Yes, my name is Grace Kinsella and I'm a filthy tweeter.

I can turn a hundred and forty characters into living sex. I can string words together in a way that will make you wet

2

your panties with lust. I can make a man blush before he even gets to the hashtag. I am famous for pithy filth.

In fact, my girlfriends and I have an online Facebook group called the Filthy Blue Birds. And we're not the only ones. The world of pithy filth is booming, friends. There are endless groups like ours. There are legions of shy girls who come alive when faced with the hundred-and-forty-character challenge. And there is a very special place online where we meet, challenging each other to achieve a new level of smexy typing.

I call that Twitter list Dirty Heaven. I made it up, like literally I'm the freaking founder. So Dirty Heaven is my kingdom and I'm the queen.

I'll stop here to take a bow.

Besides being a list, Dirty Heaven is an online competition that happens on Twitter every Saturday night across the world—yes, we have filthy tweeters from all walks of life. At 8 PM Eastern the FT's come alive and each league puts up their best and brightest. You get one tweet, one hashtag, and one chance to shine.

I don't win anymore, it's simply not fair. I'm now the judge. But back when we were first putting this together my tweets took me to Dirty Heaven time after time after time. That's back when we used to have the competitions nightly and the group was small. Just fifteen or twenty of my closest online stranger friends. Each competition we had an online muse and we took turns choosing who would benefit from our blush-inducing prose. Sometimes the girls picked models or rock stars.

I only ever had one muse and his name is Vaughn Asher.

Yes, *the* Vaughn Asher. A Hollywood legend. He started out in the boy band 2 Far Out, then when his angelic voice changed as he hit puberty he graduated into Disney sitcoms. Most child actors would fade after that, never able to make the transition. But Vaughn Asher doubled down on the workouts—gaining the title of Most Envied Body in Hollywood six years in a row from *Buzz Hollywood Magazine*—and the preteen wannabe turned into an action-hero heartthrob overnight.

Just thinking his name makes me sigh. He's so freaking gorgeous. That messy dark hair that makes him look like he just rolled out of bed. Those tight abs that just make you want to drag your tongue all over them to see if they taste as good as they look. And that package, boy. He's never done any nudes so I have to use my imagination, but my imagination is vivid. I have a very clear picture.

Besides, you know what they say about a man's thumbs, right? Well, Vaughn Asher has incredible thumbs. And large feet. They say that too.

Yes, doing filthy things to his six-foot-two frame has been my idea of Dirty Heaven for almost three years now. I'd like to say I've said everything imaginable about him, but that's not true. I never run out of ideas. It's like my brain only exists to compose a one-hundred-and-forty-character sentence that will turn him red.

That's my fantasy. That's my fairy tale. Vaughn Asher doing things to me that can only be said in a hashtag.

Chapter Two - Vaughn

#ThanksForTheFuck

"I'M afraid you're going to have to leave," I tell the dark-haired beauty crawling towards me on the floor of my suite.

Her mouth drops open and she stops crawling, but my attention is on her hair. It's dragging across the floor and picking up dust. I need to speak to the maids about the dust.

"What?" she asks, as she goes from crawling to kneeling. That has got to hurt her knees. Pressing against tile like that. "Did I do something wrong?"

She's almost perfect. Almost being the key word. She's very tall and thin, the physique of a model, really. Willowy is the word to describe her. All arms and legs. Small breasts, but they are nice enough. As is her ass. She's obedient. But—

"I can change, whatever it is. I can change."

I sigh. I hate having to dismiss the girls. It bothers me when I have to spell it out. I always tell them before we start, this is nothing but sex. But they only hear what they want to hear. Something akin to *This is more than sex, I want you by my side forever?* Maybe. I'm not sure. Whatever they hear, it's not, *Thanks for the good time, now get the hell out,* because that's what my mind is saying.

"You can keep your job here at the resort. In fact, I'll still pop in for yoga every now and then, if that's OK."

"Just tell me what I did. I'll fix it."

"I'll include a bonus in your next check if it dulls the sting."

"I didn't tell anyone about you, Master."

"I know. You did everything right." They never just take the money and leave. Ever. They never make it easy for me.

"Then why? Can't I ask why? Don't I deserve an explanation?" She's on her feet now, walking towards me.

I put up a hand and she stops. "I don't like you. It's that simple." I stand up and walk towards her so she can't take control. Her doe eyes look up at me, pleading. But my decision has been made. I'm done. I cup her face and stare down at her. "You're simply not perfect. And that's all there is to it. Your imperfections are glaring. It was nice fucking you. Good luck and goodbye."

Chapter Three - Vaughn

#NotPrinceCharming

I SCAN the guests as they pull up to the resort valet. Most are family. We have a huge family. I have seven aunts and uncles on my father's side alone. And my mother is a twin and has two older sisters. Every one of them has at least three children.

Sending that girl away this morning is still a flicker of irritation in the back of my mind. She has no room to complain. They never have any room to complain when I dismiss them. But they always do.

Some of them want the fame, I suppose. As if I'd ever take one of my submissive playthings out in public as my girlfriend. I laugh at that as I watch my family pour out of the limos down below. These silly girls and their fantasies. I've had so many of them over the years and not one ever made it to an event on my arm. You'd think they'd pick up on that, but they don't. They always assume they are the first for some reason. The Prince Charming complex, maybe. I'm their savior. They all think money is the answer, but money is the devil. Money is the problem. Money is never enough.

It takes them a while to realize this, but they all realize it eventually. This last one I'm not so sure about. One night was all it was ever meant to be. She must've been craving it. That slave-master relationship. Either that or she's been in one before, because she was ready and willing to do everything I commanded.

I feel sorry for her, but when I'm done, I'm done. And she was never my type anyway, she was just here. She was a shrug. An afterthought. A side dish. She never came close to girlfriend material.

No. The subs are never girlfriend material. They are toys. And maybe all the women I date are toys, to some extent. But none of the women I date publicly get their asses spanked red or their hair pulled as I fuck them from behind.

I crave the dirty, but only in private.

My thumb rubs circles over my brow as I desperately try to ease the tension from having to spell it out for her. Why can't they just stick to the agreement? Why do they always have to stick around afterward, forcing me to humiliate them further in the stark glare of morning daylight?

A van pulls up and I stop the introspection to observe. A van? Who in my family is arriving in an airport shuttle?

The side door slides open and two girls are inside. They are smiling and giggling. One is dark—in fact, she reminds me of that dismissed sub. But the other… I stop and catch my breath as she places one sandaled foot outside the vehicle and steps into the tropical sun. The driver doesn't even get out to help them with their luggage, just accepts the payment and drives off as soon as the door closes.

The girls stare up at the resort and I duck a little, making sure they don't spot me spying. "Vaughn," I chastise myself. "Get a grip."

They disappear inside and I'm left thinking about the girl with the blonde hair. She was pretty. Is she a guest for the party? I get out my cell and call the front desk. Javel picks up on the first ring.

"Who are those two women checking in?"

"Excuse me, ladies, I have to take this call," he says. A few seconds later a door closes and he's back. "I'm sorry, sir, they were on the approved list. They are…" He hesitates and I get a little annoyed at him making me wait.

"They're who?" I prod.

"Honeymooners. I was told not to cancel the honeymooners."

"OK, thank you." I end the call.

Hmmm. I keep my eye on them.

I PASS the evening drinking alone in what I call the Crow's Nest. It's a small alcove separate from the upstairs bar that looks down onto the front of the resort. It's almost midnight before I make it back to my house. I strip out of my clothes and dive into the pool. The crash of waves filters up from the beach that's less than a hundred yards down a pebble-covered path.

I want to fuck someone so bad. I need to bend the will of a new submissive and I need to do that soon.

Chapter Four - Grace

#SurpriseMe

JUST so you understand, my hashtag brilliance doesn't come quick and easy. It takes me some time to come up with just the right tweet. I completely understand that Mr. Asher's time is valuable and that's why I take such care in my composition.

@VaughnAsher My fantasy: The soft tropical breeze caressing my bare pussy right now is really your invisible tongue on my clit.

He played the Invisible Man in that last superhero movie, get it? I chuckle softly to myself as I sit at the resort bar. Bebe and I are on our fake honeymoon. It's a long story, but she won this trip for two to Saint Thomas in a contest and since neither of us plan on getting married anytime soon, we came together.

Her new boyfriend Steve showed up last night as a surprise and since I'm not a bitch, I told her to go have fun with him. He should've been the one here with her anyway, but I've never been to the Caribbean, so Bebe took me instead.

Anyway, back to my tweet. I still have a few characters left and it kills me not to use them all, so I ponder it a little more as I swing my foot to the bar music. Saint Thomas is a fantastic place. The beaches are lined with spectacular white sand and the water is a color of blue that I just can't describe. Our hotel is fabulous—way, way, way out of my price range—but since the contest was a honeymoon package, we have to share a bed. And now that her boyfriend Steve decided to join us, well, I'll probably be sleeping on the beach tonight because the rattan couch on the bungalow patio has my back all in a crick.

Not that I care too much that Steve is here. It takes a lot to get me riled up. I'm the kind of girl who lets things go. Steve is OK and Bebe has always been so good to me, so a night on a tropical beach is hardly a sacrifice so they can share the room and have some real privacy in paradise.

"Another drink?" the bartender asks me as he strolls by to check on this end of the bar. There's no one over here but me, so that's sweet that he's paying attention. Of course my bikini top is pretty small so maybe he's just trying to cop a look at my girls?

"Yes, please," I say as I continue to play around with my phone. "I want another martini, but this time"—I look up and bat my blue eyes at the dark, handsome man pouring drinks today—"surprise me."

"How about I pick?" a rough, sexy voice asks over my shoulder. "Let the lady try the key lime pie."

"Hmmm." I hum to myself as I continue to rearrange today's perfect dirty tweet so I get the hashtag in just the right place. "Thanks a bunch. But lime is not my thing, so"—I look up at the bartender who's got his eyebrows raised to the ceiling as he waits for my response—"I'll let you choose." I give the hot bartender a flirty wink and he lets off a hearty laugh.

"You sure about that?" he asks in his Caribbean English. "Maybe the lime is not so bad."

"Oh, no." I put up my hand and laugh with him. "I'm sure." I hike my thumb back over my shoulder. "Mr. Buttinski here can order himself a key lime pie martini. I want *you* to choose"—I look at the name tag on his resort shirt—"Dewain." I smile at him and then go back to my tweet, the matter settled.

"Have it your way, but I think I tried them all last night and this one is definitely the best. And I only bother with the best," that husky voice replies behind me. He reaches over my shoulder, pressing his body up against mine in a way that creates an explosion of chills down my arms, and then places a ten-dollar bill on the bar. "It's on me."

I swivel around on my bar stool to see who this guy is, but he's already turned away, so all I catch is a muscled back. It's tan. And hard-looking. My eyes travel south to the curve of his perfect globes. He's wearing a pair of lime green board shorts and that makes me smile.

"Nice shorts," I call out after him.

He glances over his shoulder and I catch a smirking grin before he rounds the corner and calls back, "Nice tweet."

"Oh, shit," I mumble to myself. I click out of the app and blush. "How embarrassing." At least he couldn't see my Twitter handle and Mr. Asher's handle was mostly covered up by my thumb, so he probably didn't see who it was for, either. "Eek!" I say under my breath. I hope I don't see *him* again.

"There you are!" Bebe says as she skips under the thatched-roof hut of the beach bar. "I've been looking everywhere for you."

"Oh my God, Bebe, some random hot dude just caught me composing a tweet! I think he read it!"

"Hmm," she says with a wide smile. "Did he frown or laugh?"

"I'm not sure, he was walking away before I knew he saw it." I hold the phone up and she nabs it out of my hand.

"Let me see." Her laugh turns into a squeal as she reads it. "Bare pussy, tongue, and clit all in the same tweet." She laughs again. "Girl, no man will frown at that."

"One key lime martini for the lady," Dewain the bartender says as he sets the drink down in front of me with a conspiratorial wink. "This one really is the best, the man does not lie, so this is the one I choose for you." And then he picks up the ten-dollar bill key lime shorts guy left and walks off to help a couple who just arrived.

"What's that all about?" Bebe asks.

"That bossy tweet-stalker wanted me to try this drink but I shot him down." I take a sip of the drink and minty freshness invades my mouth. I swallow and it's the perfect combination of comforting and cool. "It's good, I guess," I reluctantly admit. The bartender hears me and sends off another wink in my direction.

"Well, Steve and I are going parasailing today, wanna come?"

I scoff. "Are you crazy? I will be here at the bar if you need me."

"You can't stay at the bar all day. At least go out and beach-bum so one of those cute cabana boys can come serve you."

I promise her I will as she trots off to a waiting Steve. They can defy the laws of gravity at their own peril, I have a good book and tonight's tweet contest to get ready for. I hate that I don't get to judge the winner tonight but I was ousted in the name of vacay. Bebe thinks I have a hard time letting work go. But that's ridic. Everyone knows judging a dirty tweet contest is not work.

I have a good chuckle with myself and sip on my drink. It is delicious and when I'm done I order another. I watch Dewain add the ingredients and shake it up like a pro. I notice the bar is almost empty now that I'm not so self-absorbed in dirty tweeting.

"Where are all the people?" I call over to Dewain as he adds a slice of lime to my martini. "Why's it so empty?"

"Private party this weekend," he answers as he puts my drink down in front of me. "The entire west end of the resort has been rented out for it."

"Wow," I say as I take the first sip. Yum. "That's pretty fancy. Must be moneybags, huh?" I reach into my purse to pull out some cash, but Dewain puts a hand over mine.

"It's paid for. Mr. Buttinski left an open tab for you." Dewain gives me another one of those winks and I flash him back some suspicion.

"What's that mean?"

"Well," Dewain says, throwing up his hands in an I-surrender gesture. "He wants to make a good impression, maybe?"

"Hmmm, I dunno. Did you see his face? Was he cute? I only saw his backside and while that was very nice, I'm a face girl first." I shrug when he wags his finger at me. So I'm shallow? Sue me.

"I think many women think he's cute." And then Dewain laughs. "I'm not gay but *I* think he's cute."

I gulp the rest of my drink down. These damn things really are good. "I think I'm gonna head to the beach. Thanks for the drink. And if you see key lime shorts, tell him I said thanks!"

I scoot off my barstool and make for the door and it only takes me a few steps to remember that I forgot the thing that goes on the top of every packing list. Underwear. I've got my bathing bottoms on today, but I figure I should pick up a few pairs as I stroll by a lingerie store.

"Good afternoon!" the sales lady calls out in a sing-songy voice from across the shop. "Can I help you find anything?"

"I'm good!" I call back. That's something I would never get used to if I was rich. I'm not rich and since my job as an event planner didn't pay much before I got my new promotion, and pays only two grand more a year with that,

I'm not even close to worrying about this. But having people bend over because you're about to spend money makes me uncomfortable.

I peruse the rack of fancy underwear, check the price tag, and then promptly move over to another rack that says sale. I don't know who spends hundreds of dollars on underwear, but it's not me. I flip through everything, getting more and more desperate as the garments fly by. Nothing under fifty dollars? They call that a sale?

And then I spy some men's tighty-whities in a basket on a shelf. I grab a pair and check the price. Fifteen dollars.

OK. Still ridiculous, but they are a size small, so they will have to do. I take them to the register and sign my name and room number on the charge slip as the sales lady folds my single pair of cheap men's underwear and places them in a bag with real satin ribbon for handles.

I make a quick escape and head across the breezeway that leads to the private bungalows and I'm just looking up to see why it's so quiet when I see key lime shorts talking to a security person. The security guy looks over lime shorts' shoulder at me and I stop walking for a second.

Did I do something wrong? I'm staring at them when Mr. Buttinski walks off again.

Whatever. I have no idea what they are talking about, but I'm gonna go drop my stuff off and hit the beach so I can get back to work on my tweets. My flipflops smack my heels loudly in the stillness as I walk past the security guy, and I'm half expecting him to say something to me, but he just turns away and walks off.

Our bungalow is deep in the bungalow village as I like to call it. There are about twenty of them in a common area on this part of the resort and they have cute little winding paths surrounded by the most fragrant flowers and wispy palm trees. It almost takes my breath away. And the birds. Don't even get me started on the birds.

When I get to our room I drop my stuff off and shimmy out of my shorts so I can exchange them for a gauzy white wrap. I study myself in the mirror. This is my favorite bathing suit. It's peach so it makes my skin look a little more golden than it really is. I tie my hair up in a ponytail, grab my beach bag and stuff my tablet in there along with my phone, and then pull my shades down over my eyes and head out.

Just as I'm twisting the door handle I look down at my feet and stop in my tracks. An envelope has been slipped under the door.

Was that there when I came in?

I bend down and pick it up. The thick pink paper is clearly of the handmade variety and the fancy script writing on the front leaves no mystery as to what it is.

An invitation.

Chapter Five - Grace

#TheInvisibleGod

I STARE at the envelope and read.

Apologies, is what the actual word on the front is. Not *You're invited.* But it's written in a *You're invited* script, so it's easy to assume.

I take the card out and read the same fancy lettering:

All facility pools and beaches are closed for a private function. Sorry for the inconvenience. Please accept a full-access pass to the lazy river for the day.

Hmmm. The lazy river is not something that came in our package. Our free trip included the Spa Experience, so we have access to the Wellness Center and that's about it.

Which is bullshit. If you're on a honeymoon then you want to do the fun stuff before you fuck each other's brains out. Not let other people pound on you and stick you in a steam room.

I stuff the invitation in my bag and leave the bungalow. The lazy river is all the way on the other side of the village, so I take every winding path imaginable and by the time I finally make it over there I'm ready for another martini.

There is no one at the entrance except some kid with a resort polo shirt on. "We're closed," he says in his friendly fuck-you voice.

"I have a full-access pass for the day," I say as I hand him my invitation. "Someone just slipped it under my door a few minutes ago, so—"

His eyes get big as he stares at the paper in my hand.

"Excuse me, I'm sorry," he says as he swings the entrance gate open for me. "Yes, you are an invited guest. Please, come this way."

The place is empty. Like not a single other person here. Just me and the lazy river. How weird is it to have an entire river to yourself on an island that should be bustling with people but is somehow strangely vacant?

Weird.

The lazy river guy sets me up with a floating cabana. I'm not kidding. It comes with a cooler and a boarding platform. All inflatable. "Is this really necessary?" I ask him as he fills the cooler with ice and a variety of drinks. "I only need one for a single person. This… thing looks like it's built for a party."

He points to the invitation I'm still clutching in my hand. "The cabana raft comes with that invitation. VIP." He winks at me the same way that Dewain did back at the bar.

Hmmm. "Who's rented the resort anyway? Where did this invitation come from?"

He smiles at me and waves me towards the cabana. "You get in and I'll give you a push out into the current. Holler if you need anything."

Obviously they have been told not to talk about the event, whatever it may be. Hint taken. I throw my bag into the floating house and crawl in after it. There's a mesh sunshade that stretches out over my head and a peek hole that lets you see the water underneath.

Lazy river guy pushes me out of the loading pool and the current floats me along at a nice relaxing clip.

My eyes close automatically and my whole body relaxes back into the inflatable cushions. I relish the hot sun beating down on my body and take off my wrap so I'm just in my bikini and before I know, I'm drifting off...

"You're gonna burn," a familiar husky voice whispers into my ear as the raft rocks to the side.

I flail my arms in surprise and end up clutching onto a pair of muscular broad shoulders. "What the hell!"

"Hold still," the man laughs. "You'll tip the raft and get all wet."

I push off him and scoot away, my heart racing from the shock of having a strange man so close to me. "What the hell do you think—"

Oh. My. Fucking. God.

And I mean God. As in *the* god that is... "*Vaughn Asher?*"

His eyes crinkle a little at the corners when he smiles at me and the sunlight plays off his bright blue eyes and dark hair in a way that makes him look ethereal and brutish all at once. He hoists himself up onto the raft, dripping water all over, and then plops down next to me. His perfectly toned and tanned shoulders brush up against mine, making us cling together from the water. He flips a pair of sunglasses down over his eyes and stretches his arms out and clasps his hands behind his neck.

And then I look down. Not at his… package, which I also see because it's in my line of sight. But at his swim shorts. Which are a limey shade of green.

"Oh my fucking God," I say again. Only this time it's out loud. "You're the guy from the bar?"

"That drink was perfect and you know it."

"The bar?"

"I know, because you bought another one. Already got the tab. So don't bother fighting me on this."

"And you read my—"

"Tweet?" His smile is devilishly wicked. "In my defense, it was hard to miss."

My mind is racing as I watch his lips as he talks. I have no idea what he's saying because I'm too preoccupied with mentally calculating how many filthy tweets I've written about him over the years. Hundreds? Thousands? It has to be in the thousands.

"—name?"

My attention snaps back to the movie-star god sitting so close to me my whole body is tingling. "What?"

"I said, what's your Twitter name? I know that tweet was to me, but I didn't see it online, so you didn't post it."

"Oh thank God!" I laugh with relief. "Whew, dodged a bullet there." I pretend to swipe the sweat from my forehead and realize I'm really sweating. And so is he. Is it suddenly hot out? Or is my entire body blushing?

"So what's your handle?" he asks as he leans over the side of the raft to reach into the floating cooler. I study his back and have to physically restrain myself from touching him. I've studied every part of his body in every public picture ever released. I feel like I know that back intimately.

My hand reaches out and my fingertips do a hover trace down the length of his spine. Jesus. I might not be able to control myself.

He finds what he wants and suddenly leans back, colliding with my outstretched hand.

"Were you trying to touch me?"

"Yes," I say automatically. "I mean, no!" *Shit.* "No! Of course not. No!"

He leans all the way back again so that our shoulders are touching and then pops the cap off a beer and hands it to me. "I like that."

"What?"

"Your automatic response was to tell the truth." He flashes that movie-star smile again and I die a little inside from the cuteness of it. How old is he? Thirty-two, I remind myself. I know this. His birthday is two days after mine. But he looks boyishly young right now. Like he did back in his teens when he was doing Disney movies. He clinks his bottle to mine and takes a swig.

I'm still in shock so I just hold my beer out in front of me like an idiot.

"So what is it?"

"What?" I manage.

"Your Twitter handle?"

I do a pfft complete with a raspberry that makes me come off like a two-year-old. "Sorry, I do not care who you are, that's a name you're never getting. I've said so many filthy things about you on Twitter…" I can only shake my head. "No. Never."

"Like the one this morning? Is your pussy really bare?"

My mouth opens and stays that way for several seconds.

"Would you like to know what my invisible tongue can do to it?" he asks.

I'm throbbing.

"Or would you rather try out the visible one?"

I throw my head back and laugh. I can't help it. And then before I can collect myself he jumps off the raft and starts walking towards shore. "Think about it, Grace," he says, looking back over his shoulder as he gets to the concrete edge of the river and lifts himself out of the water. Every muscle in his back and arms is defined and rock hard as he stands up on the walkway and turns back to me, dripping wet. I glance down at his key lime shorts and see his bulge and then glance up quickly to find him smiling again. "Because that's an offer. I'd be happy to play the part of soft tropical breeze caressing your bare pussy."

And then he walks off, his feet slapping in the puddle of water his body is creating.

My mouth is still open and even though I'm still on the raft, he's not the only one sopping wet.

Chapter Six - Grace

#GodIHopeHeLikesThatShit

HOW did he know my name?

This question runs through my mind all the way back to the bungalow. I saw him in the bar and outside of the lingerie shop.

Is he stalking me?

Grace, you have lost your freaking mind! He's a movie star! He doesn't stalk nobodies, nobodies stalk him!

I shake my head and laugh as I push the key card into the reader on the door. It flashes green and I push it open. The air-conditioning makes me sigh as I kick off my flip flops and fall back onto the bed.

I met Vaughn Asher.

I scream and kick my feet. *I met Vaughn Asher!*

Oh my God, I'm having a fangirl moment. I get my phone out and text Bebe.

You are never gonna believe who I just met.

I add some hearts and flowers and then press send as I wait for her reply so we can play the guessing game.

He was every bit as much the Prince Charming in person as he is in the movies and magazines. Better even, because you never know how many of those pictures are retouched and how many of those interviews are fake. I barely got a look at his abs, but they were just as delicious as his back. And even though he was sorta dirty-talking to me, in his defense, I started it with the tweet. He is…

Lickable. Definitely fairy tale material.

I giggle and look down at my phone screen. "Where are you, Bebe?" I say to the empty room. They should be done parasailing by now. How long could something like that last? I need to tell her everything. I need to get her to tweet things to the Dirty Heaven list for me just in case he's watching for his name. He cannot find out who I am on Twitter. No.

I blush just thinking about it. Jesus, the things I've tweeted about him over the years. I would never be able to look him in the face. I tweeted about things I'd like to do to his face—hehe, I have to stop and take in a quick breath at that. The man's got a nice chin. I tweeted about how I imagine his cock looks. Another chuckle escapes. Thick and hard. And I should know, I saw it through his wet shorts.

Oh God. Whew.

The room phone rings and pulls me out of my erotic dreaming. I roll over on the bed, reach for it, and put it to my ear. "*Bueno, Señorita* Kinsella speaking."

"Miss Kinsella," a male voice says from the other end. "I have a message from Miss Chambers."

"Oh, Bebe! Where is she?"

"She is spending the night on Water Island and will be back tomorrow. She sends her apologies."

"Hmmm." That's disappointing. "OK, thank you." I hang up the phone and roll back over on the bed. I'm really not clingy, but this is a little much. I mean, we're on our honeymoon!

A soft knock pulls me out of my rant and I sit up and look over at the door just in time to see an envelope slide through.

I jump up, run over, and fling it open—I scan the pathway in front of our bungalow, but it's twisty and thick with tropical foliage, so of course there's no one in sight. I close the door and pick up the thick paper. This time the envelope says nothing, so I just take out the card.

Meet me. 9:00 Sunset Cove Beach.
Mr. B

What?

Mr. B? Mr. Buttinski? I gasp and clasp my hand over my mouth in shock. Is this note from Vaughn Asher? It has to be, that's what I called him at the bar.

Oh my God, can my day get any more fantastic? Vaughn Asher wants to… well, he never said what he wanted, only where I'm supposed to go and when.

Maybe I shouldn't go?

Ha! Like hell! I'm going. I get up and go over to the closet where my meager wardrobe is hanging. I have three sun dresses, six pairs of shorts, four bikinis, three sexy camis, two tank tops, and a pair of jeans.

A sun dress it is, I guess. I was not expecting to meet a movie star on this trip. I wasn't even expecting to get lucky. Not many single guys my age come to a resort like this. It's more for anniversary celebrations and honeymoons.

I check the time. It's only four, and I'm wiped out from the martinis and sun, so I figure I have plenty of time to catch a nap, shower, and pull myself together for a date with Vaughn Asher!

I flop down on the bed and stuff my face in the pillow as I kick and scream with excitement. I grab my cell off the nightstand and I'm already pulling up Twitter to tell my bitches before Dirty Heaven tonight when I realize I can't tweet about him! I already messed up and copped out to my past indiscretions, so there's no way he can know.

In fact, I'm not sure I want my girls to know either. I mean, they will out me in a snap. All in good fun, to them, at least. But I will die of humiliation if he ever reads half the shit I've said about him.

Once I get home and have time to process all this, I will tell them all about it. And I'll stalker-pic him all night so I have proof.

I'm smiling so big my cheeks are beginning to hurt, so I just roll over and hug the pillow to my chest, my eyes drooping as I daydream about what a night with a famous movie star means. I'm sure he wants it all on the down low. I'm nobody and he's probably only looking for a one-night stand.

Am I up for a one-night stand with a sex god?

Ha! As if. Yes. Yes, yes, and more and more yeses. I've never had a one-nighter, but if a girl needs to lose her booty-call virginity, why not do it with—wait. If I sleep with him tonight he'll think I'm cheap.

I am cheap. At least in this case. But I know better than to get involved in games. And I'm sure his game-playing skills are epic.

So no. I can't sleep with him.

At least not tonight. Tonight I should just see if he's normal or not. He could be a creep asshole for all I know. He could like choking or spanking or domination.

God, I hope he likes that shit.

Maybe he's got a special room filled with accessories. I giggle at that. I've never done anything so adventurous. I've had plenty of dates and boyfriends, but they were all pretty vanilla when it came to sex. Only one got a little crazy, but when he started putting on my underwear, I knew his brand of crazy was not what I was looking for.

But Vaughn... I reach down between my legs and find my clit through my shorts and bathing suit.

Way too much fabric between me and my pleasure, so I shimmy out of my bottoms, then let my hand wander again.

I picture all the dirty things I've tweeted about his face. How I'd like to sit on it and rub myself against his scratchy chin. How his tongue would feel lapping against my folds. How my wetness would spill out and coat his lips, and then I'd scoot down and kiss him. Tangle my tongue with his so I could share in the taste of me.

I don't usually get so excited sans vibrator, but the tingling between my legs begins to build, cresting higher until I have to pull my hand away to stop the release.

I don't want to masturbate to his image anymore. I've done that hundreds of times. I want the real thing.

God help me. Because I'm not sure I could say no if he wants to have sex with me tonight. And from what I've read about him in the tabloids, he's dirty. He's a talker, one article said. Of course that was only from a "reliable source" so it could all be made up. And another equally suspicious one said he wished he was chosen to play Christian Grey in *Fifty Shades* so he could take a girl to the red room.

My fingertips are slick with my own juices again, my hand wandering down of its own accord. And I bring my fingers to my lips and suck, picturing what it might be like to suck Vaughn Asher's dick.

And that's it.

Dreaming about blowing him is all it takes.

I gush for him. I come for him. I moan his name and buckle my back for him. My body aches for more as soon as I'm finished. I bring my fingers back to my mouth as I imagine how hot the sex might be.

How thick is his cock? How long? Will he go slow and give kisses? Or fast and hard up against the wall? Will he eat me out? Make me beg? Will I beg? Fuck yes, I'll beg. Will he have stamina? Or will he be a huge disappointment?

My eyelids become heavy and before I know it I'm dropping off as all these things flash through my mind.

I dream of hard cock.

Of my sopping wet pussy.

I dream of his fingers inside me, caressing my most sensitive spots. I picture his cock as it pushes past my wet folds and plunges into me for the first time, giving me the best orgasm of my life.

It's the perfect fairy tale ending.

Chapter Seven - Grace

#MyFirstFairyTaleDate

I JOLT awake, not sure where I am for a moment. A breeze passes over my hot sweaty body and I smell the sea.

I'm on Saint Thomas. I'm on Saint Thomas and... I have a date with Vaughn Asher! I jump up and check the time. Only eight. An hour is not great, but it will do.

My bottoms are still missing after my solitary orgasm and my fingertips slide between my legs automatically. I'm still slick. I suck in a breath as the tingling starts again. But there's no way I'm going to masturbate. If Vaughn Asher wants to have sex with me tonight, I want to be damn sure I come when it happens.

A cold shower takes care of my wanting and leaves my whole body with chills. My nipples are perky and hard when I slip the yellow sun dress over them. No bra tonight.

I look down at my pathetic pair of tighty-whitie underwear, wishing I could go commando on the bottom too, but I can't. That really sends the wrong message when you're wearing a dress, not to mention when you're on a first date.

I reluctantly pull the underwear on. They are not so bad, really, I've seen girls at the gym wear these. Not the men's variety—they were always some cute color and they were shaped for a woman's hips. But these are not so different.

The front sags over my pubic area and no matter how many ways I try to fold the waistband over, the ass sags too.

I slip them off and pull on a pair of bikini bottoms. These are better, right? Except all my bikinis are held together with strings and this dress is a little form-fitting over the hips.

I put the TW's back on and sigh. That's what I get for not making a packing list. And I have such cute underwear at home. Not the really expensive kind, but cute stuff.

I let it go and blow-dry my hair instead. It's one of my best assets. It's a color that can only be described as honey-blonde. It's thick and long, almost to the middle of my back, and perfectly straight. I love that. Some girls wish for curls when they have straight hair, but not me. I love the fact that I can let it dry naturally and it barely has any wave to it at all. And when I blow-dry it, it falls over my shoulders and down my back like a waterfall.

My makeup bag is filled with all the usual, but I opt for a light dusting of powder and some eye makeup and that's it. I've spent the entire summer bumming around in the sun on the cheap, so my tan is perfection. Why hide it with makeup?

I smile at that and adjust my girls inside the built-in dress cups. My breasts aren't overly large, but they are decent and they are natural.

I slip my feet into my favorite pair of espadrille wedges and take stock in front of the mirror.

Cute.

I've always been cute. People never call me sophisticated or glamorous or beautiful. No. It's always cute.

But it could be worse. I could be plucky or perky.

If someone calls you plucky, you're a side character. That's how they describe side characters in movies and books, right? The plucky sidekick.

I admit, I've been Bebe's plucky sidekick before. Many times. She's definitely the stock image of glamorous and sophisticated. Her long hair is dark, wavy in all the right ways, and perfectly matches her dark eyes. Everything about her look says mysterious sexy woman you want to take home and fuck.

A sigh escapes before I can stop it and a wave of self-doubt washes over me. Everything about my look says always a bridesmaid, always a sidekick, always an afterthought.

Never a star.

"Oh Jesus, Grace," I chastise myself out loud. "Stop wallowing in self-pity. You're young, you're pretty enough, you scored a fantabulous job that's waiting for you back in Denver, you have your own apartment—finally!—and you're about to go on a date with a movie star while enjoying a free vacation on one of the most beautiful tropical islands in the world."

I kick my leg up and smack my butt with my shoe. "A reminder," I tell the cute face staring back at me. "A reminder that life is what you make it. Happiness is a #Hashtag. You do not look like Bebe and that's OK because you look like *you*."

Do I have this pep talk often?

Yes. I admit I do.

It's not Bebe's fault she's beautiful. Plus, she's my best friend. We've been best friends for years and never once has she ever made me feel inferior even though she excels at everything she does. She's always supported me. She's always been there when things were falling apart. She never once questioned my past choices and she stood by me through all of it.

It's not her fault I'm so messed up.

I shake my head and my perfectly straight hair gently laps at my face.

"Snap out of it!"

And then I paint on my trademark smile and after a few seconds, it's real.

I'm going on a date with Vaughn Asher.

When I glance at the clock it's quarter to nine and I decide to head out early just in case I get lost. I sorta know where the Sunset Cove Beach is—on the other side of the lazy river—but I'm not sure which path to take to get there.

When I open the door the fragrant flowers mixed with the sea air bathe me in peace. This place really is something else. It's one of the oldest resorts on the island, but they take very good care of it. All the bungalows are updated with modern fixtures and electronics, the staff is friendly and attentive, and all the pools and beaches are immaculate. Never in a million years would I be able to afford this vacation.

Hell, I'm pretty sure this one is even out of Bebe's price range now that she's on her own. Her family is not super rich, but they are well-off. And Bebe had every opportunity growing up. But her parents believe in hard work and pulling yourself up on your own. Her family paychecks stopped the day she graduated from med school last May. She's adjusted well. Not like some trust-fund kids. She knew it was coming and planned for it all through undergrad and when she was accepted into the physical therapy program at the University of Colorado Health Science Center, she roomed with three other students in a crappy neighborhood the entire time. She saved most of her living expenses and now that she's an actual licensed physical therapist with an actual paying job at a local gym in Denver, all that scrimping and saving is gonna pay off.

My life was not so easy. I'm a few years younger than Bebe, and I have never aspired to a PhD like her. But I'm not doing too bad. I went to Colorado Mountain College, a small two-year school up in the Rocky Mountains where they specialize in hotel management, resort management, restaurant management—all kinds of recreational management, in fact. As well as culinary training, renewable energy and event planning.

That's what I do. I'm an event planner.

Yes, like weddings and stuff. But I was mostly hired to plan parties, not weddings. You have to work up to that level of responsibility. My professional life the past few years was mostly Super Bowl parties and bar mitzvahs, but I've been doing more and more weddings the past several months and I'm really good at it. I just got a new job and that is a huge step up for me.

I feel like my life is finally starting. Like the past is behind me.

All this deep thinking has me turned around on the winding paths and for a moment my heart beats fast at the thought of being lost out here in the dark. Silverware clanks on plates off to the right, so I take that path to try and get my bearings.

The path turns a corner abruptly and I find myself staring at an extravagant sit-down dinner party. There are several dozen round tables covered in white tablecloths and fancy place settings. Hundreds of guests, at least. All dressed to the nines in what I'd call summer formal. Cream-colored suits, crisp white shirts, flowing linen dresses, hair up in sparkling pins, and everything has a feel of being light and airy. Like these people are all caught up in a summer breeze.

It's a gorgeous event. There's a path that surrounds the party and I walk along it, trying my best to remain unnoticed and invisible. I take stock of the fine china, the silver on the table, the cut of the crystal that the fresh flowers are sitting in. I notice the engraved place cards, the subtle lighting, the flowing curtains of the large tent where a band is setting up for a night of dancing. Out here in the dining area there is a string quartet playing soft melodies that allow you to enjoy the music without it being overpowering.

This event is perfect and I'm jealous. Not because I wasn't invited, but because I didn't plan it. I shake myself out of that stupid funk and pick up my pace. I'm going to be late for my date with Vaughn Ash—

Wait. There he is.

He's here, at this party.

Hmmm. I stop and watch him for a few moments. He's deep in conversation with a tall, beautiful woman. Her hair is dark, like his, and she's dressed in a pale pink strapless gown that flows down her slender body and pools at her feet like satin water.

Vaughn cups her face with both his hands, his eyes intent on hers. Her eyes are glued to his lips as he whispers. And then she nods and wipes a tear. Vaughn leans in and kisses her gently on the cheek and then pulls her into an intimate hug.

I turn away, my heart beating so fast inside my chest I have to take deep breaths. I swallow down the lump in my throat and before I know what I'm doing, I'm running.

Chapter Eight - Grace

#SecondThoughtsSuck

I FIND myself on a beach. Not the Cove Beach or wherever the hell Mr. Asher invited me to. Some other beach that's finally open because obviously that party was the one responsible for closing down the resort this weekend. His party.

Why would he invite me out tonight if he's at a party already? If he's got a girl here with him? What was he saying to her? Giving her an excuse for why he needed to leave and meet me?

That's bullshit. I'm not a boyfriend-stealer. I think girls who date married or taken men are scum. I would never do that. Not in a million years.

But I feel dirty. Like—ashamed for even thinking about it.

I know his reputation. He's a flirt, if I want to be nice. He's a man whore, if I want to be honest. He's not married and most of his relationships are very private. But there are rumors about *why* they are so private. Something akin to a nondisclosure agreement.

Which, OK, that makes sense if you're rich and famous. I guess. But after what I just witnessed, I think he might have those contracts because he's hiding things.

His sexual preferences have been in the weekly tabloids more than once. But for some reason none of those stories ever affected him. Maybe people just don't care. I never did. The thought of Vaughn Asher being a deviant in the bedroom is more appealing than not, if I'm being honest. Lots of women feel that way today, so it's no wonder that these stories of his dark sexual side never touched his movie-star persona.

But I'm not into secrets. I have too many of my own to bother with strangers'. I like fun and flirty. Do I really want to know about Vaughn Asher's dark side? Wouldn't it be better to just leave him up on that pedestal I made for him and go on living in a fantasy?

I swallow down my heartache. Which is just ridiculous. I have no relationship with this guy. And he came off a little bit obnoxious before I realized who he is and changed my tune. But he *is* obnoxious. Pushing himself into my raft today and sending me this bizarre invitation to meet him on the beach.

For what?

For sex, you dumbass!

He wants to use me. And I was fully planning on letting him. But no way, not if he's got a girlfriend. Not even if he was breaking up with her, because that's almost what that conversation looked like. She was sad for some reason—he was comforting her.

I drop to the sand and remove my shoes, my toes digging in until they are on the verge of cold. "Grace," I say in a soft whisper. "You're way too impulsive, Grace. You're so eager for a fairy tale, you create one where it doesn't exist."

"It's the wrong beach," a husky voice calls out from behind me.

Vaughn. He's found me.

"Did you get lost?" he asks. He stands beside me for a moment before taking a seat on the sand. "A few of the waiters saw you on the path outside the party and said you came this way."

I can't look at him and I have no idea what to say, so there's nothing but the crashing of waves.

"This beach is private."

"Oh," I say, as I laugh a little to myself. I grab the straps of my shoes and I'm about to stand up when his large hand wraps around my small wrist.

"It's OK," he says in a soothing voice. "We can stay here." His grip pulls me down and I give in and settle back on the sand. "Did you eat dinner?"

I shake my head no.

"Are you hungry?"

Another no.

"Are you mute?" he asks with a laugh. But when I stare up at him his laugh dies in his throat. "What'd I do? You're looking at me like I'm the devil."

I take a deep breath and look away. His beautiful eyes are too distracting. I can't concentrate when I gaze at him. He steals my breath and invades my thoughts in all the wrong ways. I can feel the heat of his body next to mine. He's still wearing his suit. Not a light one, like the rest of the people at the party, but dark. A black suit.

It's an omen, I think. An omen that foreshadows the darkness inside him that I'm just beginning to see clearly. I know more about this man than a stranger should. I've been obsessed with him for years.

Maybe that makes me the dark one?

He huffs out a breath. "Did you hear something? Did you read something? I mean, you were normal this afternoon and now—" He changes position and flops down on his side in the sand, his hand propping up his face, his smile a devious smirk. "Now you're…" He stares at me in the moonlight, his eyes darting back and forth between mine. "Now you're… afraid." He lets the word hang there between us. "Afraid *of* me? Or just of *being* with me?"

I have no clue what to say, so I opt for the truth. "I saw you back there."

"OK," he laughs, a look of relief washing over his face. "So… what did you see? I'm not drunk, so I know I didn't do anything stupid. I'm still dressed, so I wasn't humping the chairs."

I chuckle a little at that.

"I didn't eat the salad"—he swipes a finger over his teeth—"so I know there's no lettuce distracting you from my disarming smile. I tipped the waiter and the band—"

"I saw you with that woman."

"What woman?" he responds too quickly.

"That tall brunette in the pink dress."

"Samantha?" he asks, sitting up with a smile.

"I don't know, is that her name?" I say back with a snarl that takes me by surprise.

"You're jealous." And now he does laugh. "You're jealous of Samantha."

"I'm not jealous, Mr. Asher—"

"Whoa," he laughs. "That's so fucking hot."

I just stare at him. "*What?*"

"Almost everyone calls me Mr. Asher, but holy fuck, hearing it come from your mouth."

I glance down at his crotch and see the unmistakable bulge of a hard-on. "I'm leaving." I get up, all the way up this time, and he does not protest. I grab my sandals by the straps and turn away. He gets to his feet behind me and I'm a few paces up the beach when he calls out.

"She's my *sister*, Grace. Samantha is my sister. She got married today and she's having second thoughts. I didn't know what to say to her so we were… having a moment, ya know? Kinda personal. I'm sorry you saw it."

I stop but don't turn around.

"I'm not usually so… I don't know, caring. But she's having second thoughts and I didn't know what to say to make it better and I was trying to help her believe it'll be OK. I think she loves him, but what do I know? I want to convince her this is normal, but I don't think it is. Because if I was getting married I would not have second thoughts. If I was the one who got married today, I'd be fucking my wife in the pool house, or here on the beach, or up in the hotel. My wedding night would be nothing but constant attention to the woman I chose to spend the rest of my life with. So I'm thinking she *did* make a mistake. But how can I tell her that?" He stops and lets out a long breath.

When I turn to look at him he's rubbing his hands down his face like this is eating away at him.

"I love my sister. She's fragile and perfect and if I told her what I really think she'd believe me and be crushed. And who am I to make her believe that? Maybe this is love to her? Maybe we just all love in different ways?"

I shrug my shoulders at him. "Oh," is all I manage. "I'm sorry."

"Would you have second thoughts?" he asks me in a soft and solemn voice. "On your wedding night?"

I shake my head and he smiles for all the wrong reasons. "No," I say decisively. "I wouldn't. Because I'm never getting married so the opportunity for second thoughts would never occur."

His smile fades. "Well, I guess you're not a romantic." It's not a question.

I'm not sure what to think of this conversation. I'm standing on a tropical beach with Vaughn Asher, the movie star, and we're talking about true love and romance. "I am," I insist. "I *am* romantic, but in a very…" I shrug. "Fairy tale way, that's all. It's not real, it's all fake. I don't mind the fake as long as I keep the fairy tale where it belongs. My fantasy."

"So why did you meet me tonight?" He takes a few steps towards me. "If you weren't daydreaming about a real-life romantic encounter—" He's close enough to see the color of his eyes now. And then his hand reaches out and takes mine. I want to pull away. In fact, I try to pull away, but he's got that grip on me again. "Then what other reason is there to come?"

I huff out a breath and the laugh comes out along with it. "You're a movie star. I'm starstuck. Can you blame me?"

"Did you think I wanted to fuck you?"

"Do you?"

"I asked you first."

"I don't pretend to read minds but I know your public persona well enough to say, yeah. I think you asked me out so you could fuck me. Am I wrong?"

"No," he says quickly. "You're not wrong." He grabs a hold of my shoes and tries to take them, but I pull back. "I'll hold them for you. And walk you back to the bungalows by way of the beach."

"This beach goes to the bungalows?" I flash him a raised eyebrow. "They're not beachfront. I know that for sure."

"No, but this beach winds around to the other side of them. We can get there from here. And I can replace my public reputation with my private one as we walk."

Well. I have to admit, I was not expecting him to be so… honest. "Will I want to know you privately?"

"Are you interested in a relationship?"

"What?" I laugh. "Oh, shit. Do you think I'm some kind of idiot? You're a movie star. I'm an event planner from Denver. I'm not that stupid."

"I know who you are and where you're from. Everyone at this resort has been background-checked, including you. So no, I do not think you're stupid. I just wanted a date with you."

"A date that ends with me being shown the door in the morning?"

He shakes his head as he laughs. "Grace, you're sending me mixed signals. Do you want to be shown the door the morning after or not? I'm confused. One second you're all swoony and the next you're hostile. I told you that was my sister. Do you want to go talk to her and see if I'm lying? You were obviously on your way to meet me when you wandered by the party and saw us. So what I want to know is how did I become some asshole in your mind in the span of a few minutes if what you saw was a misunderstanding?"

He's right. I'm being a total bitch right now. I'm angry and defensive and I don't even know why. And my surrender must show in my body language because he stops holding my hand and drags the back of his knuckles down my cheek. "Just relax," he whispers. "Come for a walk on the beach with me. It's the long way, sure. But I promise, I'll get you home and you can see part of this island not many people have access to."

I bite my lip and nod. "I'm sorry. You're right. I'm just... moody. My friend ditched me today and I'm being a jealous bitch in more ways than one. I misunderstood and I apologize. I'd love to see your beach."

I say the words and I really do mean them, but there's this instant when I watch his smile that I feel I've crossed a boundary. I'm not sure what kind of boundary it is, but I know it's going to change me. For better or worse, I think from this moment forward I will divide my adult life up into two parts. Everything that came before I met the movie star on the beach. And everything that came after.

Chapter Nine - Grace

#UnavailableToYouAsshole

"I GREW up here," Vaughn says as we walk along the beach.

I look around at all the natural beauty and try to imagine this kind of childhood. "It must've been like a dream."

"Where'd you grow up? Your background check had no childhood information on you. It was weird really—"

"Denver," I say, cutting him off. "Born and raised."

"Was it"—he looks over at me but I'm trying to avoid his stare, so I bend down and pick up a rock to skip into the waves—"a struggle?"

I really hate talking about myself, but I don't want him to think I'm evading. I don't want to give him any reason to go looking for my past. So I tell all the safe stuff. "My younger years were not bad. They were close to middle-class perfect, in fact. We were never rich, but we owned a house. A small one in the Highlands area of Denver. It's not a great neighborhood, it's still Denver and that comes with certain truths about crime and public schools. But it's nice. And quaint with all the whimsically painted Victorian houses and the small shopping district. A trendy place these days, where young professionals want to live because it's close to downtown and yet secluded from it at the same time.

"After my parents both died I sold the house to pay for college and even with my fancy new job, there's no way I could afford to buy there now. Most of the homes start at half a million. My parents bought our house back before the revitalization, so prices were cheap and the hood was bleak. But now... it's out of reach for me."

When I look over at him he's got a solemn expression. I know it well. Pity. When people hear that my parents died when I was young I get that look often. I like to get past it, so that's why I opt for telling instead of evasion. And then I always turn the conversation back around. "Is your family close? I mean, I knew you had a sister and a brother, and I've seen your brother in a few indie films, but I've never seen your sister before."

He nods as I talk. "Yeah, we're close." And his smile when he looks at me tells me that's the truth. "We bicker and shit, but it's all in good fun. We're very close. Even my father, the great Adam Asher, is a big family guy at heart. But I don't see Samantha often. She hates the spotlight. She hates the paparazzi. They wrote a story on her when she was a teenager, a real nasty one, and it about killed her. My father sued the magazine and they gave in and pulled the story before it ran. So all turned out OK. But Sam was...

traumatized. That's why we had everyone background-checked."

That whole story makes me shiver. "Why let anyone come to the resort at all? Why not just buy up all the rooms?"

He stops and waves his hand at the expansive back lawn of a sprawling beachside estate. There's a line of mature palm trees flanking a center walkway paved with pea stones that leads up to the Spanish-style house. "We own this place. The beach, the resort, the house. So we can do whatever we want with it. But—"

He looks down at me and this is the first time I realize how tall he is. I know his actual height, six foot two, because I know all those trivial facts about him from my fangirl stalking. But seeing him in person is quite different. I have to look up to pay attention to what he's saying and it makes me feel vulnerable.

"But *some* people," he stresses these words, "are on their honeymoons. And Samantha wouldn't hear of ruining them."

I laugh a little. "We lied."

"Obviously," he says back with a smile. "I wasn't sure at first, no offense," he adds with a chuckle. "You and your friend together are a fantasy come true. But the guy showing up and announcing himself as her boyfriend sorta blew your cover."

"It wasn't cover," I explain. "We just never thought about it, I guess. The rules never said you actually had to be newly married. And Bebe's current boyfriend is more of a toy than a commitment, so she brought me with her instead of him."

"Looks like that might've backfired for her." Vaughn's genuine smiles leaks through his feigned attempt at seriousness. "She seems to have forgotten about you."

"I know," I sigh. "I'm not usually a jealous bitch, but I was a little annoyed when the call came saying she was spending the night on some island."

"Well, I'm happy to keep you company and occupy all your thoughts while you wait for her to come home. Want a tour of the house?" He waves me forward and onto the little pea-pebbled pathway.

"Wow, these stones feel so good on my feet."

"They really do, don't they. You don't normally hear those three things together. Bare feet, stones, and feels good. But they are smooth and polished. It's like a foot massage as you walk." He chuckles to himself and adds, "And if you ever find yourself lying on your back, they massage that too."

"Is that right?" My God, he just admitted to fucking someone on this path.

"Wanna feel it? Here," he says as he takes my hand and kneels down on the pebbles, pulling me down with him. "Lie down, I'll show you."

"No." I pull away, forcefully this time. With enough gumption for him to realize that's never gonna happen. "No, I don't want to."

"OK," he says, getting back to his feet. "You're a tough cookie to crack, aren't you?"

"Define crack?"

"To break, to open—"

"Now you're the one sending mixed signals."

"Am I?" he replies quickly. "I think I'm sending all the right ones, to be honest."

"Why don't you just tell me what you want? Why ask me out? Why all this strange interest?"

He stares down at me with a flat line for a mouth, his eyebrows melded together in an expression of confusion. "Why *not* you? You're pretty, you're here, and you're the only beautiful woman around who is not on her honeymoon or part of my family."

Oh my God. The god just insulted me by practically labeling me 'available'. "Was that supposed to be a compliment?" I ask him. It takes a lot to undo my Happiness is a #Hashtag motto, but I admit, I am very, *very* annoyed at this point.

"Are you looking for a compliment? Because I can dish them out, Grace. I can tell you your eyes are beautiful, your ass is perfect, and your tits make me hard just picturing them inside that flimsy little piece of fabric you're calling a dress. Do you need to hear all those things right now? Do you need your ego pumped up? Because from where I'm standing, all those things are so obvious to me, I kinda figured you'd think I was some pathetic player if I said that to you tonight."

Well, thanks a lot, asshole. I'd like to say that, but I don't because I'm uneasy with all the anger I'm experiencing right now. He's affecting me in a very negative way and I don't like it. I don't like it at all. I cut right through his bullshit and lay it all out there. "Do you want to fuck me?"

"Would you like me to fuck you?"

This is going nowhere. I'm getting nowhere. And I can't take the pressure, so I blurt out, "Yes! Yes, I want you to fuck me."

He's shaking his head before I even finish. "I'm sorry, Grace. I don't work that way. I mean, yeah, look at you. I'd like to fuck you sideways, upside down, and backwards, and not really in that order because I'm a total ass man. But I don't date anyone without a NDA."

"Ah, there it is! I *knew* that was true!" I turn around and start walking back to the beach.

He does not follow and I know this partly because I don't hear the soft sound of feet on stones behind me. But also because when I get all the way back to the shore he calls out. "Hey, Grace!"

I stop but don't turn.

"Want a trial run? To give you time to make up your mind. See if I'm worth the price of your silence?"

I stop and throw up my hands but I don't turn back around. "Are you asking me if I'd like to fuck you tonight without the contract?"

"That's what I'm asking."

"No strings?"

"No." He chuckles behind me as he walks down the path. "There are definitely strings, Grace. And if we go any further, you will verbally agree to them. You'll give me a lady's word that you will not talk to the media."

Well, he's got no idea how much the media revolts me, so that's a deal I can make. I turn and I'm surprised to find him very close. "What am I not talking to them about, if I give a lady's word to take you up on the free trial?"

He takes a deep breath like he has to steady himself to answer that question, and then he lets it out and replies, "Submission."

"I don't really know what that means, so you're gonna have to explain." My heart is beating so fast at the sudden turn in conversation, I almost want to pass out. I steady myself by leaning against the trunk of a palm tree. "Will you hurt me?"

"Maybe," he says softly. "If you like that."

"What if I don't like that?"

"Then I won't do it. But how do you know you won't like it unless you try it?"

"Was all this small talk just a way to break the ice so you could get me to agree to this?"

"Yes."

No hesitation on his part at all. Just yes. I turn away and my heart pounds inside my chest, enough to make my vision blur, and before I know what's happening I'm falling to the ground. "Did you drug me?"

He laughs. "Drug you? How in the world would I have drugged you, Grace? Jesus. A little faith. I'm not a kidnapper, for fuck's sake. I'm just a kinky bastard who wants to get laid. And I want to do that with you tonight. Stop thinking so hard." He's got me by the arm and I realize I didn't fall. I almost did, but he caught me. "I can make it nice, if that's what you want."

"Just tell me why? Why me?" I force myself to look him in the eyes. "You can have anyone and I'm not the only available woman at this resort. So just tell me what you see when you look at me—and not all that bullshit about eyes and skin and whatever, but what you really see. Do I have the word victim written across my forehead?'

"Victim? What?"

"That something that says you can take advantage of me. That says I'm vulnerable and needy and I will agree to this thing you ask for because I'm desperate for someone to love me and the only person who can do that is you. That's what you want me to believe, right? I'm damaged—"

His mouth covers mine mid-sentence. A soft kiss, not hard and punishing like I imagined it. His tongue sweeps in and caresses mine and my heart slows. Slows. That erratic thumping a few seconds ago is replaced with calm serenity. With the tender touch of his fingertips as they brush against my cheek.

"Stop," he says when he pulls away just enough to allow him to speak words that won't get lost inside my mouth. "Stop all that talk, right now. I didn't realize you were so fragile. So... breakable."

"So weak, you mean."

He reaches down and pinches my ass. Hard. I squeal and try and pull away but his embrace constricts me so we are breast to chest. His hand leaves my ass and cups the back of my neck.

"I said stop." This time his tone is not soft. "And when I say stop, you obey that fucking command at all times. I don't use it often, but I refuse to listen to this bullshit spewing out of your mouth. Just because I find you attractive doesn't mean I want to abuse you or that I see you as weak because I think you might be willing to submit. It does mean I find you irresistible. That I'd like to explore our sexuality together. That I'd like to own your body, even if only for a short period of time."

My heart pounds again. Ball in my court, right? What the hell do I say? "I don't understand what any of that means."

"I know," he says, and then he kisses me gently again to calm me down. "I know. I see that now. So I'll teach you. If you agree to submit, I will teach you."

Chapter Ten - Vaughn

#OscarWinningPrick

THIS girl is a mess. A total mess. Oh, everything about her on the outside is the complete deal. She's just the right height. Not too tall, but tall enough to make holding her next to my six-foot-two frame feel like she belongs to me. Her hair is the most perfect shade of blonde mixed with darker brown strands, and it falls down her back and flutters against her bare shoulders in a way that makes me wonder what it would feel like dragging across my chest as she sits astride me during sex. Her eyes are a pale blue mixed with flecks of green. It's dark now, so I can't see them well. But they were the first thing I noticed when she looked at me out on the lazy river today. The sun made them sparkle with mischief and passion.

But this girl, confronted with my desire to have her, is falling to pieces right before my eyes. Her past is suspicious and parts of it are missing. And her sudden self-loathing and low self-worth is at odds to the woman portrayed in the background check. I know she's hiding something, but right now she still thinks her secrets are safe. So I'll play along to get what I want.

"I asked you a question, Grace. Will you agree to my terms?"

Her eyes are darting around, looking at anything but me. She begins with a shake of her head, her answer, a no for sure, on the tip of her tongue.

I stop her before she can start and take my hand to her throat, wrapping it around the smooth skin of her neck in such a way that I can feel her pulse. "Do you like to be choked during sex, Grace?"

"What?" she gasps.

"Choked," I say as I palm her a little more forcefully. She swallows against my hand and I almost come right there. Her fear is a turn-on, I won't deny it.

"No," she says, her words vibrating against my skin. I pull back, but she places her hand on mine and keeps it pressed against her, the throbbing of her heartbeat even more pronounced now. "I don't want to be choked. But..." She looks up at me and swallows again. My cock grows harder in response as I wait for her words. "But I like the *thought* of being choked."

I relax and let out a sigh. Then a chuckle. "You kinky bitch." I lean down and kiss her again, my tongue pushing against hers as my hand remains against her windpipe. "I can do that, Grace. I won't hurt you. You will trust me and always know that I won't hurt you. But if you like to be scared, I can do that. Is that what you like?"

"No, not scared. I'm not—"

Her words stop abruptly because my hand slips between her legs and my fingers pry her underwear away from her pussy and seek out her folds. She is so wet. "That's my answer right there, baby. I will always be able to tell if you're enjoying the way I arouse you with my fingers. You like this, don't you? You're dirty, aren't you?"

"Yes," she squeaks out as my fingers continue to play with her, rubbing against her opening, then sweeping back to her ass.

"Would you like my cock in your ass, Grace?"

"I don't know."

"Have you ever had anal sex?"

"No."

Oh, fuck me. "I will be your first then. If you agree." My finger leaves the hard bud of her ass and sweeps forward to touch her clit. She moans as I palm her whole pussy. "Won't I, Grace? You will let me fuck you in the ass? Me and no one else?"

She moans and I pull her hair with my other hand, yanking her neck back so she has to look at me. "Do you like me to pull your hair?"

"Yes, but not too hard." She pushes her hips against my thigh, grinding her pussy, looking for release.

I turn her around and grip her throat again, forcing her body against mine. "Hmmm, I don't think so, Grace. I get to decide how hard to pull your hair. I get to decide how hard to press against your throat. I get to decide when I take your ass and how. That's the whole idea of submission. Right now

I'm asking you yes or no to these things in general, not how you want them done to you. Do you understand?"

Her body has gone stiff in my embrace and so yes, she does understand. But she's not happy about what I just said.

"Grace, I asked you a question. If you're my submissive you will answer with a yes or no, then add Master at the end of that. Do you understand?"

Her silence is a battle I have no part of. This is the test. Either she says yes and we move on to more limits, or she says no and I end the night with one of the security agents escorting her back to her bungalow. Is my movie-star status enough to make her go against her instincts? Is she impressed with me? Does she want me? Or just the idea of me? Most women, once they get to know me, very much enjoy the sex but hate the actual man who gives it to them. I expect no different from Grace. Eventually. But it will take her some time to get tired of me, and that's what I'm counting on. A few erotic hours with this girl doing exactly what I tell her to do is exactly what I need.

"Yes, Master," she finally replies.

I chuckle and don't even try to hide it. "As if that was ever a question."

"It *was* a question, Asher," she snarls. "Make no mistake, I hand you control under the assumption that I can revoke it at any time."

"Of course," I reply, leaning into her neck so I can breathe softly into her ear. "Of course," I whisper. "You are in control of yourself at all times, Grace. But just know… you will never, *ever* be in control of me." She swallows against my hand again and my cock grows, pushing against the fabric of my suit pants and right up against the crack of her ass. I want to fuck her in the ass so bad I almost can't control myself and her thin dress is not enough of a barrier to calm me down. I growl in her ear. "Moving on. Do you like to be gagged, Grace?"

"Can I turn around and face you? Can I look you in the eye for this conversation? I mean, I'd like to see what's behind all this, if you don't mind."

"Behind what?" I ask back, a bit annoyed.

She brings her hand up to her throat and places it over mine, then gently pulls it off her neck so she can turn around. Her face is passive, not angry like I expected. Just calm. "I want to look at you to see if you're a monster or just a kinky asshole."

I laugh again, this time a little heartier, and then I shoot her the smile. My movie-star smile. "What if I'm both?"

"I'm not going to lie, Asher. I find the submission stuff sexy. I'm not sure I'm a submissive at heart, but I can get on board with some of what you're looking for. But the minute I feel manipulated, I'm out."

"Then you better leave right now, Grace. Because all of this, every bit of it, is manipulation. My goal, as your master, is to push your limits and make you enjoy things you never thought you would. I do that by manipulating you sexually. With teasing, with erotic spankings, with psychological conditioning that will allow you to let go of the monster mentality and accept the fact that, believe it or not, this shit is just fucking fun."

She huffs out a laugh and then the smile follows. "Just fucking fun?"

"Yeah." I smile back at her. "I mean, look at it rationally. If we weren't getting off on it, we'd get bored and stop. If it was really hurting us, we'd manifest that in our professional lives. I've had a lot of submissives over the years, Grace. None of them ever claimed I'd hurt them mentally or physically. An NDA does not excuse me from being punished for criminal activities. If I rape you, that piece of paper will not prevent you from seeking justice. If I break your arm, that piece of paper will not keep me out of jail. It becomes meaningless if I abuse its power. And besides, I'm not interested in hurting you. I just want to excite you erotically."

She's on board, I know she is. But she's still struggling to allow herself to say the words.

"Grace, you're not a victim if you agree. You're not a victim if you enjoy my domination. I'm not interested in forcing you to bend to my will. You've missed the whole point of submission if that's what you believe. Everything I do, if you agree to this relationship, is geared towards gaining your trust and allowing me to arouse you sexually in ways that I prefer. That's it. If I pull your hair, I'm trying to get you off. If I stroke your neck and then palm it with a little bit of pressure, I'm trying to make you come. If I stuff my cock down your throat and force you to salivate and breathe through it, you should let me do that because I like it. And because you like it as well."

My fingers play with her clit again as my other hand comes back to rest on her throat, reminding her that the whole purpose of this is pleasure. I want to fuck her right now, but I can't. Not until we get the ground rules figured out. She's not signing anything tonight, so this verbal sparring is all we have to set it straight until she's ready to commit. I take her hand and place it over the hard pulsating bulge in my pants. "You should want to submit to me because it makes me hard. It makes me want to fuck you in every way possible. It makes me addicted to you, Grace. Submitting to my whims so that I am pleased is addictive. I want that more than anything. I want a woman who will give me that when I ask for it."

"Then why all the secrecy? Why the NDA? I mean, if you're so convinced that this is good for me, and you've checked me out, then why do you have to gag me with the threat of legal action?"

"Please, Grace. I'm a Hollywood movie star. My father is a Hollywood legend. My family's production company has hands in more than two dozen high-profile projects at this very moment. What I like in private is no one's business but mine."

"You're wrong," she says, interrupting me. That ticks me off a little, but since she's not mine yet, I let it pass. "It's not just your business, it's my business too. Which means it's unfair that I can't articulate my experiences with a confidante just because your career might be impacted. You seem to think that there's only one person in this contract, and that's you. And honestly, that's a big red flag for me. Because if my feelings and experiences are that inconsequential to you that the contract is written to exploit me and favor you, then you are preying on me. Pure and simple."

"So leave," I say impulsively. "Leave. And forget everything I said to you tonight. Just move on with your life and I'll move on with mine."

She swallows under my palm again and it takes all my self-control not to flip her over and fuck her blind. Her hand comes up to her neck once again, and once again she pries my fingers from her throat. And then she smiles a big fake smile and tips her head up. "It was great to spend time with you, Mr. Asher. Perhaps we'll meet again some other day."

And then she picks up her shoes, discarded when, I have no idea, and walks back down the pea gravel path to the beach.

"You'll get lost," I call out to her. "If you take the beach. You'll get lost because you won't know which path to take back to the bungalows."

She turns around, walking backwards as she speaks. "I'm a big girl, Vaughn. A grown woman, in fact. I think I'll manage." And then she turns her back and skips down the few concrete stairs that stop at the sand.

"What will it take then?" I call again. "Grace! What will it take?"

She stops and turns. "Why? Why do you give a shit about me? Just stop and leave me alone. I'm not interested in feeding some sick pathology—"

"I'm not sick. It's not sick to have a full, enriching sexual fantasy. I—"

"See," she says cutting me off. "You're so fucking self-absorbed, you assume I'm talking about you. But I'm not, OK? Did it ever occur to you that I have my own reasons for saying no? Reasons that have nothing to do with you."

What?

"And you're so fucking clueless. Trust? You're telling me to trust you when you've never earned it. Why the fuck should I trust you? Who the hell are *you?* I mean, yeah, I admit I've stalked you relentlessly online. I've tweeted shit about you that would make porn stars blush. And it would be very easy to just let you fuck me sideways, as you put it, and then walk away with the movie-star feather in my cap. But Jesus Christ, Asher. You're an Oscar-winning *prick.*"

I laugh. I can't help it.

"I'm glad you think that's funny." And then she turns and starts her trek down the beach, muttering out, "Asshole."

I run to catch up to her and then I grab her arm. She pulls away, dropping her shoes and lifting her hands up in some kind of fake karate stance. "Don't," she orders. "Back off. I'm a certified Tae Bo specialist at the Women's Health Spa in LoDo. And I'm warning you, I will not be held responsible—"

"Tae Bo? What the fuck—"

"Yah!" She smacks me in the neck with the side of her hand and I grasp my throat, gasping for air. "Tae Bo!" she screams as I fall to my knees and choke. "Oh, shit, Asher! I'm sorry! I've never done that to a real person before! Are you OK?"

I lower my head and try not to laugh, because holy shit, she totally got me.

"Asher? Asher? Oh my God, talk to me!" She kneels down in front of me and starts shaking my shoulders. "Asher!"

I take a long breath of air, let my heart rate settle, and then I look up and grab her lethal little wrists, forcing her down to the sand, and pinning them above her head as I move my body over the top of hers. "You wanna play hardball, Hit-Girl?"

She giggles up at me and my dick is hard again. Fuck. She's all over the place tonight.

"I'm the master, Asher. I'm the master of playing games. So if you want to play with me, you should keep that in mind."

"You"—I lean down into her face and stare her in the eyes—"are *not* the master. I'm the fucking master. You got that? And if you call me Asher one more time, I'll make you pay for it later."

"Oh, yeah? How?" She bites her lip as she waits for my answer and I realize what she's doing. Evening out the playing field. Asserting control over her decision. Making me realize that if she gives in, it's because she wants to give in and not because she's forced.

I can't ask for anything more, so I silently accept her terms and move the game forward. "I'll spank you. Hard. Hard enough to make you cry and erotic enough to make you come."

"And what if I'm bad on purpose? What if my tears are fake?"

"I'll know."

"How?"

"Because I promise to never push you that far until I do know. Because by the time we get to punishments, you will trust me implicitly and I will know if your tears are fake and push you harder if they are."

"That sounds like it could take some time. So why should I care about your meaningless threats to spank me tonight?"

I smile at her and stretch my body out over the top of hers, leaning into her, pushing down on her. Hard enough that she gasps for air and my cock presses against her belly. "It will take time. But I have a long memory. I'm counting up all your indiscretions so I can dole out the consequences when you're ready."

She takes a deep breath.

"I promise, Grace. I respect you. You're not my victim. I like you and I think you're gorgeous. I love that you just cracked me in the neck and sent me to my knees. It makes me feel good that you can do that, although I'm not into physical fights, so if that shit turns you on—"

"No! No, no, no. It doesn't."

I smile big because while this night has had its share of ups and downs, it's all coming out in my favor now. "OK, then. Are you ready?"

She gulps some air, like she's not sure if she's ready to agree to my offer, but at the same time, she's not ready to walk away either. "I'm ready."

"Then let the game begin."

Chapter Eleven - Grace

#JustFuckingSpankMeAlready

GAME.

He's playing a game with me.

OK, asshole, I can play. I stare up at him and smile. "One, two, three, go."

He sits up, straddling my hips, and then leans down into my neck. "You smell good. Like the sea."

"I'm not sure what I'm supposed to do with that."

"Say *Thank you, Master.* That's what you do with that."

Oh, Jesus. This man is something else. But ten seconds ago I agreed to this, so it would be a monumental failure on my part if I didn't at least try. "Thank you, Master," I say back.

He smiles and stands up, then reaches down to offer a hand. I grab it and he lifts me to my feet. "You're welcome."

I'm at a loss now. He just stands there staring at me and I have no idea what to do. "Now what? I'm not sure what you want."

"Why not ask me, then?"

"OK." I look up into his eyes, unsure if that's allowed. Unsure of anything, really. But he's sexy. Beyond the fact that he's Vaughn Asher, the guy I've masturbated to for the better part of three years, he's sexy in another way too. His smile looks genuine right now. Like I'm amusing him. And I don't feel it to be condescending. It seems genuine. Like I give him pleasure.

I *do* want to please him, I realize. I'd like to please him. I'd like to keep him smiling. I'm probably more submissive than I'd care to admit and that scares me. Control is something I crave. It keeps my life orderly and neat. It helps me deal.

But ever since he peeked over my shoulder in the bar, I've lost sight of who I am. Snapping at him, chopping him in the throat. Who does that? Not me. That's so not like me.

Even though many seconds have passed since I agreed to ask him and no words have come forth, he's patient. He waits for me to be ready. He's still smiling, and that comforts me and gives me courage. "Master," I say softly as I continue our game. "What do you want me to do?"

He breathes out, like he was holding it in as he waited, and then he cups my face and places his lips against mine in a gentle kiss. "That, Grace. I want you to do that."

"I don't understand," I whisper back. The tide is coming in and the waves are bigger now, eclipsing my words so they are barely audible. "I don't understand what that means."

"I only respond to questions, Grace. Ask me a question and I will answer it."

Why? I want to say it out loud. *Why do I have to ask you the questions? Why can't you just tell me?* But I know why, so I don't bother. He wants me to defer to him. To submit. Asking him for things gives him pleasure. It probably excites him erotically. "Can you explain what you mean by *that?*"

He caresses my cheek with the back of his knuckles and then places a fingertip over my lips. "Suck on my finger, Grace. Gently, just very gently. Keep doing it as I talk." I bite my lip, take a deep breath and then open my mouth so he can slip his finger inside. He places it on my tongue and I suck gently as he moves it back and forth. In and out. "I want you to think about everything I ask you to do. Just like you did a moment ago when you took your time deciding if you would ask me what I wanted. I don't want you to say yes because I tell you to, Grace. I want you to say yes because you want to. Do you understand?"

He withdraws his finger and traces my lips, making them wet and slick with my own saliva. "Yes, Master," I say. My voice is low and throaty.

"Good, girl. From now on I will call you girl, is that OK?"

"Do you call all of them girl?" I ask, feeling a tinge of jealousy. And where the hell did that emotion come from? I'm annoyed at the way he affects me.

"Does it matter if I do?"

"Yes," I answer with an irritated clip to my word. "I'd like something else if that's your standard pet name."

He stares down at me for a few seconds, like my statement perplexes him. "Well, honestly, I don't call them anything. I just give commands unless we're in introductions or dismissals."

Dismissals?

"So, no, girl is not my standard pet name. You will be my girl from now on."

I nod and let out a breath. Things are getting weird. I have no idea what's happening or how I got to this place with him so fast. It was like a switch went off and here I am, his girl. He's good, I realize. He's very good at this game. He's been playing it a long time, I bet. He's the master because here I am, standing before him as his submissive, when ten minutes ago I was chopping him in the throat.

"I can read the doubts on your face, girl. So let's get the first one over with. Kneel, please."

I look up at him, stunned.

"Girl," he says calmly. "I said *kneel*."

I swallow and nod, then kneel down in the sand. I keep my head down but his fingertips find my chin and lift it up.

"I'd like for you to look me in the eyes."

I meet his gaze and realize he's got nice eyes. Not beautiful nice, they are that too, but nice as in kind. They are not the eyes of a cruel man. Which is good. If I'm going to let this man have his way with me, then I'd like for him to at least be kind.

"Good, girl. I like when you obey. Feel my cock with your hand."

I stare at the thick bulge in his pants for a moment. It pushes against his suit trousers.

"Eyes up," he says, correcting my chin with a fingertip lift. "Hand on my cock." This time his directions come out stern. Not angry, but stern, like he means business.

I place my hand over his zipper area and stare him in the eyes. He smiles and I smile back.

"Play with it, girl."

His dick fills up my palm and I wonder if I'd be able to wrap my hand completely around it. I squeeze, but it's not very accessible. "May I take it out?" I ask. I look away from his eyes for a second because I have no idea where that question came from, but his hand guides my face back to him.

"Yes, you may please me however you want for the next few minutes, then I'll ask you to do it the way I like it."

"Why not just tell me how you like it?"

"You're going to get spanked for that, girl. Not tonight, we're not ready for that. But I'm keeping a tally. Don't forget. Now what should you have said?"

"Yes, Master," I say with a smile.

He smiles back and I relax a little. "But I'll answer your question so you understand. I want you to show me how you like to pleasure me with your mouth first. So do things you like."

My doubts must be written all over my face because then he asks a question no woman wants to hear when she's confronted with a man's sex aimed at her mouth. "Do you have much experience?"

I shake my head. "Not much."

"Do you like it? Sucking a man's dick?"

"No," I answer truthfully.

"Hmm. Well, then in that case, I'll show you how I like it first. But under one condition."

"What?" He frowns at me, so I correct myself. "What is the condition, Master?"

He places his hand over mine, which is still cupping his dick, and makes me squeeze. "Fuck, you're turning me on so bad right now, Grace. The only reason I haven't come yet is because I'm saving it for your throat."

My eyebrows shoot up. I have never, *ever* swallowed a man's come. And I'm not even close to being ready to do that tonight. I know he reads that expression for what it is, but he ignores it this time. A firm declaration that I will indeed be swallowing very shortly.

"My condition, girl, if I tell you how to blow me, is that you must first tell me how to lick your pussy to make you come."

Oh, fuck. "I'm wet," I say out loud. And then I cover my mouth with the hand that's supposed to be fondling his cock.

He laughs and I smile up at him, happy that he's amused.

"Lift your arms," he orders. I lift my arms and he reaches down, grabs the hem of my dress, and pulls it over my head. I have no bra on, so my nipples perk to attention from the cool sea mist billowing up from the rising waves. He tosses the dress aside. "Stand, please."

I stand up and his eyes caress my body. His heated stare makes me writhe with want. I want him to touch me very badly. All this is happening too slow for me. I'm used to men trying to get their dicks inside me as fast as possible. I'm used to being groped and left wanting more attention. But right now, I might be getting too *much* attention. He's captivated. He reaches out to touch me, pinching my nipple so I gasp and then moan. He pulls me close to his body and then one hand reaches around to cup my ass, while the other one slips inside my panties.

"What the hell are you wearing?"

"What?" It's like a scratch across a record, that's how abruptly the erotic mood ends.

"Your panties," he says with confusion, "are men's briefs."

I laugh. "Oh, shit."

"Why are you wearing men's briefs? Whose fucking underwear are these?" When I look up at him he's livid with the thought that I'm wearing another man's underwear.

"Asher, Jesus, they're mine! I just bought them today because I forgot to pack panties!"

"That's going on the list, missy!"

I laugh. "What list?" My outburst dies because he's serious. "What the hell are you talking about?"

"You called me Asher, that's one more spanking. And you didn't call me Master, so that's two. Plus, you're wearing men's underwear. That's three."

"You can't spank me for wearing my own underwear!"

"I can and I will."

"Oh, for fuck's sake. You're being unreasonable. Just tell me how you like your stupid cock sucked so we can move on to the good shit!"

"You'll get spanked for that too."

"For what? What the fuck did I do now?"

"Two fucks and a shit, plus you gave me an order. I'm the master, Grace. Me. Not you."

"Oh, Jesus Christ. Fine." I fling my arms out to my sides like I'm being crucified and yell, "At your service, Master!"

"You're not taking this seriously," he says with a growl.

And he's right. Because I laugh. "Asher, lighten up, man. You want me to tell you how I like my pussy licked or not? Because I'm horny as fuck and I want to get *something* out of all this tonight."

He takes out his phone and points it at me, the little red light blinking that it's recording. "When we do those spankings, Grace, I will remind you of this night. I will play this video back for you so you understand each and every swat across your bare ass. And when you're crying—"

"When I'm begging for more, you mean? Because holy hell—"

"—I'm gonna laugh, and say, lighten up, Kinsella—"

"—all I want is to *get laid*!"

"—you *asked for it*!"

"OK, that's it." I grab my dress and pull it over my head, not even caring that the boob cups are all crooked. "I'm done here. I might as well just go home and get myself off." I swipe my shoes from the beach and start walking again.

"And I told you, you're gonna get lost if you go that way!"

"Well, then take me home. Now! Because I'm done playing tonight. You're a crazy jealous asshole. Telling me I'm getting spanked for wearing my own underwear. Pfft. Like hell!"

Actually, I'm not all that upset about the spankings. I'm like, dying for a fucking spanking right now. Anything. Some good cock-sucking directions. I'm even willing to embarrass myself and tell him how to lick my cunt. But he's got me so wound up, I'm out of control. I'm yelling and screaming and I'm on a damn beach with a movie star trying my best to get fucked.

And none of this is the real me.

I'm not this girl. Not in any way. I belong online with my Twitter friends. I prefer Vaughn Asher as my muse. And my heart actually beats faster as I realize this was supposed to be my fantasy and it's anything but a fantasy. It's... real life. And that's not what I'm looking for.

Vaughn weighs his options as he watches me have my internal monologue, then rakes his hand through his movie-star hair and huffs out a breath. "Fine, I'll walk you back."

"Great."

Chapter Twelve - Grace

#FreeSamplesMakeMeWet

AS soon as we get to a place I recognize, I turn to him. "Thanks, I can find my way from here." I sigh before I can stop myself because… Vaughn Asher date… *over.*

He gives me a simple nod, but his frown is all I remember as I turn my back and make my way down the path that leads to the bungalows.

So yes, here I am. Alone. As usual. Sure, I ditched the control freak… but now I'm obsessed with thinking about him. Dirty thoughts, too. Filthy thoughts about what I could be doing with him, instead of running all these regrets through my mind.

My hands wander between my legs more times than I can count and even though I want nothing more than to get off and feel that release, I stop myself every time.

Because I can't get into it. My perfect masturbation fantasy has been shattered. Who do I think about if not Vaughn Asher? He's been in my mind for years. Always reliable. Always perfect. Always sexy and hot and willing to do whatever it takes to satisfy me. I have pictured his cock entering me, his mouth on mine, his hands on my most intimate parts and tonight I had the opportunity to take everything from him I ever dreamed of.

And I walked away.

What the fuck is wrong with me?

I contemplate going after him. I fantasize that I make my way back to that beach, walk up the pea gravel path, and find him naked at the pool, the underwater lights flickering off his perfect body with the rippled reflection of the water. He holds out his arms and I walk into them, like it's the most natural thing in the world. Like he's been waiting for me, and only me. Like we were meant to be together.

But of course, the negativity starts in. Eating its way into my perfect fairy tale, curling the edges with fire and disappointment, and then leaving nothing but spent ash. I see him with other women. I see him hovering over me, making me shut up or crawl to him on my knees, only to laugh when I finally find myself in front of him, looking up to his eyes for a blink of approval.

I think the laughing is the worst. I can handle the humiliation. I can handle the hair-pulling and the spanking and the dirty words and insults. As long as I know they are all fake, I can handle all of that.

But when the line blurs between the two, then—that requires faith. And I have very little faith these days. None, in fact. I have no faith. If he laughs, then he's playing a game

I'm not a part of. If I trust him, give into his demands and let him really be Master, and he laughs?

I can't do that.

I can't feel like I'm being made a fool. A spectacle. I don't mind being his plaything, as long as I'm not his joke.

Maybe I should just tell him that?

Right, Grace. Like you'll ever have another chance with him again. You have one day left on this island, then you're back to your job in Denver. Planning birthdays, weddings, and anniversaries.

That's not true. I've been promoted. I will, at the very least, be doing corporate parties and club events. I might even be assigned some more unusual jobs—like conventions and fundraisers. I'm moving up after only two years, so why do I belittle my job? It's not insignificant.

Because, Grace, negativity is a lifestyle choice and you fly that flag proudly.

Right.

Which was why I was so pissed that he thinks my hesitation is all about him. It's not. It's about me. Who gives a fuck about him? He's rich and powerful. I can't possibly hurt him. He's got nothing to lose at all in this relationship and he knows it. His smug ass knows that if I sign a NDA, he's safe.

I'm never safe. There is no distance, no amount of running, no fairy tale or fantasy world or Dirty Heaven that will keep me safe from my secrets.

I roll over and find my phone. Three thirty. I get out of bed and pull on a sundress, slip my feet into my sandals, and then grab my key card, my phone, and a fistful of cash, and go looking for a vending machine.

Or something. Who cares, I just need to leave.

I find the cold drinks machine in the open lobby of the bar. Workers are still inside there, cleaning up or doing whatever it is that bar workers do after the drunks go home. I grab my Diet Pepsi and walk down to the beach. It's not closed anymore, the party is over. I hope Vaughn's sister had a nice night, but if what he said was true, she's probably still wondering if she made the right choice.

I do think it's sweet that he cares enough about her feelings to not influence them. The intense moment they shared earlier this evening is proof that she hangs on every word. If he says she's not in love, she's not in love.

She trusts him, Grace.

Good for her. That doesn't mean I have to trust him. The perfect world I've built for myself is at stake, after all.

I sit in the sand and open my soda, the crack of the lid and spray of bubbles familiar and comforting.

My phone buzzes and I watch it light up in the darkness. A call from an unknown number. I ignore it and drag my thoughts back to my unsettled life.

Am I really surprised that my dream man is not what I built him up to be?

My phone buzzes again. This time it's a text from an unknown number.

Answer me, Grace.

I pick up the phone and sigh, then press send for the number. It rings. He picks up before the first one ends. "Don't ignore me. I hate that."

"Oh."

"Oh?"

"What do you want from me?"

He's silent for a few seconds and for a second I think the call dropped or he hung up. But then I hear him breathing. "Did I not articulate it clearly? Did I leave something out? Did I—"

"How did you get my number?" Why does my Dirty Heaven angel have to be a total demon? I look up at the stars and shake my head at some false God. *Why are you fucking with me?*

"I have access," he says, as if that explains my question about the number. "I have needs, Grace. You have needs. You have one more day here, then—"

"How the fuck do you know so much about me?"

"That's another spanking," he says dryly.

And I have to admit, spankings are something I can get on board with. I have no idea why, but it's *so* hot. The mere image of myself lying over his knee, my ass in the air, my face pressed into the mattress while he tells me I'm bad and slaps my ass. Holy Mother, just... *yes*.

"I'm going to make that ass bright red and I'm going to make it hurt. Do you understand, Grace? You are disobeying me on purpose and I'm going to make it hurt. I'm going to pull your hair, force your head back so I can see your eyes when the flat palm of my hand smacks against the curve of your bottom, and I'm going to enjoy every wince. Every tear. And each time you flinch or buck against my punishments, I'm going to withhold pleasure. But each time, Grace"—his voice softens now, just a whisper, just a breath of air that speaks my name—"each time you stay still, my palm will soften and slide between your legs, pushing apart the lovely folds of your pussy, and I will pleasure you. Do you understand me? This is how the game is played. If you obey, if you please me, if you *submit*—then I will give you whatever your shuddering body requires to release. I'll give you a reason to scream in pleasure. I'll make that sore bottom of yours so worth it, you'll be begging me to come back and do it again. And if you're especially good, Grace, I will fuck you hard afterward."

I gulp some air and then look over my shoulder. He's standing near the concrete pathway, leaning up against a closed concession stand, looking as free and content and in control as any person I've ever seen.

And why not? Why shouldn't he feel that way? He's beyond rich, he's beyond beautiful, he's beyond talented, and he's so far beyond sexy, I'm powerless to resist his offer and he knows it.

"Say yes," he commands. "You want to say yes, so just say yes."

He's so right about that. I do want to say yes. In fact, I'm a yes girl. I hate telling people no. I really do. But for some reason, this one person who I want to say yes to more than anything else in my entire life has reawakened the no girl inside of me and I'm having difficulty understanding why.

"Say yes right now or I walk away and you never see me again. Because I require your commitment tonight or I'll just find someone else."

"I want you," I say breathlessly, my heart pounding in my chest. God, that was the total wrong move. What the hell am I doing?

"Of course you do."

"I want you, but I'm not signing that paper tonight. I need to think about it. I need to be sure."

"Grace, you have one more day left here on Saint Thomas and then you're gone. So you're wasting time."

"Wait, you said you'd punish me when I was ready, implying we had lots of time to figure this out and now you're in a rush?"

"Yes," he says matter-of-factly. "I'm in a rush because I want to fuck you, woman. I want to fuck you bad. I'm dying right now because I'm all the way over here and you're all the way over there, and all I want to be doing is fucking you. But instead I'm having this stupid conversation, convincing you, of all things, to let me pleasure you back if you pleasure me. But if you work out and you meet my needs, I might see you again. Some other place, some other time."

"Then no." I hang up the phone. Oh my God! I did it again! Where the hell are all these no's coming from?

My phone buzzes in my hand but I ignore it.

A few minutes later I feel him walk up behind me. "May I join you on the beach?"

"It's a free beach. Or is this one your personal property too? Am I just a beach to you? Something you own and enjoy at your leisure?"

"I don't own you, Grace. Not yet. So I'm asking if I can join you so we can sort this out. And that's one more spanking."

"We're never going to get to the spankings, Asher. You just admitted to it, so stop."

He chuckles. "That's it, isn't it? You want the spankings and you're afraid I'm not going to make good on my threats."

Pfft. "You wish."

He kneels down and then sits. "Grace?" I look over to him, annoyed, and as soon as I look him in the eyes, he grabs my arm and pulls me to his lap, forcing me to lie across his knees. "Would you like a taste and a promise?"

My heart is pounding in my chest. He pulls my dress up over my ass, leaving my ridiculous underwear exposed.

"Panties on or bare ass for your sample?"

OMG. I bite my lip.

"Answer me, dammit."

"Bare, please," I squeak out.

"Bare, please, what?" he asks, prodding for the word *master*.

I'm not in the mood to submit that far. But I will meet him halfway since he's giving me a free sample. I almost snicker at that. "Bare, please, Mr. Asher."

He huffs out an almost inaudible laugh and I know he's smiling.

Chapter Thirteen - Vaughn

#DirtyFilthyGirl

"YOUR disobedience is alarming, Grace. It makes me wonder if you really want to submit to me."

"I do," she says hurriedly.

And I know she does. She's having a hard time following through, but she wants to submit, that's clear. I hook my fingers under the waistband of her underwear and tug on it gently until one side slips over her hip bone. She draws in a breath, loud enough for me to know this is turning her on, and then she lets it out slowly. I slide the other side of her underwear down and leave them bunched up in the crease between her thigh and her ass.

This makes her squirm in anticipation.

"Have you ever been physically or sexually abused by a man, Grace?"

She hesitates for the slightest of seconds, perhaps wondering at my line of questioning. But then she says, "No."

"Erotically punished?"

"No," she says again. Her breathing is faster now.

"But you want to be, don't you? You want to be spanked like a bad little girl. Like a dirty, filthy girl, don't you?"

She tries to turn her head to look at me, but I push her back down into the sand and then slip my hand under her neck and palm her throat.

She swallows and my dick expands. God, I want her mouth on me. Right now. I want to fuck her mouth and come down her throat. But I want to make her beg for it and she's not even close to begging for that.

"Answer me, Grace. You insist on making me wait and that will earn you a punishment."

She grunts against my palm.

"Darling, I already have you figured out. You like the spankings. Or at least the thought of them. The erotic stimulation they will bring you. But there are many, many other ways to punish you. Ways that are not so appealing. So think before you speak."

"Yes, Mr. Asher," she replies.

OK, she's not going to call me Master, so fine. We can play that game. "Are you ready?"

"Yes, Mr. Asher."

I swat her bare bottom lightly with my hand and count out, "One," for her.

She doesn't even move.

And this makes me smile.

"How was that, Grace?"

"Um… well, what *was* that?" She turns her head, stretching her neck against my hand , and this time I let her look at me. "Was that *it*?"

"Did it not suit you?" I ask with a grin. "Was it not everything you expected?"

"Well, not really. I expected it to hurt. Or at least sting. But that—" She stops when she realizes I'm chuckling at her. "What's so funny?" she growls at me.

"You. And your silly rebelliousness at my requests. If you want a proper smacking, Grace, then follow directions." She squirms under my hold, like she wants to get up, but I place one hand over her neck and the other over the small of her back. "Hold still. You will stay like this until we come to terms." Her body relaxes and I smile. "Good, girl."

"I want you to call me Grace. And I'll call you Mr. Asher, can we come to terms with that?"

"If you do not submit, I'll get up, walk away, and never turn back. Your choice. The terms are clear, *Grace*," I say her name with a little bit of contempt to hammer my point home. "You. Submit. To me. Not the other way around."

I can almost feel her rolling her eyes and then she says, "Yes, Master," and I chuckle. "Don't laugh at me," she says, growling again.

I smack her hard this time and she yelps, her body twisting to get away from it before she can stop her reaction. "I'll do whatever the hell I please and you will shut your filthy mouth about it, do you understand?"

"Yes, Master," comes out a lot easier this time.

"OK." I put her underwear back in place and turn her over until she sits up. "Kneel right there," I say as I open my legs and point to the space between them. She scrambles a little until she's in front of me. We are eye to eye since she's propped up on her knees. "Should I allow you to look me in the eye? Or should I forbid eye contact?"

I watch her watch me as she tries to put the pieces together. Grace is a true submissive, she just doesn't know it yet, so I am patient as she works through things.

"Whatever pleases you, Master," she says quietly after a few seconds.

"You please me, Grace," I say back. "You please me." She smiles and quite possibly even blushes. I'd give anything for it to be daytime so I could see that blush. "So you get to choose. Which do you prefer?"

"I prefer to look into your eyes, Mr. Asher."

"You're bad," I say, smiling.

"You called me Grace and that means I can call you by your name. So I choose Mr. Asher."

"Who made that rule?"

"We did," she says back smartly. "Together."

"We've known each other one day, there's not enough time for traditions, Grace."

"Maybe not. But"—she smiles with mischief and I find myself eager to hear her reasoning—"we've set a precedent. So same thing. You call me Grace when you want to explain things to me, so I can call you Mr. Asher after you call me Grace."

I shake my head at her. "Fine, girl. We wouldn't want to break past precedent, so we now have a tradition. Now, what do you want to do next? Go back to your bungalow and sleep?"

"What's my other choice, Master?"

Jesus Christ. That right there makes me want to fuck her. "You're a good girl, so if you'd like to stay here on the beach with me, you may."

"OK, I choose to stay here on the beach. What will we do here?" She waggles her eyebrows at me and the grin on my face has got to be huge. Who knew she could be so sweetly manipulative? "You're the master, so you get to decide."

"I always get to decide, Grace. I don't need you to tell me that." She bites her lip to stop her smile. "Tell me about your life. Where do you work and what do you do?"

And then her mouth opens and words and sentences spill out. Paragraphs and paragraphs of details tumble out of her tender pink lips. I listen with an eager ear as she describes her new job, her old job, her loft in the city, her car, her fascination with cats—she doesn't have any because her building doesn't allow pets—and then, after she's all talked out, her pause is longer than it should be and I find her almost asleep.

"I guess I don't have to play the get-to-know-me game then. You're too tired."

"I'm not tired, I just put myself to sleep with my boring life. So, no," she whispers. "I want to hear, I'm not asleep.

My eyes are just heavy. Tell me. Tell me something about you."

"What do you want to know? The plot in the *Invisible Man 2* movie? My upcoming appearances? How much money I made this year? What kind of car do I drive? Choose."

"Certainly not any of those things."

"No? Why?"

"Asher, I can look that stuff up online." She opens her eyes and grins up at me. "In fact, I have. I already know all of that. No, I want to know what it was like to be you growing up. What was schooling on set like? What did you do on the weekends? Who was your best friend?"

I'm puzzled at her request. And now that I think about it, she never told me anything about her childhood. Only her present life.

But it's my turn to talk about me, and no one ever asks me these kinds of questions. Not anymore, at least. Maybe back when I was a little kid these were the kinds of questions they asked. But I never told the truth. I always lied.

"My childhood sucked," I finally say.

Her eyes fly open immediately. "Why?"

"Because I didn't have one. It was non-stop work. I've been working since I was five years old. I never had a best friend, or played on the baseball team, or had to stay up late to finish homework. It was all about acting. And don't get me wrong, my career doesn't span twenty-seven years because I couldn't make the sacrifices. Acting is the only thing I know. It's the only thing I do."

"You guys have a production company though, right?"

"Oh, yeah, we have our hand in pretty much every aspect of the showbusiness pot. But I'm an actor first. I do love my work, but all the sacrifices are adding up. The lack of privacy, the grueling schedules, the pressure, the politics—they all add up to an extraordinary life. And to be honest, Grace, I'd like a little bit more reality in my life."

"Huh," she says softly. "That's funny. I'm always on the lookout for a little more fantasy, myself."

I wait to see if she'll expound, but she doesn't. Just lies there, her head in my lap as I talk about everything and nothing all at the same time.

I like her, I realize once the darkness of night is breaking for the light of day. So I scoop her up and take her to her bed. I stare at her for a few moments after I place her on top of the sheets.

She's different, I realize. She's real.

I'm not sure what makes me think that or why it matters, but she's real in a way I haven't seen in a while. She's got an innocence to her, but at the same time, she seems hardened by something. I want her. I wanted the last sub too. But I never *liked* the last sub. She was just a body to use, a mind to manipulate.

But Grace…

I turn on my heel and walk out of her bungalow before I ask myself any more questions. She has one more day here at the resort and then we both have to go back to our normal lives.

It's best not to think too hard about her. I'll probably never call her again after I fuck her wild tomorrow.

Chapter Fourteen - Grace

#PleasePullMyHair

I WAKE to Bebe and Steve in the room. Bebe is right next to me, and she's not hiding her lackluster feelings for her boyfriend, because she's arguing with him in a nasty tone. "What's going on?" I ask as I roll over.

"I'm so sorry, Grace!" she exclaims. "I feel terrible for leaving you here all day yesterday and then brain case over there forgot to put gas in the boat he wanted to rent after parasailing, and we got stranded on that stupid island. We had to beg a local family to take us in. Did you know there's like, no real services over there?"

I didn't, but I'm thinking her question is rhetorical, so I don't even bother answering.

"And now *he*"—she snarls that last word out as she points to poor Steve standing sheepishly over by the door—"is mad because I refuse to go snorkeling with him today." She looks down at me and smiles her big Bebe smile. "I'm not leaving you again. It's bullshit. And I'd be so pissed at you if you did this to me, so I don't blame you one bit if you hate my guts."

I'm thinking about Vaughn and all that happened yesterday when Bebe pops in with another question. "So who did you see that you wanted me to play the guessing game with you?"

"Um—" And in that moment I know I'm going to lie to her. Vaughn never said I had to keep quiet, but if I'm going to sign a NDA, it would be a huge girlfriend mistake to tell her half the story and not the rest. She'd never forgive me. So I lie. "Oh, I think I saw like, some guy from back home. You know that one asshole who makes our drinks at the Starbucks in LoDo?"

"Oh, yeah, he's such a dick. What'd you say to him?"

She's smiling a bit. Steve is forgotten and she's all interested in my gossip.

I'm glad I'm lying. That sounds wrong, but I want to keep Vaughn for myself, and sharing any part of him with Bebe just opens him up to being fair game when we gossip.

"It wasn't him. Luckily I realized that before I said anything." My phone buzzes under my pillow and I reach for it, absently wondering how it got there when I don't remember walking home from the beach.

"Who's that?" Bebe asks, leaning over into my space so she can read the text.

The number comes up with no name, but I don't need a name to know who it's from, because it says, *Good morning, girl.*

"Just a guy I met last night on the beach. He's a local guy, so I'm not even going to bother with him."

"Hey, we have one more night!" Bebe says. "Don't cut yourself off just yet, Grace."

"Yeah, but you—"

"No! Seriously, if you found a hot man to hook up with today, by all means, go for it."

"See," Steve says from his spot by the door. "I told you she'd have something to do. Let's go snorkel and enjoy this day."

I sorta hate Steve right now, but I don't say anything because he's what Bebe and I call two-hour parking. Get in, get out, move on. "Yeah, if you guys want to go snorkel, that's fine with me." I text Vaughn a message that says, *Good morning, Master*, just to see what kind of response I get back.

My phone vibrates almost immediately, but I stuff it under my pillow until Bebe leaves. It takes me several more minutes of convincing, but she finally changes into a clean bathing suit and leaves with Steve to go snorkel. I run to the bed after I close the door behind them, and reach for my phone.

You have thirty minutes to get ready. To the left of your bungalow is a closed path. Follow that until you get to a bougainvillea-covered wall, then turn left and follow that south until you get to a clearing. Remove your clothes. Kneel down. And wait for me.

I'm already tingling with anticipation. I was too tired last night to think about sex once we decided to be friends on the beach. But now that I'm rested, I'm hornier than ever.

I shower and change into my yellow bikini and white shorts, then pull a white tank top over my head. I dry my hair to make it dead straight as opposed to mostly straight, and then put it up in a ponytail that hangs halfway down my back. I stuff my phone and key card into my beach bag, and rush out the door, eager to see what all this master stuff is about.

It's weird that I don't think it's weird. But I've read my share of sexy romance books and you can't play Dirty Heaven every weekend without at least having some kind of cursory knowledge about this stuff, so maybe I'm just desensitized. At any rate, I'm more curious than alarmed at what I'm doing. Curious as to why I'm doing it? Maybe a little. But much more curious as to what he might ask me to do. How he might treat me. And what might happen after it's over.

It's a risk, I realize. A risk that has lots of potential consequences. Because whatever happens today, it will be happening with a famous person. That part is a little surreal for me. He's so not what I expected. Maybe at first he was. Arrogant and demanding. But last night in the sand he talked for hours. And I did drift in and out of sleep for most of it, I was so tired. But I caught some of it. And nothing he said was extraordinary or special, and yet it was. It was because he was telling me things about himself that not many people would want to know. But the fact that he was talking about them makes me think they were all important moments for him.

Vaughn talked like he had years of things to say. Like he had no best friend to tell these things to, so he saved them all up for last night.

The path to the left of my bungalow is closed, like Vaughn said, but it's just a low-hanging chain with a sign dangling off it. I step over it and proceed into the thick tropical foliage. The sunlight filters through in random patterns that give the whole place a magical quality. When I get to the flower-covered wall, I turn left. The path back this way has clearly not been used for a while, because it's mostly covered by a layer of long, thick grasses. When I see the clearing up ahead I find myself holding my breath.

Am I ready for this?

Absolutely.

I step out and look around. It's not a large clearing, but it's about the size of the main room of the bungalow. There's no grass on the ground, there's too much shade here for it to grow. I like that because it keeps the temperature down.

Remove your clothes. Kneel down. And wait for me, his message said.

A couple of voices scare the crap out of me and I turn to see where they're coming from.

Oh, shit. I let out a sigh, because there's a path nearby, only about twenty yards away, and there's lots of people walking by. They must've reopened the resort after the party last night.

He wants me to remove my clothes here? There's a break in the trees, big enough for me to see the people, which means it's big enough for them to see me. I'm not sure I'm ready to take my clothes off if people can see. What if he leaves me waiting for a long time? What if people come down the path I just came from? Yeah, it says closed, but it's not really.

"Do you want to back out?"

I turn to find Vaughn standing at the entrance to the path I just came from. "I'm not sure," I answer truthfully.

"Do you think they're going to see you?"

I look over my shoulder through the clearing and then back to Vaughn. "They could."

"Do you think I want them to see you?"

I watch his face for clues. "Do you want them to see me?"

He smiles. "You're perfect at this, do you know that?"

I shake my head.

"That's the right question, Grace. And the answer is, no. I do not want them to see you. For now, you're mine."

I nod out an OK and then clear my throat to find my voice. "OK, then I should just... trust you to make sure they don't see me?"

Another very big smile from Vaughn. "Take off your clothes and kneel on the ground."

I take one more look over at the break in the trees, square my shoulders to muster up some bravery, and put my beach bag down on the forest floor. A shiver runs up my entire body as I raise the tank top over my head. Vaughn is there with his hand outstretched, asking for it. I hand it over and he folds it up neatly and places it inside my bag.

I slip my shorts off and hand them off to him as well. He folds them and puts them in the bag with the tank.

"All of it, girl," Vaughn says in a low whisper that makes my insides flutter.

I untie my bikini top, first the strings on my back, then, as the little triangles of cloth hang over my partially exposed breasts, I untie the neck and let it fall to the ground.

Vaughn smiles and steps forward. His fingertips flick lightly at my nipples until they bunch up into little hard tips. And then he leans down and picks up my bikini top, folds it up, and puts it in the bag. "You're beautiful," he says when he turns back to me.

"Thank you, Master," I say in response.

I bite my lip to keep from smiling, because his smile is wide and approving.

I decide right then… I like pleasing him. I like his approving smile. I like this. So before he has to ask, I hook my fingertips into the strings of my bottoms, and pull them down until they reach my mid-thigh. And then I stop.

I think this is sexy. Being half-undressed in front of him makes me throb with anticipation.

He clicks his tongue, and I know instinctively that it's not because he doesn't like what I've done or appreciate the fact that it's very fucking hot. It's because I didn't do it the way he asked.

And I'm OK with that too.

"You're testing me, girl?"

"No, Master," I lie. I have to bite my lip again and he has to turn his head to hide his smile.

We're both playing now and it's fun. Just like he said last night.

He walks up to me, so close that I have to tip my head to look at his face, and then he places his cupped hand on the slit between my legs. "Do you want me to fuck you, girl?"

"Very… very… badly," I whisper back.

"Get on your knees. And since you wanted to leave the bottoms on, you're going to wear them the entire time like that. Don't let them slip down your thighs, do you understand?"

"What will happen if I do let them slip?"

He looks down at me. His hand on my sex comes up to caress my cheek, leaving streaks of cool wetness as he moves. "I'll lead you forward to the edge of the clearing, lay you down on the hard ground, and eat your pussy until you scream for more. Everyone over there will hear you. And everyone over there will see you. Is that what you want?"

I have to think about it for a second, because actually, the way he just described it sounds pretty fucking erotic. He covers his eyes and shakes his head, his smile too big to hide. "Grace." He laughs out my name a little. "I asked you a question."

"I'm *thinking*, Master."

He rolls his eyes up and then takes my upper arm in a firm grip and leans down into my ear. "If that turns you on, we can start there now."

I shake my head. Fantasy and reality are two different things. "I won't let them fall, Master."

"Good, girl," he says stroking my face again. "Good, girl. Now get on your knees so I can stuff my cock down your throat and make you choke on my come."

I just stare at him.

"Now."

I stand there for a moment, thinking this through. Do I want him to talk to me like that? Is it a mistake to encourage degradation?

He places his hands on my shoulders and presses, encouraging me to follow through with his request. "Does it make you angry when I talk to you like that, Grace?"

I realize he's calling me Grace for a reason. When he calls me girl, I'm his submissive. When he calls me Grace, I'm his partner.

I drop to my knees.

"Answer me, please."

"I'm not sure."

"It made you hesitate."

"Yes, but…" I look up at him and find his attention real. He's concerned that we've already come to an impasse. "I'm not sure if it makes me angry."

"Why do you think I'm talking to you like that?" I don't know, so I say nothing. "I told you why last night. Think back."

If I pull your hair, I'm trying to get you off. If I stroke your neck and then palm it with a little bit of pressure, I'm trying to make you come. If I stuff my cock down your throat and force you to salivate and breathe through it, you should let me do that because I like it.

"You want to excite me, but you want me to be safe while pushing my limits."

He squats down next to me and cups my face in both hands. "Yes." He smiles so big I get all tingly from giving him such pleasure. "That's exactly it."

Chapter Fifteen - Vaughn

#BeggingWillGetYouEverywhere

I JUST stare at her for a few moments as I process what she just said.

Because that's the closest I've ever come to having a sub get it. Most of them say they get it. But when you reach a hard limit, they freak out, or cry, or make you feel guilty for moving forward, even though they did not safe word. I've never felt like they really… understood what we were doing. Yes, it's about sex, but it's so much more than that. It's about trust, and pleasing each other.

"I want to please you, Grace. Just as much as you should want to please me. And the ways I please you aren't always about how big your orgasm is. Sometimes I just want you to…" I stop because I can't find the right word. "I don't really know how to say it, but—"

"Accept that you know best?" she asks me, her large eyes turned up at me, so serious, so trusting, so perfect. "And just say yes?"

I nod. "It's reasonable? To want that? To presume that I'm able to give you that. And to get to that place with hair-pulling and cock-sucking?" We both laugh at that. "It's stupid. It's absurd. Hell, I'm not even sure it's rational."

"It's rational, if you look at the right way. I have never swallowed a man's semen before. And so it made me stop for a moment. But you explaining all this…" She waves her hand in the air. "It puts it in perspective. Because when you said you wanted to stuff your cock down my throat, I only felt humiliation and fear. But maybe I *will* like it? How do I know if I don't let you—" She swallows hard and shakes her head a little like she's having a hard time spitting the words out. "Take my choice away and force me to experience it." She has her eyes closed as the words come out, but then she opens them and I see her trust.

God, that's something I don't get often. A woman I just met yesterday is willing to meet me halfway. Is it wrong to accept that trust when I hardly know her? When I know she's burying secrets that might have long-term consequences?

It feels wrong, but not wrong enough to make me stop.

I reach for her hand and then stand up, placing it over my board shorts where my bulging cock is stretching the fabric. "Take me out, place my cock in your mouth, and suck me until I'm ready to come. Then I'll decide what happens next and you will accept that decision without comment."

She nods and whispers, "Yes, Master."

I want to kiss her. I want to pull her up from the ground and kiss her mouth until her lips are swollen and raw. I want to possess her, and fuck her, and own her. I want to show her how perfect she is to me right now. But that would just confuse her, so I wait for her to follow through.

She pulls the fly of my shorts apart with a rip of the Velcro and eases her small hand inside, grabbing hold of my thickness, giving it a slight squeeze—just enough to make me crazy with anticipation—and leans her head in. I shudder when her breath sweeps over my tip and then she places it on her wet tongue. "I never did tell you how I like it, but I don't think I need to. What you're doing is perfect."

She hums out a laugh and it excites me even more. I place my hand on the back of her head and push her forward. She gasps for breath and I ease up and let her take in some air. She does, adjusting to my silent demands. She doesn't take me deep, she obviously can't, so I let her do it her way and just enjoy the soft sucking, the lap of her tongue along my shaft when she pulls back, and then the teasing dance her tongue performs on the tip of my cock.

I've had girls who can take my cock all the way to my balls, but Grace's mouth makes me feel like I'm being worshiped. She wants to please me and I want to please her, so I grab her hair roughly and pull her head back. She gasps, saliva dripping out of her mouth as she looks up at me and waits for my decision.

"Stand up."

She stands, never taking her eyes off me.

I pull her by the hair and take her over to a tree. She's holding up her bikini bottoms with her fingertips, desperately trying to keep them from falling. I push her face first into the trunk. "Put your hands above your head and don't move." I wish I'd come better prepared—I'd tie her hands to the nearest bough and force her into a new limit. I realize I want to do this so she'll talk to me about it. So we can discuss how far I can go with the rope. Has conversation always been this erotic to me? Have I ever talked to the subs about it before?

Later, Asher.

I reach around and grab her breasts. They are not huge, but they are not small either. They fill my large hands and I squeeze them until she whimpers, then squeeze harder until she squeals. "Shhh, girl. The people are nearby. If you want to remain hidden, you'll be quiet." She is immediately silent. One hand dips down between her legs to assess her level of excitement. She's practically dripping. "You do realize now that I know your aversion to public fucking, we will absolutely be doing it in public every chance we get?"

"Yes, Master," she says obediently.

I want to ask her how real that is, but not now. Later. It will be a fun conversation for later.

I push my dick against her ass and she tenses up. I'm not going to fuck her in the ass now, there's no way she can stay quiet through that. But I want her to wonder. I want to see if she'll stop me.

My fingers drag her own wetness back to her asshole and I rub my tip of my cock back and forth against her clenched pucker. "Relax," I whisper into her neck. "Trust me."

It takes her almost a minute of this ass play before she relaxes and that's when I slip my dick right up into her slick pussy.

"Ohh." She starts moaning, but I cup a hand over her mouth and look through the trees to see if anyone heard her. I'm not against public fucking, but the weekend of my sister's wedding is really not the time or place. "Quiet, girl. You're calling attention to our erotic tryst." I pump into her slowly. In, as far in as I can go, then out. Withdrawing so slowly she gets impatient and tries to push back against me to make me pick up the pace. I pinch her nipple for that. "You don't get to decide how fast I fuck you, girl. You only get to accept my decisions or tell me to stop. That's it."

"I want to come," she whispers in her ragged breath. "Please, please, please. I really want to come."

"I want you to come, Grace." I wince at the name mixup. I don't want to confuse her. "Girl," I correct myself. "I want you to come, but I want to come first and I want to come inside you. Do you understand?"

"Yes, Master," she pants out.

I take that as permission. She barely has the words out before I let go. My release pulses through my cock, spilling inside her as she tries to stop her moaning, but fails completely. I cup my hand over her mouth and her hot breath only makes me groan with her. I want to come in her mouth so bad. But not yet. If she's never done it, it needs to be something special.

The last lingering spasms finish and I remove my hand from her mouth. "Your turn now, Grace. Lie down on the ground and open your legs."

Chapter Sixteen - Grace

#WinningIsntAlwaysWinning

HE'S called me Grace several times now when he should be calling me girl. But I'll think about that later. Right now, I'm eager to experience what he has planned.

A crack of thunder booms out over my head and scares the shit out of me, but Vaughn's reassuring hand comes down on my bare shoulder.

"Mmmm, I hadn't thought about what kind of fun we could have in the rain," he says in that deep, throaty master voice that makes my pussy clench with desire. And just as I look up to assess the weather, the drops start falling. I make a break for it, but Vaughn catches me by the waist and leans down into my neck to whisper, "Water won't kill you, Grace. Do as I say."

I stop and clear my head. "It's just a reaction," I say, looking up at him. "Sorry, just instinct."

"Instincts take a back seat to submission, Grace. Just listen to my voice. Now, I want those bottoms off you and this time I'm not in the mood for cute rebellion, understand?"

I nod and slip the bikini bottoms down my thighs until they drop to the ground. They land in a puddle and Vaughn taps each leg, asking me to lift my feet one at a time so he can pick them up. He folds them in half before placing them inside my bag with the rest of my clothes.

I'm completely naked now and I have to use all my self-control to not cover myself by crossing my arms.

"Lie on your back, on the ground, right here," he commands, pointing to a swelling puddle. The drops are big and thick and they sting a little on my bare skin, and the last thing I want to do is lie down in the mud. But I walk over to where he's pointing and lower myself. The mud is squishy against my ass and when I lay my palms flat, the water covers them completely.

"Good, girl," he whispers, staring down at me. "Now open your legs."

I bite my lip for this one and he shoots me a disapproving glare. The water is trickling down his bare chest in little rivers and disappearing inside the waistband of his board shorts. My eyes naturally fall to his hard bulge and I open my legs as I stare at his thickness.

Maybe it's my imagination, but I think it actually grows as he watches my pussy become exposed.

I gulp some air and the laughter of tourists on the nearby path excites me, making my insides throb with anticipation of what's coming next.

"Now," he says with a grin. "Tell me how you like it, Grace."

"Like *it*?" He cannot mean what I think he means.

"How you like men to lick your pussy. Tell me. Now." The last bit comes out angry and I wonder if I'll get another spanking if I refuse.

Not likely. He knows I want them so if I refuse he'll make me do something else.

What, I wonder? Do I want to know?

I smile before I can stop myself and one eyebrow hitches up on his forehead. But a smirk also comes forth and I know he knows what I'm thinking.

He wants me to disobey too. He has something in mind for punishment and I'd like to know what it is.

"No, Master," I say to soften my refusal. "I'm not comfortable doing that."

"Your comfort is none of my concern. My only concern is that you do as you're told, girl. Do you understand?"

"I can't, Master. I can't say those things. You should punish me."

I catch him mumbling "Oh, shit," as he turns to hide his smile. But then he clears his throat and turns back. "I will punish you by releasing you from my service. Do you want me to let you go, girl?"

"No, Master." And for a moment I fear he might actually tell me to get lost. I stare him in the eyes as he thinks, and then he holds his hand out, an open palm, to help me up off the ground.

I accept it and he pulls me up and forces me to come right up next to his chest. "I will keep you this time, Grace. But your punishment is to walk back to your bungalow like this."

"Naked?" I gasp.

"Yes, naked." He turns me around and pushes me back towards the path I came from, then smacks me on the ass very hard, and gives me a push. "Walk, girl. And don't look back. If you look back, this is over. Do you understand?"

I think he's pissed that I said no, so I nod and squeak out a "Yes, Master," as I pick my way barefoot through the long grass-covered path. When I came down this path a little while ago the sun was shining and it felt like a fairy tale—the flower-covered stone wall, the long lush grass under my feet like a cushion. But now the rain is pelting the foliage and the grass is matted flat in the mud.

Fantasy over. This is reality. And the reality is—I'm walking in the middle of a very busy resort naked.

At first I have no idea if he's behind me, but once I get to the wall I hear some twigs snapping, so I know he is.

I turn back down the closed path that takes me to the sidewalk in front of my bungalow. After a minute or two of more silence, and just before I get to the chain that I have to step over to come out of the cover of trees, he places a hand on my shoulder. "I just want you to know that your muddy ass is beautiful. It's filthy, Grace, but it's beautiful."

"Yes, Master," I say. Even though he's been calling me Grace, I've been calling him Master. I'll have to think about that a little if I make it through this test with my dignity. I stop at the chain and peek out, trying to assess if anyone is on the path.

"Do not stop, girl. Keep going, and when you get to your bungalow, stop, turn around, and put your back against the door."

I step over the chain and on the other side is a large puddle that I have to step through to get back to the path. I hear voices, but they are not in sight—the people they belong to are around a corner or on a nearby path. I'm not sure which, but Vaughn grunts at my hesitation and I continue through the puddle and step out onto the path. My pace quickens and I walk quickly down the small section of sidewalk that leads to my door. When I finally get there I feel a little relief that I made it, so I stop, turn around and then press my back against the door with a smile.

Vaughn is gone.

I fidget, shifting my weight from foot to foot as I wait. After several minutes of this torture, wondering if people will walk by and see me standing here, covered in mud and bare naked, I hear him talking to someone down the path, out of sight.

It's another man. A deep voice that has a hearty laugh to it. I can hear them as they talk low, but I can't make out the words.

I take a deep breath and wonder if he expects me to go inside.

Not likely.

The voices get closer and I know, right then, I know. He's bringing him this way on purpose. He's gonna let some strange man look at my naked body to hammer home his point.

I'm his property and he can do with me what he wants.

I watch them as they approach and then, just before they turn the corner that will give this stranger a full-frontal view of my naked and dirty body, they stop. There's a junction there. A fork in the road, if you will.

And I feel like this is a fork in the road for me too. Because if he brings that man over here, I will turn and go inside. That's a line I won't let him cross.

I take a deep breath and steady myself to disobey. They chat loudly, laughing. I can hear the conversation now. They are talking about my bag. Vaughn must have picked it up and carried it back from the clearing. They are looking inside, because the other man is asking Vaughn if he's got a naked girl stashed somewhere.

"I do," Vaughn says. "I'm going to her now."

"Don't forget lunch, dude. See you in a few."

And then the other man walks down the path that leads away and Vaughn comes into full view.

He's smiling. Quite big. "Good, girl. You have no idea how pleased I am."

I'm humiliated and confused but I'm pretty sure he's got every idea about how I feel. "I'm sorry, Master. For disobeying you."

"I'm sure you are, Grace. But we're not done here, not even close. I am a fountain of ideas, girl. You need to understand what you're getting into if you deny me again. I'm going to make this incident your *example*."

My mouth drops into a frown. "What else do I have to do?"

"Please yourself, Grace. Here. Now. And once you do that, once you make yourself come in public for me, I will allow you to go inside and clean up."

I just blink at him. He wants me to masturbate? Here?

"Hurry up, girl. I'm waiting.'

"I—I can't, Mr. Asher," I say, breaking the Master rule so he knows I need some leeway right now. "Really, I'm not kidding. I hardly ever come when I masturbate without a vibrator."

"Do you have a vibrator inside?"

"No—"

"Then you are shit out of luck, girl. Now put your fucking fingers between your legs, stick them inside your pussy, and make yourself come."

I draw in a deep breath and try to decide if I want to continue with this.

I do. I can't fucking help it. I do. I want him to fuck me, dammit. And not just because he's Vaughn Asher, the man I've fantasized about for years, but because I'm so damn horny, I just need it!

My hand dips down to my legs, but a voice on the next path makes me freeze. I look up at Asher and he's smiling. Asshole.

"Keep going, Grace."

He's confusing me with the name thing. He's calling me Grace, but he's not being sympathetic to my situation at all. I take a steadying breath and begin to stimulate myself. I watch him intently as I do it. I picture him naked to get myself wet, and then I picture him on top of me, kissing me with that delicious mouth of his. And now that I think about it, I've gotten myself off to his image hundreds of times. At least. And here he is in front of me, in the flesh. In the *rock-hard* flesh.

"Your cock is hard, Asher," I say, surprising myself.

He just smiles.

"Your cock is hard and my pussy is so, so wet. You have no idea what you're missing. You can stand there and stare all you want, that's fine with me. Because I've got what you want, even if you refuse to admit it right now. You're going to watch me play with my clit, then you're going to go back to your room and jerk off, thinking about me doing this. So I'm the one in control now, Asher. I'm the one—"

He drops my bag and walks towards me.

I gulp and keep going.

"I'm the one being satisfied, Asher. I'm the one in control, because I'm the one who will make you masturbate when you leave. So there. I win."

He cups my face in his hands. More voices and laughter come from off to the left. The rain has let up now and the place is getting busy again. "Miss Kinsella, would you like me to let you win this one?"

I nod. "I would. I really, really would."

"Will you agree to be a good girl for the next command, Grace? If I let you have your way at this moment? No matter what I ask?"

I know the answer to this, and that answer is no. No, no, no! He's setting me up, I can feel it. But I have a hard time saying no to people in the best of situations and right now all I want is to be spared the public humiliation of being caught touching myself by strangers. But at the same time, I really want to keep the game going. So of course, I say, "Yes, I will. I will, Mr. Asher. I swear. If you want I'll go inside and give it a try in my room. You can even watch, but I won't be—"

"Shh," he says with a finger to my lips. And then he leans down and kisses me gently. His tongue slips in slightly, but not far. Just a small, tender kiss that makes my whole body melt like butter. "You win then. OK?"

He pulls back, his strong hands gently resting on my shoulders, the back of his hand lightly sweeping up and down my cheek as he takes me in. "You win. Now inside is a box. Open it and follow all the directions."

He leans down and kisses me again and then goes back, retrieves my bag, and then slips it up my arm until it rests on my shoulder. He uses my key card to open my door, waving me in with a flourish of his hand.

I step across the threshold and let out a long breath of relief when I see a prettily wrapped box on the bed. When I turn to ask him what it is, all I see is his back as he makes his retreat.

Chapter Seventeen - Grace

#ThatListIsGettingLong

THE box is large, white, has a black bow, and everything about it says it's expensive.

I squeal after I close the door and then skip over to the bed and almost touch the precious, perfect gift box before remembering I'm a filthy mess of naked mud.

I run to the bathroom and look in the mirror.

Je-*sus* Christ. He saw me like this. I'm a fucking mess! I've got mud streaked down my whole body, my hair is a rat's nest of tangles and that's not easy to do with hair as straight as mine. I run the shower and jump in. I'm not sure how long I have before I need to meet him, so I wash quickly and wrap myself up in a large plush towel. I wrap my hair up next and then walk back out to the room and take in the box for real.

Yes, it's definitely out of my price range. And I'm just talking about the wrappings. God only knows what he's got inside.

I walk slowly over to it, circle it a little, like it's a dangerous animal.

When did he have time to buy me a present?

I pull on the thick black loop of satin and it slides so easily, the bow practically dissolves with one slight tug. I push it off to the side and then lift off the lid. It comes off with a whoosh of air, and then it's a flurry of white tissue paper. I rip the little sticker holding the two ends of tissue together, eager to see what kind of present a movie star gives a submissive on their second meeting, and have to gasp as I pull out the skirt and blouse.

The skirt is white flirty chiffon. It's short. Like very short. The blouse is white, crisp tailored cotton—very classic—like all the women were wearing last night at the wedding. There's a thick black belt that settles high on the waist to make the legs look longer once it's on.

He got these clothes from the gift shop. I know this because I was longing for this outfit the day we checked in. Bebe and I stopped just to look—and this was one I had my eye on. The two tags combined came to seven thousand dollars. And if that wasn't enough to give me a heart attack, I pull out a box filled with sexy shoes that have the trademark red soles of Louboutins. A classic black patent-leather shoe with a peekaboo toe and a cage of thin straps that climb all the way up over the ankle.

I set them on the bed and pull out another little pink bag that I know comes from the lingerie shop because my horrible men's underwear came in one exactly like it.

I peek inside and there's one of the bra and panties sets I looked at yesterday, in black.

Oh.

That's about all I can think right now.

Oh.

This is what it feels like to be taken care of by a wealthy man whose only desire is to turn me on and fuck me hard as I submit to his sexual fantasies.

Why the hell have I been fighting him? I drop my towel and comb out my hair in the nude. I feel so dirty, in a very sexual way, right now. I feel filthy and I want to be naked. I want to do that walk back to the bungalow again just so I can be braver. So I can flaunt my body in public and make him appreciate my boldness, the way I want to please him. And it's not because he bought me expensive presents, but because what he's asking for is something I want.

I want to surrender. I want to let someone else take care of the details for once. I want to be cared for. It's been so long since I've felt cared for.

Bebe always cares for me, but that's not what I'm talking about. She's a friend. And her family was my family after the incident with my parents. But I was too old to nurture like a real daughter would've been..

Vaughn is not nurturing me, but he is caring for me in his own way. And even though I'm excited—I love these presents, I want to go meet him now and continue to say yes to all his requests—I also feel a little… sad. Sad that this is the first time in my life I've experienced this kind of emotional reaction to a man's attention.

He's giving me something I want so badly. In a very specific way, yes, but is it wrong to enjoy it?

It's not wrong, I decide as I finish my hair, dust my face with a light powder, apply some pink lipstick, and drag some mascara across my lashes. Once that's done I stand in front of the mirror and appreciate who I am and what I look like. I'm not sophisticated and dark, like Bebe. But I'm pretty. And yes, cute. But naked I'm so much more. I'm sexual. I can see the lust in my eyes, the glow of my skin as I think about how he makes me feel, how he turns me on.

I put on my matching lingerie and immediately feel a hundred times sexier. I look at it from every angle in the mirror. And then I slip on my skirt and tuck in the blouse. I cinch the black belt high up on my waist and then buckle the incredible stiletto heels on my feet. Inside the box is also a small black clutch that looks like it matches the shoes, and I transfer my room key and a credit card inside.

I take one more look at myself and realize I have no idea what I'm supposed to do once I'm dressed. I fish around inside the box until I find a small white card.

Meet me in the restaurant lobby at one thirty. I check the clock and let out a breath of relief when I see that it's only one twenty, and then step outside, pulling the door closed behind me.

It hits me then.

I'm having a date with Vaughn Asher.

I have to bite my lip to stop the grin. I walk into restaurant knowing full well that heads are turning. But the only person I have eyes for is Vaughn. He's standing at the bar off to the right, talking to Dewain, wearing a delicious black suit tailored to every curve of his body.

Dewain nods in approval as Asher gets up and walks towards me. He holds out his hand and I take it.

"You look lovely, Grace."

I smile back, but before I can say anything, he guides me over to the hallway where the restrooms are located. "Come with me, girl," he says in his master voice, and I gulp down my apprehension.

He holds the door open to the men's room. I pass through and then he closes it behind us and locks it.

"Take off your panties, Grace."

Even though he's calling me Grace, I know I have no chance of talking my way out of this. He gave in back at the bungalow and let me win. Now it's his turn.

I lift up my flirty skirt that could blow up and expose my private parts with the slightest wind, and slip my panties down my legs, step out of them, bend over and pick them up. And then hand them over to his outstretched palm.

He brings them to his face and inhales. My eyebrows go up and he smiles.

"Fuck, that's intoxicating. Now listen, girl. I let you have your way but now it's time to perform. You owe me a public orgasm, Grace. And I want it here in the restaurant." He produces a small bullet vibrator from one suit pocket and a remote control from the other. "And I've got everything you need to be successful this time."

"No." It comes out so fast, we are both equally stunned. I take advantage of his pause, because this is the only chance

I'll get. "I'm not sure what you have in mind, but I'm not masturbating in a restaurant. I won't do it."

He scowls at me. "You will do it. You already promised me."

"So? I didn't know that what you wanted would get me arrested for being a public whore!"

"Would you just trust me, please? You haven't even heard what I want yet."

"Oh, for fuck's sake. Why can't we just have lunch?"

"I'm adding that *fuck* to your list. And to answer your question, because I gave you an order and you didn't want to follow through. This was the agreement. You do as I say and you get rewards. You disobey and you get punishments."

"But why can't you just say, *Grace, you look lovely. Let's eat some fucking food?*" I smile at his scowl and have to cover my mouth with my hand to stop from laughing. He's so easy to mess with.

"I don't appreciate that, Grace. Now bend over so I can get you nice and wet first."

"You're insane. I'm not bending over for you, and you are not"—I shake my head at the vibrator—"using *that* on me here in this restaurant."

"I am."

"You're not." I actually stomp my foot and raise my chin.

"Then you're released."

I flick my fingers at him in a mocking wave and walk out the door.

He follows me out hissing, "Grace, Grace," as we walk towards the maître d'.

I stop to beam up a smile at the very tall man standing at the podium. "Table for one, please."

"You can't afford to eat here, Grace. Charles, we're eating with my parents, thanks."

I whirl around and point my finger up at his face. "Who the hell—"

He clamps a hand over my mouth and then nods to poor Charles, who looks like he's about to go into panic mode. "We're eating with my parents, but if you'll excuse me, I need to speak with Miss Kinsella for a moment."

Charles clears his throat and waves Vaughn to a dark and empty dining room. I get a push to my back and start walking in that direction. When we're far enough into the shadows that no one can see us, Vaughn removes his hand. "We need to discuss the rules again, girl. Because there is only one master in this relationship and that's me. I give orders, you follow them, understand?"

"I'm not putting a vibrator up my vagina so you can have your fun humiliating me. And in front of your parents? What's wrong with you?"

"It's a game. They all know I play with my girls this way."

I just stare up at his handsome face. "How? How is this the person you really are?"

"What person?" he asks, but it's a flippant question and he's looking around, like he's anxious about people seeing us arguing.

"An asshole. You're an asshole. God, I feel so stupid for having this major crush on you all these years. I'm so disappointed."

He flashes me a glare and snarls, "You wouldn't be disappointed if you'd just follow directions and trust me."

"Well, excuse me for having an opinion about sticking a vibrator up my hole in a five-star restaurant in front of your *fucking parents!*"

He closes his eyes and massages his forehead, like I'm giving him a headache. "Do you want to have lunch with me or not, Grace?"

"I do," I say softly.

'Then you have to submit." He's still massaging, his eyes are still closed. If I don't give in, he's going to walk away. And even though he's an asshole and not anything like I expected, I really *do* want to have lunch with him.

"I will submit, but not in front of your parents. It's too much."

He removes his hand and opens his eyes with a sigh. "I'll find a way."

"Is that a challenge?"

"If you eat lunch with me, I'll find a way. You're mine, you agreed to be mine, and I want to fuck you. Here. In this restaurant. But I will do it when and where I want. And I will get you wet and ready in the manner that pleases me most."

I turn away so I can hide my grin. Jesus, he's intense. And he's serious. He will find a way, I believe him. "So I have no say in how I'm *pleasured?*"

"No. We discussed this earlier. You trust me and I make you feel good."

"And humiliate me at the same time."

"Were you humiliated this morning? Did anyone see you?"

"They could've seen me. And then I would've been."

"Grace," he says, taking my face in his hands and then leaning down to kiss my lips softly. I melt. If my panties weren't still in his pocket, they'd be wet from the gushing. "My attention was one hundred percent on who was on that path and where you were at all times. You're mine, no one else is allowed to see you. I made sure of it, so even though there was the possibility of being humiliated, you were not. Your job was to walk back to your bungalow naked. My job was to make sure no one saw you in the process. And I did that. And if you trust me now, all my attention will be on you and while there is the possibility that you will be humiliated, you should know that I will make sure that does not happen."

I gulp as I stare up at him. His mouth is still so close, his soft breath tickles my cheek.

"Understand?"

"OK," I whisper back. "OK, I'll trust you."

His hand lifts up my skirt and his palm passes over my round bottom. "The curve of your ass is perfect, Grace. I love it."

"Thank you, Master."

"Fuck," he sighs. "You challenge me, Grace. But knowing you're mine, that is such a turn-on. And I can't wait to spank you for all your challenging ways. I'll have your whole body across my lap, your head resting on the floor, your ass in the air"—the vibrator turns on and he slips it under my skirt and drags it over my crease, making me moan—"and I'll swat you hard enough to make you cry, Grace. I will. But I told you, if you're a very good girl, and stay still, I will reward you like this." And then his fingertip sweeps over my clit before flicking the vibrator back and forth. I moan again and then he pulls my hair until my throat is exposed. His whole palm presses against my sex, and I'm wet, but he makes sure I know I'm wet by inserting two fingers, and then he brings them up to my lips.

"Suck, Grace. When I kiss you during lunch, I want to taste your pussy on your tongue."

I open my mouth and take in his fingers, the sweetness of my own juices turning me on even more as he thrusts back and forth, the way I imagine he would with his cock if I was able to take him all the way into my mouth. I enjoy it, lap my tongue up and down and between his fingers until I make him groan. "Very good, girl. Very good. Now give me your purse."

I hand him my purse, which I've been clutching tightly. He opens it and places the vibrator inside. "When I squeeze your thigh, you will stick it between your legs, tight up against your pussy, and then excuse yourself and go to the restroom, leaving the vibrator in place. Do you understand, Grace?"

I nod and say, "Yes, Mr. Asher," before catching my mistake.

He smiles and takes my arm, not even asking for a correction. But if there's one thing I'm beginning to understand, it's that Vaughn Asher remembers everything. And he will not forget a single indiscretion. "Are you ready?" he asks as he leads me over to the restaurant foyer once again.

I nod yes and take a deep breath, not sure how I feel about this, but I'm wet, and excited, and breathless. I want more of him. He's an asshole, but he's my fantasy and I'm not ready to give up just yet. We only have one day together. One day and then I go home, back to Denver, back to my life, and I'll probably never see him again. So I'm going to try and be this girl he wants me to be.

I follow Vaughn's lead as he takes me into the restaurant. The maître d' makes small talk as we are led to the interior of the restaurant and then I'm looking at a table up near the window with an amazing view of the ocean. I can't take my eyes off the people because one man looks so familiar.

The maître d' waves us forward towards that table and my heart skips. When I look up at Vaughn, he's grinning like a boy with a vibrator remote control in his pocket. "Grace," he says, as we stop in front of the table filled with people. I recognize the woman I saw him with last night and the man at the head of the table. "I'd like you to meet my family."

The men stand as Vaughn pulls out a chair for me. "This is my father," he says, panning to the older man, "Adam Asher. My mother Corrine, my sister Samantha, her new husband Tray, and my brother Conner."

We exchange pleasantries as the waiters fill up our water glasses and ask us for drink orders. Vaughn orders for us and then in a moment when everyone else is busy chatting about wine and whiskey, he reaches over and squeezes my leg.

I reach into my clutch and pull out the little bullet, keeping it wrapped tightly in my hands. And then, as the menus come up to cover faces, I hike up my skirt and wedge the vibrator up against my clit.

Chapter Eighteen - Vaughn

#GettingRidOfThemIsGettingEasier

SHE doesn't even question me. No nod, no panic, no fight.

Hmmm. I almost wish she had. I watch her lift up her skirt and place the little bullet between her legs and then she swallows hard and looks around to make sure no one saw.

No one did, but just at that moment, Conner lowers his menu and looks right at me with squinted eyes.

Did he notice me?

I smile at him and he goes back behind his menu. Grace sits with her hands folded in her lap, looking frightened. I reach over and touch her leg and she jumps. "What do you like to eat, Grace? I'll order for you."

She smiles at me but it's fake. She's doing what I ask, but she's not comfortable with it.

Too bad.

"If you'll excuse me," she says as she stands. "I'll be—"

"Grace." I pull her back to her seat. "What should I order for you, sweetie? Fish? Pasta? Steak?"

She narrows her eyes at me but I simply smile. So she takes her gaze to the menu and scans her options. "The strawberry spinach salad, please. Now if you'll excuse me—"

She tries to rise and leave again, but I've got a hold of her hand this time. "What kind of wine?" I squeeze her leg again and then pat it. She looks at anything but me.

"Grace." My sister interrupts my thoughts, and Grace's next attempt at escape, and I realize she might be watching us closely. They all might be watching us closely. "What do you do?"

"Oh, I'm an event planner in Denver." She smiles weakly before continuing. "I got a glimpse of your wedding reception, it was lovely. Just lovely."

And now it's Sam's turn to be off her game, because she glances over at her new husband and smiles the same fake smile I just saw on Grace.

"This is boring," Conner complains on the other side of Grace. "Liven things up for me, will you, Vaughn?"

I narrow my eyes at him. Asshole. He's such a prick. He knows, he has to know. "So how's the new venture, Conner?" I throw that out to be a dick back, because we all know Conner is no actor. His indie films were offered because of his family name, not his talent.

My father grunts from the head of the table but does not lower his menu.

"Actually, Vaughn," Conner says with a smile that lets me know we are in fact, sparring, "I've started painting."

I almost guffaw at that. *Nice touch, brother. Nice touch.*

"Painting?" This gets my father to lower his menu. My mother as well, only she looks pleased. Conner does no wrong in her eyes. But my father, he's the only one who matters and now all the attention is focused on the middle child. The screwup. The wandering one. The... *artist.*

I almost laugh because I know what Conner really does for a living. But I've got an appointment with Grace's pussy. I reach into my pocket, pretending to pay attention to the argument over Conner's fictitious artistic pursuits, and press down on the mechanism that makes the little bullet pulse in a repeating pattern of long, drawn-out vibrations.

Grace stiffens in her chair, but does not look at me.

I like that reaction, the abrupt stiffening. But I'm going to make her pay for it. I depress the dial on the bullet three times and Grace immediately turns to me with wide eyes.

"Is that what you did with the money you borrowed a few months ago, Conner?" I ask, adding fuel to the fire. "Buy painting supplies and studio space?"

He shoots me a death glare and I chuckle. He's so fucking easy.

My father erupts in protest. He's looking at me and I shrug and play dumb as he rattles on and on about how my brother will never grow up if we keep handing him money.

I flash him my serious, concerned look and promise not to do it again.

Conner vehemently objects and the fight continues.

I quicken the frequency of the bullet vibrations for Grace and she actually moans.

"Is everything all right, dear?" my mother asks.

I chuckle but then a foot strikes out and kicks me in the shin under the table. I look up at my sister, who is sitting across from me. "Hi, Samantha."

She points her finger at me like *I'm* the baby in this room. "Stop it."

Grace looks over at me, her face bright red, probably thinking Sam is on to us. But that's not why she's scolding me. I'm fucking with Conner and Dad and she doesn't like it. I reach over and take Grace's hand out of her lap and raise it to my lips to give her a kiss.

Grace moves her chair back and says, "Excuse me, please, I need to use the restroom." The men all stand as she does, and then she scoots out and walks away. We sit and the fight resumes.

But I watch Grace's ass the entire time. She's taking tiny little steps, which means she's still got the bullet between her legs. I dial it up just before she turns the corner of the hallway that leads to the restrooms, and she does a little jump.

I snicker at that.

"Vaughn?" my father asks. I snap my attention from Grace and take it to my father. "Where did you meet this... Grace? What's her last name?"

"Kinsella, Dad. And I met her in the bar."

"So she's a weekend fling?"

I nod. "Yeah, it's over tomorrow. No worries, Pop. She's not joining the family."

"Then why bring her to dinner?" Conner snarls at me. "So you can play your sex games in front of us and think we won't notice?"

"Jesus, Conner," Sam says, clearly disgusted.

My mother still has her menu up to cover her face, so she says nothing, and my father shakes his head. "These games will come back to bite you, Vaughn. No matter how careful you are, no matter how many papers you make them sign, they will come back and bite you in the ass one day."

"Right, Dad," I say as I stand up. "We're going to skip lunch and have our fun another way, so see you later, huh?"

"You're a pig," Sam calls out as I walk off.

She's right, I am. But I like being a pig. I smile all the way to the restroom hallway, then dial up the bullet to maximum. I walk by the ladies' restroom door and hear her moaning in there. My eyes sweep the immediate area and then I push through the door. "Grace?"

"Oh my God, what the hell, Asher? Get out!"

"Open the stall door, Grace." Silence. "Now, girl, or the tryst is over and you can go back to your bungalow."

The lock slides and the door opens a crack. I push through and have to maneuver past the door to get inside because she's standing up in front of the toilet. "What did you do?" I demand. "Where is it?"

She swallows and looks me in the eye and growls. "In my pussy, *Asher*. Isn't that where you wanted it?"

"You're getting spanked for that."

"Whatever," she says with a wave of her hand. "Why are you in here?"

"To get you off and then we can leave. I've made our excuses to my family."

"You wanted to humiliate me? Is that why I'm here? Make me into a joke?"

"No," I say carefully, because she's pissed off, I think. "I brought you here to have an orgasm. This place is perfect, right?"

"Here, in the women's restroom at a five-star resort?"

"Ready?" And before she can answer my hand sweeps under her skirt and my fingers slide in her entrance next to the bullet. She's warm and wet. Very wet.

"Someone will hear us, someone will see us."

"I hope so, Grace, that's the whole point."

"I don't think—"

"Shut up, girl." She shuts up and I have a moment of fear that she might slap the shit out of me. Or at the very least, deny me the pleasure I've been imagining all morning.

But she doesn't. I've noticed she has a hard time actually saying no. Sure, she had a few moments last night where she made me believe she was saying no. But she's been saying yes since we met. She just doesn't realize it yet.

So I lift up her skirt and then turn us around and push her face first into the stall door. "Say stop if you want, Grace. You always have a choice."

She says nothing, so I take that as a yes.

Her breathing picks up and she puts a hand on the bathroom stall as I press towards her. She's shaking. "Vaughn, I'm not sure. I really have an aversion to public—"

"Why, Grace?" I turn her around, pull her close, and hold her tight. "Why does it scare you?"

"Because I don't want anyone to catch us."

"What will happen if they do?" I lean in so I can see her face and figure out how deep her fear runs. She's very serious.

"I know what you're getting at. Who cares, right? Nothing is going to happen, but that's not the issue."

"That *is* the issue, Grace. Is it sexy? Does it turn you on? I know it does because you're wet. So what's stopping you from enjoying yourself with me? Now. Here. Or this morning in front of your bungalow."

"I just..." She looks up at me, pleading for me to understand.

"You just don't know how to give in, Grace. I told you, I don't want people to see you naked. Your body is for my eyes only. I don't want them to walk in any more than you do, but I want you to submit to me when I ask. Even if it means it makes you uncomfortable."

She opens her mouth to protest but the door swings open and several women come in, laughing and joking. The stall walls shake as they enter on either side of us, and then the doors bang closed.

Grace takes a deep breath.

The girls talk over our stall to each other as they pee.

I place my hand on my girl's heart and it's racing, so I lean down and kiss her softly on the lips and whisper in her mouth. "You're so sexy."

She cracks a small smile, but her attention is on the girls around us, her eyes darting back and forth at the conversation bouncing off the walls.

"I want to take you," I continue, grabbing her head and tipping up her chin to make her look at me. "Tell me yes," I mouth silently.

Laughter erupts next to us.

"Say yes," I whisper it this time. She closes her eyes and nods.

My hand slides up her skirt and I palm between her legs. A toilet flushes and I lean into Grace's ear. "Enjoy it, darling."

I remove the bullet and swipe it over her sweet spot. Her eyes close again, but this time she lets out a small moan. There's enough noise in here to cover it up, so I keep going, pushing a finger into her asshole as I continue to drag the vibrator back and forth, making little circles around her clit. She's so wet there's a small slurping noise, but the second toilet flushes and Grace takes the opportunity to lean back into my chest and pant heavily.

"I'm going to fuck you," I say, just before the silence takes over.

The water in the sink covers up the sound of my belt being unbuckled and the laughter and joking of the women allows me to undo my pants. They fall to the floor with a whoosh and Grace has the most adorable look of panic in her eyes as she waits for us to be discovered.

But those girls are too busy with their own gossip to even notice. Or they have the decency to ignore it, if they do.

"I'm going to fuck you," I repeat as the door whooshes open and the three girls exit. "Say yes."

She nods her head and then whispers, "Yes," in a very small voice.

I place the vibrator in her hand and then cup her ass, lifting her up as I press her back against the stall door. She wraps her legs around my hips and holds tightly to my neck as I grab my cock and drag it back and forth across her wet opening. It slides in and she moans loudly this time.

"That's my girl, just enjoy it. Forget everything else but how I make you feel." I thrust inside her and she bites my shoulder. I take that as encouragement and do it again, making her grunt and squirm against me.

"Fuck, you are so hot, Grace." I thrust deep, but I go slow. Taking my time. She matches my pace, embracing the moment like I asked, and I reward her with an open-mouthed kiss. Our tongues dance and twist together, just like our bodies and then, just as the bathroom door whooshes open again, she comes. Moaning and biting and writhing as I hold her close and pump her hard until I spill inside of her.

She collapses on my shoulder and I lean in and kiss her neck. "I know you're on the pill, but I just want to hear it from your mouth."

"I am," she says sleepily. Her postcoital attitude is definitely something I love. And then she lifts her head and looks me in the eye as I watch her face. "How do you know I'm on the pill?" Her voice is normal, so obviously she's no longer concerned about being found out. I peek over the stall door and see no one, so we must've scared them off.

I smile as I set her down and then move her aside so I can open the stall and wet some paper towels. I hand them over to her and she cleans herself up. "I know a lot about you, Grace. And if I see you after tomorrow, I'll know even more."

I hold out my hand after she's finished and take her paper towels to the trash can. The door whooshes open and a woman with a name tag on her impeccable pastel-colored suit comes in. "I'm sorry, sir, you'll have to—" She stops and puts her hands up when she realizes who I am. And then she shakes her head a little, turns on her heel, and exits.

I look over to Grace, smirking. She's not amused. "What's wrong?"

"Are you spying on me? How do you know I'm on the pill?"

"Are you serious?"

"Do I look like I'm fucking joking?"

I point a finger at her. "Hey, I've warned you about that."

She slaps my finger down and points one up at me in return. "Have you gone through my things? Because I'm pretty sure you can't hack into my medical records to see if I'm on the pill."

I scratch my head as I ponder this. "Which is worse? Rummaging through your things or hacking?"

"You better be joking, Asher, because I'm not."

"It's a good guess. All women are on the pill these days."

"I don't believe you. And I think you went too far."

"Jesus, Grace. Can we have one hour without fighting? For fuck's sake, I hate the constant battle we have going on. Let's go hit the lazy river."

"You know *enough*, Asher—"

"And stop fucking calling me that!"

"So back off my space."

"Fine," I say as I open the door and almost walk into an orange cone blocking the entrance. When I look behind me there's a sign on the door that says, *Out of Service*. I look at Grace and laugh. "Wanna go back for seconds?"

She does not find that funny at all, because she pushes past me and walks off.

I let her go work off steam. She's so combative. I really need to come up with another way to bring her into compliance.

"You done in there, brother?"

Conner is walking towards me, so I shake Grace out of my thoughts and meet him. "I have no idea what you're talking about."

"Dad's right, you know. You're gonna get caught. Someone is gonna get you back for all your douchebaggy ways and when that happens, I'm going to sit back and watch the way you do me."

"Conner, what I do is private and none of your business. What you do is all of our business because you can't settle down."

"So I'm a free spirit, so what? I'm cool with it. And you're such an asshole for bringing up that money. I'm off the ground now, bro. I'm gonna be paying you back soon."

"Yeah, I was," I admit. But I laugh anyway. "Dad's so easy though, can you blame me?"

"You know what, V? You know what your biggest problem is?"

I shrug my shoulders. "I have too much money? I have too many girls?"

"You have it too *easy*. And one of these days, Vaughn, the shit's gonna get hard and you're not gonna know what to do. You live this charmed life and you think everything is forever. Money, girls, cars, jobs... but it's not, brother. It's finite. Everything and everyone has an expiration date."

"Whatever."

"So when your day comes, I do not want to hear your bitching."

And then he pushes open the door to the men's room and disappears inside.

I huff out a breath of air and shake my head. Fuck him. He's just mad because he never made it as an actor and I've got blockbusters lined up in post-production for the next year and a half.

And I've got Grace. He might be a little jealous of that too, because while Conner can *get* a girl, he can't seem to keep one.

I never have that problem.

My problem is how to get rid of them.

Chapter Nineteen - Grace

#IHaveLostMyMind

WHAT the hell am I doing?

This thought runs through my brain the whole way back to my bungalow.

Because I mean, what the hell, Grace? I do not even recognize myself right now. Since when do I let a man treat me like this? And yeah, I get that he's a movie star, a man I've been obsessed with for years—but this?

I admit, I'm not usually one for confrontation and I have a hard time saying no to people. But this is not me. This person cannot be me.

And what the hell was that back there? He planned for me to meet his parents so he could humiliate me.

I don't care how many ways you look at it, that's what that was. Pure and simple. He was mad because I can't be like the sluts he likes to fuck, so he made me pay for it.

Note to self, saying no to Vaughn Asher has consequences.

Right. But so does saying yes. Because saying yes gives him permission to do this shit. Is this what I am? A plaything for a wealthy man? Willing to sell myself to gain—what? What am I getting out of this tryst, as he likes to call it?

Fame? No, certainly not. He wants me to be a secret. Which is fine with me, I'm with his sister Sam on that shit. I have no desire to be in the spotlight with him or as a victim of his fetishes.

Gifts? I huff out a long breath of air. Yes, I have to admit as I look down at my clothes, I accepted a gift from him and I enjoyed it.

And now this whole outfit feels dirty.

I push my key card into the bungalow door and immediately begin taking off my clothes. I fold it all very carefully, sans underwear, since Vaughn still has those in his pocket, and place it all back inside the box. I run my fingertips across the fabric for a moment, enjoying the quality. It's something I'd never in a million years be able to just buy without guilt over spending so much.

This makes me pause, because I'm like most girls who grew up with lots of limits in place. I want more. I do, I admit it. I want more than just a working a job that takes up most of my life just so I can afford to live in a neighborhood that doesn't scare the shit out of me. I want to be taken to dinner and given presents to make me feel special. I want all those things.

But the reality of that want is that the men who are capable of fulfilling it are always asking for more than I'm willing to give in return. This present was given to me for the wrong reasons. It was a payoff. It was a consolation. It was a bribe.

Do as I say, Grace, and I'll give you the things you want.

But do I really want them if that's how I have to get them? Isn't getting them part of the journey? Aren't things like success and money and a nice big house supposed to be the result of hard work, determination, tenacity, and a little bit of luck?

This dress symbolizes all the wrong things for me. It was all luck. There's no hard work in being Asher's plaything. There's no satisfaction beyond an orgasm. I don't want to be lucky, I want to be good. I want to succeed at more than just following the sexual commands of an ego-inflated movie star.

And I'm ashamed of myself for allowing this to happen. For being drawn in, for being seduced by him.

He seduced me into being someone else.

And it's got nothing to do with the sex. Some of that is the real me, obviously, since I get off on it. That's not the problem. The problem is not me, actually. It's him.

He's an asshole.

And that sucks because the little dream bubble I wrapped around Vaughn Asher the Movie Star is being shattered right before my eyes. The reality of Vaughn Asher the Man is such a disappointment, my heart hurts.

I sit down on the bed, still naked, and allow myself to feel it for the first time.

My dream man is a huge letdown.

I let the silent tears fall and then wipe them away with the back of my hand.

But he was right about one thing, all we've done is fight since we met. In fact, the whole relationship is based on who's in charge. Not anything personal. And all that stuff he talked about last night doesn't even count, because I was asleep for most of it and that's the only reason he said all that. He thought I was asleep.

No, the only thing I know about Asher is that his cock is big, his sexual preferences are exotic, and he gets off making me do things I'd rather not.

I'm young. I'm on the verge of a promising career doing something I actually enjoy. I'm pretty enough, even in my own eyes, to know I deserve more than this. I deserve more than to be a man's casual plaything. I deserve more than to be a man's second thought. I deserve the dream. The fairy tale. I'm worth it.

A breath comes out and with it, heartache. Because as much as I hate to admit it, I'm so fucking sad that he's a dick. I kneel down to my bag and rummage through it to find my last pair of clean shorts and tank top and then dress quickly. I drag a brush through my hair and I'm just about to flop down on the bed when there's a knock at the door.

My stomach and heart both twist up with that small noise.

Vaughn? It must be him. Do I want to answer it?

I roll my eyes and sigh. As if there was ever any question.

I get up just as the second knock comes, and straighten my tank top. I have no bra on, and my girls are perky, but this morning he fucked me in the woods, so whatever. I walk over to the door slowly to make him wait, and then twist the handle and pull it open.

It's a woman.

No, I take that back. It's a girl. College-age maybe, and she's dressed up in a tan skirt suit with a ruffly white blouse peeking through her cropped blazer.

OK, what the hell is this? "Can I help you?" I ask in my most annoyed voice.

She smiles stiffly at me, like she's some kind of uptight librarian. Her hair is pulled back in a severe bun like a ballerina might wear, her jewelry is large and gaudy like a grandma might wear, and her suit skirt is too short. A micro mini. "Ma'am," she says, "Mr. Asher asked me to drop off your paperwork. He'd like me to notarize it and then bring it back to him immediately."

I almost choke. "Excuse me?"

She pushes her glasses up her nose and tilts her head up. "I'm not privy to the details, ma'am, but he said the two of you had agreed to a contract." She pulls a tablet out of her messenger bag and starts tapping on the screen with a stylus.

"Who are you?" I ask, annoyed. Something is wrong here. Something about her is—

"I'm Felicity, Mr. Asher's lawyer—"

—off.

"I handle all his business arrangements. And he asked me to come here and have you sign the NDA the two of you discussed over the weekend."

"Lawyer?" Ha! I laugh. "You're like twelve years old."

She pushes her glasses up again and crinkles her nose. "I was a child prodigy, Ma'am, it's not my fault I'm young."

And that's when I realize what's wrong with her. She's made up. She's fake. She's... she's... *acting*. She's dressed like a lawyer might look on TV. Like she just walked out of wardrobe.

And suddenly all that heartache at finding out my dream man is an asshole disappears and is replaced by rage.

"Look, Felicity, if that's your real name. I'm not sure what kind of game *Mr. Asher*"—I seethe the name out—"is playing with me, but it's over. So you can take that tablet and that NDA and go tell him to shove it up his ass. Maybe that will give him the sexual satisfaction he's looking for."

I slam the door. Shaking. My whole body is trembling as I realize how big a joke he thinks I am.

How dare he? How dare he send this girl, who is probably one of his many, many, many sexual conquests, to my door to ask for my signature?

And I'm sure he does want that signature. He did all kinds of questionable things with me this weekend. He wants to make sure I'm silenced before he goes back to his life in LA.

Well, fuck him!

Chapter Twenty - Grace

#Follow

I HAVE to sit on my bed and breathe deeply to calm myself down. I'm so angry but beyond that, I'm so humiliated. Vaughn Asher is a complete asshole and I feel so dirty I want to take a shower. I want to get out of this room.

No, this resort. I want to go home. Like right now.

I'm leaving. I walk around the room and pick up all my things, stuffing them into my backpack, then hit the bathroom and grab my incidentals. There's a pad of paper on the desk and I scribble out a note to Bebe.

Had to go back to Denver, emergency at work, they need me tomorrow. Love you—Grace

I can already hear her when she reads this. *A party-planning emergency that requires you to leave a tropical island so you can work on Labor Day?* She'll never buy it, but I don't care. I take a long steadying breath, hike the backpack strap up over my shoulder, and leave the bungalow. I take the path that takes me to the main hotel, ducking out of sight when I hear voices, just in case they are Vaughn or one of his minions, and make it to the valet area where there are a few cabs lined up waiting for fares. The valet is busy, lots of people checking in after the resort was closed for the wedding, so I walk past the guys unloading luggage and approach the first cab in line. "Airport?" I ask.

"Get in," he says in his Island accent.

I do get in. And as soon as I settle into the backrest I relax and breathe a sigh of relief.

It takes a while to get to the airport even though this island is small and we're not that far from the central business district of Charlotte Amalie. It's all the way across the bay and there are times during the forty-minute ride through the coastal traffic that I think I could've gotten there faster if I was swimming. But finally, the cab pulls up into the departures area and I pay him and get out.

A few seconds later, I'm alone at the airport with no ticket home.

Inside it's a madhouse. It's Labor Day weekend and people want to get home in time to enjoy the holiday tomorrow before they have to go back to work on Tuesday. I get in the ticketing line and wait patiently as one by one we inch forward and finally, after an hour and a half, I'm next in line.

My phone buzzes in my pocket. I take it out and check the message.

Where are you? From an unknown number. Which by now I know is Vaughn.

I consider not answering, but it's best to just get it over with. So I text back. *At the airport, on my way home. Thanks for the fun. Bye, Grace.*

And then it's my turn at the ticket counter, so I stuff the phone into my pocket and ignore the incessant buzzing as I concentrate on what they are telling me.

"First class? No, I can't afford first class. I just want a coach ticket to Denver."

"Miss, we have one seat left at a discounted price as it leaves in thirty minutes. You have five minutes to make up your mind and you can make that flight with the complimentary premium security access checkpoint. It's eight hundred and seventy-two dollars. The next available flight is tomorrow."

My phone rings in my pants and I grab it and press answer out of habit before I remember that I'm avoiding Asher. "Grace," he says, his voice urgent. "Stay right where you are, I'll be there to pick you up in ten minutes. Stay put, do you hear me, Grace?"

I press end and look the ticketing woman in the eye. "Book it. Here's my card."

I have exactly one thousand one hundred and two dollars in my bank account—that includes savings—but I do not care. I refuse to let that asshole find me stranded here at the airport like a child.

Fifteen minutes later I'm through security and I'm walking down the aisle to the only seat left in first class. I drop down into my seat, the window, so the woman next to me is put out, and stuff my backpack under the seat in front of me.

I breathe a huge sigh of relief. I hope I never see that man again. I never want to see his face, like ever. Even on TV. I'm not going to see *Invisible Man 2*, even though *IM1* was my favorite movie last year. I am over it. Totally one hundred percent over it.

In fact, I grab my phone and bring up my Twitter account real fast. I look up for the flight attendant and he's busy making coffee or something in that tiny galley kitchen, so I open up my account and start deleting tweets. I just want to erase Vaughn from my life. My fingers are flying down my profile page, but there's no good way to delete them all without deleting my whole account. I consider that, out of desperation, and I'm just about to give in and do it when the flight attendant stands over my row and tsks his tongue.

"Airplane mode, please. And I can see your Twitter page, so I know you're not in airplane mode."

He waits there, tapping his foot, until I go into my settings and flick that little tab to airplane mode.

Well, whatever. Vaughn has no idea who I am on Twitter, but as soon as I get to my stop in Atlanta, that shit is going.

I plug my headphones into my phone and bring up my tunes, then settle back into my oversized seat and try and enjoy my first, and probably only, first-class experience.

A few hours later, after I've been served lunch, champagne, orange juice, a hot towel, and a movie—*IM1*, it's the only one playing—I'm satiated, relaxed, and even a little bit giggly over my ridiculous weekend with movie star Vaughn Asher. It's sort of a blur, and sort of surreal. I mean, did I really get fucked by him in a tropical forest? Did I really put a vibrator against my pussy in the company of the great Adam Asher?

I laugh out loud and several people look over at me.

It was sorta fun, but Jesus, I'm glad it's over. I'm not his type, he's way too much ego for me, and we really did fight the entire time. I prefer my quiet, predictable, low-conflict life and the only dates I see in my future are virtual ones on Saturday night Dirty Heaven twitter chats.

The plane lands and phones begin dinging as everyone switches them off airplane mode. I stretch out, ready to get off this plane and find my next gate so I can just go home to Denver. I fish out my phone to check my messages. Bebe is gonna be pissed off when she gets that note. I switch the phone off airplane mode and it begins dinging.

A balloon bubble pops up on my home screen telling me I have twenty-two messages.

What?

I swipe my finger to go into my messages app and look at them.

Unknown number.

Unknown number.

Unknown number.

Unknown number.

They go on and on like that. More and more and more.

My email app dings and I press that to take my mind off what might be happening on my phone. I have fifty-two new emails from Twitter.

I open the first one and it takes me a few seconds of staring to realize what I'm seeing.

Vaughn Asher (@VaughnAsher) favorited one of your Tweets!
Vaughn Asher (@VaughnAsher) favorited one of your Tweets!
Vaughn Asher (@VaughnAsher) favorited one of your Tweets!
Vaughn Asher (@VaughnAsher) favorited one of your Tweets!
Vaughn Asher (@VaughnAsher) favorited one of your Tweets!

On, and on, and on. Down to the very last new email for today.

Vaughn Asher (@VaughnAsher) is now following you on Twitter!

I scream.

People startle and flight attendants come to help me. But I fall back against my seat, unable to process what just happened to my life.

I've been outed. He knows. Every last dirty thing I've said about him over the years—from *I wish I could slide my pussy against your scratchy chin* to *You have long thumbs, I hear your cock is three times that size*—he knows them all.

And then my phone dings a message.

I force myself to look down.

I can't wait to play Dirty Heaven with you this weekend— Vaughn

I die of humiliation right there. I just die.

SOCIAL MEDIA SERIES BOOK TWO

NEW YORK TIMES BESTSELLING AUTHOR

HUSS

Chapter Twenty-One - Vaughn

#HappinessIsHacking

I CHUCKLE to myself as I lounge on my couch back in LA. I've been watching Grace's Twitter feed for twenty-four hours now, ever since I sent that tweet, but she's gone silent. Black, they call it. Dead.

I laugh again.

"What're you smirking about?"

I sit up and peek over the back of the couch. Felicity's back is to me and she has the fridge open, staring at it. "She's hiding," I tell her.

"Of course she is, you just embarrassed the fuck out of her—"

"Felicity, language, please."

"—in front of her entire community of online friends. What'd you think would happen?"

I stare at my adopted daughter for a minute, noticing how tall she seems. She is all legs. I hate it. "Your skirt is too short. I hope you're not going to wear that out of the house."

She glares at me over her shoulder. "It's a tennis skirt, Vaughn, relax. I told you, I'm trying to get better at a sport this year so I can be all jocky and shit." She finally grabs a sparkling water and slams the refrigerator door with a sigh.

"'Jocky and shit?' First of all, language. Second—" I have to stop here and think about my word choice for a moment. Twenty-year-old girls are sensitive to any criticism, and while I do not think what I'm about to say is a criticism—it's the whole reason we met—I do not want her to take it the wrong way. "I love the non-jocky version of you. So whatever jock you're trying to gain attention from does not deserve you if he can't appreciate your nerdy side."

I smile. That was perfect.

She comes into the family room and plops down on the overstuffed chair across from me with a whoosh of cushions. The bottle cap snaps as she opens it and the fizz bubbles into the air. "I hate you."

"What?"

"*I love the nerdy you,*" she says in a fake voice. "Of course you do. You're seeing me in a non-sexual way—"

"Oh, Jesus, Felicity, please—"

"—but I'm trying to get laid by a hot dude, OK?"

"OK, this subject is over."

"Yeah, let's just talk about your current relationship, that's much better. And you know what, you adopted me at sixteen. It barely counts. I'm your best friend, not your daughter, so stop with the parenting, V. I can't take it." She takes a long swig of her water and then wipes her mouth. "Anyway, having me figure out who she is on Twitter for you is one thing. The games you're playing are not nice. She's gonna flip out. And all seven thousand members of Dirty Heaven Twitter group will see every bit of it."

I let out a long breath. I have to admit, playing this game with Grace has really injected some fun into my pathetically boring movie-star life. I have been busy most of the year with production schedules and charity benefits, but most of the sex has been... disappointing. I've had no real romantic fun until this past weekend. Grace has got me all distracted and bothered. I hate that she left the island before we could have a real date. Fucking her in the forest is not the same as seducing her and making her submit to me in private. Public is fun, but private has so many, many more options.

"Oh, by the way," Felicity says, "your douche of a brother called. Says he's gonna be gone on a business trip for a couple weeks and he'll pay you when he gets back."

I make a face at the change in subject. Fucking Conner and his business deal. If my parents knew what he was up to, they'd flip. But I promised not to tell them while he gets it off the ground, and I'm a man of my word.

"What's that all about, anyway?" Felicity asks.

"Nothing," I say to stop the conversation. "I don't want to think about Conner."

"Well, I'm gonna dig up some info then. I barely know anything about him."

"Felicity," I say in my stern father voice. "Do not hack into his stuff, do you hear me? He will know."

"How's he gonna know?" she laughs. "I'm careful. You know I'm careful."

"It's not ethical, anyway."

"Pfft," she says. "Please. You have me hack stuff all the time, V. Like your new girlfriend's Twitter account? Ringing any bells?"

"That's harmless fun, Felicity."

"What I'm doing is harmless too. And it's fun. For me." She smiles broadly as she takes a sip of water and it dribbles out of her mouth. "Besides, I'm pretty sure Miss Kinsella will not be thinking it's so funny when you start playing for real. She's gonna be mortified. She might change her name and move away to escape the public humiliation you're about to unleash."

"It's not public. It's her Twitter account. She hides behind that FilthyBlueBird handle for a reason. So no one knows it's her."

"Whatever you say, boss." And then she looks at her watch and gets up. "Well, I've got a two PM tennis match scheduled to perfectly coincide with my future man's football practice so I gotta jet." She walks over and then leans down to peck me on the cheek. "Later, V."

"Be good!" I call after her. "And be safe if you're going to—"

"Vaughn! That's too far." She waves me off with her hand as she skips down the hallway and a few seconds later I hear the door to the garage slam.

I sigh. She's so different from the girl I found sitting in a jail cell a few years ago. Brought in on felony hacking charges after she broke into my production company's database looking for dirt to sell to online Hollywood tabloid shows. She was living on the streets. No parents, no home. No money. No future.

I wanted to press charges, teach her a lesson and make her pay for it all at the same time. I was still reeling from a lackluster performance in an independent project I helped produce a few months earlier, not to mention the constant headlines in Buzz Hollywood accusing me of living some kind of dark, sordid double life. I wanted to make her pay.

Luckily Samantha talked me out of it after learning what Felicity's situation was, and I ended up not pressing charges. But I still wanted to teach her a lesson. So I made her work for me as my personal assistant that entire summer and decided to become her foster parent.

She changed my life. It went from shallow and empty to meaningful in one day. Like seriously, her first day at the studio with me. She had my whole life arranged on a tablet before lunch. She was quick and personable, and funny. She's so funny. She lights up my life. We were inseparable that summer. People started calling us Velicity, that's how attached we became. It's like we were destined to be best friends.

When the end of the summer rolled around she started asking me weird questions. Would I get rid of her some day? Would I send her to another family to live with if she was bad? Would I get married and forget about our friendship? Would I have new children and replace her?

God, it killed me to hear her asking these questions. And of course, I reassured her without question. I might be a dick, but I believe in commitment. Once I'm on board with something, I'm in. I believe in the long haul. I believe in sticking it out. People who make it past my initial aloofness, and not many do, so I can't hardly blame Felicity for wondering, but those who do get inside, I am loyal.

I just couldn't imagine living with that level of uncertainty Felicity was displaying. So I adopted her. Sent her to the best school for the duration of high school and just as I suspected, she was brilliant. She made up for all the previous years of poor education with perfect attendance and she graduated *summa cum laude* right on time. Colleges came knocking and she was admitted to my alma mater, the University of Southern California, without me even pulling strings or writing an extra check.

Now, she's a senior. Psychology with a minor in criminal justice. Still has perfect grades. Still has perfect attendance. And even if she had none of that, she's still perfect to me.

Yes, Felicity has certainly changed my view on life. The past four years have been the best, even though my love life has seriously been lacking. I count up the number of submissives I've had in that time. At least fifteen. Some of them were so bad at it, I never got past the first oral sex. All were stand-ins for the real deal.

I've had plenty of public girlfriends too, and those I do not fuck. It's a business arrangement my agent sets up. We go out to eat together, shop once in a while, attend functions—but, you know, public things.

I don't take the subs to any of that stuff. And to be honest, I've never had the desire.

I think I can count two authentic girlfriends in my life and both were in my teens. My co-star at Disney was matched up with me for some awards show and we actually did hit it off. We're still friends now, but she's... well, a movie star. Egomaniac, selfish, pampered, and self-sufficient. She never needed me.

I like to be needed.

The other real girlfriend crashed and burned at eighteen. Been in and out of rehab about a dozen times. It's too bad, she was so cute as a teenager. But that one was clingy. Too needy. I like to be needed, but not for stupid things like waking up on time every day. I want to date a grownup. That girl never quite grew up, no matter how old she got.

After that, eh, I could take them or leave them. You'd think it'd be easy to find a soulmate as an internationally famous movie star. But it's not. People just want to use you. They want something from you at all times. They want money, they want introductions, they want help.

I never know if they like me for me, or just for what I can give them. It's hard to separate the two because if you really want to make a relationship work, you have to be invested.

I try not to be invested. I admit that says I'm not trying to be in a relationship. Which is why I have the submissive girls. They do what I say, and while I certainly do hand things out, they don't get to *ask* me for anything.

One-way streets. Those are the best kind of relationships for me. I tell them up front I'm not invested.

I'm shallow, I'm using them, I'm a controlling asshole. Take it or leave it.

Very few leave it. Well, that's not true, they all leave it eventually. When I kick them out the door. When I drop their asses off at the airport. When I stop taking calls, or answering emails, or reading messages. I don't need to change the locks, they never come home with me anymore. Not since Felicity. This is a sex-free house. For both of us. No boys here for her, no women here for me.

Nada. This place is our safe haven from the world and that's how it's gonna stay.

My tablet dings with an incoming third-party Twitter notification.

@FilthyBlueBird has unfollowed you.

I laugh. "Oh, Grace, Grace, Grace. You think you can slip me that easily?"

Grace @FilthyBlueBird – 1s
OMG, I have a stalker! What do I do, #BlueBirds?

You'd think a woman using Twitter this regularly for a few years would understand how it all works. I can still see her tweets when she unfollows me. I have to stop and laugh a little.

MovieStar @VaughnAsher – 30s
@FilthyBlueBird Who is this stalker? I will set him straight.

And then the usual happens. Within minutes, there are dozens of @replies. Mostly from her girlfriends on the Dirty Heaven list, the #BlueBirds. But some random stalkerish fans of my own are in there too.

@VaughnAsher is @FilthyBlueBird your GF?
@VaughnAsher if you're the stalker, you can stalk me any time!
@VaughnAsher who is @FilthyBlueBird? Can I be your blue bird?

They get worse from there. Invitations to fuck them. Sit on my face. #SOHF is a code word for that on Twitter. @FilthyBlueBird uses that one a lot. And I've got to admit, that's something I'd like to imagine. More than imagine, actually. I'd like to lick that sweet little pussy until she's dripping down my chin.

Fuck. I'm horny. I reach for my phone and press Grace's number in my contacts. She picks up on the first ring.

"What the hell are you doing?" she growls at me.

"You left so suddenly, Grace. I didn't have a chance to—"

"Get off my Twitter feed, Asher. Now!"

I chuckle. It's one of those full-of-myself chuckles I do when my power is looming over people. "Now whyever would I do that, Miss Kinsella?"

"Because, Vaughn, I'm just a girl from Denver who has absolutely no interest in signing your contract. It was a fun fling, but it's over now. So leave me alone and stop stalking me on Twitter! My friends are all going to see—" She's interrupted by a continuous litany of pinging from my tablet and I admit, at this point in the conversation, I've got a hand over my mouth to stop the laughing. She screams on the other end of the line.

I can see why. She just got bombarded with tweets asking about me.

"Oh my God. What do I tell them? What the hell am I going to tell them?" She screams again. "Fuck! Bebe just found out, thanks a lot! I never told her about you, now she's going to know I was with you on the island."

"So?"

"So? Jesus, have you no sympathy for me at all? She's my best friend and I lied to her! I fucked a goddamned movie star and I didn't tell her! How can you—"

"Grace?"

"—be so fucking cold, you jerk!"

"Grace?"

"Oh. My. God. Do you hear that? That's her now! She's calling on the other line!"

"Answer it, I'll wait."

"Answer it? No! I'm—"

"Grace?"

"What?"

"I'll tell them all it was a lie if…"

"If what?" she growls at me through the phone.

"If you have phone sex with me, right now."

"Holy shit, you are insane!"

"Oh! What's that ding? Bebe again? I don't suppose she's very happy with you leaving the island the way you did either. I sense a girl fight coming. I almost wish I was there so—"

"Fine! Fine, fine, fine, I'll do it. Just quick, say it was a lie."

"No can do, Miss Kinsella. I need satisfaction first."

There is a pause then. A blank in her freaking out. But the entire time I can hear her Twitter dinging the incoming messages. She sighs. "OK, you win. Just tell me what to do, I've never done anything like this before." Her breath is all ragged and fast. It's driving me wild. I wish she was here so bad. I'd strip her naked and bend her over the couch back, then finger her pussy until she screamed.

"Make me come. It's that simple. With words, Grace. Make me come with words." I close my tablet cover and it makes a little snapping sound as the operating system goes to sleep. "Did you hear that? That was me putting my tablet aside. I'm not in the least bit of a hurry to stop the Twitter chatter going on right now. But if you are, my girl, then by all means, you can make it snappy."

"You're lucky I'm not there. I'd make it snappy. I'd snap my teeth on your manhood so hard, you'd—"

"Now, now. While I do love the image of your mouth on my cock, your plump lips wrapped around my shaft, sucking while your hands pump me hard and fast—the teeth are not working for me. So leave that part out."

She growls again and my pants become a little tighter as she decides what to do. "Why? Why do you like to embarrass me?"

"I'm not trying to embarrass you. Why do you think that?"

"Because you want me to talk dirty to you, you want to fuck me in public, you want to drag me kicking and screaming outside my comfort zone and you want to laugh at me while you do it. I don't like that."

"First of all, Grace, take a nice deep breath and then sit down, lean back on your couch or the pillows on your bed, and relax for a moment. Can you do that?"

She groans on the other end of the phone. "Fine, I'm sitting on my couch, completely relaxed."

I smile as I picture her all tensed up. She's probably pacing. "Take a deep breath, I said."

She inhales deeply, holds for a moment, then lets it out in a long, slow stream.

"OK, now listen to me. I am not laughing at you at all. I'm enjoying you. You make me smile, OK? You make me laugh, yes, but in all the right ways. You bring me… joy. Do you see the difference? I'm not trying to embarrass you. I'm trying to stimulate you."

"But why does that have to be in front of the whole world?"

I sigh and narrow my eyes as I try and work through what she's saying. "I'm surprised at this direction you're going, to be honest. I mean, look at it from my perspective, Grace. You've been online for years. Years! Typing out every dirty sexual fantasy about me in public. You do understand that, right? Or have you deluded yourself into thinking no one is watching what you're doing? Maybe you think this is just a friendly chat with a few friends, but that's not the case, Kinsella. Your Dirty Heaven thing is quite big. In fact, on Saturday nights, you are a Twitter star. So how can you blame me for assuming that you have a fetish for exhibitionism?"

She's silent on the other end.

"Am I right? Or did I totally miss the boat on this? Because I just assumed, after reading that tweet in the bar, that we were into the same thing."

"So you *do* like public sex!" She says this like it's a gotcha moment and I practically throw up my hands.

"Grace, how could you be my online stalker for years and not realize that? I admit, it's reading between the lines, but there are so many lines to read between. Every few months there's a report about my deviant behavior. Don't you read *Buzz Hollywood*?"

"I do, but—"

"But you assumed they were lying?"

"Well, yes. Of course. I mean, I'm not naïve, I figured the NDA was legit. But I just always gave you the benefit of the doubt."

I am silent. I'm seriously without words. "You... did?"

"Of course, Vaughn. I had you wrapped up in this tight fantasy bubble. You were like, my prince. You were the perfect man. And I know that's not real. I understand you're a human being, but..."

She trails off and I'm not sure I can fill in the silence, so I don't even try. I let it hang there. *We* let it hang there.

"Are you still there?" she asks.

"Yes," I breathe out. "Just thinking."

"About how stupid and pathetic I am?"

"No, Grace. That's not what I'm thinking. I'm thinking… it's been a long time since someone was so honest with me."

It's her turn to be silent now.

"Grace?"

"I'm still here."

"Tell me, truthfully, if you don't mind. Why don't you have a boyfriend? Why do you waste your Saturday nights on me?"

"Why not you? I mean, you're hot. And you're so easy." She giggles. "I mean, you have such a long public history, you know? I can do a search and somewhere, someone has an answer to my questions about you. I like that. And your pictures are everywhere, so I can make cute graphics with comment bubbles over your head."

"I'm public."

"Yeah, you're—" She stops as the pieces fall into place. I have never had a conversation about this stuff with a woman. None of them. "That's why you like the public stuff? Because you're an open book?"

I let her think about this for a few seconds. "Makes sense, though, right? I mean, look, I've been in the media since I was five and started doing commercials. Primetime sitcom series for six years, then the band when I was fourteen. I've been on display my whole life. What's one more asshole watching me during a private moment?"

"Is it an addiction? Have you ever had sex in private?"

I laugh. "Of course."

"But you thought I like the public stuff too?"

"I know it excites you, Grace. I felt your pussy and it was wet every single time. So why fight it? Why give me such pushback?"

"Because it makes me feel... dirty."

"Aren't you? Aren't you the filthy blue bird? Isn't that the public persona you've been cultivating for the past few years?"

Silence from her again.

"It's not real to you, is it? All that Twitter stuff. It's fake to you. Is that why you don't have a boyfriend? You prefer the illusion?"

"That's actually not why."

But her tone is hostile, so maybe that's not exactly why, but there is a reason why she doesn't have a boyfriend. And it's got something to do with this Twitter stuff. Somehow, some way, it's related.

"I just don't have time for one."

"Right. But you have time to chat online every Saturday night for hours and hours? You know, for someone who is extremely self-righteous when it comes to my bad behavior, you sure do have some good excuses to justify yours. At any rate, dirty is just a word. Exhibitionist sex can just as easily make you feel sexy. But for some reason you choose something negative."

"Are you going to stop the Twitter chat or not?"

Her abrupt subject change is a signal that she's done with the personal stuff, and that's OK with me. I'm about finished as well. With the personal stuff. I'm just getting started with the sexual stuff.

"I told you. Make me come with words, over the phone. And I'll put a stop to the chatter."

"Why can't you just be nice and do it without the phone sex?"

"Because I want you, Grace. And this is a good way to get what I want."

She's quiet for so long I almost think she hung up. But then I hear a small breath of air and I know she's about to give in. "Grace," I whisper, breaking her silence on the other end and unzipping my pants at the same time. "I've got my hand on my cock, ready to go. Forget about Twitter and think only about me." She takes a deep breath on the other end of the line and I know... I can just feel it. This will be epic. "Talk to me, Grace. If you were here, what would you do to get me off?"

Chapter Twenty-Two - Grace

#MrsInvisibleMan

I TAKE a deep breath.

"Grace?" he asks, a softer tone this time. His breath is heavier, like he's relaxed. *Like he's jerking off,* the cynical person inside me corrects. "I'm ready. I have my hand on my dick and you're in front of me. What are you doing?"

I take another deep breath and then I swallow. Should I really do this?

"What're you thinking?" he asks.

"I'm debating," I tell him truthfully. "On whether or not I should cross this line with you."

"So letting me fuck you in a tropical forest on Saint Thomas wasn't crossing a line with me?"

"It was," I interject. "But that's different. That was a fantasy fling, this is reality. This is my life, Vaughn. I have a real life and those people on my Twitter feed are friends. You're playing with my life. You're..." I shake my head a little. I should not be having this conversation with him. I should not be letting him into my head at all. He's a fun dream guy in the sex department, but as a real human being, Vaughn Asher is an asshole. I don't want to go any further in this demented relationship and giving in to his demands right now would be a monumental mistake.

"I'm what?" he asks.

"You're using me."

"I'm not using you. I think we both had fun on the island. We can both have fun right now."

"You're forcing me to have phone sex with you."

"I'm not forcing you—Grace, please. If you don't want to, just hang up and I'll never call you again. How's that?"

"But if I do that, you won't make things right, will you?"

"Oh," he says with a chuckle. "I get it. You *want* me to force you. You want me to take away your decision in this matter, because you want to do it, you just want to go on pretending you don't."

I'm silent. Because he's right. I want it both ways. I want the excitement of what he's asking—what he's offering. But I don't want to take responsibility for choosing to allow him to treat me this way.

And that's worse, isn't it? Because I'm lying to myself. The least I can do is be honest. So I swallow down that fear and take another deep breath to steady myself. "I'm staring at you from across the room."

"Mmmm," he growls through the phone. "Why so far away?"

"Because…" I bite my lip to stop a smile. "Because the length of your cock has taken me by surprise. I never got a good look at it, and…" I stop to think. "And it's very hard."

"It is. It is *so* fucking hard right now. I wish you were here, in front of me."

"What would you want me to do?"

"Only what you're comfortable doing."

Well, that makes me smile. "I'm walking over to you, slowly, so you can appreciate my body. I'm naked." I giggle as soon as the words come out.

"As am I. How do I look?"

"God," I say. "You look like a god." A god I'd like to lick from top to bottom. But I don't say that. I've written that. I've written worse, but I can't say that out loud to him. I just can't.

"Are you still nervous?"

"Yes," I reply too quickly.

"OK, then since we've just met and this is our first time, maybe you shouldn't be allowed to touch me."

"No?"

"No. Maybe you should only be allowed to touch yourself. Kneel down in front of me, Grace."

I don't know what to do. Do I really kneel? Is this all pretend and we just say we're doing things? I don't get it.

"Are you kneeling? Don't lie to me. I want you to kneel down and picture me naked, sitting on a black leather couch, my hand on my shaft, pumping up and down in a slow rhythm."

"I'm sitting on my bed." I figure this game might be fun, but only if I play along. "But I'm getting to my knees now." I stand up and kneel down on the rug that lines the long edge of my bed and then put the phone in front of me and press the speaker icon. "I'm kneeling now."

"Mmmm. And you put me on speaker, like a filthy little blue bird."

"Now what?"

"You want me to do the talking?" he asks with an incredulous tone. "When you're the one who needs the favor? Sweetie, please."

"Mr. Asher," I say in a low husky whisper. "I want you to tell me what you want so I can please you."

He chuckles. "If I do, and I take care of the Twitter frenzy, you will owe me twice, darling. Do you really want to stack these favors like that?"

"Yes," I say back immediately. "Because I have no idea what to do, OK? I just don't. I've never done this before, I'm out of my element, and I'm starting to get horny."

I hear that smile from a thousand miles away. "Are you naked?" he asks, his voice a little bit rougher.

"No, I'm just in shorts and a t-shirt."

"If I take control, you will follow all my directions?"

"I swear."

"OK," he agrees too quickly and I have a wave of nausea wondering what that might mean. "Strip, grab your vibrator, and return to that kneeling position. And Grace? Don't bother telling me you don't have a vibrator. Now do

186

as I say and describe to me in detail as you follow my directions."

"OK, I'm standing. And now I'm pulling my shirt over my head." I do that and drop the shirt on the floor.

"Do you have a bra on?"

"No."

"Stop for a moment and play with your breasts. Tell me how they feel, so I can imagine I'm the one touching them."

I cup my breasts and squeeze. "They're soft, and they overfill my palm. "

"Mmmm. They overfill mine too. I love them."

"If you were here, I'd want you to suck them."

"If I was there, I'd lift them up to your lips and make you suck them yourself."

Oh.

"Do that, Grace. I'd like you to do that."

"I can't," I laugh.

"You won't. OK, moving on. Take off the shorts."

My brows knit together as I ponder what that quick capitulation might signify. "My shorts are unbuttoned so I'm pulling them down over my hips." They fall to the floor with a soft whoosh. "Now they're around my ankles."

"Do you have panties on?"

"No."

He chuckles. "Do you go commando often?"

"Yes. I don't see the purpose of underwear when mine are so skimpy they barely count. What's the point?"

"I'm not complaining. Now get your vibrator and tell me what kind it is."

I walk over to my night stand and pull the top drawer open. "It's a Lelo. It's in a black satin drawstring bag. It's pink, and it's the Gigi."

"Does it feel good when you use it?"

"Yes, it better, it cost enough."

"Who do you think about when you use it, Grace?"

"You."

There is nothing but silence.

"Asher?"

He clears his throat. "Kneel down on the floor, spread your legs, and place the vibrator against your clit."

"I'm kneeling. My legs are open, and—" I pause to turn my Gigi on. "And it's touching my clit."

"What setting do you start it on?"

"Full."

"I'll let that go this time, since this is all new. But when I get a hold of you and your Gigi, it will never be set on full power, Grace. A toy is used to stimulate you for me, not to get yourself off."

Whatever, I think to myself. "Yes, Mr. Asher," I say back to him. I'm never going to see him again and as fun as this could be, that shit right there is a mood-killer.

"I know you disagree, but that's only because I'm not there. You think the toy is what makes you come, but it's the visions of me that make you come. So, if we're together, you won't need the toy, Grace. Not for orgasms. Only for stimulation prior to my cock entering your ass or your pussy."

Whoa. OK, I'm back. "I'm wet," I tell him.

"Of course you are. You have a vibrator up against your pussy and we are discussing the limits."

"Wait, what? Limits? We're not talking limits, Asher. We're phone-fucking one time."

"Lie down on the floor."

I huff out some air. He's got me right now. I need him to stop that Twitter chatter before it gets worse.

"Stick the tip of the vibrator into your pussy, get it nice and wet, then remove it and rub it across your clit."

I hesitate. I don't make any noise, I swear. But I can hear him groan on the other end, like he knows. "Jesus," I say, giving in and doing as he says. "Fine."

"It's not supposed to be torture, Grace. It's supposed to be fun. And you know what? If you're really not into it, then fuck it. Never mind."

I get three quick beeps to let me know the call has ended and I just stare up at the ceiling. "What the fuck?" I pick the phone up and press redial. He picks up on the third ring. Like he was busy.

"What?" he barks.

"You're like a little girl, you know that? A spoiled little girl who throws a tantrum when she doesn't get her own way. I was playing along, Asher. But I've never done this stuff before and it's embarrassing." I huff out a disgusted sigh and then end my tirade with a, "Fuck you," and the technology-age equivalent of a phone slam. A pointer finger press of the *End* tab.

"Asshole." God, why do I let him make me so angry. He's such a—

My thoughts are interrupted by a string of pings from my tablet. Great, what the fuck did he say now? I grab the tablet and check the Dirty Heaven list.

MovieStar @VaughnAsher – 1m
@FilthyBlueBird my deepest apologies. A hacker took over my feed but it's in control now. Sorry to interrupt your fun.

Oh, so now I get the passive-aggressive bullshit? I don't think so.

Grace @FilthyBlueBird
@VaughnAsher – the party just started, don't be too quick to leave. #FantasyOrReality

MovieStar @VaughnAsher
@FilthyBlueBird I figured you'd be embarrassed by all the dirty tweets coming out of your #FilthyBlueMouth.

A slew of tweets flood the stream, all dirty. Hashtags start appearing that would make a porn star blush. *#TakeMyButtVirginity #SOHFSlipNSlide* There are even some I coined that play off his movie roles like

#ThatsNotMyHand #ItsTheInvisibleMan and
#IManUltimateStalker #WatchMeSquirt
#OnYourInvisibleTongue

Grace @FilthyBlueBird
@VaughnAsher – #MrsInvisbleOnline and that's the way I like it.

MovieStar @VaughnAsher
@FilthyBlueBird Do it any way you like, Blue Bird. Sing for me, I'm waiting to be wowed.

Shit. I giggle a little at this. OK, maybe I'm not so good with phone sex, but I'm the filthy Twitter goddess. I can be dirty and spontaneous with the best of them. And besides, he invited me in front of the entire world. It's like a challenge.

I bite my lip as I think up a good tweet.

Grace @FilthyBlueBird
@VaughnAsher – This blue bird can sing #WithYourCockInMyBeak

MovieStar @VaughnAsher
@FilthyBlueBird Hmmm, I recently had that pleasure. #Fantastic #BackToNatureFucking #MissingSomething #You

I stare at that last tweet. Me.

A flood of tweets follow that message, but I close my tablet and sit on the bed. He did that on purpose. He took away the suspicion and rebuilt it on a whole new level.

My phone buzzes. I stare at the message flashing unknown number at me and then even though I know I shouldn't answer that call—that giving in to him is the worst idea possible, that he will take over my life, probably in every bad way imaginable—there's no way I can deny him.

"Yes," I say softly into the phone.

"I liked that. It was fun. We are now @mrinvsman and @mrsinvsman. Private profiles who only follow each other. Log in tomorrow night at eight your time using 'bluebird' as your password."

And then I get the three beeps.

My phone vibrates a message a few seconds later. I look down and this time the number comes up.

I will ignore you as FilthyBlueBird from now on. But you're still mine, #MrsInvisibleMan.

What if I don't want to play? I text back.

Then don't. A pause from him. Then—*Do you want to play?*

I like being asked.

That's not an answer.

Yes.

Are you still naked?

Yes.

I get a smiley face in return. *Be naked tomorrow at eight your time, #MrsInvisibleMan.*

Chapter Twenty-Three - Vaughn

#SisterSecrets

GOD, that girl, I think as I press the end tab on my phone. She's got me. Somehow, she's grabbed my attention like no other woman I've ever met. She's naughty and mouthy and I love it. And I realize I've got a stupid grin on my face.

I snap out of it when my phone rings and Sam's face lights up the screen. I smile a very different kind of smile and press accept. "Why are you calling me on your honeymoon, princess? Are you ready to divorce Tray already?"

"Do you think I should?"

"What?" Fuck.

"I mean, it could be an annulment, right? Do they still let you do those things?"

"Sam, what's going on? What happened?"

"Nothing happened, Vaughn. I'm just so unsure of this. I mean, I've never been so unsure of anything in my life. I can't eat, I can't sleep. I can't…" She stops and huffs out a breath. "I can't sleep with him, Vaughn. I just can't do it."

"Wait, you've never slept with him before?"

"Of course not!"

"Oh my God, you're a virgin?"

"I'm insulted that you're surprised!"

"Sorry, it's just…" I guess it all makes sense. My sister has always been a prissy thing, but I've always assumed it was an act. "It wasn't an act?"

"Why would I lie about this?"

Shit, I can think of like a billion reasons, but I keep that to myself. "I wonder if Felicity is still a virgin. Dare I hope she's been as frigid as you?"

"Is that supposed to be funny?"

"Sorry. OK, well, look, sis, it's pretty normal to be… ah… Jesus, can't you find a girlfriend to talk to about this shit?"

"I already talked to them! They're on his side!"

"What side is his? He did something, didn't he? I'll kill that asshole."

"He didn't do anything, he's just… Vaughn, he's just not the prince I've been waiting for. And I know, I just feel it to be true, that if I sleep with him as his wife, I will be making the biggest mistake of my life. Bigger than marrying him. Because I've been saving myself for the perfect guy. And I'm sorry, I know Mom and Dad paid a fortune for this wedding, but I can't do it. He's not my guy. He's not."

She lets out a long breath and waits for my reaction. I know whatever I tell her, she will take it very seriously. So I really need to tread carefully here.

"Sam, first of all, your happiness is the only thing we care about, OK? Mom and Dad do not give two fucks about the cost of the wedding. So don't let that be a determining factor. But before you make up your mind, I just think you should stop comparing Tray to some fictional guy who doesn't exist. Because, honey, he's not out there. We're all assholes. We're all the same. We don't think the way you ladies do. We're not perfect. And I'm going to tell you the truth, I don't like Tray. I don't think he's good enough for you, so if you want to ditch the guy, by all means call the plane, pack your shit, and leave his ass on Saint Thomas. But before you do anything, Samantha, I want you to make sure. Because this really isn't something you can undo. A man's not going to forget that you had these second thoughts on the honeymoon. So if you walk away, be sure."

She's silent for a long time. Almost a minute. But I'm patient. I let her think. She just needs someone to listen to her and if I'm the only one who will, then I'll wait all night for her to be ready to speak again.

I've always worried about her so much as she was growing up. She's a fragile person. One prone to sadness and guilt over things she has no control over. The state of the world. Injustices in faraway countries I probably couldn't place on a map. Kids who have no parents. She was a huge reason why I didn't press charges against Felicity. I was so angry when that girl hacked into my personal business, I was ready to do just about anything to get even. But Samantha calmed me down. Made me see things differently. Made me see Felicity as the desperate teenager she was instead of the criminal I was trying to make her out to be.

I owe Sam for that. Because my life was a hollow shell before that girl came into it. And every day since has been better than the last. No matter what happens during my day, seeing Felicity at the end of it—hearing her smart-ass mouth, listening to her crazy plans about meeting guys, watching her change from a suspicious and angry teen to a brilliant, confident, intelligent young woman…

Well, that's what life is about.

Sam sighs on the other end of the line again. "OK. I'm going to have dinner with him in an hour and I'll give him a chance. I'll stop comparing him to my perfect guy and see him for what he is. A nice-looking man with a good job who loves me."

"Jesus, is that how you see him?"

"Yeah, why?"

"Well, look, Sam, I'm no expert on how women should feel about men. But on your honeymoon you should want to spend every minute with him. You should be gazing into his eyes, declaring your lust, for fuck's sake. You should absolutely not be on the phone with your brother."

"God, Vaughn. I don't love him. All of that makes me tremble with fear and apprehension. And I have played sick every night since the wedding so I didn't have to sleep with him. I'm almost out of excuses. He's going to want to sleep with me tonight, I just know it. And I don't want to. I don't want him to touch me, Vaughn."

My sister doesn't want him to touch her. That's enough for me. "I'm calling the airport."

"What?"

"I'll take care of it, sweetie. OK? I'll call the jet. You pack your things right now, and go get in the taxi. I'll have someone meet you at the airport and bring you home."

She starts crying and I want to jump through the phone and hug her, that's how bad this tears me up. "Sam, you're gonna be all right? I'm gonna take care of it, OK? Just do as I ask and then call me when you get on the plane so I know you're safe. Understand?"

"OK," she squeaks out. "I'm going now. I'll call you on the plane. And Vaughn? Thank you. Thank you so much for this."

"It's no big deal, sis. It's what brothers are for."

We hang up and I sit back against the couch and let out a long, sad sigh. I just sit there for a few minutes, running all this over in my head, then I press the pre-set for the jet service and arrange the plane. Then I call the airport concierge and tell them to meet Samantha outside departures and escort her to the jet.

And once all that is done, I speed-dial Conner. He picks up on the first ring.

"Yo, bro. What's up?"

"Samantha is leaving Tray. I just set up the jet so she can leave without telling him."

"Fuck, what happened?"

"She doesn't love him. She felt pressured to accept his proposal and make it work. She hasn't slept with him and he's making her shake just thinking about it."

"Fuck."

"But that's not why I called. I need a favor, Conner. And I need it to be done very discreetly. Can you do that?"

"Please, brother. Discreet is my middle name. Conner Discreet Asher at your service."

I tell him what I want and we hang up after he gets the details.

God, I just hope Felicity doesn't end up with a guy she can barely stand because she feels pressured to accept a proposal. I should've sent her to a public university. Get her away from the arrogant rich kids who flow with the money at USC.

I ponder all the mistakes I might've made with Felicity in the four short years I've had to influence her life, and come to the conclusion I'm a failure. No matter what I do, it probably won't be enough to protect her from getting hurt. Not in love, not in life, not in anything.

My phone rings and I press Sam's happy face to answer. "Tell me good news, sis."

"I'm on the plane." She starts to cry and I almost lose it.

"Do you want me to tell them to forget it?"

"No! These are happy tears, Vaughn. Just thank you. So much for being the best brother ever. Thank you. I don't know what I'm going to tell Tray—"

"I'll take care of Tray. I'll see you when you get to LA, now get some rest."

I look up Tray in my contacts and press in the numbers. He picks up on the fourth ring. "Yeah," he says, his voice almost completely drowned out by the club music in the background.

"Tray, Vaughn Asher here. I'd just like to let you know your marriage to my sister will be annulled. I'll send you the court date. If you try and contact her, I'll take legal action. Have a nice night out clubbing."

I press end on the phone and wait for the callback. But he doesn't call back.

And while that's good in the short term—I won't have to deal with him, he seems to have gotten the message— that's not good for the long term.

Because a man who doesn't fight for his new bride when she gets cold feet and walks out on the honeymoon will probably turn out to be an asshole.

Chapter Twenty-Four - Grace

#YouAreCaredFor

VAUGHN invades my dreams and they are some of the sexiest dreams I've ever had. I dream about his hard chest, the curve of his muscles, the scratchiness of his jaw, the thrust of his cock inside me—making me wet, making me shudder, making me—

My alarm goes off on my phone and I reach under my pillow to find it. I swipe the screen and it goes silent and then I glance at the time and weather, like I do every day, and get a pleasant surprise.

Good morning, #MrsInvisibleMan.

Wow. I smile. I'm smiling like… huge. It almost feels like we're friends now. I stare up at the ceiling for a few seconds. Vaughn Asher is texting me good morning. And he's calling me MrsInvisibleMan. It's weird that he's calling me that, but I started it last night with the *#MrsInvisibleOnline* hashtag. I tap the screen to pull up the keypad and type out a response.

What kind of perks do I get for being your Mrs?

He texts back immediately and I bite my lip as I wait, my eyes glued to the little *typing* message.

I take care of what's mine. Whatever you want.
Haha. Then I will get you my list. :) I gotta go to work. Toots.

I throw the phone down and get up so I'm not tempted to stay in bed and chat with him. I have to mentally shake myself for a second, because it's just so surreal. I'm starstruck and yet not all at the same time. Last week this man was the star of all my sexual fantasies. And this week I know him intimately.

Not as intimately as I'd like, it's been a strange introduction. But holy hell, I had sex with him. Twice.

Yeah, it was the same day, and they were both on vacation. But still. Twice.

And he's still calling—and texting, and messaging—so that means he wants more than sex. Right? I'm not delusional, am I? He's definitely interested in something else, because for whatever reason, he's making sure he leaves a lasting impression. And he might even be going out of his way to make it… well, maybe not good. But certainly satisfactory.

I take care of what's mine.

That's not something a man says when he's looking to move past a one-night stand.

Am I way off here? Is he just blowing smoke up my ass? But why do that? I'm nobody.

Maybe that's why he wants you, Grace? Because you're safe. You're secret. You're invisible.

But I even met his parents. Sure, it was the briefest of meetings. I barely said hello. But I met the famous Adam Asher. And his weird brother Conner. And his beautiful fragile sister, who really did marry the wrong man, even I picked up on that.

I take a shower and my fingers wander down to the cleft of my sex. I consider it for a moment, but I pull back before I even get started. If I'm going to be twexting with Vaughn Asher tonight, I want to be aching for release.

Thirty minutes later I'm heading out the door and out of habit I head to my car, but just as I'm clicking the door locks, I remember—I don't have to drive.

Yes. I even do a fist pump.

The full meaning of my promotion hits me and I allow myself a wide, broad, beaming smile as I walk back into my building, exit the front door, and find myself out on Wazee Street. It's always been a dream of mine to be able to live and work locally. And now that I'm working in our Downtown office instead of the Cherry Creek office, I can do that.

I walk up to the Sixteenth Street Mall and the free mall bus is just pulling up. My Starbucks is only a block and a half down, but what the hell? How many people get to take the mall bus to work? I get on, stand, weaving a little as the bus moves, then get off on the next stop with a grin. My Starbucks is only a few steps away and my new work—right across the street.

I do a little happy dance in my head and pull the door open on my favorite coffee establishment. I keep my coffee money on my handy Starbucks app, so I pull that up as I stand in line and wait my turn.

And this is when my dream comes crashing back to reality.

I spent almost all my money on that first-class plane ticket home and I won't be paid for another week. I have to make a car payment in a few days, and that right there will wipe out my whole account. I will be short, in fact, once I pay insurance. The prepaid balance on my Starbucks card is even worse. I might not even be able to afford my coffee right now. If my memory serves, my card might have about three dollars left.

Maybe I can sell my car? Then I wouldn't have that payment. Two payments if I stopped my insurance.

I dig through my purse, looking for change.

"What can I get you?" the overworked cashier asks me.

"Um, just a venti Coffee of the Day, thanks." I look longingly at the muffins as I wait for him to fill up my cup. That's one perk of getting cheap coffee. They fill it up for you as you wait. "And a blueberry muffin," I add quickly once he sets down my drink.

"Four seventy-five."

I flash my app under the scanner and gather up my nickels and dimes. I know I don't have that much on my card.

But he hands it back with a receipt and says, "Next!"

I take my coffee over to the milk station and add in three sugars and half-and-half, still thinking about my card balance.

I guess it's my lucky day. I smile again as I stir my coffee and put a lid on it. My step is a bit lighter as I walk out the door and enjoy the crisp fall air as I stroll across the street to my office.

The downtown office of Big Guys Events, of which I am now an employee, is run by Scott Baker and his brother, Blake. They own the Cherry Creek office too, but they call that one Little Lady Events, and it's run by the bitchy sisters, Leah and Ali—gag, they are a *Mean Girls* movie waiting to happen. I was never a favorite of theirs, so I was a little surprised when I got promoted up to Big Guys, but hey, I'm just living, breathing proof that hard work pays off.

The Big Guys are super-cool. We hit it off immediately at my interview and I'm hoping they give me club events to manage as my first gig. Big Guys handles a bunch of those, all of them hip, trendy rock clubs that have up-and-coming bands playing every weekend and special events once a month.

I'd be the special events girl. I wouldn't be dealing with rock bands, thank God. Just planning one or two fantastic parties for each club every month.

Whew.

The reality of that is sort of stressing me out as I pull open the door to our building and push the button for the elevator. Our building is six stories tall and only has our offices on the top two floors. The bottom floor is a sandwich shop, but there's a separate entrance for that.

The doors open so I get in and hit the button for the fifth floor for a quick stop at my office—squee—before I have to check in with the Big Guys on the top floor for my assignments. The doors open and Flora, the main receptionist, greets me with a wave as she talks to someone on the phone through her headset. My office is the last on this floor. It's small and dark, but I do not care.

I flip on the light and stand there for a moment to let it sink in.

I've made it. I'm here. And even though the thirty-two-thousand-dollar salary isn't a lot, it's two thousand dollars more than I was making in Cherry Creek.

So squee again!

I sit at my old desk and take out my laptop and set it up next to my new desktop so I can check my mail.

I have a bunch of spam and an email from MrInvisible. I have to smirk as I open that up.

Enjoy your first day!

Wait. Did I tell him I started a new job? Did I give him my email?

"Grace?" Flora calls from outside my door. "You have a delivery."

"Delivery?" I get up and peek out the door and spy the most ginormous bouquet of flowers I've ever seen. They are like two feet tall and four feet wide, I'm not even joking. "What's that?" I ask, walking up to the reception desk.

"Flowers, obviously." Flora says, peeking out from behind them and pushing up her nerd glasses. "You have a great guy, I'm so jealous."

"Um, yeah. He's really great. I don't know if I can even carry—"

"I'll get them, Grace," Scott says as he walks up to us. "I was just coming to see if you were in yet." He grabs the massive arrangement with ease, since he and Blake really are big guys, and walks it down to my office. He sets it down on the only table and then turns to face me. "We have a serious problem," he says.

"Oh?"

"Yes, now listen, I don't want you to think we're taking advantage of you, but Grace, you're the only person who can do this job."

"What job?"

"The wedding," he huffs out. "I know we don't do weddings here, and the whole reason you wanted a promotion was so you can move away from weddings, but this is John Blazen's fiancée. And Johnny went to school with us—with my sister, specifically—and wants us to handle the wedding, but the new Mrs. refuses to use Leah over at Little Lady."

"Blazen? He's the new quarterback for the Broncos?"

"Uh, yeeeahhh," Scott says back, like he can't believe I had to ask. "This wedding is the event of the year and it's happening in two weeks. But Leah pissed off the future Mrs. Blazen, and now she wants Big Guys to handle everything. So…" He hesitates and shuffles from one foot to the next. "Will you do it?"

"How come I've never heard of this wedding?"

"Total hush-hush," Scott says as he wipes his brow. He's really sweating my answers. Which is ridiculous. I never say no. I'm a yes-girl. And besides, like I'd really turn down my first assignment. It's something I do well and they need me. "Blazen just got raked over the coals by his ex after that whole cheating scandal, and didn't want the media to know about it until after it's over."

"OK, I mean, sure, Scott. Whatever you guys need."

He claps me on the shoulder—hard, like he must do to his brother—and beams a smile at me. "That's great. I'll make sure your club events are all taken care of this month. The wedding's in Vegas in two weeks. I'll have Flora get all Leah's preparations over to you, stat, and you can set up a meet-and-greet with the future Mrs. Blazen today."

Before I can ask if the future Mrs. Blazen has a name that might not reference the husband she doesn't yet have, Scott is off, being his usual boisterous self to my new co-worker Adam.

I let out a deep breath. OK, for a first assignment, a wedding is right up my alley. It's a good thing, really. It will give me time to settle in without the pressure of setting up club events on top of it.

Just one wedding in two weeks.

How hard can it be?

Plus, it's a celebrity wedding. Sorta. The Broncos are superstars in this town, and everyone knows of Johnny Blazen, both on the field and off. He's a huge playboy and his recent divorce from second wife Amber was a scandal this town will never forget.

At least until they have the new wedding to gossip about.

"Here you go, Grace," Flora says as she hands me a thick paper file. "This is the hard copy of receipts and stuff that Leah sent. She said to tell you good luck. Apparently Mrs. Blazen is pretty difficult."

"Oh, great." I smile at her. "Hey, by any chance, do you know Mrs. Blazen's first name?"

"Um…" Flora stops to think. "No, actually. I think she refers to herself that way."

And then she's gone and I'm alone in my office with my new assignment. I flip the folder open and find Mrs. Blazen's number, key it into my phone, and then hit send.

"Hola," a chirpy woman says on the other line. "Future Mrs. Blazen here."

"Um, hi, Mrs. Blazen, this is Grace Kinsella from Big Guy Events. I'm your new—"

"Yes, Grace. We've met down at Little Lady Events. I'm thrilled to see you've been moved. I asked for you specifically a few months ago, but Leah refused to let you be my planner."

"Oh, I had no idea. I just—"

"I have time to meet in an hour, can you come to my house in Park Hill?"

"Sure—"

"Great, see you then."

And the call cuts off.

I just stare at my phone for a few seconds and then it rings in my hand. I press accept automatically without looking at the number. "Big Guy Events, Grace Kinsella speaking, can I help you?" Shit, I just answered my personal phone with my business greeting.

"Miss Kinsella, this Mr. Whitman at the bank."

"Yeah?" Double shit, I bounced a check.

"I just wanted to personally let you know that your savings account conversion has been completed, and I wanted to check to make sure you didn't need anything else before I leave for the day. My mother is not well and I'd like to—"

"Wait, what's going on?"

"Oh, my mother, she's a diabetic and she's got a toe infection, so I have to go take her—"

"No, I mean…" I roll my eyes. "I'm sorry to hear that, so yes, of course you should go—"

"Great. Your new interest rate on your savings has been doubled." He stops to chuckle. "After all, with a deposit like that, we offer special perks to our best customers."

"Perks?"

"You have concierge service now. I'm your personal attendant and I will attend to everything you need, Miss Kinsella, but tomorrow, if that's OK?"

"Yeah, sure, but—"

"Great, call me at this number whenever you need anything. Just not—"

"Today, yeah, I get it."

"Thank you," he sings back at me. And then I get the disconnect beeps again.

Jesus. Can life get any stranger? These flowers are not mine, this bank concierge is not mine, and this celebrity wedding is not... well, yeah, that one is mine. I smirk at that, but still. Weird.

Well, since Mr. What's-his-face can't be bothered today, I will sort that bank stuff out tomorrow. And I still have forty minutes before I need to leave to meet Ms. Blazen, so first thing first.

How much coffee money do I have left?

I press my Starbucks app on my phone and walk over to the flowers as I wait for it to load. There's a card, and I'm just pulling it out of the little pink envelope when my balance comes up.

I stare at it.

Then at the card in my hand.

You are cared for.

Then my balance. Four thousand, nine hundred and ninety-seven dollars, sixty-three cents.

What? How? I look back at the flowers and see Asher's little V initial. What the fuck? Who the hell puts five thousand dollars on a Starbucks account?

And that stuff with the bank?

I pull up my banking app on my phone and log in. It takes a few seconds, which is not good, because the time between that and when it loads only gives my heart time to beat faster, so that when I actually see the balance in my savings, I have to grab a hold of the table to keep from falling over.

I have thirty thousand dollars in my savings account.

Chapter Twenty-Five - Vaughn

#TheGiftThatKeepsOnGiving

MY mind wanders all day. Grace, Grace, Grace. That's all I think about as I listen to my agent go on about upcoming projects, promotions, and charity functions.

I nod for everything.

"Yes, sure, Larry," I tell him when he asks if I'll attend the *IM2* premiere.

"You will?" he asks, surprised. He's holding his phone, glancing down at it every few seconds even as he talks to me. "I mean, you've been making such a big deal about it these last few years."

"Hell the fuck no! I'm messing with you. I can't stand the paparazzi and the fanfare. I'm sick of it. I've lived in the public eye for twenty-seven years, and that's not including the first five years where the public eye was only Adam. It's tiring. I'm at the point where this really is a job, ya know? I'd like to go home at the end of the day and just... be with people in a *normal* way."

Larry looks at me suspiciously, one brow hitched up on his forehead, one eye squinting. "You're seeing someone?"

"What? No, hell no. I'm not seeing anyone."

"You have a girl at your place, don't you? I'm coming over tonight to check. Are you shacking up?"

"No, Larry. Look, all I mean is that I need space. I need... time *off* maybe."

"Time off? Are you kidding me? V, your career is at its height. You're in your prime. You have roles coming out your ass. *IM2* is the beginning. All those stupid roles are behind you and now is the time to take on projects that are meaningful and fulfilling. You can't quit now."

"I'm not talking about quitting, I'm just talking about doing... something else. Like relaxing. Enjoying what I have for a year."

"A year? No, you can't—" His phone buzzes in his palm and that distracts him away from my conversation just long enough for me to wave a hand at the waitress to get the check. "I have to take this, do you mind?"

"You go, I'll pay. Talk to you next week."

He pats me on the back as he answers his call and then walks out.

We've had this weekly lunch every Tuesday for ten years. Larry is my best friend as well as my agent and I know he's just looking out for my career, but the truth is I don't want to think about my job, or the premiere of *IM2*, or the appearances I'll have to do to promote it, or any of the other endless things that come with being a movie star in Hollywood.

I need to get the hell out of Hollywood, actually. I think that might be my problem.

"Here you are, Mr. Asher," the waitress says as she hands me the check. I pull out my card and hand it over to her and go back to my thoughts, looking out the window onto Santa Monica Boulevard. *Grace.* That's all I want to think about today. Tweeting with Grace tonight. And who would've thought that this simple thing could make my day?

I wonder if she got my flowers, or realized I've padded her bank account with money? Or the Starbucks card?

I'm still smiling at all of that when my phone buzzes and speak of the angel, she's calling me right now to thank me! I press accept. "Calling me at work, tsk tsk tsk," I say playfully.

"Asher," she seethes and I actually sit back in my chair at her tone. "Who the fuck do you think you are going into my private accounts? Just who the fuck?"

"Whoa, Grace, not the thank you I was expecting."

"Thank you? Are you crazy? I'm writing you a check and giving all that money back. How dare you! I will not be bought. I will not have you giving me money with the presumption that I owe you something, understand? I will write you—"

The waitress discreetly slips the bill back on the table and I hold my hand over the phone and mouth *Thank you, bring the car,* at her.

"—and you will stop with this. Do you understand?"

"Grace, listen carefully, because you're missing out on the experience of what just happened to you. OK?"

"How dare you discount my feelings on this—"

"Listen," I growl at her. "You had your say, now I will have mine." She huffs out some air and I can almost imagine the eye roll she's giving me in Denver and that just makes her all the more desirable. But she needs a firm hand right now, because she's being emotional and reactionary. "It's a gift. I'd like to help you out. In your pursuits or dreams. Whatever. Use that money any way you want. There are no expectations tied to it at all. If you write me a check I won't cash it, so don't waste the time and effort it will take for all your self-righteous indignation. It's pointless."

"I don't want your gift. And I've changed my mind. I'm not tweeting with you tonight."

"You are."

"I'm not. And who the hell puts five thousand dollars on a Starbucks card? It's ridiculous!"

"What's ridiculous about it? It's a payment card, now you have money to pay."

"It's five years' worth of coffee, Vaughn. Starbucks could go bankrupt in five years. The world could end in five years. You have no idea what will happen in five years. So it's a waste of money."

"You're right, anything can happen in five years. But…" I hesitate, take a deep breath, and then say it. "But every day for the next five years you will walk into Starbucks knowing I'm still caring for you. Every day for the next five years you will think of me at least once. So it's not a waste of money, it's a gift that keeps on giving. For both of us. Because once a day I will know for certain that you are thinking of me. And once a day you will know for certain that I'm thinking of you. How is any of that ridiculous?"

Total silence on the other end of the line.

"Grace?"

"I don't even know what to think about that."

I shake my head in confusion as well. "What's to think about? I don't get it."

"It's too much. And the money, Vaughn, please. It's sending me all kinds of mixed messages. I don't understand what's happening. All of this is just too much!"

"Too much how? Your constant objections to everything I say and do are sending *me* mixed messages. Jesus, do you even like me? From the way you react to everything I do, I'm going to have to say no. The money is not complicated, Grace. You must worry about bills, you don't make very much. So why is it too much to take that worry away?"

"You're trying to buy me."

"Buy you for what? That doesn't even make sense."

"It does to a poor person." And then she hangs up.

And that is bullshit. I redial and get ringing. One, two, three, four, voicemail. "Grace, call me back."

I take my credit card and stuff it in my wallet as I exit the cafe, sliding my sunglasses down over my eyes, as I head into the paparazzi. They bombard me with questions, cameras clicking, people touching me. The crowds gather, but the valet is there, and then the security from the restaurant comes to help—this is the cafe to the stars, they know how to deal—and I slip into the Range Rover, check traffic, and pull out onto Santa Monica, heading west.

I'd like to forget about her.

That's a lie. I'd like to fly to Denver right now and fuck that girl until she relents and lets me boss her around.

I chuckle a little because she hates the bossing. I get it. Lots of girls hate it. But I'm half joking about it with Grace. I can take no for an answer, but not all the fucking time. She wants to say no to me just to say no. And while I like to spar with her, it bugs me that she's so combative. Can't she see I'm playing? I'm not sure if she's pretending to be offended by the money, or if she really is.

Isn't that why she works? Isn't that why everyone works? To make money and pay bills, and do new things, or take care of kids?

I'm not out to offend her. I just wanted to help her

I dial her phone again, and again, it goes to voicemail. "Why can't you just say thank you? Why can't you just feel good about the money? Why can't you just enjoy it?" I hang up and wait to see if she calls me back.

I don't want to squash her independent nature and I like her feistiness. I wonder how feisty she can be in bed when she's not getting fucked publicly. I'd like to find that out and I'd like to find that out right now.

But I put on my blinker and turn right at Laurel Canyon to head up into the hills. I've got meetings and she's got a job. I try and remember how long it's been since I was dating a woman with an actual job. Someone who was not paid to hang out and wait for me to show up.

Wait, did I just refer to this as dating?

We're not dating. I shake my head and laugh. I don't date, and not only that, long-distance relationships never work. And I'd never date a girl in Denver, for fuck's sake. Denver. No. Colorado is a place you go on vacation. You ski there, you don't date girls there. You might fuck some girls there, and I do plan on fucking Miss Kinsella there. But that's not dating. I don't know what this is, a friendship maybe. But it's not dating.

I check my phone to see if I've missed any messages, but no. She's not calling me back. That's OK. I will leave her alone so she can work today, but if that woman thinks I'm going to walk away from our sex tweeting tonight, she's mistaken.

Ten minutes later I pull up to the gates of my modern mid-century home and the security guards let me through with a smile and a wave. I have a tuxedo fitting later this afternoon, but the tailor comes to the house, so I plan on spending my day at the pool thinking up ways to make Miss Kinsella blush and wiggle with one hundred and forty characters.

Chapter Twenty-Six - Grace

#SomeAssholesAreBrilliant

I THROW my purse down on the table near the front door, kick off my heels, and flop down on my couch. Exhausted.

Walking to work this morning was fun and exciting, but the reality is that I need my car during the day to meet people. So all that musing over living and working local was just bullshit. I can't ride the bus to meet clients. It's stupid. Just stupid. It took me forever to get over to Park Hill today, and I was totally late because I had forgotten that I didn't drive. And instead of going home and picking up my car, I insisted that I try to get around without one.

Denver has no real train system, so public transportation is not an option like it is in bigger cities. So now I live two blocks from work and I'll still have to drive every day.

The future Mrs. Blazen—who actually does have a name and it's Kristi—was a mess. A total mess. All that fake happiness on the phone was just that. Fake. She tried to force the smile with me too, but in person you can see she's having a very hard time dealing. She's pregnant for one, and that's why all this hush-hush stuff with the wedding, and she's far enough along for everyone to know that she got herself knocked up by this Blazen guy months before the divorce was final.

She was on the verge of tears the entire time. Everything I asked, from what kind of music she liked to what color flowers she would prefer, her eyes filled up. I can't say for sure, but I think some of that is the pregnancy hormones and some of that is guilt. And she deserves to feel guilty. Women who sleep with married men are scum in my mind.

As are men who cheat.

I didn't actually meet the infamous Johnny Blazen because he doesn't live there with Kristi, he still lives in the house he shared with his previous wife in Cherry Creek. I'm hoping I can get all the way to the wedding without meeting him, actually. He seems like an asshole, and the future Mrs. Blazen, who does actually call herself that, could do a lot better in my opinion.

At least the wedding should be relatively easy to plan. They're eloping to Vegas. Well, technically they're eloping, but it's going to be planned to the nines. No drive-through wedding for Kristi and Johnny.

No, a fountain terrace affair at the Bellagio is what Kristi wants. And why she needs me to do this is puzzling, because the Bellagio has its own wedding coordinator.

My phone buzzes and I cringe. I've been thinking up excuses all day for Asher. Jesus, that man has some nerve. But when I glance down at my phone, it's Bebe, so I smile and say, "Hola, bitch. Tell me my life is fabulous so I don't forget how long I've worked to climb my way up to the bottom rung of the ladder."

"Awww, the poor baby. She chats with a movie star last night and she's feeling down today because her life is ordinary? Please. Your life is fantastic. And as much as I like to know about the new club parties you'll be planning—I want regular invites, by the way—I'd like a little more info on this whole Twitter hacking that took place. Is that crazy or what?"

"Totally crazy," I say, trying to feign excitement. I don't want to talk with her about Vaughn. Meeting him was nothing like my dreams. He's pushy, controlling, pompous, and rude.

And he put thirty-five grand into my accounts today.

Thirty-five grand. That's more than I make in a year and he just put it into my bank and on my Starbucks card. I could put a down payment on a house with that—

"Earth to Grace? You still there?"

"Sorry, I think I lost the connection for a second. I don't really know how that hacking stuff happened. I didn't talk to him or anything, so—"

"What's wrong?" Bebe says. Why did I think I could fool her? "You should be jumping up and down with excitement over this. Bitch, you tweeted with Vaughn Asher, the man you've been cyber-stalking for years. And you're not fangirling!"

"I know!" I say back, trying my best to be excited. "But today was a crapper. My first day on the new job and I got a high-profile client who makes me sad in so many ways I can't explain it. And I can't even talk about it, because I had to sign a NDA to work with her."

"Oh, Jesus. NDA, that's some serious shit."

"Yeah." And it only further reminds me of Asher and what he's offering. How do I go through twenty-three years of life never even saying the words non-disclosure agreement out loud to being asked to sign two of them in the same week?

At least the one for work is acceptable.

"—you hear me?"

"No, sorry, my mind wandered. What?"

"Steve and I are going to the mountains this weekend, wanna come?"

"Can't, I gotta work on this new event. It's taking place in two weeks and I'm the second planner, so I have a lot to do."

She buys it, but the truth is, the future Mrs. Blazen has almost everything set up. I will not have to work very hard at all for this event. But the thought of being third wheel for Bebe's fun trip to the mountains is too much. I can't do it.

We chat for a few more minutes. Mostly it's Bebe bitching me out for leaving the island and not telling her, and I agree, that sucked. I do not deserve to even defend myself because it was bullshit. And then we make up and say our good laters.

I set my phone on the coffee table and close my eyes, but no sooner have I done that than the door buzzer goes off. "Jesus, can't I just get a moment?" I drag myself up and go over to the front door and press the intercom. "Yes?"

"Delivery for—" There's a pause, like the guy is reading something. "Mrs. Invisible M? Is that you? It said apartment four, but—"

"It's me." I sigh heavily and then press the door buzzer. I open my door and stand there, waiting for the delivery guy, because if I sit back down, I might fall asleep. I can hear him trudging up the stairs, huffing like he's out of breath, and then he comes into view and smiles at me. "It's heavy!" He walks down the short hallway to my place and stops at the threshold and thrusts the pretty-papered, ribbon-tied box at me. I take it, groan from the weight, then set it down by the door. I shuffle though my purse to find the few dollars in change I didn't need to spend this morning on coffee and hand it over. He smiles, does a short bow, and turns on his heel.

I close the door and slump down to the floor next to the box. "Now what in the hell is this?"

My phone buzzes across the room on the coffee table, so I get up and grab it.

I'm calling you in thirty seconds, pick up.

Bossy Man is back. I ignored his earlier messages. I mean, not really, I listened to them and I fumed about them. But I didn't call him back like he demanded. But when the phone rings thirty seconds later I press accept. "Yes," I say curtly.

"Open the box."

"Oh," I say with a hint of disappointment. "That's from you?"

He grunts. "Who the hell did you think it was from?"

"I'm kidding, you jealous jerk."

"Just open the box."

I walk back over to the package and untie the ribbon. "I like the gift wrap," I say, as I pull on the long satin strands.

"Is it pink?" Vaughn asks, sounding earnest.

"Yeah, a very bright pink. It's pretty." He sighs, like that makes him happy, and my stomach flutters. For all his caveman tendencies, he's actually charming at times. I take the lid off the box and peel back the white tissue paper, not expecting anything specific, because the weight of the box was a dead giveaway this was not lingerie or candy. "What is it?" I ask, staring at the bundle of papers. "We're not really married, @mrinvsman, so I know they're not divorce papers."

"No, you said you'd never marry—which is disturbing, if I'm honest, but that's a conversation for another time. Just open them."

I pull out the first heavy glossy folder and read the logo. "Front Range Fosters. I don't get it."

"It's a charity, what's not to get?"

"No, I mean, why did you giftwrap me a folder with this company's info?" I pick up the folder underneath. "Or the Denver Foster Kid Alliance Scholarship Fund?"

"Because I wanted to give you choices."

"Choices for what, Asher? Just speak plainly, I have no idea what you're talking about."

"Donations. You said you didn't want the money, you'd probably do something stupid with it, so I figured I'd channel that anger into the right direction. So pick one, and I will give that money to the charity of your choice."

I swallow down the tears as I look at all the charities in this package. They are all for foster kids until I get to the last one for the Colorado Sibling Fund, and then I almost can't breathe. "How?" I ask him as calmly as I can. "How did you come up with these charities?"

"Is it more of a transgression to admit to stalking or hacking?"

"Asher," I growl.

"Fine, I might've peeked at your charitable donations for the past five years."

I close my eyes and let out my breath, calm returning. "OK," I say, taking one more moment to gather myself. "Well, that was very nice of you. I'd like to split it then, and give each one the same amount."

"I'm smiling, Grace. I'm smiling very big right now." It sounds genuine too, like he's a little boy giving a grownup something that came from his heart. And maybe for the first time since I met him, he is speaking from his heart and not his dick.

I smile back, but I don't tell him.

"OK, so we're still on for Twitter sex in an hour. I sent a gift in the box—"

I check the box, and sure enough, there's another gift-wrapped box in there with the same pretty ribbon.

"—but it's to be opened after we're finished. Be online as @mrsinvsman at eight. And be naked."

The line goes dead before I can even answer. I'm a little bit stunned. He sorta stuns me. He's overpowering, and controlling, and bossy. But at the same time, he's got this charm about him. And he's very confident. Like he's in charge of things. Like he takes care of things. Makes everything OK. And I have to admit, he took the money back graciously and made me feel important at the same time.

It was a brilliant move and suddenly this day is exciting. Like it should've been all along.

Vaughn did that.

The movie star I'm secretly tweeting with has made my day and it's got nothing to do with the dirty sex I want to have with him.

Vaughn Asher might, just maybe, be a decent guy.

Chapter Twenty-Seven - Vaughn

#KiddingNotKidding

THE summer wind is just enough to make the low eighties temperature perfect as I sit outside on the terrace and sip a glass of Cuvée Elisabeth Salmon, 2002. Champagne is a drink I not only enjoy, but appreciate for the complexity of flavors and scent. And as I highly doubt Grace has had the pleasure of the 2002 vintage of this particular house, I'd like her opinion on it.

I check my watch and notice the lights that are strung up along the exterior of the terrace. It's pretty. Romantic even. Perfect for our Twitter date.

I have to chuckle to myself. Is that strange? To be excited about a Twitter date when the sole purpose is to get her to open up to me sexually?

Why not, though? People communicate in all kinds of ways in this age. Twitter is just another method of making a personal connection. One hundred and forty characters and a well-placed hashtag might just change my life.

And I have to admit, just the idea that Grace has been stalking me for so long, thinking about me as she's touched herself… well, it's more than a compliment. It's a turn-on.

I check my watch again. What is she doing? Preparing? Is she naked yet? Probably a more apt question would be will she actually accommodate that request?

I pick up my phone and find the note app. I've been composing filthy tweets all day. Tweets like:

My fingertips are dragging up and down your calf as my head dips between your legs.

But that's too much like phone sex and I don't want this to be like phone sex. I want it to be… different. I like the thought of my head between her legs, and I'm sure, from what I've read of her dirty tweets about me over the years, it's definitely one of her fantasies. But it needs something more. A hashtag, for sure. That's Twitter sex 101. Are there rules for Twitter sex? I don't think so, but maybe there needs to be? Guidelines to challenge and excite at the same time. Am I too competitive?

I'm sipping from my glass as that thought crosses my mind and I almost choke on the expensive champagne.

Is this a competition? What am I really trying to accomplish with this night? Her one-hundred-and-forty-character orgasm? A next date? Something else? The NDA contract and six months of dirty sex at my whim?

All of the above?

None of the above?

Some of the above?

Yes on the written orgasm. That makes me grin like a fool. I don't even know why it's so damn hot, but it's making me hard just thinking about it.

Yes on the date too. I've seen her sexually, now it's time to see her in other ways.

Do I like her? Like, for real like her? Or do I just like her body?

That I can't answer. It's a step ahead of what I'm capable of knowing at this point. I know only what I've dug up on her life. And I have to admit, there are some sketchy things about her past that have thrown up big question marks. Her childhood for one. It's missing. If she went to private school, then that would explain her missing school records. Hell, my childhood school records are pretty scarce as well. But I was trailer-tutored on set most of the time. The one year I did attend a real school, it was super-private and only for the elite.

Grace doesn't seem to come from money, but what do I know? Her parents were named Kinsella but they were a much older couple who died a year apart while she was in high school. I had Felicity do a property search for real estate records in the Denver neighborhood Grace said she grew up in, but it came up blank. So I'm not sure if she's lying when she says she sold their house, or I'm just missing something about her past.

I feel it to be both. Something is just a little bit off about her background check. She has no criminal record as an adult. I could dig deeper into her juvenile record, but is it really necessary to pry that much for a few sexual encounters?

I check my watch again, impatient with waiting. Why did I give her a whole hour? How long does it take to take off your clothes and open up a laptop?

OK, back to my tweets. They are inadequate. I need to up my game. I type one out on the notepad app on my phone, this time playing around with the hashtags.

#MyScratchyChin between your legs *#MindAboutToBeBlown* as my tongue caresses *#YourSmoothSkin*

That's more like it.

My laptop on the patio table pings a new tweet on my timeline.

Girl @mrsinvsman – 1s
@mrinvsman – As you commanded, I'm *#BareForYou*

My whole day is instantly better. God, this girl just lights me up. I forget the planned tweets and just reply to her.

Master @mrinvsman – 5s
@mrsinvsman - I expect obedience.

Girl @mrsinvsman – 1s
@mrinvsman – *#GoodGirlTonight* Tell me what you want.
;)

Master @mrinvsman – 3s
@mrsinvsman - #FlatOnTheFloor #LegsOpen #FingersWet

There is no answer after this request and my heart beats a little faster at the prospect that she does not want to play with me tonight. I want her to play. A few seconds after this private admission, a ping.

Girl @mrsinvsman – 2s
@mrinvsman – *#DoneDoneAndDone* Now your turn, unzip and let loose. I need a pic to continue.

Oh, that little bitch. That sneaky, delectable, horny, filthy little bitch. I laugh quietly as I consider the fact that she might have Twitter moves I've never even dreamed up yet. I unbutton and unzip my pants and my thick cock springs forward. I fist it, pumping two or three times just to get myself erect, then I scoot back and let the full length of my manhood fall across my flat, muscled stomach. I hold up the phone and snap a pic, sync it to my laptop, and attach it to the tweet.

Master @mrinvsman – 3s
@mrsinvsman - #LikeALollipop NOW.

God, what I'd do to her lips around my shaft right now.

Girl @mrsinvsman – 2s

@mrinvsman – #TwirlsAndSwirls

Her tweet comes with a picture too. A high angle looking down on her face. Fingertip in her mouth, tip of her tongue seductively touching, lips puckered appropriately, fuck-me eyes at half-mast, and just the slightest hint of her open legs.

Jesus fuck. She is hot. And she is one hundred percent naked. I was almost afraid to let myself believe she'd really be playing along, but she is. She more than is, she's into it.

I put my dick away and stand up, tweeting as I move across the terrace.

Master @mrinvsman – 3s
@mrsinvsman - I want to fuck you.

Girl @mrsinvsman – 2s
@mrinvsman – #ImYours #TellMeWhatYouWant

Master @mrinvsman – 3s
@mrsinvsman - More pictures. I want more pictures. Send me your three best and then I'll call you.

I go inside and stop in front of the stairwell, wanting to see the pictures before making another move. The first picture comes through. It's a picture of her hand covering her pussy. Nothing explicit at all.

Master @mrinvsman – 3s

@mrsinvsman - Need to do better than that.

Another picture comes in a few seconds later and this time it's her arm over her bare breasts, covering up her nipples. She's playing with me now.

Master @mrinvsman – 3s
@mrsinvsman - I'm not happy.

Girl @mrsinvsman – 2s
@mrinvsman – You are spoiled and impatient.

But attached to that tweet is what I wanted. Her. Open to me. Bare for me, as she put it. Legs spread. Fingers slick with her own juices. Pussy shaved.

She's delicious.

I dial her number as I go downstairs. She picks up on the third ring, sounding breathless. "Was that what you wanted?"

"No," I say in a low growl. "Answer the door."

"What?"

I knock.

"You're here?"

"Open the fucking door." I end the call and wait.

The chain on the other side of the door slides across the track and I watch the door handle jiggle with an apprehension I've never felt before. My dick is so hard as I anticipate seeing her, I grab it just as she opens the door.

She stands there naked, her eyes wide, her arms down at her side. I come in without being invited and close the door behind me while I reach for her hand and place it on my hard thickness. "Take me in your mouth."

She looks at me, her upcast eyes so fucking sexy, I want to explode right now. And then she lowers herself to the floor in front of me and releases my cock from my pants.

"Like a lollipop, Mr. Asher."

Fuck, that turns me on.

Her tongue darts out, licking my tip so softly, I moan. It sweeps out and grabs that little pearl of liquid and flicks it right into her mouth. She licks her lips, her eyes still trained on mine, like I own them. And then my cock disappears inside her. Her face pushes forward and takes me in, not all the way, but holy fucking shit, the heat of her breath and the slickness of her saliva drive me wild. I run my fingers through her long blonde hair and then grab it tightly, fisting it, pulling up as she watches me but never does her mouth stop sucking, never does her hand stop pumping.

"Do you like it rough, Grace?"

She shakes her head.

"No?"

She pulls her face from my cock and the cool air rushes in to replace the heat. "No, Master," she says in a demure voice I've never heard before.

She's playing along. She's fucking playing along and this excites me so much, I let out a long breath and grab her harder. She moans and then her fingers go between her legs and start rubbing her clit in small circles. It occurs to me then that we need a safe word. We don't have one and she's saying one thing and meaning another. This might get out of hand.

I'll be careful. I'm not ready to spoil the mood we've got going with serious talk, so I ignore that flashing red light and force my cock back into her mouth. She gags and then I yank on her hair, hard, and force her to stand.

"Miss Kinsella," I say as I push her against the wall and thrust my knee between her legs to make her open up. "You will like it rough by the time I'm done with you, won't you?" I pull her hair, forcing her chin up and her eyes on me again.

"Yes, Master," she says.

I turn her around and push her face against the wall. "Listen, little blue bird, you're mine now. I own you, baby. I will pay for you and you will accept my money without question from now on. Do you understand?" Her naked body stiffens as I press against her back. "Grace," I growl into her ear. "Say yes or I'll walk out and leave you breathless and wanting."

She turns her head so she can get a glimpse of me. I'm pushing her limits. A few seconds ago this was a game and she was somewhat in control, but I'm well on my way to dominating her, and she knows it. She's not sure it's right to give in, but she wants to. I know she wants to.

"Yes," she says, her ass pushing back against my cock.

"Tell me I can fuck you any way I want."

"Fuck me, Asher. Fuck me any way you want."

I don't even bother correcting her use of my last name. In fact, it turns me on. I fist her hair again and pull, making her take a few steps towards the living room until we reach the couch. It faces the window, but it's dividing up the room with the back facing the apartment entrance. I walk her forward until her thighs come in contact with the cream-colored fabric of the couch, and then I push down on her head until she bends over with a whimper.

I slap her ass so hard she jumps, but I place my hand on the small of her back to keep her in place.

"Do you like the slaps, Grace? Tell me truthfully. On the ass?"

"Yes," she says as I slap her again.

"On the face?"

She says nothing to this so I lean down and kiss the small of her back. "It's a heat-of-the-moment slap, Grace. Usually when my cock is in your mouth. Do you like those?"

She shakes her head no and a shiver runs up her body. Like she's frightened.

I stroke her softly. "OK, I won't do it. But"—I pull her hair again so she has to look at me—"I like it. And just so you know, I'd never do it hard enough to mark your cheek or make you feel like it was violence. None of this is violence, do you understand that?"

I slip my hand over her round ass, stopping to probe her bud. I expect a squeal of protest, but only get a groan that makes me suck in a breath of air through my teeth. "I don't want to hurt you, it should all feel good in the end. Unpleasant at times." I kick her legs open. "Slightly demeaning." I slap her pussy from behind and make her jump. "But always, *always*"—I reach around and grab her nipple as I press my chest against her back—"erotic." I twist it a little and she writhes underneath me, so I let go.

I know this is a lot for one night. It's almost crossing a line. But unless she tells me to stop, I'm going to keep going.

"You've heard stories about me?" I ask her as I push her face into the couch. Her head turns to the side automatically so she can breathe and she nods. "I hate that you're not using words, the words are half the turn-on for me. But I don't want to scare you, so I'm going to let it go."

"I've heard stories," she says, fighting my control with a lift of her chin and giving me what I want at the same time. Grace might be a true submissive, but she will not submit easily because she hates that part of her.

That can be very fun for me. If she wants spankings and nipple clamps, I can certainly abide. "You like ass-play. You like spankings. You like restraints. You like toys." I smile at that last part. "You know I like toys. Did you enjoy getting off in front of people at the restaurant?"

"No," she says, surprising me. "I thought it was rude to do that in front of your parents. You were trying to humiliate me."

"Yes, and?"

Her mouth drops open and she stares at me like I'm an asshole. She tries to stand up, in fact, but my hand is still holding her down at the small of her back. I lean in and kiss her mouth. "I like that," I whisper. "I like that and I'm not going to apologize for it. Because this is *our* relationship, Grace. Us. It has nothing to do with them. And if you really hate it, then I won't do it again. But answer me honestly. Did it turn you on?"

She swallows hard and nods her head. "It did. It was exciting."

Yes. I knew it. "OK then," I say, continuing my soft whisper in her ear. "If it excites you, I should be allowed to do it."

"I don't want to be caught. I don't want to be humiliated. I don't want to be embarrassed."

"Of course you don't, dirty bird. That's the fucking point, isn't it? The thought of getting caught having a mind-blowing orgasm in front of strangers is what makes it so fun. And really, how bad would it be if people knew I pleasured you? Is that something you're embarrassed about?"

She takes a deep breath and lets it out with a shrug of her shoulders.

I don't accept that as an answer, so I remove my hand from her back and pull her up by her hair. She has not said one thing about the hair-pulling, so that's not going to stop. I yank it to make her move her feet, and then I tug her over to the door and open it.

"What—"

I cover her mouth with my hand and bring her out into the building hallway with me. "Take out my cock," I instruct her.

She messes with my pants for a second, looking around wildly, and then my cock appears. She licks her lips as she stares at it and it jumps a little in anticipation of what we're going to do.

I slip my hands around her waist and pull her close. "Grace," I say softly in her ear as I let go of her hair and begin to stroke it. "Listen to me. None of what I do sexually is about humiliation or control. It's about excitement. It's about breathtaking sexual experimentation. It's about trust." I cup her face for this part, because she needs to hear it. "I'm speaking softly now because public sex is about *not* getting caught, even though we *might* get caught. Do you understand?"

I reach between her legs and drag a finger across her sopping wet crease, then slip inside her. She moans through my hand still covering her mouth, and I almost lose my shit right there. Her hot breath against my hand as I press it against her face. Her panting, her heaving chest, the small sounds that leak out.

"Quiet," I chastise her in a low voice, even though I love it. I love everything about what we're doing right now. "I'm going to make you come here in the hallway and you're going to be quiet. If you're not quiet"—I point to her neighbor's door—"someone will come look. And they will see us. And I will not stop what I'm doing. I will finish fucking you right in front of them if it comes to that. So if you don't want to get caught, remain silent. Because if you make noise, I'm going to assume you want people to watch."

I check her pussy again and it's even wetter than before. I smile at her and she smiles back.

"Do you want to be watched, Grace?" I remove my hand so she can speak.

She swallows hard. "Not now, but maybe. Someday."

I kiss her mouth tenderly. "I'd fucking love to try that with you. I will arrange it. But right now, I'm going to fuck you in the hallway. Do you want me to fuck you in the hallway?"

She bites her lip and looks over my shoulder, her eyes darting about wildly as she tries to make a decision. And then her attention returns to me and she nods. "Yes," she says, breathlessly.

"Face the wall and place your hands flat against it, above your head," I command. "Do not move." She obeys and I'm already pushing my throbbing cock between her legs. "In the ass?"

She gasps and tries to turn around to look at me.

"Kidding," I say as I ease my dick into her wet folds. I don't enter her, just rub it against her, bumping up against her clit with each thrust, making her bow her head and stifle her moans of pleasure.

She's ready to come right now and so am I, so the next thrust forward, my cock slips right inside her. I thrust upwards and she moans loudly.

I cover her mouth and lean into her neck. "That's the only time I'll do that, Grace. The next time I'll assume you want to be seen."

My motions become faster and harder and with each forward movement, she lets out a little squeak. My hand wraps around her stomach and then drops to find her clit. Her hands stay put on the wall, like she was ordered, but her whole body is writhing, desperately trying to make contact with me in every way possible.

I feel her body tense and I thrust deeper, burying my balls up against her pussy. She bucks her back... and opens her mouth... and screams.

Chapter Twenty-Eight - Grace

#BeMineGoesBothWays

IT takes me a few seconds to realize the primal noise ringing in my ears belongs to me.

Oh God, oh God, oh God.

That's all I can think about as Asher pounds into me. His thick, thrusting cock fills me up over and over again, pressing me against the wall. A whoosh of a door down the stairwell stops my moaning and writhing, and I stiffen. "Someone's coming."

But Vaughn's motions never slow. In fact, he speeds up, his movements becoming punishing, entering me with brutal force and then pulling back so abruptly all I can think about is the emptiness he leaves behind.

Voices now, laughter. And I recognize them. The guy who lives across the hall from me. In fact, now that my needs have been satisfied, I realize I am pressed up against their door.

"Vaughn, they live here! Stop!"

He slows, moving inside me more gently. "Why would I stop? Why would I care if your neighbors see me fucking you? You wanted this, remember? Tell me why I should take you inside."

"I don't want them to see me," I say simply. "Please, I don't want them to see me."

He turns me around, lifts my ass up, cupping my cheeks into his hands, and then he holds me close to his chest. "Grab my pants, please." He says it with a chuckle but I do not see one thing funny about what's happening. I can hear my neighbors' feet shuffling up the stairs, and we're on the third floor, it won't take them long to get here.

As soon as I have hold of his belt, essentially holding up his pants as his cock stays firmly inside me, he starts walking down the very short hallway and rounds the corner. There's a laundry unit a little farther down, and for a moment I sigh out a little relief, thinking we will go in there. But he stops, turns me around, and places me against the wall again.

I have a straight-on view of the stairs. "What the fuck are you doing? Go down the hall a little so they can't see me."

"Get on your knees."

"Vaughn!" I plead. They are almost to the top of the stairs. We are so busted. "Please!"

"Suck my cock and I'll make sure they never see your face."

I just stare at him.

"Now. And if you bolt inside, our fun ends permanently." He pushes on my head until my knees bend and I'm at his feet looking up at his beautiful movie-star face.

"I want you to suck my cock and I want them to know it's you because you disobeyed and made noise. But you are still mine, so I do not want them to see you. Now do it." His voice is low, barely a whisper, but his intent is clear. Begging is not an option. And I can see their heads as they climb the last few steps.

I grab Vaughn's hard thickness and open my mouth. As soon as my lips cover his head, he moans. The laughing neighbors stop, clearly noticing the sexual act going on at the end of the hallway.

"Uh," the guy says. "Wow, blow jobs in the hallway? Really?"

I look up at Vaughn's face and his fingers brush against my lips as he says, "Shhh." And then his hand leaves my face and he flips the guy off behind him.

"Prick," the guy's girlfriend says. "You sick fuck, we should call the police."

Vaughn responds by crouching down, pulling his slick cock out of my mouth as he descends, and then kisses me on the lips.

The door slams down the hall and he smiles as his tongue thrusts inside me. "Now, continue." He stands up and guides my face to him once more. I open and he thrusts, filling me up again. This time I take a deep breath through my nose and tip my head back. His hand finds my throat and he feels for the movement of the muscles in my neck as I swallow the pooling saliva and then he's inside me. Completely. His entire cock is inside my mouth, his large balls tight up against my chin. A few seconds later the warm

Social by JA Huss

rush of salty semen gushes down my throat as he tips his head back and growls out, "Fuck, yes. Fuck, yes."

I swallow him. Every bit of him. I'm breathless and elated, and humiliated, and turned the fuck on so bad, I start rubbing my clit and then the release finds me again and I moan out my whole body trembles from the shock of it all.

A few seconds later he pulls me up by my hair. I'm still trying to catch my breath when his lips cover mine like he wants nothing more than to have his mouth on mine, drawing heaving breaths together, celebrating our pleasure with the seal of a kiss.

"Grace," he says breathlessly, "That was so fucking perfect. You are so fucking perfect. Thank you, baby. Thank you for trusting me to get us through that." He grabs the back of my neck and presses his lips to my forehead in a gentle kiss that has my head spinning. "Come, on baby. We're not done yet."

He tucks his dick back into his pants, and then takes my hand, giving me a small, reassuring smile as we walk back to my apartment. The door is still open, I realize, so any hope of that neighbor not knowing who I am is totally out the window.

"He never saw your face, Grace."

I roll my eyes and shake my head as he closes the door behind us. And then I look up at him, his expression still so clearly hungry for *more*. For more playful fun. For me. And then his hand is between my legs, his fingers pushing inside me, so slick with my wetness they slide around.

"You liked it?" he asks, his words so low and soft that I feel another gush between my legs as he plays with me.

I let out a long exhilarating rush of air and nod. And then I laugh. "Jesus. That was…" I look up to him, for guidance maybe. Or reassurance. He nods and in that moment he gives me both. He gives me just what I need.

"Fun? Sexy? Dirty? Hot? Fucking incredible? The way you sucked my cock, Grace… Christ, I want to pull my dick out and come on your face just thinking about it."

I bite my lip and drop to my knees, my legs open a little, just enough to give him a peek at my swollen and sopping wet clit. I swallow hard and look up at him. "Do it, Mr. Asher. Come on my face." And then I open my mouth and wait to see what he'll do.

He only hesitates for a moment, and then he's unbuckling his pants and pulling out his half-hard cock. He sticks it back inside my mouth and this time I put my hands behind my back and take a deep breath as he begins to face-fuck me. It starts slow and gentle, but he speeds up, almost losing control, his hips thrusting harder and harder.

"Oh, yes. Grace, you have no idea how good you feel. You have no idea."

He grabs my hair again, but instead of the tight fist, he weaves his fingertips through it and strokes my scalp softly, all the while whispering comforting things, showering me with pretty words that make me feel special. "Your pussy is so tight, it grips my cock like a fist. Your lips wrap around my cock so perfectly, I never want to take it out. That's it," he says, guiding my head to pleasure himself. "Just like that," he moans as I let him in farther, gagging and choking. And then he throws his head back and withdraws from my mouth. I stay open, looking up at his face. But his eyes are closed and when he comes a second time, he misses my tongue and it squirts on my cheek, then he aims down and the rest of his pleasure spills out across my chest.

He fists my hair one more time, asking me to stand, and I do, still watching his face. I want to see the moment he opens his eyes. But he spins me around and wraps me up in his arms, hugging me tightly, burying his face in a mess of hair, breathing hard on my neck. So hard that it tickles my ear and causes a shiver to race up my body.

An embrace that is something other than sex. Something more than sex. Something I can't quite recognize, let alone define.

"Come, shower with me," he says after a few seconds of ragged breathing from both of us. "And then I have a surprise for you."

"A surprise?"

"The box," he says as he nods to the wrapped package still sitting on my coffee table. "You have to open that box and then I'm taking you somewhere."

"You are?" I ask, as he leads me down the hallway, searching out the bathroom. I point to the closed door across from my bedroom and he opens it and feels around on the wall for the switch. The fluorescent light takes a moment to flicker and decide if it wants to work, and then flashes on with an intensity that makes me blink.

"Oh, Grace," Vaughn says. "This is not a bathroom. It's too small to allow us to fuck. And there's no tub." He turns back to look at me and drops my hand so he can loosen his tie and drag it over his head. He reaches over my shoulder, the warmth of his arm pressing against my bare skin, and checks the back of the door, finds a hook, and then hangs it up and goes to work unbuttoning his dress shirt. My eyes are transfixed by his fingers as they nimbly undo each button, starting from the bottom and working his way up.

I gulp a little as his chest appears. I've seen it before, of course. But here in my tiny, extremely inadequate bathroom everything is different. It's not the vacation fantasy. It's not a one-night stand. It's not a… relationship.

What is it?

"Why do you have that look on your face?" he asks me as he shrugs off his crisp white shirt and hangs it on the small hook with his tie. I have a moment of panic that the hook will distort that perfect garment and ruin it.

"What?" I have to take a deep breath because my heart is beating so fast. Why am I feeling like this?

"What's wrong with you? You look… afflicted."

I swallow hard. And shake my head. "Nothing, I'm just hungry."

"Oh." He reaches for me, pulls me into his chest in another one of those hugs, and then leans into my neck. "Let's wash up and you can change. We're going to eat."

"We are?"

"Yes, baby. I have to feed you. You need to eat."

"Who are you?"

He laughs so loud he startles me and I step back a pace. This makes him stop and frown. "Tell me," he says in the authoritative tone I'm used to. "Tell me what's going on."

"What are we doing?"

He stares at me with that famous intent gaze, his deep blue eyes bearing down on me with confusion. I think I'm sending it right back, because I'm so off balance I might faint. "We're fucking, Grace. We're fucking, we're showering, we're eating, we're discussing. In that order. We've just checked off number one and we're about to complete number two. Then we will go eat and have a conversation. Clear?"

I nod. OK, I can deal with that. I move over to the shower and turn it on. The stall is barely big enough for me, let alone the both of us together. So I jump in before the water is even hot and begin to wash myself, taking care not to get my hair wet so I don't have to worry about it.

He finishes taking off his clothes and steps to the shower, ready to get in. But I put a hand up. "I'll be done in a minute and then you can get in alone."

"You must be joking."

"No," I say with chattering teeth since the water is not quite hot yet, "there's really no room—"

He physically moves me backwards until I'm pressed up against the cold tile wall, and steps in. He sucks in a breath at the water temperature and then adjusts it, standing over me to shield me from the cold. A few seconds later the hot water steams up the tiny stall, and he turns to me with a bar of soap and a wicked grin.

"I made a mess. It's my job to clean you up." He lifts up my arm and rubs the soap up and down the length of it, paying close attention to the crevice of my elbow and my ticklish armpit. He chastises me with a simple, "Shhh," when I giggle and pull away. And I bite my lip and let him continue. He does this for every limb, his deft fingers slipping between my legs and into my folds to massage my clit with the sweet-smelling suds. I groan, I can't help it.

"One more fuck before we call it a night? I don't know when I'll be able to come back again."

I look up at him and imagine him as Vaughn the man and not Vaughn the movie star. What would it be like to have a relationship with him? Like a *real* relationship? Is he this attentive all the time? Or does he just want something from me?

I shake my head no to his offer.

He grins. Not a big, wolfish one, but a slight, sympathetic one that tells me he knows. He can see right through me. He knows I'm having some kind of... emotional experience.

"Grace," he says softly as his fingers slip between my folds. "Relax, let me do this for you. It gives me pleasure."

I close my eyes and shake my head again, grabbing his hand and taking the soap from him. I lather myself up after that, quickly, as he watches with a keen and still hungry eye. And then I slip under his arm and rinse off in the water. When I open my eyes, he's staring at me with a smile.

"What?"

"Why do you have such trouble accepting kindness?"

"Is that what you're calling this? An act of kindness?"

"What do you call it?"

I just stare at him, because even though it's an obvious response to my question, I'm at a loss for words. "I'm finished," I say instead.

"As am I," he says back.

I shut the water off and step out onto the ragged blue bath mat. We both reach for the towel at the same time. There's only one, I always leave my hair towel in my bedroom after, and he gets there first.

"Shall we fight over the towel too? Do you enjoy this battle? Or is this true insecurity?"

"Oh, God. Just give me the towel."

"Why do you insist on making me repeat myself? I told you, I made a mess, so it's my job to clean you up. I'm not done yet." And then he brings the towel to my chest and gently presses it against my body, like I'm a fragile piece of art and rubbing me too hard might break me.

This from a man who was dragging me around by my hair and stuffing his cock down my throat not ten minutes ago.

And as I'm still thinking this, he dips his head and his mouth is on mine. Not a kiss so much as a caress, like the towel against my breasts. His tongue slips in and tangles up in mine, the water from his face drips into my mouth, making the kiss wetter than normal.

I close my eyes.

He moans, "Yes, that's my girl," into my ear.

I swallow hard and lean into him.

"You're mine now, Grace. Can you feel it?"

I want to say no, but his lips caress me into submission. I want so, so badly to say no. But I can't. Because I'm a yes-girl. Because a wave of heat rushes through my body and I'm rendered speechless and weak. Because my knees buckle and I begin to fall, but Vaughn scoops me up into his arms, never ending our kiss, and he holds me tight until I finally look up into his eyes and give him what he's waiting for.

"I can be yours," I say, my chest all aflutter with my uneven breathing.

"No," he says, his steely gaze dropping to my breasts, making me feel exposed and vulnerable. "Not you *can*, Grace. You will." His eyes dart back and forth, searching mine for acceptance, or surrender, or maybe just attention.

"I will be yours if you'll be mine."

Chapter Twenty-Nine - Vaughn

#WinWin

I IGNORE her statement and instead carry Grace into the living room and sit down on the couch, keeping her head in my lap. She wriggles, but I tsk my tongue at her. "Stop now. Just sit still. I need to explain something before we go any further and I need you to be OK with this, or we'll have to part now as friends."

She takes a deep breath. "I already know what you're going to say." I want to look away from her accusatory look, but I can't. I need to make this very clear, so I urge her on with a nod instead. "You're not mine. You'll never be mine. And no matter what *you* do, I'm your plaything and I'm not allowed to stray."

I nod again and she shakes her head and looks away. "I'm sorry, Vaughn." She pushes my hands off her and tries to get up, but I flip her legs up near her head and then smack her bare wet ass with a crack.

She squeals, wriggles, blushes, and pants all at the same time.

Jesus. I need to keep her long enough to get to the spankings, that's for damn sure. This was just a tease. "Don't move, we're not done. I can negotiate. Your characterization is harsh." She draws in a long tight breath that turns into a long, sad sigh. I've upset her and I feel a little wave of sympathy wash over me. "I don't have girlfriends, Grace. Your position is one of a kind. Does that help at all?"

She laughs, but it's not a happy laugh. "No. You make me sound like an employee. I don't need another job."

"What do you need?" I ask quickly.

"I don't know. Something… more than what you're offering. This… position, as you call it, means that I'm your *kept woman*."

"Is that so bad?"

Her laugh is a bit heartier this time. "You're joking, right?"

"Grace, you're thinking about it emotionally. Think about it objectively for a moment." She puts a hand up to silence me, but I grab it and wrap her little clenched fist in mine. "Hold still and be quiet."

"Quit ordering me around, Asher. And let go of my legs." She kicks and wriggles some more until I let them fall back down. I'm desperately aching to flip her over on my lap and turn her ass red.

But I need to set this up right. I need to keep my wants to myself until she's willing to comply with my unique demands. One step at a time. "Oh, we're back to Asher, are we? Fine, girl. What's wrong with two adults having consensual and erotic sexual encounters? It's an outlet, Grace. A way for you to explore new sexual boundaries. A time to draw new lines, make new limits, and try new things." She makes to protest but I cover her mouth with my hand. "Shush, I said. It's a way to do all those things while remaining under my care and protection."

"See?" She pushes my hand off her mouth. "This is where you lose me with your caveman shit."

"Language, please. And it's not caveman *shit*, it's necessary. The world is filled with unsavory characters, Grace. Especially those who would take advantage of you sexually. I will not take advantage of you. We can talk more about that later, if you agree to be faithful. But now that I've awakened your sexual curiosity, it's my duty to ensure you don't allow yourself to be drawn into another man's influence."

"But your influence is fine? How does that makes sense to you?"

"Because I'm famous and if you talked, you could ruin me. With or without a NDA, this is your hold over me. I'm trusting you to keep our life together private."

"Secret, you mean."

"If you prefer to use the word secret, by all means. But I prefer private. Something between the two of us."

"Except the people across the hall, they're in on it too."

I bend her legs forward and slap her hard and quick across her exposed pussy and then stick my fingers inside her, moving them in and out slowly as the shock wears off her face. "Did the people across the hall see you?"

"No," she moans. "But they knew what was happening, and they knew it was me. So what's the difference?"

"The difference is they will remember *me* being an asshole, flipping them off. Not you on your knees with my dick in your mouth. Because that's private. When I slap your pussy, that's private. When I pull your hair and come down your throat or on your breasts"—I lower her legs again and look into her eyes—"or whatever else we do. All of that is private. I don't want anyone to know about it."

"Is what you want to do to me that disgusting?"

"No, for fuck's sake. No. It's… beautiful. It's an agreement of trust. You allow me to dominate you sexually, and in return I make sure you're safe as you push yourself outside your comfort zone. You will never be forced, but most of the world sees my sexual preference as disgusting, and violent, and degrading to women, and it's not. It's consensual. It's highly erotic and it's a kind of escapism that doesn't come around very often."

She's silent for a moment, thinking presumably. "OK, but listen, that's not what's bothering me. I don't think I should have to be faithful to you, especially when I don't know how often you'll be around to"—she offers me a shy smile—"take care of my needs. And yet you can go out and get laid if the mood strikes you. I won't agree to it. Either we both follow the same rules, or I'm not interested."

"We can't both be in charge, Grace."

"I don't need to be in *charge*. I just want to be treated as your *equal*."

"We can't be equal, because I give the orders and you obey them."

"In bed? Or in life, Vaughn? Because those are two very different things. In bed, fine. Be the caveman. But in life, no. I'm sorry, I'm in charge of that. I make my own decisions and you live with them."

I tilt my head back and stare at the ceiling for at least a minute. I expect her to get tired of waiting. To struggle to get up, release herself from my all-encompassing embrace. But she's patient as I think this through. I'm not interested in someone who wants to whore around when I'm not present, but Grace doesn't strike me as promiscuous.

"I want a weekly STD test from you," I say without giving in to her demand. Let's see how far this goes. "I will set up a private service to check."

"Absolutely not!" she huffs in disgust. "You're not getting control over my health care."

"Then how can I be sure you're clean if you refuse to be exclusive?"

"You're the one who's not using condoms, Vaughn. I haven't had sex in eight months, I'm not a whore or a porn star who needs to be checked for sexually transmitted diseases on a weekly basis."

I smile at her. Eight months. "Who was the last boyfriend?"

"Who was your last *slut*?" she retorts.

I wince. "You're not a slut, I know that."

"Then don't insult me with a demand for weekly STD testing. It's not like I'd even have sex with anyone else, it's just not fair that you expect me to be exclusive and I'm not allowed to expect the same from you. That's bullshit."

"The only other option is for me to stop seeing other women and I just told you I don't do that."

"Then this conversation is over."

She makes to rise up out of my lap, but I hold her down again. That's the third time in five minutes I've had to do that, and so far this conversation is not easing my mind that she will accept my offer. "You will not fuck anyone else. You are mine."

"Then you will not fuck anyone else either. If you agree to that, then I will be yours."

I stand up and set her on her feet, then point to the box. "Dress, please. My clothes are still in the bathroom. We will have dinner and discuss limits and the NDA. You will sign tonight, Grace. Understand?"

I expect her to balk at that order, assert her independence and put up a fight. But she simply smiles and says, "Yes, Master," as she turns her back to go get the box.

Chapter Thirty - Grace

#SheepskinRugsEnoughSaid

HE doesn't move to go get his clothes. Instead he stands still behind me. I can feel his heated stare on my body even though I can't see him. I could feel him get excited when he spanked me. And holy shit, was that amazing or what?

I have to be honest with myself, I want to sign that damn agreement. Everything about this night has been erotic, and hot, and I'm so ready for him to fuck me again, I am starting to think I'm abnormal.

"Bend over, Grace. I want to see your pussy."

Oh. Fuck. I take in a deep breath. No, I gasp for air. I can't draw it in fast enough, that's how turned on I am with that request.

"Do it, please. I'm asking nicely. Bend over, like you're going to tie your shoe, but keep your legs straight."

I nod yes without turning around and then gulp down another fortifying breath. I bend at the waist and the air rushes in as my ass opens and exposes my soft folds to him. His hand rubs the round curve of my ass and then dips between my legs. "Will you ever be satisfied?" he asks as he flicks my clit.

"I was just wondering the same thing. I've had more orgasms in the past hour than I have all year."

His fingers withdraw from between my legs and then he bends down and he traces them across my lips. I open my mouth and taste my own sweetness. "I want to eat your pussy so bad right now, but we have to discuss the contract and have dinner." He pauses and I can almost imagine the smile on his face at procuring my compliance. "And an impromptu lesson in obedience."

Before I can ask what that means, he grabs my hair roughly and pulls until I stand up and face him. "Good, girl," he says once I'm looking him in the eye. "Does it hurt when I pull your hair?"

"No," I tell him honestly. "It's a little uncomfortable, but it doesn't hurt."

"Good," he says as he leans in. His scent, the soap from my shower, the leftover cologne from when he dressed this morning, and even the slightest hint of something sweet that I can't place—all these things rush in as his lips gently touch mine. "It's a delicate balance, Grace. The pain and discomfort playing off the desire and pleasure. Pulling your hair and smacking your pussy should make you uncomfortable and turned on at the same time. Otherwise I'm doing it wrong."

I gulp and nod. "It does. I mean, you're doing it right."

"Good." His lips touch mine again and then he pulls back. "We'll never get out of this apartment if I don't stop touching you, but I'm finding it very difficult."

I place a hand on his chest, fully intending to push him away, but I feel his beating heart and I'm distracted. It's fast. A staccato rhythm that betrays his excitement inside, while the cool man on the outside maintains control. He places his hand over mine and I look up at him. "I make your heart beat faster."

"You do," he says with a smile. A genuine smile. "Now get dressed and we'll eat. I'm starving." And then he turns and walks down the hall to retrieve his clothes.

I take my attention back to the box. The satin is smooth and silky under my fingertips. I pull lightly and the bow instantly dissolves into a river of pink ribbon that looks so delicious I'm trying to think of a reason to keep it next to my skin.

"Hurry," Vaughn calls from the bathroom.

I nod, even though I know he can't see me. It's to keep myself on task, because everything in this room is making me think of sex. I'm imagining that ribbon tied around my head, covering my eyes. Or binding up my wrists, so Vaughn can fuck me constrained.

Jesus, get a grip, Grace.

I lift off the lid and pull back the thick tissue paper to reveal the complete outfit I was wearing on the island. The bra, the shoes, and the bag included.

"You left," Vaughn says from behind me. "Before we got the details worked out. And this was the outfit I imagined you in when that happened." When I turn he's buttoning up his cuffs and something about that strikes me as hot. "I want you to wear this tonight because we *are* striking our deal. There are no panties. Go bare. I'll need access."

The tingle between my legs is immediate, but I turn away and try to keep my mind on what I'm doing. He watches me, I know, but he stays silent as I fasten up the button on the crisp white shirt and then pull on the flirty chiffon skirt and cinch the belt around my waist.

His hands wrap around me, taking me by surprise and making me teeter for a moment as I'm trying to step into the shoes. "I've got you, baby."

"Thank you. Just give me a moment so I can check my hair and—"

"No," he replies, pulling me towards the door. "You look well-fucked. Well-fucked and satisfied. Just the way I like you."

We leave the apartment, me sans purse even, but I don't even bother objecting. He's in charge, I'm sure that involves making sure I get home. So I just give in. I surrender and let him lead me down the short hallway towards the stairs. I expect to go down, but he points up.

"Dinner's on the roof, sweetness."

I'm caught on the affectionate term he just used, so I don't even bother to ask any questions about that, just follow him up the flight of stairs that lead to the roof. Standing at the door is a middle-aged man dressed in a smart, black suit.

"Mr. Asher," he says in a low voice. "Servers have been notified."

"Thank you, Robert."

And then Robert opens the door and Vaughn whisks me out into a fairyland of white lights and beautiful flowering plants. Tropical plants, I realize as I take it all in. And palm trees. There's even a shallow pool of water with a sand beach.

I laugh and look up at Vaughn's delighted face. "How did you do all this?"

He shrugs, a very boyish gesture that tells me he's pleased and relieved at my reaction. "Money does this, Grace. Money can do anything. But none of this would matter if you hadn't seen it. If you hadn't appreciated it. So I'm thankful to have money, because it helps me make moments like this. Come on," he says, urging me forward. "Let's sit at the table."

I follow him over to a long rectangle table covered in thick white linen and set with a pale-colored china and crystal glassware. "Oh," I say as I realize what I'm looking at. "It's only set for one."

Vaughn takes a seat in the chair and then points to a sheepskin rug at his feet. "No, sweet thing, it's set for two. Sit here, at my feet."

I'm stunned. He wants me to sit at his feet? Like a fucking dog!

"Grace," he says sternly, probably reading the disgust on my face. "Trust me. Just do as I ask and then you can feel any way you want about it when I'm done. But let me show you what this means."

I sigh, but I give in and kneel down on the rug. It's ivory white, very soft, and very thick. And even though everything about kneeling at his feet is wrong and I'm not going to change my mind about that, my fingertips caress the silky fur as I situate myself.

I look up at Vaughn and he's smiling.

I smile back.

"Spread your legs, sweets. Spread them wide and pull up your skirt a little, so I can see your pretty pink button poking out of your lovely folds."

Damn. I watch these words come out of his mouth and I'm stunned at how they make me feel. Because even though he basically just said spread 'em, it's the gentle nature of his request that makes all the difference. I can hear his breath speed up, like his heart is racing as fast as mine. And I can feel the heat radiating off his body in front of me.

I look over at the table and spy a selection of sex toys laid out on top of a black satin cloth. I hike up an eyebrow and look over at Vaughn, but his gaze remains stoic, not willing to end the play to explain.

It's my call, that look says. Obey or not.

My fingertips reach down for the hem of my flirty skirt and drag it up to the top of my thighs. The cool night air rushes in and my whole body shivers. Vaughn is mesmerized as he watches, his eyes fixated on my sex as it's revealed.

"Like that, Mr. Asher?" I ask him in a low voice that makes me feel vulnerable and powerful at the same time. "Can you see me?"

His gaze rests on my exposed pussy for a few more seconds and then he tears himself away and finds my face once again. "That's perfect, love. That's perfect. I'm going to reward you for that, but first I'm going to ask you to decide how the servers will see you as they bring our food."

He stops, waiting for a protest from me. But I'm far too turned on by the soft rug and submissive position to doubt that whatever he does tonight, it will be spectacular.

"Perfect," he says, reading my silence as willingness. "You can sit on my lap with a toy inside you, facing forward with the skirt covering the parts of you that now belong to me. Or you can just sit like you are at my feet. Covered up, of course."

It should be such an obvious choice, right? I should immediately say, covered up at your feet, not secretly getting fucked by an assortment of sex toys.

But even though that's what the angel on my shoulder is saying, the little sex demon on the other side is begging me to say lap.

"Grace? I didn't think it would be a difficult question."

Neither did I. "Lap," I say quietly.

"Why?" he asks through a huge smile.

"Because I might like it. And I know you planned this." I wave my arms to the magical fantasyland he's created on this dingy rooftop terrace. "And I want to experience this night the way you planned it."

He chuckles and smiles. And even though I've seen every public picture they have of this man, I've never seen that smile.

"Oh, you are so unpredictable, Grace. I can't get enough. Now, stand up, turn around, and bend over."

I do as I'm told. I'm far too turned on at the moment to put up a fight. I want to see what he can do. I want to see how he can make me feel. I want, I realize, to experience him in control. Fully in control. When I bend down in front of him he sucks in his breath and then leans in and blows it out and the warm currents of air travel across my exposed pleasure zone. His finger dips inside me, wiggles briefly to make sure I'm wet, and then he drags my juice up to my asshole.

"The toy goes in here this time, sweets. So just try and relax." I do my best as he plays with me, dragging the lubricant up to the tight bud of my ass, and then without warning, he slips something inside me with a firm thrust that stirs every last nerve ending awake.

I expected it to hurt more, but it's so fast, the initial pain is already wearing off when he pulls his hand back. "Good, girl," he says in a deep throaty voice that lets me know he's getting off on this as much as I am.

"I am a good girl, Mr. Asher, please be nice."

"Mmmm," is all he says as he licks me, a long sweep up my slit that ends just before it reaches my newly opened ass. This makes me bite my lip to stop a cry of pleasure. His tongue circles the toy and my entire body shudders with a chill.

"Now we make it exciting," he says as the toy inside me begins to vibrate. He pumps his cock with his free hand behind me. The rhythmic slapping of skin combined with the sudden vibration inside my ass almost has me over the edge, but his calming hand on my hip steadies me. "Straighten up and sit back onto my lap."

I swallow hard, then stand up and step backwards, stopping when I hit his legs. And then his cock is at my slick entrance. Hard and thick, almost pulsating along with the toy inside my ass.

"Sit, Grace," he says in a low whisper. "Sit down on my cock."

I ease down and he fills me up. "Ohhhh, holy fuck—"

My nipple is twisted and I try to scoot away, but his hand is firmly around my waist, holding me in place.

"If you say that word again, I will gag your mouth. Do you understand, sweets?"

"Yes, Mr. Asher." It comes out so fast and so automatic it takes me by surprise.

"Now, sit all the way back and get comfortable," he says as he arranges my chiffon skirt so it covers me up.

I adjust myself, hesitant to sit back as he commands, because the anal toy makes the whole experience very, very different from any sexual experience I've ever had. He gives me a few seconds to decide to comply, and then he just pulls me back until I'm against his chest.

I let out a long moan. "Asher," I whimper. "Asher, I'm going to come."

The nipple twist doesn't make me scoot away this time, instead it brings me closer. Vaughn's hand leaves my breast and grabs his phone from the table, typing out a message. And a few seconds later, the doors open and several servers appear on the roof with trays of covered dishes.

"I want you to come, Grace," Vaughn whispers discreetly into my ear. "But right now these people are serving us food. So you will not come until they leave."

As the last word comes out the intensity of the vibrations in my ass increase. I close my eyes, take a deep breath, and do my best to stay in control. There seems like an endless supply of silver domes plated being arranged on the table on the other side of the sex toys. The servers have the good sense to ignore everything around them and just concentrate on their jobs.

Finally, they exit the terrace and it's just Vaughn and I again. "You did so well, Grace. So well. Now tell me, are you ready to eat?"

"No, I'm ready to come." I turn, shifting in his lap enough to make me moan. "May I come, Mr. Asher?"

"No, baby. Not yet. Bring your arms up and hold me here." He positions my hands so they are behind me, grabbing onto his messy and deliciously sexy hair.

That turns me on harder. I close my eyes and just enjoy it. And just when I know there is no possible way to withhold my orgasm, my back buckles and my head drops back onto Vaughn's shoulder.

"Come, baby," he whispers in my ear. "Come for me, come for me, come for me."

I come for him. And then Vaughn stands up, his cock still inside me, and swipes the table clear of the sex toys so he can bend me over and fuck me from behind.

Chapter Thirty-One - Vaughn

#SecretsMakeUsEven

MY God, her ass cheeks from this angle make the perfect heart shape that drives me wild. Her slit glistens from her excitement, and when I tap the end of the plug in her ass, she clenches. "This is the most beautiful sight in existence, Grace," I tell her in a soothing voice. "So, so beautiful." I lean forward to allow the tip of my dick to enter her briefly before pulling back. Her ass follows along, desperate to keep me inside her. "Do you like this?"

"God, yes," she pants out, her words really just a stream of air as she presses her cheek against the tablecloth.

I thrust a little harder and this sets her off. Her face tenses up, her back goes rigid, and her mouth opens to let out a loud moan. She is unable to control herself. And that's what I want. A woman who will give in, let go, and enjoy the ride as much as I do.

"Hold still, baby. Hold as still as you can. I want you to enjoy this. I want you to fully experience it. So just hold still and let me take you."

She stills her wiggling bottom and adjusts so her forehead is cradled in her hands on the table.

"Oh, I think we can do better than that, Grace. Spread your arms out."

She slides her palms across the linen, making a path through the different bowls and covered plates, and then I thrust hard, making the whole table jump and the water splash out of the crystal glassware. I thrust again, making her hands fist the tablecloth.

"Yes, I love that, please fuck me harder."

"Oh, baby, you haven't seen anything yet." I pound her with my hips, our skin slapping together, the table practically bouncing. "Keep still and I will blow your mind right now, you sweet thing." And then I reach down, pull out the anal plug, and replace it with my hard cock. She groans loudly and tries to rise up off the table, but I push her down, grab her hair, twisting it around my hand, and thrust deep inside her.

"Oh, fuck, yes!" I growl. "Your fucking ass feels spectacular." I reach around her hips, my fingers desperate to find her pleasure spot, and when I do, I rub her wild as she bucks and screams and twists her body, desperately trying to maintain control.

But we're too far gone. It's over. I pull out and shoot my semen up and down the back of her blouse in long sticky streams as she collapses on top of the table and pants her little heart out.

"Perfect," I say, just as breathless as she is. I grab a napkin and dip it into a water glass that is now only half full from the rocking table, and then clean myself up, tuck my dick back in my pants, and then stand her up and turn her around. "Here, baby. Kneel down on the rug. Relax." She falls to her knees, her breath still ragged with release, and she looks up at me with half-mast eyes that make me want to take her all over again. "I've ruined that blouse, let's take it off." She looks down and watches my fingers as they undress her. One button, two buttons, all the way up to the last one between her perfect breasts. I lift the shirt away from one shoulder and let the soft cotton fabric slip down her arm. I repeat that with the other arm, and then she's only in her black bra and skirt.

"Put your hands on your thighs, please."

She obeys and I sigh a little with her compliance. She catches that, I'm sure, because she looks up at me and smiles. This night is going so much better than I ever anticipated. I wasn't sure if she'd be mad about me showing up by surprise or not. It's so hard to predict what might set her off. She is clearly a smart woman capable of many things. She probably thinks she doesn't need a man. But she's wrong. She does. She craves it, I can tell.

I straighten out the tableware as best I can, moving all the covered plates so they are within arm's reach, and then settle back in my seat with Grace between my legs. I lift the lid off a small dish. The scent of meat fills the air with a puff of steam. "It's still hot, good," I say more to myself than her. I pick up a small bite-sized piece of tender beef and bring it to her lips. "I'm going to feed you, Grace. Open your mouth and take the meat."

She complies and my heart swells a little. I wasn't sure how she'd take this, to be honest. She might've got up and walked out, spouting off about how she's perfectly capable of feeding herself. But perhaps she's catching on? Or perhaps I just wore her down and she's too satiated and relaxed to care that I'm hand-feeding her.

"Why am I feeding you, Grace? Why not just let you sit at the table with me?"

She looks up at me with her big blue eyes and smiles as she chews, taking her time before swallowing. "Asher, I don't know and I don't care. I'm hungry and tired. You could do almost anything to me right now." I wince and she catches it. "Wrong answer?"

I nod, but stay silent.

"OK," she says, pausing to think this time. "Let me try again." She looks down at the sheepskin rug, her fingers caressing it for a moment, and then tilts her chin up so she can look me in the eye. "You… want to be responsible for me?"

I positively grin. "Dear Lord, you are perfect." I lean down and kiss her gently on the lips and then grab another piece of meat and place it in her open mouth.

She chews slowly again, and then swallows with a heartfelt, "Mmmmm."

"That's why I gave you money, Grace. Not to buy you, but to care for you. If you want to give it all away, that's your choice, But there will be more money in your account the second it goes below thirty thousand. That's the threshold. Thirty thousand dollars is enough to leave me and move on, so that's the dollar amount I need to stay in your account."

"What?" she sputters, shocked by my words.

"Leave me, Grace. I'm not bribing you to stay. I want to make it very clear you are not being paid to stay. You are being paid to leave. I want you to be OK when you're ready to walk away. When we get tired of each other. I want that money to be there for you so you never have to wonder if you can afford to break off our arrangement."

Her shoulders slump over and she bows her head in defeat. I hate to spell it out so callously, but it needs to be said. She needs to accept it or she needs to take the money and move on. "Do you agree?"

"Can I think about it?" she asks quietly, her head still bowed. "And let you know?"

"Of course," I say back and lift her chin up with my fingertips. "Are you very hungry?" I ask her as I grab another morsel from the plate.

"Yes," she says, a little bit defeated. "I really am. I feel starved."

"You have to go slow, so you can enjoy it. Otherwise you might eat too fast. And that will never do. You can't enjoy our time together if you're busy scarfing down food. Just be patient and know that you will be satisfied when we're done. Even if it takes longer to get there this way, understand?"

"OK," she says.

I don't like her defeated attitude at all. I prefer feisty Grace over this demure imitation. But I need that contract signed tonight, and this was the only way to get that. "Now tell me about your day, sweetness. Tell me about your new job."

"It's just a job. I don't want to talk about it with you. If you're not really interested in me as a person, and this is just about conquering me during sex, then I'm not interested in sharing my day with you."

"That's not all I'm interested in, Grace. I'm just trying to be honest with you, that's all. I don't want to hurt you. I want us to enjoy each other. I think we can have a nice relationship."

"Relationship?" she huffs. "This isn't my idea of a relationship. A relationship doesn't come with walking-away money."

"So give it all away."

"You'll just put more in my account."

"So give that away too. Give it all away. When it ends, you can give that last thirty thousand away as well. Problem solved. You can spend every minute with me practicing your role as a philanthropist."

"This isn't—" She looks up at me and swallows. "You're not anything like the man I fantasized about."

"Hmmm, I think being unrealistic is a trademark of all fantasies, don't you?" She doesn't answer, just stares up at me. "But since we're talking about it, you're exactly the kind of woman I fantasized about."

"Is that my consolation prize?"

"Grace," I say, placing the meat from the plate up against her lips. She opens and takes the morsel, chewing slowly. "You're sending me mixed signals again. Did you think this was a serious relationship? Did I lead you on?"

She shakes her head and then swallows the food. "No, it's just not very romantic to be told you're getting money to walk away."

"Ha!" I say. "I am the romantic one in this arrangement, Kinsella. You're the one who never wants to get married! You practically admitted you're not romantic. I sent you flowers today. I sent you a happy-first-day message. I arranged this perfect evening of sex, and fun, and food. Not to mention the titillating conversation. What more do you want?"

"I want it to be *real*," she says defensively. "And not something fake. Not something you do because you're looking to get something in return."

"Real? Really? Then why do you keep comparing me to your fantasy?"

She sighs and then collapses back onto the rug, her long legs stretching out on either side of mine. "OK, never mind. My feelings don't count. I get it."

I lie down next to her, propping my head up with my elbow. "I never said that. Why are you so conflicted? Just have fun, for fuck's sake. Just enjoy this. Smile, be happy. Tell me about your day."

She eyes me suspiciously with a sidelong glance. "If I tell you about my day, then you have to tell me about yours."

"Deal," I say quickly.

"All of it. Even secret stuff."

"What kind of secret stuff?"

She lets out a long sigh and then smiles. "I don't know." She laughs and the tension releases. "Personal things, so I don't feel so... impersonal."

I drag a stray length of hair out of her eyes and tuck it behind her ear. "I can do that. Every time we meet, I will tell you something no one else knows. Will that make you happy?"

She nods. "Tell me something now. Something that happened today that no one else knows."

"Hmm." I lie all the way down next to her and fold my hands over my stomach. "No one knows how happy you made me today." I look over at her and she's shaking her head.

"Nope, that's not gonna work. It can't be about me."

"OK, I have this adopted daughter—"

"Daughter?"

"Uh, yeah. I mean, she's not my daughter, but I think of her as one. Felicity's a senior in college. I adopted her when she was sixteen. So anyway, I hired my brother to hack her phone today so I can keep track of her."

I look over at her and her mouth is gaping open. "Oh my God, that is so wrong."

"I know. It's a secret. You wanted one, so there. You got one. I'm spying on Felicity because I'm a controlling asshole who can't let go. I wish she'd been mine from the beginning. It makes me sad to think that she had all those important moments in life and I missed them. I get torn up inside when I think about how many shitty birthdays she had before she came into my life. Or how many Christmases she had to endure with no family to love her."

We sit there in silence for a few seconds and I wonder how she'll take this.

"I think," Grace says in a low whisper, "I think that's the sweetest thing I've ever heard."

"Good," I say with genuine relief. "I've redeemed myself. I just hope Felicity doesn't find out, she might not think it's so sweet. Now," I say getting to my feet, and then pulling her up as I sit in my chair. "Come back here and tell me about your day while I feed you."

And she does. Pausing every few sentences to take in the food I feed her, but then picking up right where she left off after she swallows it down. I take that time to feed myself, cutting my own steak and enjoying her conversation as I listen with an attentive ear while I chew. And then I tell her about mine. About lunch with my agent. About production schedules, and other mundane things that people talk about at dinner. We trade off that way, her talking while I eat, me talking while she eats.

We've already found our stride.

By the time we've finished everything on the plate, she looks exhausted, but I don't want to deny her dessert if she desires it, so I let her choose. "I have berries, sweets. Do you want some berries before you go to bed? Or are you too tired for dessert?"

She sighs as she looks at the door to the building. "I am tired, but I don't want to go to bed just yet, so berries, please."

"Here, come closer. Place your head on my thigh. Rest and let me feed you some raspberries."

She does as I ask, situating herself snugly between my legs and placing her cheek on my thigh. I can feel her hot breath though my trousers and it's turning me on again. But we're done fucking. She'd be too tired to enjoy it properly.

I take a raspberry from the bowl and bring it to her nose, "They smell delicious, don't they?"

She inhales and closes her eyes. "Mmmm, they really do."

I place the berry against her lips but she does not open her mouth, so I trace the soft fruit along the thin line. The berry bruises easily and the juice bursts forth, staining her lips with a few drops before her tongue darts out and licks it off. I place the berry on her tongue and she closes her mouth, chewing slowly in a way that lets me know she's enjoying herself.

"Are you happy with our evening, Grace? I don't want to spoil this, but I want you to sign the papers tonight. I think this date sets our standard. If you agree, you can expect more nights like this. Although how often, that I can't promise."

I offer her another berry, but she tightens her lips and gives me a small shake of her head. Having her mouth in my lap, so close to my cock—well, that's something I could get used to. And I have to admit, I haven't gotten so much pleasure from a date in a very long time. Maybe ever.

Tonight, after all the sexual frustrations were put behind us, we melded together like a key in a lock.

"I've had the best time tonight, Vaughn," she says as she opens her eyes and gives me a smile. "Really. All of it was perfect. But I'm still not sure what you want from me."

"This, Grace. Tonight. That's what I want from you. Why is that so difficult?"

"It's not what we're doing that's difficult. It's how I feel about what we're doing that's difficult."

"I understand. You might feel used, or degraded, or out of control. But you're looking at it the wrong way. You just need to trust me to take care of you. Give in, let me lead, and I swear, I'll make you happy. I'll take you places beyond your wildest expectations. Both figuratively and literally. We can travel, if you want. We can stay here. You can come see me in LA. We can meet on Saint Thomas again. Whatever. All that is up for negotiation."

She sighs and closes her eyes again, staying silent as she thinks things through. I play with her long golden hair, picking up the strands and letting them slip through my fingertips. I stroke her head a little, petting her like one might a small kitten. Her breathing deepens and for a moment I almost fear she's fallen asleep.

"I'll sign," she finally says, easing my fears about slumber.

It's almost unfair to ask her now. She's too tired. But her capitulation elates me. I lean down and kiss her on the head and then send off a text as Grace resumes her silence in my lap. A few moments later the rooftop doors open and the notary steps into our magical world. Grace stiffens and begins to rise out from between my legs, but my hand, firm on her head, tells her to stay put. She's either too tired to argue or is playing out her role as my sub. Either way, I'm happy when her cheek remains on my thigh as I talk.

"Grace, this contract"—I reach out and take it from the woman standing a few paces off—"states that everything we do together, from phone calls to text messages to Twitter conversations, every single interaction we have, is private and you agree not to discuss any of it with anyone unless given explicit permission to do so. Do you understand and agree?"

"Yes, Mr. Asher, I agree."

"Good girl. Here you go, sweets. Sign your name and then Mrs. Lancaster will fill out her book and sign after you. May I send in a server to get your identification from your apartment, Grace? An ID must be presented to make the contract legal."

She sighs again, but she agrees.

And fifteen minutes later, we have our documents. Two originals, both signed, both binding. I dismiss the notary and pet Grace's hair again. "Are you ready for bed?"

"Yes," she says sleepily. "I'm ready for bed."

I scoop her up in my arms and carry her down the stairs. She's fully asleep by the time I get her inside and strip off her bra and skirt. The new luxury sheets on her bed, along with the fluffy down comforter, envelop her in a puff of white cotton. I had a team of workers come in and transform her bedroom while we were on the roof, fucking and dining.

I kiss her on the head one more time and then pen her a quick note and leave it on her bedstand on top of her copy of the NDA.

I look at her one more time before I flick the lights off and make my way downstairs to the waiting limo that will take me down to the Centennial airport where my private jet awaits.

I'm not sure when I can come back, that note said. But I've taken liberties to ensure she's well cared for in my absence.

I smile all the way to the airport. Grace Kinsella is mine. All. Mine.

SOCIAL MEDIA SERIES BOOK THREE

BLOCK

NEW YORK TIMES BESTSELLING AUTHOR

HUSS

Chapter Thirty-Two - Grace

#Don'tWantToLoveHim

I WAIT for Vaughn's footsteps to fade and the front door to close behind him before I let the tears stream down my face. This is a huge mistake, I already know it, and the ink isn't even dry on that contract. This is a huge mistake because this night was perfect. *This* Vaughn Asher was the man of my dreams. Attentive, distant, rough, gentle, sexy, mundane, soft, hard, silent and talkative. He's everything a girl loves and hates in a man, all wrapped up into one complete package. I loved our dinner. I loved him feeding me. I loved the sweet scent of that raspberry when he pressed it against my mouth, the way the flesh broke and the juice spilled out as he traced my lips. I loved the tender steak he placed on my tongue and the time he gave me to chew it completely before expecting me to talk. I love that he filled my chewing time in with talk of his own day.

And even though almost none of what he told me about production schedules and agent luncheons made any sense, I loved the tone of his voice and the laughter in his speech as he recalled it for me. I love that he listened to my day and even asked questions about the Big Guys. Not quite jealousy questions, but protective ones.

I love that he fucked me hard and soft. I love that rug he had me kneel on. The soft sheepskin was a delight on my weary legs. I want that sheepskin right now, and for half a second I contemplate going back upstairs to see if it's still there.

I love Vaughn Asher.

I don't want to, I really don't. I want to convince myself he's a selfish asshole who will use me up and throw me out. And he will, I know he will. He's done it to every girl who came before me, and there have been a lot of those.

But I love him. I've been dreaming about him for years. I've had fantasy dates with him that didn't even come close to the night he gave me this evening. And I'm hopeless. Hopelessly in love with a movie star who made me sign a contract to see him again.

The tears stream out now. Tears of contentment. Tears of joy. Tears of fear. Tears of shame. Tears of submission.

I cry long rivers of regret, but with every new breath, I am secretly thankful for my good fortune. I'm secretly thankful that I was the one Vaughn Asher chose to use this time. I'm beyond excited that I will be part of his life in this pathetic way.

I hate myself for it.

But I can't say no. I'm a yes-girl and I *want* to say yes to him for everything. Yes, use me. Yes, fuck me. Yes, take whatever you want. I won't be telling him no. I don't have it in me to deny myself this chance at my fantasy, even though I know what's coming.

I just have to trust in him. Have faith. That when he's finally done with me, he'll toss me aside gently and I will walk away with enough pride to keep my head up and my self-worth intact.

THE dawn breaks far too soon after a night of being well-fucked and dined to perfection. And I'd like nothing more than to stay in bed and feed my delusions of Vaughn professing his undying love for me. But I have daily meetings with the future Mrs. Blazen for the next two weeks until the wedding. Today we're going to the Botanical Gardens to look at flowers.

Why aren't we visiting florists like normal people? I have no idea. But the Big Guys told me to give her whatever she wants. This is a big deal to them and the people of Denver.

They actually said that. The people of Denver. Like the soon-to-be Mrs. Blazen is the goddamned First Lady of this town.

They take their football seriously here. Personally, the only reason I know of any Bronco football players is because some of them own car dealerships and have billboards up all over town. But Kristi Almost-Blazen seemed nice when I met her yesterday, so I'm going to tuck away the cynical side of me and just give her the benefit of the doubt.

She's picking me up, so I'm waiting outside my office building at ten sharp when my phone buzzes and a message from Vaughn comes through.

Fabulous time last night. I'm still internally reliving parts as I have breakfast with Russell Mame.

Oh, fuck.

How do I process this? He's thinking about me. Does it mean anything? Does it mean he likes me? Or that he just wishes he was fucking me again?

I'm hopeless. I'm going to be reading between every line there is. Every word will be scrutinized. Every text pored over. Every phone call revisited in my mind at the end of the day. Every touch cherished. Everything about him will stay with me.

I'm going to be obsessive, I just know it.

Russell Mame is his co-star in *IM2*. He's the bad guy. Or the good guy, if you think the Invisible Man is the bad guy. Either way, he's the adversary and he's another Hollywood legend. I wish I was in that restaurant right now. I wish I could meet his friends and listen in on their conversations.

Am I crazy?

Jesus. This is not starting well at all.

Twitter tonight at eight mountain time.

That little bit of reality pulls me back from the edge of my fantasyland cliff. *He's real, Grace.* I pinch myself and then wince. I'm just about to text back when the white Mercedes SUV pulls up. Kristi rolls down the passenger window and slides her sunglasses down with a smile. "Hop in, girlfriend! We have flowers to choose!"

She's entirely too chirpy for me this morning, but that's my own damn fault. I'm so mad at Vaughn for making me love him. Damn him. Damn him to hell. Why did he have to be so perfect last night? Why does he have to text me this morning and make me read into things? Make me wish for more than just sex. For...

Don't think it, Grace.

"What's wrong?" Kristi asks as I get in and pull my seatbelt across my chest.

I sigh. "A guy."

"Oh," she says with sympathy that I'm not sure is real. "I completely understand."

I highly doubt that, since she's engaged and the only reason we're spending time together is because I'm her wedding planner.

"I would try and put it on the back burner, ya know? Just forget about the bad and focus on life. Because whatever it is he's doing" —she looks over at me and lowers her sunglasses again—"it's his problem, not yours."

"Maybe," I say back. "But I'm letting him do it. I gave him permission. So really, it's all my fault I'm so..." So what? What am I really feeling? "Sad, I guess."

She puts a hand on my shoulder and gives it a squeeze. "I really do get it. And I don't blame you if you can't let it go, so go ahead, you can mope today. I don't mind being a listener if you need it."

Well, that was nice of her. "Thanks, Kristi. I appreciate that. But no, I'm not going to let him affect my days. He might be able to turn my nights upside down, but my days belong to me." I reach in to my purse and turn my phone on silent, then toss it back into my bag. "I'm incommunicado today. So there!"

"That's the spirit, girlfriend!"

That lasts for like thirty minutes, because the second Kristi goes to the restroom in the visitor center of the Botanical Gardens, I check my phone. My heart skips—like literally skips—when I see the message from Vaughn.

Prepare. In nine hours I blow your mind with surprises.

Surprises, hmmm. He left all sorts of surprises in my apartment last night as well. Boxes and boxes of gifts, and the new bedsheets and comforter did not escape me either. It might've been my best night of sleep ever. I'm just not sure if it's because I was fucked unconscious, because of the new bedding, or because living a fantasy is exhausting. But either way, dragging my butt up out of bed was difficult.

I text back, I can't help it.

You're #OnMyMind, is that good or bad?

I press send and then immediately wish I could take it back. I should not discuss my feelings with him. He's made it very clear we're just fucking, and the fact that I'm having feelings is going to put an end to this as soon as he figures it out. In fact he might be debating that right now. *Should I cancel our tweet date?* he's probably wondering. *Is she getting clingy already?*

Way to go, Grace.

My phone buzzes and I look down.

I'm smiling, Grace. You made me smile.

What's that mean?

And then my phone dings a noise I've never heard before and an alert comes through.

FaceTime, Accept?

I didn't even know I had FaceTime. I press accept and a view of Los Angeles appears. "Are you alone?" Vaughn asks.

"Yes," I giggle back.

His face comes into view and he grins at me. "You look nice today. What are you up to?"

I bite my lip and look around. I'm fucking FaceTiming with Vaughn Asher in public. "Um…" And then I spot Kristi coming out of the bathroom. "I'm looking at flowers with a client. And she's coming back from the restroom, so I can't really talk."

"Mmmmm," he says back. "I want to fuck you right now."

"Shhh," I say, looking around to make sure no one can hear him.

"Tweet me something special when you ditch the friend." And then the screen goes black and cycles back to home.

"Who're you talking to?" Kristi asks when she rejoins me at near the ticket line.

"Oh, no one. I got a call from the office but it's nothing important." We get our tickets and make our way through the gardens. It's a lovely place, and Kristi is quite knowledgeable, pointing out all sorts of plants that have absolutely nothing to do with weddings. I do my very best to pay attention, but most of the time I'm tuning her out.

Vaughn is the only thing on my mind. Vaughn is the only person I have room for today. And the impromptu FaceTime break only makes it worse. My mind is spinning with questions. What does he really want from me? What do I really want from him?

I think about that all morning and by the time I'm finally able to ditch my client and concentrate on the movie star pursuing me, I have to accept what's real.

I like him. I want him. I want more than sex, I want feelings. And these small gestures that probably mean nothing to him are going to drive me mad. Because it's impossible for me not to read into it. When a man leaves you gifts and pays attention to you during a workday, that typically means he likes you. He wants you. And yes, I know Vaughn likes and wants me, but it's only for sex.

I don't want him only for sex, I want him in every way imaginable. I want him to love me.

That thought stops me dead as I step off the elevator on the fifth floor of Big Guys. No, no, no, no, no. That's the worst possible thing that can happen to me.

"Grace?" Flora asks from her reception desk. "Are you OK?"

I shake myself out of it and start walking again. "Yeah, sure, I just remembered that I forgot something." I flash her a smile and try to get to my office as fast as I can.

"Oh, Grace, wait!"

I turn and she's holding out a message.

"Your banker came by. He said you need to stop by and see him."

I take the message and call out a cheerful, "Thanks," over my shoulder. When I finally reach my office I close the door and sit down.

I cannot fall in love with this asshole movie star. I just can't. He's going to use me up and throw me away. It's a done deal. I need to get a grip on these feelings fast.

I resolve to do that. I make a firm commitment to accept this arrangement for what it is, but in that very instant, my desktop computer dings a new email from my work account.

It's from The Invisible Man.

I click on it.

It's a picture of me at the Botanical Gardens. I'm leaning down to smell a rogue daisy in a greenhouse filled with rare hothouse orchids.

The message reads:

You are the white daisy in that greenhouse. Your beauty is simple, your confidence strong, your feelings genuine. I love it.

What the fuck?

Is he stalking me from LA? How is that possible? How did he get that picture? How did he get this email? Jesus, is he crazy? I get out my phone and press the number he called from earlier. He picks up on the second ring.

"I already know what you're going to say, Grace. I'm sorry."

"You damn well better be, mister. What the hell is going on?"

"It was too much, wasn't it? The message was too personal. I apologize."

"The message?" I'm confused. "You mean the picture. And the fact that you have my work email and I never gave it to you."

"The picture?" Now it's his turn to be confused. He chuckles. "Darling. I have security on you. They send me updates. It was in the agreement. If you're mine, you have to have security and I can ask for an update any time I want."

"You're spying on me."

"No, I'm keeping track of you. Spying would imply I'm doing it secretly. And please, your email at Big Guys is GraceKinsella@bigguys.com. It was not that difficult."

He's fucking spying on me.

I end the call and sit back in my chair. Well, that takes care of my movie-star crush. I'm so over that crush. He can kiss my ass, thinking he can have people follow me around and take pictures. It's invasive. It's degrading. It's manipulative. It's—

My email dings again and it's another message from Vaughn. I click open and there's a selfie picture of him standing in front of his view of LA holding a white daisy to his nose. He has the most adorable boyish smile on his face. This message says:

Now we're even.

And then another one comes in as soon as I finish reading that one.

You can call it whatever you want, but I'm not going to stop. I like getting updated. I like knowing what you're up to. I want to know more about you, Grace.

How much more?

Shit. What if he starts digging?

I call him back and he picks up on the first ring this time. "Miss Kinsella."

"Mr. Asher, I don't want to be spied on. I don't want you fishing around for information on me. I don't want to get these creepy feelings everywhere I go, wondering if I'm being watched."

"You are being watched, and that condition is non-negotiable." He says this in his authoritative tone, but there's an edge to it that causes me to hesitate in my retaliation. "Grace, if the media ever finds out about you, you will be a target. I'm being very careful, but they are relentless motherfuckers and I have a movie coming out in two weeks. They want dirt. They want filth. They want proof that I'm some abusive prick and they want nothing more than to plaster pictures of whatever they can find out all over the tabloids. This is a security issue for me *and* for you. I will not give in on this point. I won't. And I don't want to hear about how you'll walk away, because Grace, I have a whole night of erotic spankings planned."

I laugh and then cover my mouth and try to compose myself so I can spar properly. "Mr. Asher, I will be polite and accommodating and call the spying 'security', but you have to stop looking in my past. If I want you to know personal things, I'll tell you."

He's silent for a few moments and my mind is spinning with thoughts and questions. Will he back off? Will that make him look harder? Will he demand answers? Will he send me to therapy?

Where the hell did that come from?

"OK," he finally says, letting out a sigh of resignation. "OK, no more digging. But the security stays."

"I accept that deal."

"But Grace" —he pauses for a moment—"is it bad? Your past? Is it bad?"

I have to sit down for that question. Because his voice is not filled with pity, he doesn't know what happened to my parents, so that's not it. But the sympathy catches me off-guard. And I've never told this story to anyone. Not anyone. Oh, Bebe pieced together most of it, but that just excused me from ever saying the words out loud.

"You can tell me, sweets. I can keep a secret too. And I don't judge. I'm a good listener."

"It's nothing, Asher," I say back, minus the melancholy threatening to take over. "Really, just back off and let it be. You're getting your way about so many things, please just let me have my way about this."

Chapter Thirty-Three - Vaughn

#DamageControl

IT surprises me how affected I am by this turn of events with Grace. Plenty of submissives over the years have had personal problems, and while I would listen if they brought these troubles up, I never cared to understand what the issues were about or how they affected the woman I was fucking.

But Grace pleading with me to allow her some privacy about her past, in combination with the fact that it's missing from all public record—that's… odd. And troubling. And it makes me worry. Not about me. But about her.

What kind of indiscretion could it be? Should I allow her to keep that secret? Or should I go digging and break my promise? Will me not knowing affect her protection, should the media ever discover her?

Well, the good thing about that is if I'm having a hard time finding out about her past, so will they. But the bad thing is, what if they do find out and they take her by surprise?

I speed-dial Felicity. I know she's in school and she hates me bothering her on the weekdays, but I need absolute discretion in this matter and she's the only one I can trust.

It goes to voicemail, so I leave a message, hang up, and then access the picture the security team sent me from the Botanical Gardens.

Grace is so sweet in this image. And she is like a daisy surrounded by rows and rows of orchids. Because her beauty doesn't need to be cultivated. She doesn't need special conditions to thrive. She's what people in the biz call a natural beauty. No makeup, no hair products, no fancy clothes required. Just her in whatever she throws on. Her straight honey-colored hair and her flawless peach skin.

But the tremble in her voice just now, when I asked her about her past and she retaliated by calling me Asher… that concerns me.

My phone buzzes in my hand and I feel relief when Felicity's face appears on my screen. "I need you to dig up Grace Kinsella's past."

"Oh, I totally forgot to tell you, V. I did, but all her juvenile records have been sealed. It's very difficult to find those because they are expunged, and lots of places don't have the juvenile records digitized after they are sealed."

"So you can't do it?"

She laughs. "Please, I can do it. It's just a big deal. How bad do you really want it? Because it will take a significant amount of time and planning. And probably bribes," she adds.

"How long if you start now?"

"I dunno, weeks?"

"Start now. If it gets too difficult, let me know, but I think it's very important that I know. And Felicity?"

"Yeah?"

"If someone knew about her sealed records—knew where to find them, for instance—how hard would they be to get?"

"Well, in LA, probably pretty hard. But in Colorado? Who knows how they run things out there. Could be really easy. Like maybe one person has complete access and there's no paper trail when you go into the file room. Or it could be just as tight as here."

"OK." Yeah, that's not good. "Please do this for me and make it a priority."

"No problem, V. I'm on it."

The line disconnects but I'm too deep in thought to bother putting my phone away, so I just stare out across the valley and suddenly wish I could fly back to Denver tonight. I speed-dial my office. "Janet, can I cancel my day tomorrow?"

I have to pull the phone away from my ear, that's how abrupt her laugh is.

"Mr. Asher, you have a fundraising meeting with your father at eight AM, remember?"

I sigh. "Never mind." I pocket my phone and walk over to the glass wall that lines the terrace, resting my forearms on the thin ledge, as I ponder my feelings.

She's fine. Nothing's going to happen to her. I'm careful. I've been doing this for years and no one has ever gotten a speck of dirt on me. They won't find her. I've only been to see her once.

Which means, even if my day was clear tomorrow, I can't go. I need to keep the distance between us because if the media finds out about her, we have to call it quits.

That's always been the rule, and even though I've never had to put it in practice, I will if necessary.

My phone buzzes again and I'm surprised to see Conner's face lighting up my screen.

"Yeah," I say into the phone.

"So which one of you assholes is spying on me?"

"Aw, fuck."

"Seriously, Vaughn? You need to spy—"

"It's not me, it's Felicity."

"That kid? Why the fuck is she digging through my shit?"

"Because she thinks you're a douchebag and she wants to mess with you."

"Whatever. I'm not the one bringing a girl to meet Mom and Dad with a vibrator up her hole. And you know, it's real interesting that Felicity is taking all this interest in me while she should be doing damage control for you. Did you forget that Sam invited *Elite Lifestyles Magazine* to the wedding so they could do a spread on her? Because they saw that whole brunch debacle."

"What? Sam never told me that. Since when does she do interviews?"

"Since her dickhead husband made her."

"I gotta go." I end the call and go back inside to make myself a drink. Holy shit, this day went all to hell. No wonder Sam was so upset the night of her wedding. If Tray wasn't still back on Saint Thomas having a non-honeymoon for one, I'd kill that asshole.

I pour four fingers of Scotch and sit down at the bar out by the pool. Something is very wrong. Something is very, very wrong. I can just feel it. It's like a snake, slithering up behind me, just waiting for me to be complacent so it can strike.

I take a long swallow of my drink and then speed-dial Ray, my security coordinator. "I need you to double up on the Denver client and get a team to dig up information about the reporter who attended my sister's wedding last weekend."

"On it, boss," Ray says.

"Check the Denver house for bugs and steal her phone."

"No problem."

"Discretely. And then put it back so she thinks she misplaced it."

I end the call and swallow a long gulp of Scotch just as my phone buzzes in my hand. The number comes up unknown so I ignore it and take a seat on the couch to think things through. The magazine reporter is a wild card I was not anticipating. And fucking Conner knew all along back on the island. That's why he was talking shit to me about getting discovered and having all my dirty deeds come back to haunt me.

But he'd never turn on me. We might fight a lot, but we're brothers and that means something. All growing up Conner was the only real friend I had. Sam was too young, Conner was too young too, but when you're isolated from the world for your own protection, well, you take what you get. And Conner was what I got.

He was secluded from the craziness that my father and I endured for being famous. He went to a real school, he had real girlfriends, he experienced a childhood. I, on the other hand, had celebrity fundraisers for social events. Or wrap parties overflowing with drugs. Or red-carpet events where the sole purpose of the paparazzi was to make me look bad.

This is the kind of shit I've been building walls against my entire life. And every time I think I have it all under control, it spirals.

My phone buzzes again, this time to signify a voice mail. I absently grab it off the table, my curiosity getting the best of me, and press the icon for messages.

"Vaughn," a crying woman says from the small speaker. How did she get my number? "I have to talk to you, it's an emergency. Call me back at the hotel spa number."

No. This is not good. Something is very wrong.

I delete the message and pull up email instead. I hate to do it, but I can't see Grace tonight. I need to think this over, figure out what's going on, get my bearings, and make a plan of retaliation.

Sweets, please accept my apologies. Leaving town on business, don't know when I'll be back.

Damage control. If this magazine reporter is on to me, it's better to cut that shit off now and lie low. I take another swig of my Scotch and kick my feet up on the table. There's not much choice. This is my life. No matter how hard I try to be normal, no matter how far away I think I am, it's never far enough. That traditional family I never had is just a dream. My life, for better or worse, is a string of side-show events that prohibits me from having a real relationship.

So fuck it. Why bother, right? Why bother fighting it. I'm lucky—at least I have Felicity, even if that relationship is about as unconventional as it gets.

I grab my phone and press Felicity's face so I can fill her in on the reporter and tell her to leave Conner alone. The call rings through to voice mail. I know she's in school and won't answer, but it was worth a try.

I stare out at my ten-million-dollar view, lost in thought.

Why can't I ever get what I want? Just once I'd like to get what I really, truly want. I want to fly back to Denver and sleep over at Grace's house. But I can't. Something is cooking and getting sloppy now will have consequences. Once the paparazzi has you on target, they never let go until they get what they want. They're always around. Waiting in trashcans. Hiding in bushes. Following me three cars back. And they know one of these days I'll get drunk, or sad, or desperate and I'll fuck up. Then they'll get what they've been tracking for years. Proof that my private life is nothing but a long string of sexual debauchery.

I down the rest of my drink and pull up my agent. That rings through to voice mail as well—figures—but this time I leave a message. "Larry," I say with a slight slur from the Scotch. "Set me up with a beautiful date for the *IM2* premiere and I'll go."

Chapter Thirty-Four - Grace

#PrinceJerk

VAUGHN never calls again. It's been two weeks of silence after he canceled our last Twitter date. Nothing. And I'm pretty sure the spies are gone too because last night I met my co-worker for a drink thinking I could draw Asher out with jealousy.

But no. He's gone. And what did I figure? That I'd be the girl to change him? That I'd be the girl he falls in love with? That I'd be the girl who could claim his heart, even though countless others have tried and failed?

I'm an idiot.

For years, my Dirty Heaven was Vaughn Asher. I lived and breathed for those Saturday nights and ever since I met him in person, my fantasy faded away, one disappointment at a time.

He's a jerk.

He's a sexual deviant—and even though I did like that date we had, a BDSM relationship was never part of my perfect fantasy. I didn't exactly dream of wedding bells and diapers, but it was a monogamous partnership kind of dream. I would live in Denver and build my career, flying out to see him in Hollywood every weekend for parties and fun. Then he'd fly back with me on Sunday nights to fuck me in ways that did not involve kneeling at his feet or having bite-sized morsels placed on my tongue. He'd kiss me goodnight on my doorstep like the perfect Prince Charming and fly home for a week of hard work and I'd do the same here in my own little corner of the world.

And although I think he might be on board with the distance that I prefer in a relationship, his unique sexual requests are not part of my long-term plan. That is vacation sex. That is one-night-stand sex. That is not partnership sex.

So it's better this way. I'm perfectly happy like this. I'm going to find myself a new fantasy prince and give him all my Dirty Heaven attention. Maybe a younger one this time. Someone more my age. Someone who doesn't need to prove his sexual prowess with games.

"Earth to Grace?"

I'm going to forget all about Vaughn Asher, wipe him right out of my life.

"Hello?"

Which is easier said than done when those stupid fucking *Invisible Man 2* posters are all over this fucking airport.

"See something you like up there? Because that's my soon-to-be husband."

"What?" I look over at Kristi who is handing me a cup of coffee from the Starbucks while stuffing her face with a blueberry muffin. "No!" I laugh. "No, I was looking at the *IM2* poster next to Johnny Blazen's Broncos."

"Oh, yeah, that Vaughn Asher is a dream. I'd do him." She chuckles as we drag our luggage onto the moving sidewalk that will take us down to the end of the concourse to the gate. The Blazens have hired a jet to shuttle Denver friends and family over to Vegas and they keep all the small airlines on the very edge of the concourse, making the walk a long one.

Hmmm. "He's OK, I guess. Not quite my idea of a dream though. So speaking of the soon-to-be hubs—why isn't he flying with you instead of me?"

She paints on her life-is-perfect smile like she's been doing for the past two weeks and swallows hard. "He's got football stuff tonight, so he's going to fly in tomorrow."

"Right. Football season." I don't get it. Their relationship is not what I expected. He's never around. Always something about football. And she always makes excuses for him. They don't even live together. And maybe some couples like that before they get married, but she's *pregnant*. If I was pregnant—and I won't be, so this is a total hypothetical—I'd throw a fit if my husband wasn't there. I'd never put up with this.

Add in the fact that she practically let me make all her wedding choices for her, and I see a pattern emerging.

Kristi soon-to-be-Mrs.-Blazen has no mind of her own.

"You know, Kristi, it's your wedding, so it would be expected for you to throw a little fit to get him here the night before. I mean, what about the bachelor party? Isn't he dying to sneak into your room and ravish you inappropriately?"

Holy shit, why did I use that word?

"It's different when you're dating a famous person, Grace." Her voice is pleasant and her smile is still fake as we get to the end of the slidewalk and heft our luggage back onto the tiled floor. We have to walk the rest of the way because we are out of moving sidewalks.

"Oh!" Kristi exclaims, pointing to a bathroom. "I wanna pee again, just in case."

"You just peed after we came through security."

"I know, but I hate to pee on the plane. One last time before we board. Here, take my luggage."

I start to sigh but cut it short. *She's a client, Grace. Be graceful, like your name implies.* I lean up against a wall to wait her out, but the buzz of my phone snaps me out of my irritated funk. I pull it out of my purse and stare at the screen.

Unknown number.

My heart rate speeds up immediately, but at the same time, I get a very sick feeling in the pit of my stomach. Vaughn. It has to be Vaughn.

I press the accept tab with a nervous smile. "Hello?"

"Miss Kinsella?" an unfamiliar voice asks me from the other end of the line. "Are you Grace Kinsella?"

"Who's this?"

"Miss Kinsella, my name is Jasinda Gonzales, I'm Vaughn Asher's girlfriend, and I've noted a pattern of calls to this phone and I'd—I'd just like to know if he's cheating on me?"

My head spins so bad I almost fall down. "Excuse me?"

"Are you near a TV, Miss Kinsella?"

"What?"

"A TV, or the internet. Because *Buzz Hollywood* is running a story on us right now, and I think you should see it."

"Who the hell are you?"

"I told you—"

"I know what you said, but I'm sorry, you have the wrong number. I have no idea what you're talking about."

My shaky finger presses end and I just stare at the phone in my hand.

"Everything OK?" Kristi asks, taking possession of her luggage.

I look up at her, stunned. And I lie. Because I'm a good liar. I've been telling lies since I was a kid and my world fell apart. I'm good at faking OK. "Fine," I say cheerfully. And suddenly I become Kristi soon-to-be-Mrs.-Blazen. I'm the one with the fake smile and feigned happiness. "Come on, we're gonna be late if we don't rush it. Can't be late for your wedding!"

I let her chat the rest of the way to the gate and then thankfully we are there and the flight attendants take over. Everyone is already on the plane—all of them family and friends of Johnny, minus Johnny, of course. And even though the fact that Kristi has no friends or family of her own on this plane should raise a red flag, or at the very least make me pity her, I can only think of one thing.

Vaughn was cheating on someone when he was with me.

Of course he was, you idiot! He's a fucking movie star!

The large corporate jet seats twenty, and all seats are filled, but thankfully almost everyone is seated on the long couches that line each side of the aisle. I settle into one of the few chairs near the front and try to calm my racing heart.

I need to see that webpage. I need to know what that woman was taking about. I fish around in my bag for my tablet and quickly do a search for *Buzz Hollywood*. It feels like an eternity before the page loads, but then—there he is.

My Vaughn is on the front page. A split picture of him and a dark-haired beauty who reminds me a lot of Bebe.

Jasinda Gonzales.

Asher's pregnant girlfriend accuses him of infidelity and sexual abuse. Mr. Asher could not be reached for comment.

Sexual abuse.

Pregnant?

My stomach turns and I bolt up, looking for the bathroom.

"Ma'am," a flight attendant calls out to me. "We're getting ready to take off, please return to your seat."

I push her out of my way and rush into the bathroom compartment. It's bigger than a regular plane bathroom, thank God, but it's still stifling and in that second I know I'm going to throw up. I fall to my knees, flip the head lid open, and puke.

I lose time as everything sinks in. The setup, the lies, the sexual conquest—that I willingly gave in to—and the NDA so I can't talk about it.

I shake my head and laugh. I fell for him. I fell for my dirty Prince Charming. I swallowed him whole in more ways than one.

"Grace?" Kristi's concerned voice asks from the other side of the door. "Are you OK? We need to take off but we can't do that until you're in your seat."

Great.

I take a deep breath and pull on my everything-is-fine disguise. "Fine, fine!" I say cheerfully. "I just got a wave of nausea, that's all. It's gone now, be right out."

"OK, come sit with me if you want. There's room on our couch."

My answer is the gushing of water from the sink, so hopefully that means Kristi has left to take her seat. I cup my hand under the tap and bring some cool water to my lips. I pat my face and straighten my professional blazer in the mirror, then paint on my smile as I pull the latch back on the door and emerge.

No one even notices, not even Kristi, so thank God for the little things. I scoot past the pissed-off flight attendant and take my seat. "You have to put that on airplane mode, ma'am," the bitchy attendant snaps. "You're holding up the departure."

I grab my tablet from the floor, the web page at *Buzz Hollywood* still showing the story of Vaughn and his lies, and do as she says so she will leave me alone.

I don't remember anything about that private corporate jet flight to Vegas. All I know is that I'm walking past a bar on our way out of the airport when I glance up and see Asher's face on the TV.

It's *IM2* premiere night and he's walking the red carpet. Not with me. Not with the woman carrying his baby. But with the biggest party slut in Hollywood.

His ex-girlfriend from when he was a teenager.

I want to get sick again, but I can't afford to do that. I have to deal. I have to pretend life is perfect.

I'm still living the fantasy.

My Prince Charming is out there somewhere, his name just isn't Vaughn Asher.

Chapter Thirty-Five - Grace

#CalledOutByKristi

THE limo ride from the airport to the Bellagio is agonizing. I sit between Kristi and her future mother-in-law, across from her future brother-in-law, and beam out the fake smile I perfected ten years earlier at her future father-in-law.

I nod my head. I laugh when they laugh. I add in cute little quips when the conversation calls for it.

I start drinking. Heavily.

And when we get to the hotel I go straight to my room. I have one hour to dress and prep for the rehearsal dinner. I need to change into my midnight-blue sheath dress and my discount shoes. It's professional, not at all flashy. And while the shoes are pretty in a Target sort of way, they do not have red soles.

And that makes me sad all over again, because I really fell for the shoes Vaughn bought for me on the island. I have them with me, but I can't. Not after the ultimate betrayal I just saw online. And that phone call. That woman, Jasinda, she thinks I'm the other woman.

I hit the minibar, grab a few bottles, fill a glass with ice, and fall back on the bed with my laptop.

Don't do it, Grace, that little voice in my head says. *Don't look.*

But of course, I absolutely am going to look. I pull up the webpage and just stare at the picture of Vaughn. It was taken recently because it's a promo for *IM2*. He's smiling and happy. His female co-star is in the picture with him, but they cut her off so they could do the side-by-side shot of the girlfriend.

I scroll down to read the article.

Ms. Gonzales says her relationship with Vaughn Asher began almost a year ago on the island of Saint Thomas—

I pour the contents of the little bottle into the glass and take a long swallow before I can continue reading. Of course she met him on Saint Thomas. It's where he gets all his girls.

I wipe my mouth and return to the article.

—where he propositioned her to become his sexual submissive in exchange for money and gifts. "I was required to sign a nondisclosure agreement," the teary-eyed Gonzales explains. "He told me people won't understand the type of sexual relationship we have together. He said what we had was special and not something he did with just anyone. But I've seen him with other submissives on the island. Many of them.

He has a sexual appetite that can't be quenched and he insisted that he not have to use a condom, so of course, I find myself pregnant."

Is he the father?

"He is," she says as the tears roll down her face. "I haven't been with anyone else but him. And whenI told him about the baby, he was very excited. And at first that made me happy, but I now know he's unfit to be a father. I need him out of my life and I will fight for the right to raise our child alone."

I close my laptop and guzzle the rest of my drink.

What did I think? How did I think this movie-star fling would end? I mean, wake the fuck up, Grace! He's a user. He says whatever he needs to in order to get his way. He probably has girls stashed all over the world. He probably has dozens of kids, because that whole not using a condom thing she said, that's true. He never used one with me.

And Jesus Christ, I need to get myself to the doctor as soon as I get home to make sure I'm not infected with some sexually transmitted disease.

I make myself another drink and then strip out of my clothes so I can change into my dress. I struggle with the zipper for a few minutes, but finally contort my body enough to pull it all the way up. It feels tighter than it was at the fitting last week. My body is slim, so the dress looks good, but I really need to put all this Asher stuff behind me and get back into my normal exercise routine. It doesn't help that Kristi has been taking me out to lunch with her every day, and she eats like a pregnant woman.

I smile at that. I like Kristi, but I hate her husband-to-be. I've still never met him. He's much too busy to concern himself with a wedding. I've spent the last two weeks with her planning the big day and that jerk has yet to show up for so much as a cake-tasting. Kristi and I, on the other hand, have been inseparable and she's starting to feel like a friend. We've come to Vegas four times on day trips to iron out wedding details, and everything is perfectly planned, but I can honestly say that this wedding is a disaster waiting to happen.

My phone buzzes and I reach over and pluck it off the nightstand.

"I'll be up in ten minutes," I tell Kristi, before she can even say hello.

"OK," she laughs. "We have time, but I'm lonely. I'll do your hair when you get here if you want."

Her request betrays her nerves. Hell, I'd be a bundle of nerves too, if I was marrying Johnny Blazen. If I didn't see him play football last weekend, I'd think he was fake because I've never seen them together. "Sounds good, Kristi. Be right up."

I end the call and grab my purse and then catch my reflection in the hall mirror and stop dead.

I look… tired. Wounded. Used up.

Depressed maybe. My moods have steadily gotten worse since my last interaction with Vaughn. I've missed Dirty Heaven, and even girls I hardly talk to online have started sending me direct messages asking if things are OK. Bebe, thankfully, has not noticed much because she's traveling with the competing members of whatever they do over at her sports club.

"Grace," I say to myself in the mirror. "You…" But I have no pep talk to give myself on this night. I have nothing positive to say. So I just turn away and leave the room.

Kristi is up in one of the upper-floor executive rooms, so I get in the elevator, flash the keycard required to access that floor, and massage my temples with my fingertips to try and ease the tension headache creeping up on me.

The doors open and I step out and knock on the door right across the way.

A faint, "Come in," is called out to me from inside. The door is propped open with the metal swing lock, so I push through and close it all the way behind me. When I enter the living area, Kristi is setting up a curling iron on the wet bar. She's so damn cute, she makes me smile. "What the hell are you doing?"

"Sit," she says, pointing to the bar stool. "Did you know I was a makeup artist at Channel 9 before all this crazy Blazen stuff started?"

I shake my head and take my seat. She produces a brush and begins to stroke it through my long hair. "Well, I was. Before Johnny asked me to quit and stay home to be a mother. That's where we met, you know? I was doing his makeup before he went on *Good AM Denver*, and we hit it off." She lets out a long sigh and begins to twist up strands of hair in her nimble fingertips.

"I didn't know that. I never watch local news. Too depressing because my neighborhood is always on there.

Things I should know, but really don't want to know. Ya know?" How the fuck would she know? She lives in Park Hill. "Do you miss it? Being a makeup artist?"

"Sometimes," she says with a smile I can see in the mirror behind the bar. "I'm bored at home, ya know? I can't wait for this wedding to be over so we can live together."

"Why don't you live together now? I mean, the cat's out of the bag, right? You're pregnant, you're getting married. Why not just get that party started?"

"Hmmm." She pins up a section of hair before continuing. "He wants us to start out right."

"It's kinda late for that, don't you think?" I want to stab myself for speaking up. "Sorry." A look of hurt crosses her face in the mirror and a wave of guilt flows through me. "I'm just being a cynical bitch, I guess. I mean, normally I'm not one to rock the boat. I hate confrontation, so I'd never say anything. But this is your wedding, Kristi. This is your *life*."

She laughs nervously. "I hate confrontation too, so let's just drop it and have a good time."

"But how do you cope? I mean the fact that you broke up his marriage? How do you trust him not to find another woman to take your place?"

"You don't even know him, Grace. You have no idea what kind of man he is in private."

"Huh," I grunt sarcastically. "Where have I heard that argument before? Oh, right. The last guy I slept with, he was like that too. *Oh, the private me and the public me are two different things*," I say in a fake voice.

"Well, Johnny is a famous football player, so in his case, it's actually true." She pins up the final strand of hair and then begins to curl them.

My blood is beginning to boil, because seriously. I grab a flute of champagne on the bar that's been set out for us and give it a good long guzzle so I can control my building rage. "Kristi, I've never even met the guy. And I'm the wedding planner. He's never around. I've been with you every day. When do you see him?"

"I just explained, Grace. He wants to keep it low-key until after the wedding. And I have no problem with honoring that request. I think it's romantic and" —she actually stops to swoon here—"gentlemanly. He's a gentleman."

I almost snort my champagne.

She curls the last strand of hair and then holds her arms out wide. "There, that's pretty, don't you think?"

I look at my updo in the mirror and shrug. "Yes, thank you. But look, I'm not trying to start a fight, but he's playing you, can't you see that? He's a liar. He's had how many wives before this? He was cheating on his last wife with you, Kristi! How the hell do you not see that he's not any good?"

"Stop, OK?" Her face is turning bright red and the tears are building in her eyes. "There's so much about me—about *us*—that you don't know. And I can't talk about it so…"

"You can't talk about it because he's got a gag order on you, Kristi! Can't you see that? Why is that so hard to understand?"

"Grace, I don't know why you're so angry, but you don't understand. You only have his ex-wife's side of the story. I know the whole story. He and I, we know the whole story. And I'm not discussing this with you. It's my wedding eve and I want to enjoy it."

I stand up and smooth down my dress with the palms of my hands. I'm shaking, I'm so enraged. "Maybe it's wrong to tell you things, Kristi. But I consider you more of a friend these days than a client. So I'm just going to come out and say it. He doesn't love you, do you understand that? You're pregnant with his child. He got caught cheating. He's desperate for damage control to save his football career. He's a lying, worthless cheat and you're falling for it one hundred percent. He's playing you, Kristi. Asher is playing you!"

"Who?" she asks, equal parts confused and outraged. "You're crazy, Grace. Maybe you've had too much to drink, but I don't want my night to be ruined because you're having some kind of emotional breakdown!"

"Breakdown!" Oh, she didn't. "You think I'm crazy or something? Is that what you think? Because you're a joke around Denver, Kristi. People talk behind your back and laugh. Haven't you seen them pointing at you, the hushed whispers? The snickering?"

"You've lost your mind, Grace. Seriously."

"OK, you know what? You go ahead with your fantasy life, Kristi. OK? Because I'm living in reality right now and I see the writing on the wall. He's not here today because you're not important. He's not here because he doesn't want to be here. It's the night before his wedding and who gets married on a Thursday?"

"It's football season, Grace! He works on the weekends! How is that any different from anyone else who works on the weekends? He can't just call in on Sunday and say, *Sorry, coach and teammates who depend on me, I'm not showing up for the game today*. That's insane!"

"You're insane if you think this is normal."

"Define normal? Just because it's not normal for you doesn't mean it's not normal for us."

"Whatever, Kristi—"

A beeping noise comes from the foyer as a key card is fed through the lock. We stop our fight and look over to watch the handle turn and the door open. And who walks in?

Kristi squeals and runs over to her soon-to-be husband and he wraps his arms around her, kissing her on the head. "Sorry I'm late, babe." He looks over to me and smiles, stepping forward with Kristi hanging on his arm, his hand outstretched towards me.

I take it and shake.

"You must be Grace?" he asks with that winning smile they flash on TV every chance they get. "John Blazen. Nice to finally meet you. Kristi has talked about you non-stop for two weeks now, she's your biggest fan. I can't thank you enough for taking over the wedding and making her happy."

He actually beams a smile down on her and...

I wilt.

I die right there on the spot as I play all my nasty words back in my head.

I'm an asshole.

I bolt out the door and for once in my life, luck loves me. The elevator is open and waiting so I can make my shameful escape without having to explain myself.

There is only one place to go when your life implodes.

The bar.

Chapter Thirty-Six - Vaughn

#NotYours

MY phone buzzes in my pants more than two dozen times during the premiere of *Invisible Man 2*, and each time I check it, just waiting for that one call. But each time I'm disappointed. Unknown numbers, known numbers... but none of them are Grace.

The movie screening ends to resounding applause and I allow myself to feel a moment of satisfaction at what we've accomplished. The Invisible Man is a complex character. You never know if he's the good guy or the bad guy, and most of the time he's both. Moviegoers like to have a clear villain. They like to know who the hero is. But the Invisible Man can't be boxed up like that and that's why I can relate to him.

Am I good?

Am I bad?

Am I both?

Social by JA Huss

Are all those things Jasinda is telling the world about me true?

I didn't read the entire article at *Buzz Hollywood Online*, but I did read the one *Elite Lifestyles Magazine* ran today. And that one drew very clear parallels between the story Jasinda is weaving and all the past reports. Complete with a full-spread timeline. Like they're piecing together the clues in a murder mystery.

My date for the premiere—my Disney ex from back in my teens, who is mostly known for her sex tapes and trust-fund money these days—clings to my arm like a leech. I only brought her to take all suspicion off Grace, and even with my world crumbling around me, that seems to have worked.

My phone buzzes again and this time it's Ray. I pry the girl's fingers off my arm and excuse myself, walking out the emergency exit. I do not end up outside, but in the bowels of the theater's backstage. "Yeah," I say into the phone. "Any news?"

"She's been drinking all evening, Vaughn. She's in the Villa Privé casino hanging on the arm of some corporate guy from San Diego. But I don't know how you're going to get in. It's a private rental."

Two weeks. I've forced myself to stay away from her for two weeks, doing my best to keep her out of this. I felt it coming and I'm never wrong about these things. But I can't do it anymore. She has to have seen the tabloids. She has to be drinking because of me. I am a coward if I don't set this right. A coward and a dick. She deserves to know the truth.

I *need* her to know the truth. When I decided to pull away from her, my understanding was that it would be temporary. But this doesn't feel temporary anymore. This feels like my last chance.

"The staff said she's talking about your tabloid news today, but they didn't tell me exactly what she said. You want me to subdue her and take control?"

Fuck.

"Boss?"

"No, I'll take care of it." I end the call and dial up my pilot, which goes to voice mail. "We're going to Vegas. Tonight. Fuel the jet."

I don't go back inside the theater, I'll never escape if I do. Instead I push my way out the back doors into the alley and call my driver to come pick me up a few blocks away. It's a forty-minute drive up to the airport and by that time the pilot is on his way, but not there yet.

I board the jet and collapse back into one of the leather seats with a sigh.

"Rough day, Mr. Asher?" the attendant calls from the small galley near the front of the plane.

I ignore her and she takes the hint and shuts up.

I spend the next two hours with my knee bouncing, my head pounding, and the internal dialog with Grace running through my mind continuously. The car delivers me to the front of the Bellagio and I get out, button up my suit coat, and straighten my sunglasses.

My personal concierge steps forward with his hand outstretched as I pass between the Asian lion statues that flank the entrance. "Mr. Asher," he says with his best customer-service smile. "I'm so happy to see you again. What brings you here on such short notice tonight?"

"Carl, I have a woman inside Villa Privé and I need immediate access. Her security detail tells me she is drunk."

Carl smiles that smile he gives me just before he says no. So I interrupt him with a squeeze of his shoulder. "Carl, listen. I know the rules, I know the party is private, I know the security is tight. But I'm going in to get my girl, do you understand me? I'm not leaving here without her. You do whatever it takes to make that happen and I will make sure you still have a job when it's all said and done."

His smile falters and then disappears. He knows he has to try at the very least. He's paid to try and give me whatever it is I ask for, even if it's something outrageous like this. "Yes, OK, let me see. Let's go to the villa level and make a plan."

We walk briskly through the lobby and I keep my sunglasses on, but the finger-pointing starts immediately. People start calling out my name, yelling insults, and a few women actually rush me and the security guards have to form a wall to stop them from getting too close.

Carl and I ignore everything, never slowing our pace, until we leave the bustle of the public areas behind and stop at the elevator.

We both exhale a long breath.

"Rough day for you, huh?" Carl asks as we wait.

"This is my life and I know people will never believe this, but it sucks. I am always guilty and never proven innocent."

He just stares at me for a few seconds and then the elevator dings and the doors open. He nods, telling me to enter first, and then he follows. The doors close and we pretend to listen to the elevator music as we go up.

"This girl is important to you?" Carl asks, his eyes trained on the digital numbers counting off the floors as we rise. The ride is short so the car dings again and the doors part.

"I've disappointed her today, Carl. I'm sure this is happening because she saw the news. And I need a chance to set it right."

He nods at me as we exit and then waves me into a lounge. "Have a seat, Mr. Asher. I will make my case and be right back."

My phone buzzes just as I take a seat on a plush burgundy couch. Felicity. "Please have good news," I say into the phone.

"Well," she says, "define good."

I shake my head. What else could go wrong today?

"I found out where Grace Kinsella is from. A tiny farming town in northeastern Colorado. I also found out something else."

She stops talking and I get a sinking feeling in my stomach. "Do I want to know?"

"No, Vaughn, I really don't think you do. But since I know you're gonna to ask, let's just start with her real name."

Shit. This cannot be good.

"Does Daisy Bryndle ring any bells?"

"Should it?"

"Depends. Did you turn on a TV at all ten years ago? Because Daisy Bryndle's family was murdered back when she was only thirteen. Daisy went missing and then showed up eight months later and spent the better part of a year locked away in a secret location. She was charged with the murders and was all over the news for months, then poof. Gone."

"What the—why isn't she in jail?"

"Apparently the charges were dropped after a Denver lawyer stepped in. That lawyer, Marjorie Tamren, is her friend Bebe's mother. They changed Daisy's name, legally adopted her at age fifteen, and her juvenile record was expunged and sealed when she turned eighteen. I couldn't get a hard copy, but this info comes from someone close to her as a child."

A set of double doors open and Carl appears.

"I gotta go, Felicity. Thank you."

"Hey, I'm glad to help. And I can relate to this girl, ya know, V? I can relate to her."

"I know, kid. I know. I'll see you tomorrow." I end the call just as Carl walks up. He's got a tight smile on his face and I can't tell if that's a good or bad sign.

"You've been accepted into the game, Mr. Asher, but I cannot guarantee that you will be able to get to the girl. She's... quite wrapped up with our special guest at the moment."

Fuck. "What the hell does that mean? If he's got his hands on her, I will—"

Carl puts both hands up in a stop motion and looks around nervously. "Mr. Asher, please," he whispers. "This entire area is wired up to off-site regulators. They will not allow you to distract from the game. You are in there to bet, and if you can get your girl while you're at it, that's fortunate for you. But fighting over a woman in this suite is absolutely out of the question. There are armed guards inside, Mr. Asher. I have to take your cell phone and you need to put up three hundred thousand dollars to enter the suite." He thrusts a clipboard at me. "Sign here and we'll withdraw the funds from your account."

I hand over my phone and sign for the bank transfer. I look nervously over Carl's shoulder at the door he came out of. "She's in there?"

"Yes, sir. They are playing craps at the moment. The suite patron has stipulated a minimum playing time of one hour." I nod as we approach the double doors and he stops and waves me forward as someone on the other side releases the lock. "Good luck," Carl says as I walk through and enter the suite.

A loud cheer goes up from a considerable crowd of about twenty people surrounding the craps table. I take them all in. Men in expensive tuxedos—at least I'm dressed for the part—each with a woman on their arm. Most are in long expensive gowns flashing diamonds.

Except one.

I have to chuckle at her. My Grace is wearing a knee-length dark blue dress that is probably part of her everyday work attire. She has no diamonds, her hair is out of place, and her cheeks are ruddy with excitement as another cheer goes up.

A tall middle-aged Asian man with striking green eyes leans down into her neck to whisper and she throws her head back and laughs again.

Clearly she is not torn up about my bad news today.

Green-eyes notices me and gives me a nod to signify this is his room and I'm here as his guest. I nod back and he calls out. "Mr. Asher, I'm honored."

Grace practically gives herself whiplash trying to find me, and I admit, that gives me a little thrill. "What's he doing here?" she whispers. But she's looking right at me, so it's not hard to read her lips.

"Come, Mr. Asher. My good-luck charm is still hot." He nods to Grace, ignoring her question about me.

I walk over to the table and begin greeting other people. They nod and shake my hand as I put on my polite public persona. I take up shooter residence, opposite of the Asian man. But my eyes are only on Grace as I try to assess her state of mind.

Stunning. Check.

Even though her dress is not a designer gown and her neck is bare of flashing jewels, she is the star of this room. Her hair is piled up on top of her head in a way I've never seen before and it allows me to stare at the sweeping line of her neck. The strap of her black bra is showing and even though I'd love to see more of that, I don't like the fact that every man in the room is probably thinking the same thing.

Drunk. Check.

Her cheeks are flushed, and not just from the winning. Her eyes are a bit glassy, enough to have me worried. And once I look closer, they are puffy and red. She's been crying. She's leaning into the Asian man, who is way too old for her, steadying herself so she doesn't teeter.

Angry. Check.

Her forehead is a field of furrows as she purses her lips and squints her eyes. Just seconds before, her face was relaxed and excited. But now the hurt I've caused her today is coming through loud and clear.

"Grace," I say in a soft, gentle voice to let her know I'm not here to start trouble. "You look beautiful."

She smiles up at her date and ignores me.

"I'm Damian Li," the Asian man says, his green eyes brilliant and his smile genuine. "Welcome to my suite. Do you know my date tonight?" He looks down on Grace and she continues to beam a smile at him.

"Intimately, actually," I tell him back with a straight face. Might as well get this out in the open. "I'm here to win. Shall we?"

Li doesn't even flinch.

"Place your bets!" the dealer cries.

My dealer places my three hundred thousand dollars' worth of high-value plaques on the apron in front of me. Li places the equivalent of fifty thousand dollars on the Pass Line and I match him by pushing my chips into the Don't Pass Line with a smile. The other players make their bets, but I don't pay any attention to them or the amount of money flowing in here. Li's hand is on Grace's hip.

I see red, but I take a deep breath. Wrong time, wrong place.

The dealers flips the puck to white and the game is on. Li picks up his dice, jiggles them in his hand, and then with a flat palm offers them to Grace. She leans in and kisses them. I zero in on her lips, fuming when they touch Li's skin. When I look back up to his face, he's smug. "Good luck from the lady," he says loudly.

Everyone cheers.

"You bet against her, Mr. Asher," he says, nodding down to my Don't Pass Line bet.

"I always bet the House first time out, Mr. Li."

He throws the dice and rolls a seven. The whole room erupts in cheers. Except for me. Because I lost.

"Ha," Grace says in a voice pitched too high, "loser! That's what you get for betting against me."

I smile at her as I push another fifty thousand dollars into the Don't Pass Line. Li doubles his money and holds out his palm for Grace to kiss. This time she looks me right in the eye, takes his hand in hers, stroking her thumb up and down the length of his fingers, and then leans in and touches her lips to his skin once again.

I fume. Anger manifests as heat and pulsates through my entire body. "Grace," I growl, but at the same time Li throws the dice and rolls snake eyes. Everyone but me lets out a collective groan. My chips double and I've made my money back.

"Shall we raise the stakes a little, Mr. Asher?" Li asks me, his grin a little too wide. "And move over to baccarat? Minimum bet of fifty thousand?"

"I'm in," I say as his hand rubs against Grace's hip once again. She leans into him and I have a brief second of panic that maybe they really know each other. Maybe she's dating this guy. I've left her alone for two weeks, Ray can't know everything about her. It's possible she had plans to meet him here.

"With a private non-monetary wager as well. My date for tonight."

"What?" Grace squeals. "You can't bet me!"

"She's not a piece of property, Mr. Li."

"No, Mr. Asher," he says back evenly. "She's not. So stop treating her like a gold watch."

"I didn't buy my way into this game to retrieve a gold watch, Mr. Li. I told you, I'm here to win."

"Win back the girl?" he asks with a lightness in his voice that really pisses me off. "Too late for that." He pulls Grace in close, his large hand across her hip. "She's mine and I'm not ready to give her up just yet."

"Oh, I assure you, Mr. Li. Grace Kinsella is not yours." I smile and a small laugh even comes forth. "She's mine in every way imaginable."

"Holy shit, you're both a couple of asshole cavemen!" Grace says too loudly, sipping on a glass of champagne that has materialized in her hand while Li and I have this pissing contest. "I don't belong to anybody but me!" And then she storms off, handing her champagne to a waiter as she makes for the door.

A few of the women in the room cheer her on, but their partners quickly divert them to another game and a few seconds later Li and I are staring each other down from opposite ends of the table.

"You have a one-hour minimum in here, Mr. Asher."

My attention is fixed on Grace, who walks out the goddamned door.

"So let's make that wager. And if you win, you can have her. If I win, she spends the night with me and you are escorted off the premises." I recoil and he grins a little wider. "Don't worry, someone will be scooping her up momentarily and taking her to the bar to await the outcome."

The doors close after Grace exits.

"One hand of baccarat. If I win, I get to leave immediately and you back off."

"One?" He tsks his tongue. "Where's the fun in that? That has no risk, Mr. Asher. You're wealthy. Whatever you lose or net in here will not affect your bottom line. No, I'm afraid we'll need to raise the stakes higher. At the very least the best of ten hands. You see, your risk is leaving her alone out there. She's been drinking, she's angry, and she's in Vegas. Ten hands of baccarat, played swiftly, might take ten minutes. But she can make a lot of decisions in ten minutes."

I could stand here and argue with him, but why bother. If I play and win, I could have her back under my control in a matter of minutes. If I play and lose, well, at least she won't be picked up by a stranger. If I do nothing she's got a sixty-minute head start on me. I can't even call Ray and have her followed because I don't have a phone. She could disappear. Someone might get her and who can tell what might happen. I have no choice. "I accept."

Chapter Thirty-Seven - Vaughn

#SheDeservesBetter

WHEN Li waves his hand, his people close the doors to the baccarat room and we approach the table. I set my rack of chips down and wait to see how he wants to play this.

"Place your bets," the dealer says.

"How interesting should we make this game, Asher?" Li asks.

"It's your game, Li. You said best of ten. You bet first and I'll match. That will be our ante."

He allows a small grin as he walks over to the bar and asks for a snifter of brandy.

I watch him. He's very confident. But everything about him—the way he dresses, walks, talks—everything says he's got a reason to be confident. And it's more than money. Hell, I've got money. Lots of money. But I don't think I've ever walked around like that.

Why is he taking such an interest in Grace? She's beautiful and she's sweet. But why her?

"One hundred thousand," Li says, bringing my attention back to the game. He pushes ten neatly stacked chips to bet the player.

I grab ten chips from my rack and place them on the banker.

"Do you like to bet against me?"

"Banker always has a higher advantage, Li. I'm sure you know that."

"Ah, it's making sense now. You hate risk, Asher? And yet"—he cocks his head at me, like he's thinking through some elaborate theorem—"you find yourself in a world of risk right this very moment." I make to answer him but he puts up a hand. "Not this, Asher. Miss Kinsella. Do you know where I found her?"

I just stare at him.

"In a hallway, sobbing her eyes out." He narrows his eyes at me. "Over you."

Who the fuck does this guy think he is? "Not that it's any of your business, but that was a misunderstanding. I haven't had a chance to explain what's happening yet. But once I do, she'll see past it."

"Past it?" He sneers at me. "She's just a thing to you, isn't she? She really is a gold watch. You think you own her."

My jaw clenches and I want to fuck this man's world up in so many ways. But I've spent my whole life dealing with assholes like him. I'm a professional. "I only own what she's willing to give, Mr. Li. Regardless of what you read or watch on the tabloids, the decision to stay always belongs to them."

"Hmmm. She was a fountain of information in the twenty minutes we sat and had drinks before this suite was ready."

I clench my jaw again. What the fuck did she say?

"She told me," Li says, "that you threw her away."

"I didn't throw her away. I made a decision to keep her safe. I've got... a situation brewing. I don't want her caught up in it. She's misunderstanding, that's all."

"Hmmm. Then you are a poor communicator, Mr. Asher."

"Probably, yes."

"I think she deserves better."

I laugh loudly. Too loudly. "Is that right?" He nods and smiles, but says nothing. "You have no idea what you're talking about. I am determined to have my say tonight. And once I do, she will understand and be right back in my arms."

"But maybe you don't deserve that chance."

"Who the fuck are you, Li? The fucking guardian angel of second chances? Fuck off and let's play."

That smile again. That motherfucking overconfident smile. "Let's liven the game up, Mr. Asher. Let's see how badly you want that second chance. How much you're willing to risk for it. Every time you lose I'll have my associate make Miss Kinsella an offer and if she accepts my offer before our game is over, then she's mine to keep."

"She's never going to be yours."

"You're probably right. I have a daughter her age, so I'm not really interested. My point is that if I win this game, she will *not be yours* because my offer will take her to places beyond your reach. I'll introduce her to a whole new life. Give her a chance to find a nice man who will treat her well and not make her break down in a hotel casino hallway because her lover threw her out like trash."

"And how do you plan on getting her to accept your offer?" I growl.

"A job offer. In Hong Kong where I do a lot of business. She has a useful profession. Everyone needs someone to coordinate events, right? Even you, maybe."

"She'll say no," I reply with confidence. "She likes her job, she has friends, she's rooted in Denver."

"Perhaps. But each time you lose, the offer will increase by thirty thousand dollars. How long will she hold out when the salary offered is in excess of a hundred grand?"

My jaw clenches along with my fists. "Why are you doing this?"

"I thought you liked to play games with your women, Asher?"

I just stare at him.

"When I took her into the bar, we watched the *Buzz Hollywood* interview with, what's her name? The soon-to-be mother of your child? Jackie, Jacey, Jennifer—"

"Jasinda."

"Right, right. *My* Grace was very upset. And she was a little bit drunk at the time. She mentioned an NDA—"

Fuck.

Li laughs. "And then she mentioned *so* much more." He shoots me a smile. "So, since you are an avid game player, let's play." His jovial nature disappears and a ruthless businessman takes over. His smile drops into a straight line, his face becomes passive, and he builds superiority with a squaring of his shoulders and a raising of his chin. "You do not deserve *any* woman, let alone her. So if you lose, I steal her away with an offer that will change her life, I call up *Buzz Hollywood* and repeat everything she told me, and I take your money."

My heart rate increases as I realize what he's doing. "And if I win?"

"If you win you keep my money, you keep your girl, you keep your secrets, and I will make sure she is safe and accounted for until you arrive to beg her forgiveness for being an asshole." He glares at me through squinting eyes. "Women are not chips, Asher. Love is not a game. You think money buys everything but you're wrong. Your money can't buy love and that girl deserves love."

"Do you know who she is?"

"I know everyone in this room."

I can't tell if that means he knows her hidden past or if he's completed the cursory background check that I did before I asked Felicity to dig deeper.

"Is it a bet?"

I clench my jaw as the words come out. "It's a bet."

Li looks over at the dealer and nods.

"No more bets," the dark-haired woman says as she waves her arm across the table to signal the start of the game.

She deals out the cards, one for the player, which is Li, and one for the bank, where my bet is placed. Li has a ten of clubs, which is zero points in baccarat. The bank gets a nine and a ten, which is a nine, since tens and above are worth zero. Nine is the highest score you can get.

"Bank wins," the dealer says. "Congratulations, Mr. Asher." She smiles at me as she stacks my winnings next to my bet.

I wonder if these employees sign an NDA for the casino. I make a mental note to ask Carl.

"Place your bets," the dealer calls again. "Hand number two, Mr. Asher."

Jesus, she's keeping track. When I look over at Li, he's smiling so big all I can think about is putting my fist through his teeth. I let my chips stand, almost three hundred thousand dollars now, and Li replaces his ten chips. This time he bets on the bank, like me.

"No more bets," the dealer says. She waves her hand again and then lays out the cards. This time the player wins. I just lost three hundred thousand dollars.

I look over at him and smile. "You're bad luck. And we both lost, so is that a tie as far as the job offer goes?"

"You wish," he laughs back. "You lost, that is the only requirement. You should pay better attention to the rules." He pulls out a pad and paper and writes a quick note, then beckons the doorman over. "Pass this to my attendant, thank you." He looks over at me. "Don't worry, I offered her less than her current salary. This time."

"Place your bets," the dealer calls out. "Mr. Asher, this is hand number three."

I put a hundred grand back on the bank. I'm not a big gambler, but I do know betting the bank is the safest option.

Better odds than betting the player and much better odds than betting on a tie.

"I will bet against you and see if your luck theory holds, Asher."

"Whatever."

The hand is dealt and I sigh.

"Player has six, bank has four. Player wins!"

The dealer takes my money again, and now I'm out four hundred thousand dollars. I'm starting to sweat, so I loosen my tie and unbutton my shirt.

Li writes another note and hands it to the waiting doorman. He smiles up at me as the man leaves to deliver the message. "Sixty thousand, plus a fully furnished condo with the best view in Hong Kong."

"Bets, please! Hand number four for Vaughn Asher, movie star!"

I squint my eyes at the woman and she shrugs.

"Condo, Li? There was no condo offer in the deal."

"There was no mention of perks at all, Asher."

Fucking cheater. I place another hundred thousand dollars on the table, with the bank. I win that hand, gaining back almost two hundred grand. I let that bet stand, and that goes to the bank again. Now I'm back in business and Grace has not gotten another offer.

"Bet again, Asher!" the dealer cries out. This makes Li laugh. "Hand number six, num… ber… six." She calls it like she's a barker in a midway side show.

I take back four stacks of chips and let two stacks ride. "On the bank," I say.

I cringe as the cards are presented. "Player wins!" the dealer calls out, taking my winnings with her.

Li writes up his message and tears the piece of paper off the pad with a lavish gesture. "Ninety thousand plus a condo, and her own personal driver."

"Fuck," I mutter under my breath. My heart is starting to beat faster. What if I fucking lose?

Li laughs. "How about another level of risk, hmmm?"

"Why would I do that?" I seethe at him. "I've won three of six. I've got an even chance. Why the hell would I raise the stakes now?"

"Because higher risk has higher reward, Asher. Let's forget best of ten, eh? We have four hands left. I match your wager and bet with you for hands one and three. You match my wager and bet with me for the second and fourth hands. Deal?"

"But you still get to make an offer if I lose?"

He grins, and this should make me extremely suspicious, but I'm desperate to get the fuck out of this goddamned room. I check my watch and I've already been in here forty-five minutes. I could end up being tied up more than an hour since I have to play all ten hands.

"Since your luck really is running on empty," Li says, "I will forgive the first three hands if you lose. But if you lose the tenth hand, you have to leave the hotel tonight without her. Not even a goodbye. Not even a phone call. And you may never contact her again. But if you win the last hand, even if you lose the first three or she accepts my offer, then I'll back off."

I'm silent as I weigh my options.

"Decide, Asher. Your time is ticking."

"OK," I reluctantly agree. I know he's setting me up, but I'm too worked up over Grace to see how. I just need to get the fuck out of this room and go find her. The thought of walking away and never seeing her again... well, shit. I can't let that happen. But I can't let Li take her away either. That last offer was pretty sweet. "Deal."

"Place your bets," the dealer calls. "Hand number seven, Mr. Asher. Lucky number seven."

I put one hundred grand on the bank.

Li matches me like he promised.

The dealer deals the cards.

"Win to the bank!" the dealer calls. "Congratulations, winners! Place your bets. Hand number eight, players. Hand number eight, what will it be?"

Li moves his three hundred grand to bet the player, and I do the same.

The player gets dealt a three, the bank gets dealt a seven, the player gets dealt a five, and the bank is dealt a ten. "Player has eight, bank has seven, player wins! Congratulations, winners!"

"It seems," Li says as the dealer doubles our chips, "we might make a lucky team." He winks and I scowl.

"My turn to bet," I say.

"Hand number nine, Mr. Asher. Only two more left, make it count!"

I put all my chips, all six hundred thousand dollars, back on the bank. Li copies me with a satisfied smile.

"You really don't like to take risks, do you, Asher? You'd make a horrible businessman."

"Don't kid yourself, Li. This whole night has been a risk for me and I run more businesses than you'll ever know."

"No more bets!" our animated dealer calls out. Like there's anyone else here making bets. She deals the player and the bank their two cards and adds up the scores. "Three for player. Eight for bank. Bank wins! Congratulations, winners!"

"Holy fuck. We just made one point two million dollars."

Li grins up at me. "We could win a lot more, Asher." He pushes his chips to the top of the table and then stands back a little, like he's proud of himself and needs to take it all in for a moment.

"You have got to be fucking with me." There are only three ways to bet in punto banco, the version of baccarat that we're playing here. You can bet the player wins and double your money. You can bet the bank wins and almost double your money. Or you can bet that there will be a tie and make eight times your money.

You are more liable to win betting on the bank than the player. Only a fool bets on the tie because the odds are heavily against you. And only a fool with nothing to lose bets one point two million on the tie.

I am not a man with nothing to lose, I realize. I am a man with everything to lose.

Li is silent, watching me.

I look at the dealer and she shrugs. "You guys are lucky."

"We are lucky," Li says. "Together at least. Bet with me, Asher. Let's pool our luck. You have to anyway, it was part of the wager."

"How about I just give you the money, Li? If we win the tie, the payout is eight hundred percent. I will give you all that—almost ten million dollars. I will pay you ten million dollars to let me get the fuck out of this room and go find Grace Kinsella."

"Put your chips in the tie bet, Asher," he says without emotion. "Have a little faith."

"Faith in what? Stupidity? That your purpose here is to fuck up my life?"

"You said she was yours when you arrived at the craps table. Well, prove it. If she's yours, certainly the universe knows of your claim."

"Your hour is up, Mr. Asher," the nosy dealer says. "But you agreed to play ten hands so as soon as you finish, you can leave."

"I can leave, but if I lose this hand I have to walk away."

"I thought you liked games, Vaughn?" His use of my first name, like we're friends, sets me back. "You're so used to getting what you want. So used to paying people off with money. You walked right into this. Come on, put your chips on the tie and let's play this out like men."

I have no choice. None at all. I push all one point two million dollars' worth of chips into the tie bet and hold my breath.

"No more bets," the dealer calls. "Last hand, all bets on tie." She waves her arm across the table and then slides the first card out of the shoe and places it face up on the player's side. Ace.

She repeats this for the bank. Ten. Which is a zero in punto banco.

The player's second card is an eight. "Fuck," I say loudly. That gives the player a score of nine, the highest score possible and an almost automatic win.

The bank's next card is a five.

"Bank score of five requires a third card." The dealer swipes out another card from the shoe and flips it over.

My whole worlds stops. I am still holding my breath, unable to exhale the stale oxygen coursing through my veins. Why the fuck did I let myself get into this situation?

How could I bet a woman in a card game?

I swear to God, I'll never do it again. I'll never be this asshole again. Just let me win my—

"Four! Bank has nine, player has nine." The dealer looks up at me. "It's a tie! You win! Congratulations, winners!"

I look over at Li and he's smiling. "I told you, Asher. We're lucky together. Let's do business. I'll call you next week. Your Grace is down in the private villa bar with her friend. I'll have Carl take you to her."

He shakes my hand as I try to understand what just happened. My mind is blank. My whole body is in overdrive, my heart is beating wildly, I'm sweating, and relieved and stressed out all at once.

I nod my head at him as I walk to the door, leaving all my money on the table. Someone will take care of it for me. I'm too shaken up to even think about the money.

All I think about is how close I came to losing her.

I can't lose her.

I will never let that happen again.

Chapter Thirty-Eight - Grace

#I'mOnHisTab

"ONE minute I'm enjoying my night being a good-luck charm for a filthy rich old guy and the next fucking Vaughn Asher is ruining my night." I take a long sip of my giant margarita. "Can you believe that asshole followed me to Vegas? I'm working and he's gonna ruin my job."

"Mmm-hmm," the bartender says absently. "I hate it when Vaughn Asher shows up on his movie premiere night and follows my ass around Vegas. Fucking sucks."

I narrow my eyes at him. "Are you making fun of me?"

"Grace!"

I look across the bar and spy Kristi, waving at me frantically.

"Ah, fuck. And her." I point to Kristi, weaving her way through the crowd. "She's supposed to marry Johnny Blazen tomorrow, but, pfft. I don't see it."

The bartender stops washing the glass. "So let me get this straight. You" —he points his wet glass at me—"think you're being stalked by Vaughn Asher. And she" —he points to Kristi who is almost at the bar now—"thinks she's marrying Johnny Blazen tomorrow."

I take another long draw on my margarita. "That's right."

"No more drinks for you."

"Grace!" Kristi says as she places her hand on my shoulder as she tries to catch her breath.

"Let me guess," the bartender says, pointing at her stomach. "That's Johnny Blazen's love child you're carrying, right?"

"Oh my God, is he psychic?" Kristi squeals.

"You're cut off too."

"I'm not drinking!"

"Out, both of you. You're both on drugs."

"Come on, Grace. Come back to the rehearsal party with me, please. I need your support tonight. Please. His family is so unhappy with me. They're not excited about this at all. I need you." She gives me a pouty face that would make a six-year-old proud.

"Kristi, I told you what I think. Marrying him is a big mistake."

"Why though? Please, if you know something I don't, just tell me. Because I seriously love him, Grace."

"Well, of course you do, he's a famous football player. He's got a ton of money and he's hot. But can you honestly say he loves you back? I mean, he won't even move out of the house he shares with his ex. She owns it, the divorce is final, and he's still living there."

"She's not there though, she's in the Caribbean—"

"Oh." I put up a hand. "I can't even go there. The fucking Virgin Islands are where all my troubles started!"

"But Grace, did you hear rumors or something? Please, we're friends, right? You can tell me."

"Kristi, how are you so dense? The man is twenty-four years old and he's been divorced twice! You will be his third wife. You got pregnant when he was still married," I say, pointing down at her baby bump. "You were a cheater! Women all over the world are cursing your cheating name. You cannot seriously be blind to all this!"

"But all those things have a really good explanation, Grace. I mean, sure, the divorce thing is real. And yeah, I'm nervous about being the third wife and all. Especially since we're having a baby. But—"

"Oh, fuck," I interrupt Kristi. "Her again?" Vaughn Asher's girlfriend is on the TV. She's poking her belly, lifting up her shirt to show the cameras her pregnancy. It looks like she's puffing out her stomach on purpose if you ask me.

"Four months," she says, answering the reporter's questions about how far along she is.

"Oh, I know," Kristi says, leaning into me. "She's been on TV all damn day. I'm so sick of her. Who cares, anyway, right?"

I shoot Kristi a look. "Well, you would say that, you're the other woman. Johnny got you pregnant while he was still married. And now this woman is accusing Vaughn Asher of cheating on her. It kinda hits home, don't you think?"

"I honestly don't see how our situations are the same, Grace. I mean—"

"Are you serious?" I just look at her with my mouth open. "OK, I have nothing for that. It's so obvious, if you can't see the similarities, I can't help you. And God only knows how many girls Vaughn Asher has slept with. Johnny and Vaughn are two cheating assholes who deserve to have their pricks chopped off!"

"Why are you so hung up on Vaughn Asher? I mean, seriously—"

"Because, *Kristi*..." I seethe her name. It's filled with venom. Directed at the wrong person, I admit. It should be directed at Vaughn or myself, because there's no way a man like Asher is not involved with a woman every single minute of the day. "I'm Vaughn Asher's *other woman*. Just like you are Johnny Blazen's. But unlike you, I have the good sense to know what a ho I am, and—"

"That's enough, Grace." I turn around and Vaughn is standing behind me, his arms crossed over his chest. "That's e-fucking-nough."

"Oh my God, you're Vaughn Asher's girlfriend?" Kristi squeals, shaking me by the shoulders. "Oh my God, oh my God, oh my God!"

"I am not his girlfriend, Kristi! Jesus, wake the hell up! That"—I point up at the TV where the bitch is still talking about the future Baby Asher—"is his girlfriend right up there!"

"Kristi, is it?" Vaughn asks in his I'm-the-reasonable-one-here voice. "Grace is my girlfriend, that bitch is the lying ho. Grace." He turns back to me. "She's not pregnant with my baby. I slept with her once, six months ago, so there's no way that baby is mine. I made it very clear there was going to be nothing more between us before I met you on Saint Thomas and she obviously took it badly. I did not sleep with her that night. I dismissed her. She's a liar. You, Grace Kinsella, are the only woman I've slept with since we met."

"I don't believe you," I sneer.

"I don't care. You're drunk so I'll just explain it to you again tomorrow when we wake up."

"I'm not going home with you."

"Oh, yes, Miss Kinsella, you are. Because you have no idea what I just went through to make sure I could have you tonight. There's no way I'm letting you go now."

And then he hoists me up and swings me over his shoulder.

"Send her tab to my room," he calls out over the cheers from a crowd of men as we pass. "She's with me from now on."

Chapter Thirty-Nine - Vaughn

#HappinessIsNotAGuarantee

GRACE pounds her little fists on my back, demanding to be put down.

"Will you come along nicely? Or should I carry you all the way upstairs?"

She lets out a groan as I walk, bouncing her along. "I'll walk nicely."

I set her down and she straightens her dress, looking around at the people who are now staring at us. She smooths her hair and then squares her chin and shoulders, steeling herself for a confrontation as she looks me in the eye. "I'm not going to your room, Asher. That much is for damn sure. And if you pick me up again, I will scream."

And then she turns on her heel and makes her way towards a restaurant. She approaches the hostess, and then she disappears inside.

Jesus Christ. She tires me out. I just spent the worst hour of my life trying to win an opportunity to see her tonight and set things straight, and she blows me off like I'm some… some… some nobody. I scrub my hands down my face and go after her. Again.

Why, Asher? Why are you so fixated on this girl?

I look around at all the women in this hotel. So many to choose from. I spot ten or fifteen who would be candidates for my sexual attention. A few even catch my surveillance and openly flirt. But I don't want them. I want the one who just walked away from me.

I huff out a breath and follow her. "Good evening," I tell the hostess. "I'm meeting the woman who just came in. I'll just—"

"I'm sorry, sir. The lady said you were harassing her and asked me to call security if you tried to follow her."

"You're kidding, right? She and I are dating."

"I'm sorry, the lady said she's not interested and wants to be—"

"I'm sure there's a misunderstanding. Perhaps she meant someone else?"

The hostess gives me a sneer. "Is there another Vaughn Asher who looks just like you? Perhaps you're his twin brother?"

"Ha ha." I peek past the hostess turned security and spy Grace at the bar, chatting with the bartender. This restaurant is quiet and almost empty. "Look, just let me in so I can talk to her, OK? Obviously you can see we're having a little fight—"

"Little fight?" The hostess laughs. "Dude, your girlfriend is pregnant and you've been cheating on her with that woman, who said she knew nothing of your secret life. So—"

"None of that is true, OK? I just need a minute to explain what happened to Grace and then she'll see I'm the victim here. Me! I was never dating that bitch on TV and she certainly isn't carrying my child since I haven't slept with her in six months. She's a fraud, a liar, a gold-digger! I'm innocent and you, ma'am, are helping to perpetuate her plan to ruin my life. That woman," I say, loud enough for Grace to turn around, "is the one I'm interested in. Grace," I call. "Just listen to me for a moment." I look back at the hostess. "Five minutes. Just give me five minutes and if Miss Kinsella wants me to leave, then I will. But I'm tired of fielding strangers who think they know what the fuck is going on when they don't. I'm having my say tonight, whether you want me to or not."

The hostess crosses her arms and sneers. But just then a man in a suit approaches looking like he's the manager. "Can I help you with something?"

"Yes," I say calmly. "That woman at the bar is my girlfriend. There was a public accusation against me today that is false and I need five minutes of her time to state my case. That's all. Five. Minutes."

He looks me up and down. "*Invisible Man?*" He smiles. "Oh, yes! I love that movie! You rocked that shit, right?"

"I did." I give the hostess a smug look all the while beaming my movie-star smile at the manager. "So look"—I check his name tag—"Mr. Sollen, I just need a moment. That woman at your bar is the only reason I'm in Vegas right now. I need to talk. Please."

I stare at him as he weighs his decision.

When was the last time I had to beg someone to give me what I want? When was the last time I was denied? Maybe Conner was right. Maybe my life has been too easy and when things get hard, I just bail and don't know how to cope.

"OK," the manager says. "Five minutes. But if she makes a scene, I'll have to call security and have both of you escorted out."

"Deal." I give him a we're-all-in-this-together clap on the back as I move past him, straightening out my jacket. I head towards the bar and Grace isn't even paying attention. She's chatting up the bartender, who sees me coming and excuses himself as I take a seat two stools away from her.

"Hey," I say in a low voice. "I'm sorry for picking you up back there. It was presumptuous to think you'd talk to me tonight, let alone come up to my room."

"Another margarita," Grace calls out to the bartender.

I catch his eye and hold up a finger. "Scotch, please. Top shelf."

"I'm not interested in your excuse, Vaughn. Truly." She looks me in the eyes for the first time tonight. "Truly, I am not interested. I'm not playing a game with you. I'm not playing hard to get. I'm not *pretending* to be pissed. I'm not even pissed. I'm just not interested. You're not the man I thought you were. And I get that I was invested in the fantasy version of you. OK?" she says, shaking her head a little. "I get that. It was my fault for turning you into some kind of

Prince Charming. So it's not fair that I had such high expectations of you. I'm sorry that I blamed you for something I caused."

The bartender delivers our drinks and takes Grace's empty glass away. I take a sip of my Scotch, then gulp it all, and slide my glass on the bar. "Another, please." The bartender nods and moves off to get that. I put my head in my hands. "Grace," I say, rubbing my temples. "Just for the fun of it, tell me what that Prince Charming version of me was like. How do I not measure up?" I look up at her, but she's staring down into her pink drink, playing with the paper umbrella. "Was I nicer? Was I more generous? What is the real Vaughn Asher missing?"

She meets my gaze for a moment, but it's a fleeting one. Her eyes drop back down just as quickly and she shrugs her shoulders. "I don't know. The fantasy was… charming. Not just in a princely way, either. But really, really charming. Saying witty things, and being at ease with himself and others. He jokes with me and makes me laugh. You…" She doesn't look at me, just continues to stare into her drink. "You make me sad. You make me feel inadequate. You make me feel stupid and small and pathetic."

Fuck. "How though? How did I do that? Because that was not my intention. OK?" I reach out and cover her small hand with mine. "I never wanted to make you feel like that. I wanted to excite you."

She looks up at my eyes and I almost wish she hadn't. Her expression is overflowing with disappointment and she looks tired. She does look sad. She looks like she cried very hard earlier and the makeup can't quite hide that. "You wanted to excite *yourself*, Vaughn. You wanted to please *yourself*. Not me. Everything you did, from picking out those clothes to putting money in my bank account, all of it was for your benefit. You lie to yourself, I think. You're one long string of self-serving lies. I don't know how you do it, or how you get so many girls to play along. But all your best intentions were nothing but really good deceptions. And even though I know in my heart" —she clenches her fist and holds it over her chest—"that the fairy tale is fake, that it doesn't exist and I'm setting myself up for disappointment, I don't care. Because I deserve that happy ending, Vaughn. I do. You might not think so. You might think I'm just some silly girl who has no right to expect so much from a man. But I don't care. Maybe that man doesn't exist and maybe I'll spend the rest of my life alone, waiting for my prince. I don't care. I refuse to play this game with you."

And then she reaches into her little clutch purse to grab her credit card and wave it at the bartender. "I'm done, Vaughn. And for what it's worth, I do believe you about that girl on the TV. Thank you for the charity money. I will make sure it goes to worthy organizations and send you the receipt so you can claim it on your taxes."

The bartender shakes his head at me as he takes her card and I cup my chin with my hand and rub the shadow covering my jaw. My mind races with ideas, desperately trying to find a way out of this.

But Grace has made it clear she's not interested in my games.

"Grace," I say softly as she signs the credit card slip and tucks her card back into her purse. "Would you like to have dinner with me? Here?"

She stands up and straightens her dress and then looks me in the eye. "No, Vaughn. I would not."

I reach out and touch her shoulder, gently, and this is just enough to stop her from turning away. "Grace, please don't leave. Just listen for one more minute, OK? Because… because… I might not be your prince, but I think you're my princess. I swear, I never knew I was looking for one. I just always knew that the women I was with before didn't mean anything to me. But Grace, when I was up in that private suite and you were sent away, I realized something. I realized that I like you. A lot. And I don't know what that means or where that leads, but I like you and I want to keep seeing you. I want to know you better. I want a chance with you. I'd like another chance to be your prince. I realize I'm a pretty bad substitute, but I can be fun. I can joke. I can make you feel all those things you crave, Grace. I know I can."

She looks up at me with a tear in her eye and shakes her head. "I don't think so. I think if I give you another chance you'll break my heart, Vaughn. I'll believe in you because that's the kind of girl I am. I'm hopelessly naïve. You'll tear me up and leave me, just like you do all your girls. And I don't think I can survive that. I really don't. I think…" She swallows hard. "I think if I invest in you, and believe in you, and give my heart to you…" She looks up at me and the tear slips down her cheek. "And you broke my heart? I think I might never recover from that."

"So it's better to just never take a risk at all, then? It's better to turn me away and protect your heart, even though what I give you might make you whole and complete? Because I don't think that's right, Grace. I think that's worse than living with a broken heart. Even if we fail at this and that fairy tale ending eludes us, we will be living it for as long as it lasts. Isn't it better to live?"

She smiles, but it's strained and filled with sadness. "No, Vaughn. It's not always better to live. I know better than most. Sometimes living is the worst thing that could happen to a person."

"What?" I'm not sure that remark makes sense but she turns away and I react by grabbing her and pulling her close. Pull her right up to my chest. "Grace, please. One dinner. There's no risk, sweetness. None. Just dinner. You need to eat, let me feed you." She looks up at me and I know we are both imagining our date on the roof of her apartment. "Not like that, Grace. Just a normal dinner. With normal dinner conversation. I owe you a secret, remember? Tell me about your day and I'll tell you about mine. I think we both had a pretty bad day. Don't you want to talk to someone about it?"

She shakes her head no and I'm desperate here. I'm failing. I'm fucking failing. She's dead set on walking away and there's nothing I can say to stop her. "Please, let me tell you about mine, at least. OK? I need a friend, Grace. I have none to talk to."

"I don't want to hear about your problems, Vaughn. I have enough of my own."

She tries to turn away again, but I hold tight. "OK, fair enough. No problems. Then... then... let me tell you about my dreams. Dreams, Grace. Did you know that all growing up I wanted to be a surfer?"

She laughs and I have a glimmer of hope. "Yeah," I say. "A fucking surfer."

She cocks her head, maybe interested. "Do you surf?"

Now it's my turn to laugh. "No. I mean, I did try, but holy shit, I was terrible at it. And to be honest, I sorta hate the ocean."

"I've always wanted to snorkel and dive. But I've never had the opportunity."

"Dive, huh? I tried it once but it was for a movie role I never got, so I never did it again. But I bet... I bet you'd be great at it, Grace. I bet I'd like it if we did it together. We should've gone diving on Saint Thomas instead of... well, what we did."

Her shoulders relax but I respond by clutching her tighter. "Have dinner with me. Please. Let's talk about dreams."

She's shaking her head no before I'm even done talking. "I'm afraid to do that, Vaughn. I really am. Because that might breed hope and I don't want to get my hopes up about you. I just... I just don't trust you. I think that the minute I get comfortable, you'll leave me."

"I don't know how to fix that, Grace. I can't tell you anything that will make you believe me. I can only show you, and you won't give me a chance to show you because you don't think I deserve it. So how can I change your mind if you don't give me another chance?"

"Even if I did give you another chance tonight, and even if it was amazing, there's no guarantee that tomorrow will be just as good. What if we wake up and things are worse? I can't do it."

"Just listen. No one has guaranteed happiness, Grace. That's absurd. Your bar is impossibly high. How can I predict the future and promise you good days for the rest of your life? It's not reasonable. And you know that. You're only telling me these things to make excuses. To make me go away. If things suck tomorrow, then we deal with them. Like people do. One date, Grace. Right now. We've never had a real date. In public, I mean. We're in public. This restaurant is cozy and quiet. And I bet they have good food here. Have dinner with me. If you don't want to talk about your dreams, listen to me talk about mine." She bows her head into my chest and I rest my chin on her head. "One dinner. Just give me a few hours of food and conversation. That's all I'm asking."

She's still and silent in my arms. Very wounded. Very suspicious. Very vulnerable. And so very, very, very much in need of a win.

"Tonight you win, Grace. You win. I'll be yours if you'll be mine."

Chapter Forty - Grace

#TrustTheFuture

I LET Vaughn lead me to a table. The hostess gives me a funny look, thinking what, I can only imagine after the fight I put up to keep Vaughn away from me.

But of course, I gave in, didn't I?

I bet they all give in. He's a man who does not respond well to no. I'm not sure I like that. In fact, I'm not sure I like anything about him in real life.

"Drinks?" the hostess asks as she places the menus down in front of us.

"Another margarita for me, please." If I'm going to do this, I definitely need alcohol. Otherwise I'll overthink every word he says and assign hidden meanings to things that should be taken at face value.

"Mineral water, please," Vaughn says.

Hmmm. He's in Mr. Responsible mode. "How was your premiere?" I ask him politely. "I saw you on TV." And apparently I am not quite drunk enough to dampen down my venom because he shoots me a look.

"Valencia is just a friend, Grace. Not even a real one at that. Just a publicity date."

I cock an eyebrow at that. "Good to know. Just one question, Mr. Asher. Do you have any authentic relationships? Any? A friend? Your brother? No? He's a player in your game as well? Your daughter? Oh, no, another player. She's a little young to be your legal counsel, don't you think?"

He sighs. "*This* is giving me a chance?" He stares at me. Like I'm the one who's disappointing him right now, instead of the other way around.

My drink arrives and I take a sip. A long sip. My head is fuzzy and I am good and buzzed, but I've got some time before I'm drunk. And if ever there was a day that required a spin before bed, it's this one.

I plan on being good and spun before I black out tonight.

Vaughn grasps his water glass with both hands and twirls it slowly, like he needs to be doing something. He clears his throat. "Um, well to answer your question, no. I don't."

I look up from my menu and find his eyes. He looks lost.

"I don't have any friends. So everyone you see me with on TV, they are a negotiated business deal. I mean, I guess my agent, Larry, he's probably my best friend, but we don't do things together. Like hike or boat or—"

"Surf," I say with a smile.

Vaughn laughs and that smile he's famous for warms up my stone-cold heart for a moment. He does have an incredible smile when it's genuine. "Larry actually does surf, but he doesn't invite me."

"Why not?"

He shrugs. "I always say no, so why bother asking when he already knows the answer."

"I can't imagine a life without my best friend. I haven't seen her very much these days. We're going in different directions, it seems. But Bebe and I have been besties since I was fifteen."

Vaughn is silent for several seconds, like he's thinking about that. It makes me a little bit uncomfortable, so much so that I feel compelled to divert the topic to something else. The problem is, I'm not sure anything is safe right now.

"What are you thinking?" he asks softly. "Tell me."

I shake my head no. "You are the one who has to talk, not me. I'm here to listen, remember?"

He nods. "OK, you're right," he says as he studies my face.

What does he see? God, that bugs me when people look at me like that. Like they know all my secrets. It makes me so uncomfortable. I forgo the straw in my margarita and lift the wide glass to gulp, the salt sticking to my lips.

"If you were serious, the movie premiere went really well. I'm happy with my performance. Do you think you'll go see it?"

"A few weeks ago I was dying to see it. The man of my dreams was the star."

"And now? I'm your worst nightmare and you've lost interest?"

"Not exactly."

"I've disappointed you and you're hurt?" I nod and he nods with me. "I'm sorry. I… I don't know how to be me, Grace. The real me, I mean. I'm so used to being him, I might've lost me along the way. What exactly did you like about the fairy tale me? And I'm not fishing for compliments, OK? I'm seriously interested. What did you see? If this is the guy I am"—he gestures to himself—"then how did you get beyond it when everything out there in the public eye is fake?"

I turn my head and concentrate on a point off in the distance. Another couple having dinner. They are comfortable with each other. Talking easily. Smiling easily. "There was this picture of you. It was taken about four years ago, I guess. And you were at a charity function for foster kids." I stop for a moment to choose my words carefully. "And you were sitting on a couch somewhere, surrounded by kids—"

"*Trust the Future.*"

"Yeah," I say, smiling. "That was it. That was the name of the charity. And you looked so freaking happy in that photo. I thought to myself, now that man might make me want to marry. And then I went looking for more information and I found a video of that day. You were playing X-Box with those kids. Some violent shooter game that most parents would throw a fit over. But you looked like you were having the best time. You looked real that day."

"I love kids."

"I can tell."

"I want a shitload of kids," he says, almost wistfully.

"Is that your dream? Marriage and children?"

He nods slowly, pressing his lips together, probably expecting me to object since I told him I was not interested in marriage. But I don't. It's not my place to stomp on his dream.

"I just don't get it, Grace. If you want the prince, why don't you want the marriage?"

I take another gulp of margarita and finish it off. "Because," I say, picking up my menu. I'm not hungry anymore but I need something to do with my hands. "Because regardless of what you think, I realize there are no princes, Vaughn. And you're right, it was unfair of me to expect you to be perfect." I stare at him. Hard. My eyes are narrowing, I just know it. Because it sucks to admit I've been foolish for all these years. Looking for a phantom man who will spoil any good relationship I ever have because my expectations are too high.

He studies me for a moment and again, I find myself squirming under his scrutiny.

Can he see through me? "Excuse me?" I stop our waitress as she passes by. "Can I get another margarita?"

"That's not why, Grace."

Jesus. I need that drink. "Of course that's why. I think I know my own reasons."

He's shaking his head as I defend myself. "You don't want to marry because then you might have to actually be happy."

"What? Seriously, Asher. You're totally wrong. I was—I am—a very happy woman. I was socially complete before I met you, believe it or not. I realize I've been all over the place emotionally since the island. But that's not me. I'm happy, and well-adjusted, and, and, and *happy*."

Fuck.

"But that was the fantasy, right? The fantasy made you happy. This is reality and you're lost in reality."

"Why are we talking about me? The deal was that we talk about you."

"What do you want to know? Ask me anything."

But nothing seems safe. Everything feels like a trap that will throw me backwards into the past. That will unravel all the raveling I've done over the past ten years and leave me frayed and filled with holes.

"I want to get married," he says. "And I don't need her to be a princess, Grace. I just need her to love me for who I really am. And then I want a bunch of kids. And I want them to have the perfect childhood filled with jumping in puddles, and playing in mud, and bad grades because their personalities require them to rebel and be themselves. I want school plays and coaching football, and standing out in the rain to watch a track meet. I want to bring my wife breakfast in bed for Mother's Day and I want to receive handmade gifts of painted macaroni from my three-year-old."

I just stare at him.

"I want normal. I lived the fantasy and it's not as perfect as it seems."

I have no idea what to say, but luckily, the waitress brings my drink. So I take a really long sip and then set it down on the table and stare at it.

"What do you think of all that, Grace?"

"I think…" I look up at him. My eyes are watery from the alcohol or maybe from the serious conversation that makes me think of my own childhood. "I think I'd like to give the fantasy a try first."

"Take it for a test drive?"

"Yes. Just to see what it's like."

"You need to be able to compare?"

I nod.

"Because you've lived normal and it's not as perfect as it seems?"

"Yes."

"Come upstairs with me, Grace. And let me give you a free sample."

I huff out a laugh. "Does it come with spankings?" I try and joke to break the seriousness of his offer.

"No," he says, shaking his head slowly. "No, the fantasy doesn't come with spankings. It comes with gentle, tender lovemaking. And flowers and chocolate-covered strawberries. Soft sheets, and softer music. No dirty talking or blindfolds or sexy lingerie."

"Sounds pretty boring."

"Mmmm. It is. Come upstairs and let me show you how boring."

And then he stands up and comes around to pull my chair out. I stand up and he hooks my arm in his. "Grand Lakeview Suite," he tells the waitress as we walk out. "Bill it to the room."

Chapter Forty-One - Vaughn

#StickAroundAndFindOut

"I CAN be romantic," I tell Grace as I open the door to my suite and flatten my hand on the small of her back. "But everyone's definition of romance is different." I close the door and watch her as she moves forward through the foyer and into the large room.

"Nice view," she says in a low voice.

"Yes, I always enjoy a room with a view. And doesn't everyone want to see the Bellagio fountain when they come to Las Vegas?" She just shrugs. "Sit, Grace. I'll be right back with a drink."

"I'll have a margarita," she calls out as I retreat back to the foyer and call the butler service using the control panel by the door. I meet him outside in the hall and give him my requests, then go back inside. Grace is standing at the windows, her back to me.

"Tonight is not a night for margaritas. Do you like pink champagne, Grace?"

She turns and smiles. "Doesn't everyone?"

I take her in as I approach. Her dress, for being something she wears regularly to work, is a beautiful dark blue that hugs her curves and makes me crazy. Her hair is still piled up on her head, but there are long spiraling strands that have fallen out. They frame her face, making her look just the tiniest bit unkempt.

I love that. I love that her oh-so-together persona has a crack in it.

Her face is flushed pink. Maybe from the alcohol or maybe from being alone with me. Her skin is glowing in the low lights and she looks like a vision of perfection one might only see behind the lens of a specially filtered camera.

"You are the most beautiful woman, Grace."

"I might be drunk."

I smile wide as I walk up to the bar and check the refrigerator for some champagne. Inside is a selection they stock based on my personal preferences. "Do you want to skip the champagne?" I ask her as I pull out two crystal flutes.

She walks over to me, her shoes clicking lightly on the marble floor. "No, I might need more than usual."

"You can't be around me unless you're drunk?" I ask with a smile as I pop the cork on the bottle and pour.

"It helps me keep things in perspective. And when I wake up tomorrow I'll have a reason to push this night away and forget it ever happened."

I stop pouring and just look at her. "What?"

"You want to dominate me, right? I don't want to admit I want to give in. So a few more drinks will give us both what we want, but in the morning I can justify my behavior. Blame it on too much alcohol."

I shake my head. "No more drinks for you then." She laughs but I'm serious. "I'm not on some conquest, Grace. That's not what this is about."

She joins me behind the bar, reaches past me, and grabs a champagne glass. She lifts the pink bubbly to her lips and takes a delicate sip. "Mmmm. This is good, what is it?"

"Billecart-Salmon Brut Rose 2002. It's one of my favorites."

She takes another sip and licks her lips. "I like it. If I stay and have sex with you, will you spank me?"

My smile is tight. She's got the wrong idea and I don't know how to change that. I've set our relationship up this way, after all. I'm the one who gave her all these preconceptions. Preconceptions I'm desperate to change right now.

I grab my champagne and put my hand on her back, once again guiding her into the main part of the room. "Come, tell me what you think of the view."

"I'd rather talk about what you plan on doing to me tonight, actually." She takes a long sip from her glass, finishing it, and then setting it down on a table as we make our way to the window.

I sigh with frustration. "I want to talk to you, Grace. I want to apologize for what you saw on TV today. It's a lie. It's like you witnessing me comforting my sister back on her wedding night. It's not what you think. And I don't want to be judged by that woman's accusations. At least..." I set my glass down and then cup her face in my hands. "At least not by you. I could care less what the world thinks, but please, don't let that woman's bitter revenge taint what I'm trying to do here."

"Why is she bitter, Vaughn?" Grace's jaw clenches and her lips form a tight line. "What did you do to her?"

"Nothing." I laugh, a little bit uncomfortable. "I mean, I fucked her a while back. Six months ago. And I did see her on the island a few weeks ago, but I made it very clear that I was done with her. We did not sleep together on the island. I just dismissed her and gave her thirty thousand dollars so she could move on."

"Thirty thousand dollars?" Grace asks. "You mean like the thirty thousand dollars you put into my bank account? Holy shit!"

"It's not the same—"

"How is it different, Asher? Jesus fucking Christ! Is that your standard payment to keep people quiet?" She turns and slaps me in the face. Hard.

I just stand there. Stunned.

"You're a pig, Vaughn. I can't... I just can't—"

She pushes past me, making a move to flee, but I grab her wrist and pull her back. "Stop for a minute. OK?"

"Why? Every minute that passes you get worse, Vaughn. Everything I thought was the real you, it's all fake. It's all pretend. It's all—"

I lean down and kiss her angry mouth. She pulls back and I let her, but I wrap my hands around her waist and press her hips to my groin, keeping her close at the same time.

"Stop now. I heard you downstairs. I get it, I'm a dick. But I'm trying my best, Grace. I'm trying my fucking best to change that opinion you have of me. I'm sorry we started this relationship the way we did. I'd like to start again. So just be quiet and let it happen. Forget about the past. Forget about the money. Forget about the spankings and all that other shit. And just fucking listen to what I'm saying. Watch what I'm doing. And tomorrow, if you want to walk away after I give you my best effort, well, then go. I won't stop you. I won't come after you. I'll respect your decision and leave you alone."

"Ha," she laughs. Her face is right in front of mine and I can see the panic building as she struggles to get free, but can't. "You're not fucking me tonight, asshole. There's no way."

"You're right. I have no intention of fucking you tonight."

She wriggles in my hold, her little fists pushing against my broad shoulders. She's small when pulled tight against me.

"But you will be in my bed. And you will let me make love to you."

"Like hell," she says, still resisting.

I stroke her cheek to calm her down. "Grace, listen. Just be still and listen to me. I like you. I can't stand the thought of you not being in my life and I want to have something more with you. Now settle for a moment. Just get used to this. Let me hold you close."

She lets out a long breath but she does settle against my chest. I wrap my hand around her head and bring her even closer. So her cheek is pressed against my suit coat. "I wish I could take this coat and shirt off and feel your cheek on my bare chest. I'd like to feel your breath as you calm down. I'd like to feel the thumping of your heart as it slows. But I'm afraid if I let you go, you'll get away."

She stays still against me, thinking.

"Will you leave me?"

"Will you leave *me*?" she asks back.

"Stick around and find out."

"Fuck," she huffs. "What the hell do you want from me, Vaughn? It's not enough that you insulted me with your NDA, your money drops in my bank account, the public fucking on the island, the humiliation of making me blow you in my hallway, making me eat out of your hand as I sit at your feet, and then having to watch one of your many whores on TV tell me I'm breaking up her relationship. For Christ's sake, what more do you want to do to me?"

"It's pretty clear all that makes me a monster, right?"

"How the fuck could it not?"

"Did you like the sex, Grace? And be honest."

"Yeah, I liked the sex. But a relationship is more than your stupid sex games, Vaughn. Life is more than the fun stuff. Life is the serious stuff too. And I don't think you do the serious stuff. I like the fun just as much as anyone, but it's another lie. Because if we were together, then most of our time would be spent having regular sex. Doing things like working, and cooking, and all that stupid bullshit that comes with a relationship."

"How would you even know what comes with a relationship?"

"Says the fucking kettle to the pot!"

"Have you ever had a normal relationship? A long-term one?"

"Have you?"

"No!" I shout, making her jump. "No," I repeat, softer this time. "That's my whole fucking point. I want all that boring stuff and I want to try it with you. And you're what? Too fucked up to even hear me? Should I just put you to bed and try this conversation again in the morning when you're sober and rational?"

"I'm not drunk. I'm just angry."

"With who, though? Me? Because of the girl on TV telling lies about me? Because of all the fantastic sex we had? Because I gave you money to donate to your favorite charities? Because I won you in a game of baccarat? I mean, what exactly is pissing you off here?"

She laughs. Her whole body shakes against mine and she laughs. "You *won* me?"

"Oh, please, don't take that the wrong way. Of course it was fake, Grace. A symbolic gesture between me and that Li character you were attached to at the hip. So spare me your feminist self-righteous bullshit. I can't take anymore. You have no idea what you want. You want the fairy tale? The prince, the money, the fantastic vacations and travel? Private jets, probably. That's fairy tale stuff. Stuff I can actually give you. So you say you want all that, but then when I offer it up, I'm using you. I'm disrespecting you. I'm—what were your words on the island?—I'm an Oscar-winning prick." I let go of her and push her off me. "Just shut the hell up with your conflicting emotions for once, Grace. Give in and say yes. You never want to say yes."

"God, how can you even say that?" She crosses her arms in front of her and rubs her shoulders, like she's chilled. "I *never* say no. I *always* say yes. You're the only person ever who makes me want to say no."

"And why is that? Can you at least answer that honestly?"

She stops her rubbing and lets her arms fall to her side. And then she turns her back and walks over to the bar, grabbing her empty champagne glass along the way. She fills it up, takes a sip, then fills it up again and guzzles it down.

She places her hands over her face and drops her head for a moment, and I'm almost positive she's trying very hard not to cry, but then she brings her hands back to her sides and turns to face me.

"Because, Vaughn, you scare the shit out of me. That's why. You want honesty? Fine. You scare me. You were my dream guy, OK? You were everything I ever wanted. And you're here and it's not real." She shakes her head, like the whole idea that we're in this room together is incredible. "You're here in front of me, offering me something I want more than anything else in this world. And I'm too scared to try because I know you're not the dream guy I made you out to be. And I'm going to get hurt. And I'm going to get used.

And I'm going to regret it if I let you in. Do you understand that? I'm going to regret it."

"You're setting yourself up to regret, Grace. How do you not see that?"

"You've been complaining about my fantasy since we met. You want me to be rooted in reality and not heap these expectations on you. So fine, that's where I'm at. And that means this fight, Vaughn, all this fighting we do… that's our reality. It's unfortunate, but true."

I sigh and walk over to the bar to pour myself another drink. I take a long sip, then guzzle it, just like she did a few moments ago. "It doesn't have to be that way, Grace. We don't have to make this our reality."

"It's a personality clash, Vaughn. It can't be helped."

I turn back to her, shaking my head. "It's not a personality clash, Grace. It's an issue of trust. You don't trust me to be careful with your heart. I don't trust you to be honest with me about your feelings. It's got nothing to do with our personalities. Our chemistry is just fine. I really like you. I'm attracted to you in every dirty way imaginable. You say you've been fantasizing about me for years. You respond to my sexual requests and are willing to meet me halfway. You signed an NDA for me. So I know you're interested. I know you like me. Why can't you just admit it to yourself?"

She walks over to the couch and sits down. Her head falls back against the cushions and she lets out a long sigh. "I don't think it can work."

"Why?"

"Because…" She closes her eyes and stays silent.

"Because why, Grace?" I take a seat next to her and pull her in my lap. She scoots down and places her head on my thighs and tucks her hands between her legs like a little girl going to sleep. I stroke her hair and wait her out, and with every brush of my fingertips past the smooth skin of her neck, I feel her relax a little more.

"Because I'm scared. It's so much easier to want things than it is to have things. Because having things means you have to keep things."

It's my turn to sigh now. "That's true. The more you have, the more you have to lose."

"Exactly."

"You have to take that risk, though, Grace. What good is living if you have no real joy?"

"I like to experience my joy from afar."

"Don't be stupid," I chastise her. "That's not living. I'm here, right now. You're here. I want this. I want you. And all you have to do is say yes and we're together."

"We're together how? I'm your whore you fly in to see in Denver whenever you feel like it? You never called me again after last time. Why would I trust you this time?" She makes to get up but I hold her steady.

"Grace, I have a very good reason for that and I'll be happy to explain everything, but not tonight. It's too much for tonight and we've been drinking. That is a sober conversation if ever there was one. Tonight, just let me take care of you. Let me make love to you."

"If I let you do that"—my heart skips at the possibility that she will give in—"then what happens if you disappoint me again?" She opens her eyes and stares me in the face. "I can't take it, Vaughn. That's why I push people away. I've lost a lot in my life and I can't go through that again."

I know she lost her parents, but the revelations from Felicity make me question everything. There's something very wrong with my Grace's childhood. Something very, very wrong. We need to have that conversation soon, but not tonight. Tonight I just want to make her happy. "I won't fuck it up, Grace. I swear." She shakes her head just as the door chimes. "I swear, just settle down for one night. Enjoy yourself." I lift her up off my lap and she sets herself back against the couch cushions.

"Just trust me now, please." I get up and walk over to the door to let the servers in. A team of six bustles past me with carts piled with silver trays and they proceed to set the table with linens and silverware. Grace takes it all in. She says nothing, but her eyes dart all over the place, not missing a thing.

A few minutes later the team of servers leave and I close the door and turn back to her. She walks over to the table and stops in front of it and looks down at the large sheepskin rug. Then she slips her shoes off and steps forward, digging her toes into the plush pelt.

"There's two place settings," she says, her focus on her feet.

"One for me and one for you."

She looks up. "Then why the rug?"

"It's just an option."

She sinks to her knees and then lies down on it. I walk over to her and sit in the chair. "Why are you on the floor, Grace?"

"Because I'm tired, Vaughn. I'm exhausted. And it feels good. I just want to lie here and do nothing."

I kneel down next to her and turn her a little so I can unzip her dress. She doesn't protest, so I lift up her arm and slip it through the sleeve. I repeat this for the other arm, and then I pull it down to expose her black bra. "Lift your hips for me, sweets." She does and I pull the dress down her legs, then past her feet. I fold it nicely and place it over the back of a chair.

"It feels so good," she says, her fingertips threading through the soft fur.

My hands press against her calves and then I slide them up her legs and loop my fingers around her panties. "Not commando today?"

She smiles but her eyes are closed.

I pull them down her thighs, exposing her sweet pussy. It makes my dick so hard, I can barely think. I spread her legs and lick her inner thigh. She moans and her hands automatically come to my head, pressing me into her slick sex. I lap at her clit, then suck as I finger her softly.

"Why do you feel so good?" she whispers. "Why do I want you so bad?"

I lick her again, and then I push her legs up, bringing her knees up on either side of her head, and I probe the soft bud of her ass for a second before dragging my tongue up her crease. She wriggles and moans, so I stop. "We're going to eat first." I pull her up so she's sitting, then reach behind her and unclasp her bra, letting her full breasts fall free. I palm one, squeezing, but not too hard. It's a time to be gentle. There's time for other stuff later.

"Do you want to sit at my feet or in a chair?" I stand up and take off my coat. She watches me and this makes me very hard. I drape my jacket over the chair, on top of her dress, and then I pull my shirt out of my pants and begin unbuttoning it from the bottom up. Her eyes never leave my fingers.

I remove my tie and shirt and place them on top of my jacket.

When I turn back to Grace, she's got her fingers between her legs. "I'm dying for you, Vaughn. I hate you and I'm dying for you. Why do you make me feel this way?"

I squat down and cup her face with my hands. "Because you like me, Grace. You like me and I like you. We're in like."

"We can't be in like," she whispers back. "Like should not be filled with so much discord and fighting."

"Like is passion. And what we have, Grace, is not discord. It's passion. There's a difference." I watch her as she thinks about that. "I'd like you to sit on my lap. Will you sit on my lap for dinner? And if you get too tired you can sit at my feet and fall asleep with your head on my thigh. Your hot breath against my cock."

"Will you fuck me?" she asks in a sweet voice.

"No, baby." I reach for her hand and pull gently, bringing her reluctantly to me. I sit down in my chair and guide her onto my lap. One of her hands goes between her legs as I lift the lid off the plate closest to me. There are two steaks, both cut up into bite-sized pieces and grilled to a perfect medium-rare pinkness in the center. I pick up a piece with my fingers. "Open, Grace." She opens her mouth and I place the juicy meat on her tongue.

"Mmmm. I'm hungry." She chews slowly and I take this time to feed myself. We alternate this way for a few more bites, then I hand her the champagne flute and she sips. We do this over and over again. Not talking. Not fighting. No expectations or awkwardness.

Just… nourishment.

Her head is pressed against my bare chest. My hands play with her breasts between bites. I squeeze when I want to hear her moan, and then when the last bit of meat is gone and the champagne glasses are empty, I dip my fingers between her legs and find her slick and ready.

"I won't fuck you, Grace," I say, bringing my wet fingers to her lips. She opens and sucks, her tongue doing a little dance against my skin, heightening my already raging desire. I'm so fucking hard for her. "But I'll make *like* to you." Her eyes open and she looks at me, still suckling on my finger. "Should I do that, sweets?"

She slips from my lap and drops to her knees at my feet. And then she rests her head in my lap, her hot breath penetrating through the fabric of my trousers, just like I imagined.

"I'd like that," she says quietly. "I'd like that very much."

I move her slightly, just enough to stand up. And then I reach down and scoop her into my arms. She laughs a little, but her eyes are closed. She's very tired. And maybe drunk. But I won't wait. This is a moment you don't cut short. This is a moment you relish and prolong.

So I take her weary body to the bedroom and lay her gently on the bed.

"I've never had sex with you in a bed before," she says sleepily.

God, that actually hurts. "I'm ashamed of that fact, Grace. I will make sure we spend lots of time in bed from now on." She stretches her arms above her head, not trying to be alluring at all, but simply because it feels good. She presses her cheek against the soft white pillow and her whole body relaxes as she lets out a long breath of air.

"I'm tired."

"Too tired for sex?" I ask her as I remove my trousers and fold them over the back of a chair. "I'm not in a hurry."

She opens her eyes and gives me a smile that actually makes me swallow down a bit of apprehension. "I'm not too tired. But just don't make me work too hard."

I slip onto the bed next to her and my dick grows from this simple act. I position myself over top of her burning body and lean down, angling my mouth to kiss her.

"Mmmm," she moans.

"Mmmm," I reply. I tongue her and get an enthusiastic response, so I grip her head and clutch her to me. Our passion increases, the kiss lingers, the want grows… and finally we have to pull apart to take a breath.

I lift my hips up and angle my cock between her legs.

"No kinky shit?"

"No kinky shit, Grace. You want to know what everyday sex with me is like? This would be it. Me. You. In bed naked. I don't need the dirty words or the public performances. I don't need to make you submit or humiliate you. I just need you, Grace. That's it."

I slip inside her and she moans, her fingernails digging into my shoulders as I fill her up. He legs spread wide for me and I thrust, gently at first, then her hips match my rhythm, pressing against me, asking for more.

I give her more.

I give her everything she wants. I love her slowly. I take my time and whisper in her ear. "You're so perfect," I tell her. "You're all I want," I insist. "We don't need the fairy tale when this is our reality."

She stills underneath me and when I look down at her, a tear slips out of her eye and rolls down the curve of her perfect cheek.

"What's wrong?" I ask, leaning into her ear. "What did I do wrong?"

She gives me a slight shake of her head as she presses her eyes closed. "Nothing," she says with a sniff. "It's just so perfect and I… I don't ever get the happy ending, Vaughn. If I let myself think I can have it, if I believe… I'll be so crushed when it disappears."

"It's not going to disappear, Grace. I promise. Don't let your fear ruin this, sweets. Just accept it. Enjoy it. Please."

"I have so much inside me, Vaughn. So many bad things inside me that I'm trying to move past. And I think you're right. I'm too afraid of failure to allow anything good to happen to me."

I drag a piece of hair out of her eyes and kiss her nose. I know her past is something we need to deal with, but not now. Not tonight. This night is not about the past, it's about the future. "You can't fail, Grace. You're a winner." She smiles. "And besides, I'm not going anywhere. I promise. I will never treat you badly again. I'm sorry. I promise, what we have is good. What we'll have in the future will be good too. Just trust me."

I move inside her and she responds by wrapping her arms around my neck and her legs around my waist. I plunge deeper. "Be mine, Grace. For real. Just tell me you'll be mine."

"I'm yours," she says, breathless as our lovemaking increases pace. "Just don't leave me, Vaughn. Not again."

"Never again, baby. I promise. You'll see."

I press myself against her, thrusting deeper as our bodies rock against each other. Her hands come up and grab my hair, making me crazy with my desire to fill her up and make her mine. My mouth and hands drift down to her soft breasts and I suck and squeeze them, making her writhe under me, squealing with desire.

And that's all I need. A confirmation that the way forward is filled with endless nights alone with her in bed like this.

"You're mine," I whisper in her ear as my balls tighten up, readying for release.

"I'm yours," she says back. Her legs squeeze, her pussy clamps down on my cock. And we find simultaneous perfection together in that moment.

Chapter Forty-Two - Grace

#TrustMeI'mAProfessional

I'M jolted awake by the nausea and spinning. Something has died inside my mouth. I try and open it, but there's a shitload of cotton in there too. And the fucking sun is blazing down on my face.

No, wait. That's the light on the nightstand, I think. This room faces west. And it's morning, right? Sun's in the east in the morning. I try and crack my eyelids, but there's no hope of that. I reach up to pry my mascara-crusted lashes apart. Little flakes fall on my cheek. I sit up and Vaughn's arm tumbles off my stomach. I force my eyelids open so I can at least look at him.

God, that man is beautiful. I sigh and the stench of my own bad breath wakes me up. There is no way he will see me like this. I throw the covers off, trip over an empty bottle of champagne, and then fall onto the soft sheepskin rug.

How did that get in here? I thought we left it in the dining room.

I get up and make my way to the bathroom, closing the door softly behind me so I don't wake Vaughn.

I look in the mirror. I'm a fucking mess. My eyes are ringed black like a raccoon from the makeup I never took off. My skin is pasty white with a healthy shade of green. And my head is fucking pounding. I look down to my outfit. "Hmm." I'm wearing a flirty white cotton nightgown that hits me high on my thigh. It's got some sweet eyelet lace and a pink satin bow between my breasts.

Cute. But where the fuck did this come from?

My stomach does not care, because right now, all that fucking champagne is sloshing around inside me and I need to hurl. I rush to the separate toilet room, smack the door closed, and barely make the porcelain bowl before emptying the contents of my stomach against my will.

"Oh, God, I will never drink again. Just make this all stop."

I hurl again. God hates me.

After waiting several minutes to make sure that the sickness has passed, I get up and wash my face. There's a new package of toothbrushes, so I brush and rinse with mouthwash. And when all of that is done, I feel slightly better. Well, enough to go searching for a coffee machine.

I leave the bedroom with Vaughn still asleep, and tiptoe my way out into the living room. There's a buzz coming from my little purse and I dash over and grab my phone. "Fuck!" Seventeen missed calls from Kristi. It's her wedding day! Oh, my fucking God. It's almost one in the afternoon. I'm her planner and I'm going to fuck up her whole day!

My phone buzzes in my hand again and I quickly press accept. "Kristi, shit, I'm so fucking sorry!"

"Where are you?" she demands.

"Um, with Vaughn, in his room. Hold on, let me check the room number." I run to the door and throw it open. "It says Lakeview Room."

"I'm just down the hall. Stay right there so I can see you."

"OK. Shit, I swear, I'll fix this, OK? I can be dressed and ready in thirty minutes—"

"Never mind that." Her voice is booming now and I realize she's coming down the hallway. A second later she rounds the corner and comes into view. "Grace!" she says, her voice filled with despair as the tears stream down her face.

"What? What happened?" She's a wreck as she comes up and throws her arms around my neck. "Tell me, tell me!"

"I can't do it."

"Can't do what?" But I know what, and my stomach sinks inside me. I feel sick again.

"Marry him, Grace. You were right. He's not... he's not into me, right? He's just doing it out of guilt or something. Public image, like you said. He's a bastard asshole. Making me get married on a Thursday! And... and... and... not taking part in any of the planning! I can't do it. I can't. You were so totally right! Thank God I have a friend like you, Grace, I don't know what I'd—"

"No," I laugh. "No, no, no. You can't… I was drunk, Kristi. Totally fucking smashed. You need to forget every word I said. Please!"

"No," she says, shaking her head. "I can't do it. I don't think we're right for each other. I don't want to be wife number three. Oh my God! What was I thinking? I'm going to ruin my life if I marry Johnny, I know it!"

"Wait, why? Just calm down and tell me why. Did something happen last night? Did he come see you and—"

"No, he didn't come see me! That's part of the problem. You said he should be sneaking in to get a look at me if he cared. And he didn't. He doesn't care about me at all. I'm just a way to tie up his loose ends!"

Oh, Jesus Christ, I have done it now. I put my hands together like I'm praying and touch the tips of my fingers to my forehead. "Kristi, please. Be calm and listen to me, OK? I don't know Johnny. I saw him for the first time yesterday evening. I have no clue how he feels about you or why he wants to marry you. Only you know that stuff and honey, this is called cold feet. Lots of people get this, it's not new. Do you love him?"

She gets a look of pure panic on her face. "I don't know! I'm so emotional these days because of the baby. I can't tell what's real and what's not."

Welcome to the club, I feel like saying. But I don't. I'm the professional here, I need to act like it for once. "Listen to me, Kristi. I'm a love-life loser, OK? I know nothing. At all. So forget everything I said yesterday and just ask yourself… do you really want to throw this day away over cold feet?"

She takes a deep breath and appears to gather herself. "I don't know. I don't know anything, Grace. Tell me what to do."

"Go back to your room and take a moment. I see your hair and makeup are done, so all you have to do is touch it up and then go down to the dressing room like we planned and let them get that dress on you. OK?" I hold her shoulders gently and give her a small shake when she doesn't answer. "OK? We're going to get you ready and you're going to calm down. Just go get your stuff and I'll meet you down in the dressing room in thirty minutes. We can do this."

She looks warily at me.

"Kristi," I say firmly. "You're getting married today. You love this man, he loves you. And this wedding is that expression of your love." I wait but she just continues to stare. "Right?" I prod her.

She takes a deep breath and lets it out slowly. "Right."

"I'll meet you in the dressing room in thirty minutes. OK?"

"OK," she says with a pouty frown on her face. "OK. but please, Grace, don't be late. I still might need some support and I have no family here. I can't exactly talk to his people about this, ya know?"

"I know. I'll be down there in thirty minutes, I promise."

She bobs her head in agreement and then turns away.

Whew. Crisis averted.

Chapter Forty-Three - Vaughn

#Unraveling

I TURN over in bed, still lost in my dream about Grace. She's in a white dress surrounded by twinkling lights and there's music playing. I take her hand and draw her to me, my eyes never leaving hers, and then I cup her face fully in my palms and kiss her mouth in a way I've never done before. So thorough. So soft. So lingering.

And she lingers too, like this kiss is the first.

We kiss like it's the first time ever.

I reach out to her in bed, unwilling to leave the dream, yet wanting her close. But all I get is empty sheets.

I bolt up. "Grace?"

"In here," she calls and my racing heart immediately calms down. She comes out of the bathroom a few seconds later, brushing her hair. "It's Kristi's wedding day and she's freaking out. I need to get down to the dressing room and calm her down."

"OK," I say, swinging my feet out of bed.

She glances down to my morning wood and smirks. "Apparently you are not the invisible man this morning."

"Completely visible," I joke back. "We need to talk, Grace. Before you run off for this wedding. I just need you to understand that whatever it is, I'm here for you."

"What are you talking about?" She bends over to slip on her shoes and I ogle her ass. "You're here for me about what?"

I grab my trousers off the chair and slip them on. "Your childhood."

"My childhood?" she asks, her attention immediately on me. "What about it?"

I just stare at her. "You don't remember?"

"Remember what? Jesus, Asher, I don't have time for this. I have a wedding—"

"Asher? Why are you getting defensive with me? Last night we were talking and I asked you about your childhood and you insisted that if I dropped it, you'd tell me as soon as we woke up."

"I did no such thing," she says, walking out of the bedroom.

I follow her out. "You absolutely did. Last night, we were celebrating with champagne after we had mind-blowing vanilla sex—"

"Well, champagne makes me crazy drunk. That's why I started drinking margaritas. You should just forget everything I said because chances are I was talking out my ass."

"Fuck that."

She whirls around at my language. "Excuse me?"

"Fuck. That. We had a fucking awesome night, Grace. And then you wake up this morning and tell me to forget about it because of some stupid excuse about champagne? Fuck that."

She gives me a short laugh. "You can drop all the f-bombs you want, Asher. I've got nothing to say about my childhood. It was perfect. My parents were perfect."

"Obviously not, Grace. They're dead. So something happened and it's affected you and your ability to commit. You told me so last night."

Her mouth flies open to make a perfect O shape, like I just stunned the shit out of her. "I just explained to you, I don't remember anything and I know for a fact I must've been wasted out of my mind if I was telling you that kind of stuff. So sorry, I'm not talking about my childhood."

"If it was so goddamned perfect, why are you hiding it?"

"I'm not hiding it! I told you back on Saint Thomas, we were middle-class perfect. And you know what?" She points her polished finger up at my face. "Fuck you for bringing my dead parents into this. That is so rude."

She makes for the door and I grab her by the wrist. "You're not leaving here. You don't get to just say, *Whoops, I can't remember last night*, and walk the fuck out."

"Watch me," she snarls back. "And that hurts," she says, yanking her arm. I let go of her wrist before I leave a bruise and she walks towards the door.

"Grace, wait."

"I can't, Asher! I have a fucking wedding to get to, OK? I'm here working, ya know. I have a job. It's a fucking weekday, for fuck's sake. I'm busy." And then she pulls the room door open and walks through.

I follow her. "Just hold on a second. How much do you remember about last night?"

She punches the button for the elevator and taps her foot. She's still wearing that blue work dress and in the light of day, with her hair brushed out and all her makeup washed off her face, she does, in fact, look like a woman going to work. "Nothing," she rockets back, before she even thinks about the question.

"That's not even possible. Tell me the last thing you remember."

"Dinner, at the restaurant. After you won me in a poker game."

Fuck. You have got to be kidding me. "It was baccarat. And I know you remember more than that. We came up here, we had dinner up here. Remember? We didn't eat at that restaurant. We came up here and you sat in my lap—"

"And then I told you about my childhood? I highly doubt that, Asher. I don't talk about it. It hurts too much. I lost my parents and then I moved on." She whirls around to look me in the eye for this part. "I do not talk about it. So if you are trying to trap me and make me think that I promised to tell you things, that's not going to happen."

I just stare at her. I'm living a nightmare. I'm seriously living a nightmare. Where do I even start to explain? We had all these conversations and now she can't remember? "I already know what happened, Grace. I told you last night, Felicity found some things locked away in your juvenile record—"

She slaps me across the face. "You're spying on me!" She slaps me again, harder. "How fucking dare you spy on me! It's one thing to give me money to dole out to charities, or fill my Starbucks card up with enough cash to buy five years' worth of coffee. But to actually have that girl dig through my sealed fucking records! You have gone too far, buddy."

The elevator dings and the doors open. It's empty, thank God. Grace storms in and then turns around, trying to block me from joining her. "No way," she says, her arms outstretched across the doorway, trying to prevent me from entering. "I need to go to work and you're not following me there."

I push right past her and then grab her hand before she can storm out of the elevator. "Let go," she says. "Or I will scream."

The doors close and I let go as we descend. "No, I'm not letting you run away this time, Grace. You're mine now and I'm responsible for you. We're having this conversation and your friend's wedding can wait."

"It's my job, Asher—"

"Quit fucking calling me that. It's insulting and you know it."

"Oh, now I have to call you master in public too?"

I scrub my hands down my face and let out a long breath. "Look, let's just start this day over, OK? Last night was so perfect, it's a shame to spoil it. We can talk about your childhood later."

"We're not talking about anything, Asher. In fact, I think this whole movie-star crush thing has run its course. I'm not gonna see you again."

"What? You're crazy. So I know what happened to you. Who cares? Just talk to me about it. I know they let you off and the charges were dropped."

Her mouth literally falls open.

"Grace, I told you I know."

"What do you know?" she growls. "What do you think you know?"

"I know that whatever happened, you didn't kill them." She turns completely white and I almost get sick watching her come to terms with this. "Grace, just calm down, would you? It's OK, I know there has to be a good explanation for whatever happened. So just tell me what it is."

The doors ding open and we find a crowd of people waiting for the elevator. Grace darts out, stopping to look left and right. "I didn't want to come to the lobby."

"We never pushed the button, it brought us here." I take her arm gently and lead her away from the crowds. I have no shirt on, and I'm regretting that immediately. I'm regretting coming down here at all, because people are beginning to recognize me. "Grace, come with me. The media is probably around. I don't want you—"

"Mr. Asher!" they start yelling from down the hall.

I look back at the elevators, but none are available. "Grace, stay close, baby. We gotta make a run for it."

She yanks free from my embrace and turns to point at me again. I draw back a little, afraid she's gonna start with the slapping. "I'm not going anywhere with you, you spy! You have no right to pry into my personal life. None. I'm appalled and sickened that you would stoop so low. Kill them? You think I killed them? Fuck you! Just fuck you!"

She starts crying and then the paparazzi are upon us. Cameras flash and questions are begin shouted.

"Mr. Asher, what will your pregnant girlfriend think of this new development?"

"Vaughn, over here! Give us a statement about last night!"

They go on and on like that. I grab Grace and pull her through the crowd. "Come on! We can grab a taxi at the front and get out of here." She fights me all the way, but I hold firm this time. I might bruise her, but if I let go, they will swarm us and who knows how badly she could get hurt if that happens.

"Vaughn!" she screams. "Stop. I have to go to work!"

Fucking work. How the hell does she think she's just going to go back to work today? Jesus, it's like she forgot everything that happened last night. I drag her into the main lobby, heading straight for the door, when another barrage of paparazzi ambushes us.

"Grace! Grace!" they start calling, and this is when I know it's gonna get ugly.

"Don't stop, Grace. Just keep going. Don't say a word."

"What?" she shouts up at me. "What's going on?"

"Is it true you murdered your parents, Grace?"

She stops dead. She just shuts down. This question is like a slap and all I see in that moment when she realizes her secret is out, not only to me, but the world, is blind panic.

I see my sister Sam, so fragile at age sixteen when the media found out a secret about her too. But Sam has us. Sam has our father, the powerful Adam Asher. Sam had the support of professionals who knew how to handle these things. And Sam's secret was never told.

But Grace...

I see her life changing before her eyes. Maybe even ruined.

I see humiliation, and fear, and depression.

"Why did you kill them, Grace? Did you kill your brother too? Did they do something?" The media is relentless. They never stop. Once they draw blood, they circle like sharks.

She shuts down, so I swoop her up into my arms and push my way through the crowd, aiming for the valet area. The flashbulbs are going off—so many pictures, that's all I think about. I don't even want to imagine the headlines tomorrow. She will be all over the news. Her private life gone, ripped away like it surely must've been back when she was a teenager.

History repeats.

"Don't worry, Grace," I whisper into her ear. "I'll handle everything. I have lawyers and a team of PR people who will manage this for us."

She kicks her feet, twisting wildly in my arms, making me lose my grip and forcing me to set her down before she falls.

"Get off me, Asher!" she screams. "Just leave me the fuck alone. Do you hear me? You asshole! Ten years I've lived a nice quiet life and a few weeks with you unravels my whole world. I fucking hate you!"

"Grace!" a voice yells out from the valet area. "Grace! Over here!"

Grace turns, searching for the voice. And then she bolts off in the direction of a white Mercedes SUV.

The media follow her and suddenly the space around me is empty.

Grace climbs into the car and it speeds away.

She's gone.

Again.

Chapter Forty-Four - Grace

#BuryThemDeep

"WHAT are you doing?" I ask. Kristi weaves around a camera crew and flips them off in the rearview after barely missing running them over. "We're gonna kill someone. And you're supposed to be getting married!"

"No! I can't do it, Grace. I'm not gonna do it." She's wearing a white terrycloth robe and her hair is a bit disheveled from the excitement. "I gotta get out of here, like now."

I hold on as she takes a corner at a crazy fast speed. "Slow down!" She peels out onto the Strip and we promptly get stuck at a red light.

"Shit!" she says, her little fists slamming against the steering wheel. "Shit, shit, shit."

Yeah, if you're trying to get somewhere fast in Vegas, you don't take the Strip. She honks her horn and then changes lanes, waves her fist at someone behind us, gets over another lane, and then turns right at the first street and then doubles back around behind the Bellagio.

"Where are we going?"

"I know someone here, Grace. We can go stay with him until we figure out what to do." She reaches over and pats my hand. "We'll get through this. Don't worry."

I settle back in my seat as she gets on the 15 freeway heading south. "I can't believe that just happened. My life is over."

And then I realize who I'm saying this to. A pregnant woman who just walked out on her wedding. I reach over and pat her hand and her tears roll freely down her face. "We'll get through this. Don't worry."

She nods at me as she tries to control her sniffles, and then she starts shaking her head no. "What just happened to you back there, with the cameras and stuff…" She looks over at me and I recognize that look on her face. Fear. "That's gonna happen to me too. As soon as they realize that Johnny and I have been lying about everything."

I just stare at her.

I don't ask her anything else.

Secrets aren't meant to be shared.

Secrets are meant to be buried and ours are perilously close to resurfacing right now.

So we do the only thing we know how to do. The same thing people with secrets the world over do once bits and pieces poke through the surface.

We throw more dirt on top and hope for the best.

Chapter Forty-Five - Vaughn

#NoOneShouldHaveItSoGood

I MANAGE to get back to my room after Grace takes off in that SUV. I don't even know who was driving, but it was someone Grace knew.

I call Conner and he picks up on the first ring. "I need help, dude."

"I just saw it, Vaughn. You're all over the fucking news already."

"How the hell did they find her? How the hell did they even know we were dating? It was all very discreet. Last night was the first time I've seen her in weeks."

"It was Sam's dickhead of a husband, Tray. I just got off the phone with him. He's blackmailing us. He says he's got a list of your past girlfriends on record about your nondisclosure agreements and he knows what happened to Grace ten years ago."

"What the... Did he tell you?"

A pause on the other end.

"Conner, dammit. Did he tell you?"

"He told me some. And believe me, V, you do not want this to get out. I think we should pay him. I think Grace might actually be in danger."

My whole world spins. Just when I think I've got it all figured out, bad luck can't touch me and life is good… it knocks me down and kicks my ass.

"Is it bad?" I ask in a low voice that betrays my fears. "I need to know, Conner, even though I really don't want to know."

"It's bad. It's so, so fucking bad. I've already called Felicity and she's on her way to Vegas now. She'll meet you in your room in a few hours. Just hang tight until then."

I end the call and slump back into a chair that has a view looking out over the Bellagio fountains and I sit for a few minutes. Running last night over and over in my head.

It was *so* perfect.

Conner was right. Life has been too easy for me. No one should have such an easy life.

But it's all coming due now. Because last night I did something I will most certainly regret and when Grace finds out, she might never speak to me again.

END OF BOOK SHIT

So it has been FOUR YEARS almost exactly since I started writing this series. And it's weird to look back on it all because even though I had a lot of success with Rook and Ronin series and this series did very well for a short period of time, it's Rook& Ronin that everyone still talks about. Social Media gets lost in the fray because I write so fast and have, at this point, released more than fifty books.

But these books – God, every time I think back on them I have to smile. Because Vaughn is such a dick in the first couple. And it's really only at the end of Block that he starts to change his stripes. So lots of people hated Vaughn. Of course, if they stopped at Follow or Like, they probably still do. But if they kept reading… if they kept going and just gave him a chance—he pulls it out in the end.

Social Media has some of my very favorite sex scenes, some of my favorite comedy scenes, and definitely some of my most emotionally twisted scenes. (You have read MEDIA, the bundle of the final three books, to get that.)

And generally, when readers get to the end of novella six, Home, they love Vaughn. I hated Vaughn in the beginning too, but characters have to start out flawed or they have no goal to aspire to. So I made Vaughn Asher extra special flawed so he had lots of ways to spread his wings and soar.

When I started to reformat this this bundle I had an EOBS about what my typical day looks like. And I was going to just copy and paste it into this new edition because my day is pretty much the same now as it was four years ago, but there are some differences.

So there's a new look at a typical Author JA Huss Day. (This is my actual TODAY – it's five-thirty PM as I type this, so not quite done yet, but I can make a reasonable prediction as to how I will spend the remaining hours before I go to bed…

MY DAY - MAY 2018

4:30 AM – Wake up and let the dogs outside. I used to wake up at 6 back in 2014, so as you can see, my days have gotten longer. I make coffee, sit down in my writing nook, and check social media. Today was extra special stressful because I have two chapters to finish in The Boyfriend Experience and it needed to be sent to my editor before noon. Little factoid – I'm still using the same editor! So that hasn't changed.

5:00 – coffee and social media done, I start writing. Today I wrote about 3000 words and was finished by 8:00 AM.

8:00-8:30 – more social media time. Checked Twitter and Facebook and made a teaser announcement that I had written the end for Boyfriend book to post.

8:30-9:15 – Feed the donkeys. This hasn't changed either. I did it a little early today, usually I feed them around 11 AM, because that's when my morning writing break is. But I was done writing today since it was "The End" day. I also take my dogs for a hike on the ranch and that's about 30 minutes.

9:15 – I have the house cleaners coming today, so I gotta clean before my house cleaners come. So I start cleaning the kitchen (they don't clean my kitchen, just floors and bathrooms and I want the whole place to look nice when they leave, so I clean the kitchen before they come.) Back in 2014 I stressed out about house cleaning A LOT! In fact, when I look back at the old EOBS my day was riddled with guilt for not cleaning the house. So getting housekeepers to come every two weeks was something that has really helped me. I also did some laundry and planned my lunch.

9:30 – House cleaners come and start while I finish the kitchen and laundry and then make some teasers for The Boyfriend Experience and check email. It's Monday and Johnathan McClain and I are writing our new book together, so I answer three emails from him and because we're very behind on Giveaway mail, I start on the mail.

11:30- 1:30 – House cleaners are done, laundry is done, kitchen is clean, and dogs are happy. I do the giveaway mail and send Johnathan his list (because he has all the Julie & Johnathan books)

1:30 PM – I finally get a shower, make lunch, eat, and then work on more teasers for Boyfriend.

2:00 – I take a nap. I've been up working since 4:30 AM, so I need a break. A huge thunderstorm with hail wakes me up at 3:00, so that's the end of that.

3:00 – I've got everything checked off my list for today except reformatting these Social Media books. So I hunt down old files, make new files, new headers, and try my best to make sure I don't fuck up my Whispersync when I upload new eBooks, because the audiobooks are already online.

That brings me to 5:30 PM – which is when I started writing this EOBS. When I'm done with this I will reformat the Social paperback, adjust my new cover, and then do that all over again for the second book, Media. I also check email (entertainment lawyer has sent me the book rights contract for The Company TV Series Johnathan and I are doing, so there's some back and forth on that.)

This is what I will do with the rest of my day and if I'm lucky, somewhere around 11:00 PM I will be ready to upload new files and covers and I can forget about Social Media for another four years.

So I don't know what people really think writers do, but as you can see, writing is a very small part of it. Most of my day is doing publishing tasks, email, social media, and stuff everyone else does – like cleaning and taking care of animals.

But tomorrow – tomorrow I write words with Johnathan on our July release and start a NEW BOOK called Play Dirty!

Because that's my job.

I am an author – and this is what that looks like.

:)

FINISH THE STORY OF GRACE AND VAUGHN IN BOOK TWO, MEDIA.

Thank you for reading, thank you for reviewing, and I'll see you in the next book!

Julie
JA Huss

About the Author

JA Huss is the New York Times Bestselling author of 321 and has been on the USA Today Bestseller's list 21 times in the past four years. She writes characters with heart, plots with twists, and perfect endings.

Her books have sold millions of copies all over the world, the audio version of her semi-autobiographical book, Eighteen, was nominated for a Voice Arts Award and an Audie Award in 2016 and 2017 respectively, her audiobook, Mr. Perfect, was nominated for a Voice Arts Award in 2017, and her audiobook, Taking Turns, was nominated for an Audie Award in 2018.

She lives on a ranch in Central Colorado with her family.

www.ingramcontent.com/pod-product-compliance
Lightning Source LLC
Chambersburg PA
CBHW020503260626
47156CB00006B/1847